UNDEAD SAMURAI

BAPTISTE PINSON WU

Copyright © 2023 by Baptiste Pinson Wu

All rights reserved.

No part of this book may be reproduced in any form or by any electronic or mechanical means, including information storage and retrieval systems, without written permission from the author, except for the use of brief quotations in a book review.

Ebook ISBN: 978-4-9912768-7-3

Paperback ISBN: 978-4-9912768-6-6

Cover by Damonza

Map by @Saumyavision/Inkarnate

❀ Created with Vellum

To Raphaëlle,

*They'd better make a movie of this one
so that we can watch it together.*

GLOSSARY

Daishō 大小: A pair of swords worn by Samurai, usually consisting of a *katana* and a shorter *wakizashi*.

Fundoshi 褌: Japanese undergarment.

Geta 下駄: Japanese sandals elevated on one, two, or three "teeth".

Hakama 袴: Loose, pleated trousers.

Jitte 十手: A hooked weapon used by the police during the Edo period.

Kabuki 歌舞伎: A form of Japanese theatre born in the early 17th century.

Kaede 楓: Japanese maple tree.

Kanji 漢字: Japanese system of writing based on Chinese characters.

Kashira 頭: Cap at the end of the *katana's* handle.

Kenjutsu 剣術: Term designating the ensemble of Japanese martial arts involving blades, armor, horse riding, and firearms.

Kotsuzumi 小鼓: An hourglass-shaped hand drum.

Kusarigama 鎖鎌: Weapon made of a short sickle connected to a chain ending with an iron weight.

Kyonshī キョンシー: A type of reanimated corpse, based on Chinese culture.

Kyūdō 弓道: Japanese martial art of archery.

Mizugumo 水蜘蛛: Devices used by shinobi for crossing water.

Naginata 薙刀: A polearm with a curved, single-edge blade.

Ōdachi / Nodachi 大太刀 / 野太刀: A sword used by the Samurai. Longer than the *katana*.

Onna-musha 女武者: Female warriors.

Saya 鞘: The sheath.

Shinobi 忍び: Another word for *ninja*.

Shitagi 下着: Shirt worn by members of the Samurai class.

Shōgun 将軍: Military leader of Japan and de facto ruler of the nation.

Sōhei 僧兵: Buddhist warrior monks.

Tantō 短刀: A single edge dagger worn by Samurai.

Tengu 天狗: A legendary, often dangerous creature, usually depicted with wings, a red face, and a long nose.

Teppo 鉄砲: Arquebus.

Tsuba 鍔: The hand guard of a sword.

Wakizashi 脇差: The shorter sword in the *daishō* set.

Waza 技: Martial arts techniques.

Yōkai 妖怪: Supernatural creatures in Japanese folklore.

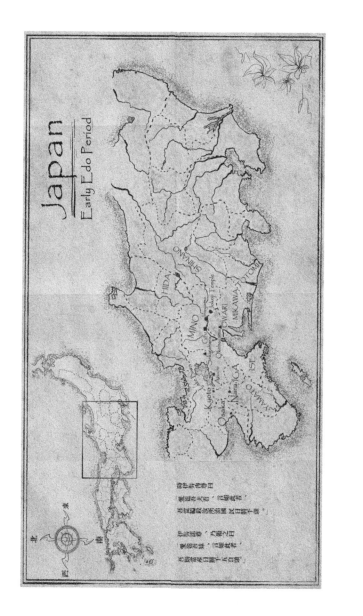

時伊弉冉尊曰
「愛也吾夫君、言如此者、吾當縊殺汝所治國民日將千頭。」

Upon this, Izanami no Mikoto said:

"My dear lord and husband, since you said so, I swear to strangle to death a thousand of your people each day."

伊弉諾尊、乃報之曰
「愛也吾妹、言如此者、吾則當産日將千五百頭。」

Then Izanagi no Mikoto replied:

"My beloved younger sister, since you said so, I will each day give life to fifteen hundred people."

日本書紀
Nihon Shoki

PROLOGUE

Okehazama, 1560

They came with the storm, using the crack of the thunder to mask their advance, and the howling wind to cover their shouts. The earth shook under the hooves of their mounts, yet even as screams spread into the camp, Yoshimoto Imagawa remained on his stool inside the square of command, confident in the overwhelming superiority of his army. Still the screams came, closer and closer by the second. The daimyō was used to soldiers dying, but this was not it. This was the sound of lambs being slaughtered.

A young soldier brushed the flap of the square open and rushed in, not even taking the time to kneel, panic disfiguring his otherwise unmarked face. A knot formed in Yoshimoto Imagawa's throat upon the sight.

"My lord—" the young soldier said, but an arrow sprouting from his forehead cut his words and his life short, prompting Yoshimoto to his feet. A second jutted from the soldier's throat before he was on his knees, and when he finally tumbled over, the first enemy riders burst through the curtain of the square, trampling the Imagawa crest.

The guards sprang to action. Being the only sober warriors in the camp, they fought valiantly, and with even more bravery than usual for their lord's presence by their side. Yoshimoto and his second in command drew their blades and joined this bitter battle as well, slashing through those impudent fools who dared to challenge the might of the Imagawa clan. No one in Owari, or in Japan, could hope to overcome the thirty thousand men Yoshimoto was leading toward Kyōto. This, the daimyō believed, was the last stand of the Oda clan. Yoshimoto had expected some resistance from the local clan, of course; they had resisted the Imagawa for generations, after all, and honor would not let them bow without a proper fight. But this was stupid. He had ten times the Oda numbers, and his men were strong from easy victories. The Fool of Owari had thrown caution to the wind and led his feeble forces inside the maw of death for nothing.

"Push them back!" young Matsudaira Motoyasu, his second in command, shouted from the depth of his lungs, his blade gleaming red and the rage of war in his eyes.

The guards responded to his enthusiasm with shouts and cheers, and Yoshimoto congratulated himself once again for marrying his niece to the young man.

The daimyō struck a samurai of the Oda clan with a clean cut that nearly took his leg off. The samurai shrieked and buckled, his broken knee unable to support him, and Yoshimoto lifted his katana above his head to bring the killing blow, but it never came. More horses tore through the square, opening the camp to Yoshimoto's view for a brief second before a dark mare rammed him backward. In this instant before the horse uprooted him from his stance,

Yoshimoto Imagawa realized the unquestionable truth of his situation. He had been crushed. His army was no more. The camp was on fire. Hundreds upon hundreds of warriors were fleeing through the valley, leaving their comrades to be butchered. The chaos was so fierce that men bearing his colors and emblem fought each other everywhere the eye could see. How did Oda Nobunaga manage such an attack? the daimyō asked himself as his last two guards helped him to his feet.

"Nobunaga!" Yoshimoto shouted as he recognized the man sitting atop the dark horse.

Nobunaga Oda, the Fool of Owari, climbed down from his mare, the five-petaled quince flower of his clan shining in its golden splendor on his chest. Nobunaga crossed the small distance to the defeated daimyō with slow and measured strides, taking pleasure at the sight. Yoshimoto Imagawa was flanked by his two guards, the three of them being the last armed men from their side within the square. The young Matsudaira was on his knees, blood pouring from his broken nose, but defiance still vibrating in his warrior's eyes. An Oda samurai had his knee on the back of the young man, while another kept his blade at his neck, yet Matsudaira snarled in a challenge. Nobunaga's grin infuriated Yoshimoto to the point that he discarded the idea of seppuku. He would die, butchered by those pissants, if it meant killing the *fool* responsible for his defeat. Nobunaga was not even armed. Instead of a sword, the young daimyō of Owari rode to battle carrying a *kotsuzumi* drum. Yoshimoto spat with rage at this insult. The rumors were true, Nobunaga had no sense of honor. He was not a true samurai. Luck and boldness had made him victor here, but to think that he would disrespect his enemy with a musical instrument made Yoshimoto cringe with rage.

"*Kisama...*" Yoshimoto cursed through his teeth.

Nobunaga responded to the insult with a smirk. Other than the shrieks echoing here and there and the burning structures tumbling down, the camp was silent. Nobunaga lifted the drum over his right shoulder with his left hand, allowing a look at the colt's skin spread on the instrument's head. The *kanji* for death had been painted in a rusty color over it, and Yoshimoto shivered at the sight. Nobunaga squeezed the red cords around the drum's body to tense the skin and hit the ridge in a high-pitched note. Just once.

"I expect you to die with honor," Yoshimoto whispered to his two guards.

The one on his right nodded. The one on his left displayed the same resolve. But just then, as Yoshimoto shared a last glance with this honorable warrior, the guard's eyes opened in a stupor, and through his chest appeared a blade. The guard looked down at it with something like curiosity. They had left no enemies behind. Curiosity was replaced with fear, then pain. Yoshimoto checked over the dying guard's shoulder and gasped.

There, in the growing darkness of the evening, stood one of his own soldiers. His eyes were white, his skin gray, but the most prominent of the young man's features was the arrow jutting from his forehead, still slick with blood. The daimyō recognized the soldier who had meant to inform them of the attack, and the second arrow sprouting from his throat confirmed it. Yoshimoto's breath remained in his lungs. The soldier had died, fallen by two lethal missiles, he had seen it. But here he was, standing, expressionless, even as he drove his katana deeper into his comrade's back.

"Impossible," Yoshimoto whispered as the dead soldier's empty eyes slowly lifted to meet his. The daimyō saw death in them. Not just his death, but the death of all things. And suddenly he understood how Nobunaga had overcome him so easily. The *fool* had used his own Imagawa warriors against them.

There was another hit of the *kotsuzumi* as the guard fell forward, and all around Yoshimoto dead warriors rose slowly, hands wrapped around their blades, just as they had fallen. Their joints made impossible rattling sounds as they were forced back to an unnatural second life, and some even whizzed malevolently as the air left their bodies through their fatal wounds. Yoshimoto heard the teeth of his last guard chattering and thought he smelled the pungent odor of piss coming from him until he realized the heat along his own thighs. The dead stood, their bodies rocking with the memory of breathing.

The guard fell to one knee, shaking blade pointed at Nobunaga.

"Don't...don't," he said, shaming himself with this show of fear.

Nobunaga's smile vanished and was replaced by a frown. He hit the drum once more, with the same note as before.

Yoshimoto saw a flash as another undead slammed into the kneeling guard and dropped him on his back. Except that this dead warrior held no blade, his arm having been cut off during the exchange. Lacking a sword, he instead used his teeth, which he plunged directly into the throat of the screaming guard.

Yoshimoto whimpered as the dead warrior's head shot up, ligaments and strips of flesh stuck between his teeth connecting him to the guard who gurgled in a pool of his own blood.

"How about you?" Nobunaga asked the young officer as the undead soldier finished the job without passion by ripping the open throat with his fingers.

Any trace of defiance was now gone from young Matsudaira's eyes; all of it had been replaced by fear and submission.

"Please," the young man sobbed as his head touched the ground, his whole body trembling with shameful spasms. "Please."

Nobunaga walked to the young officer and dropped his hand on his back. Matsudaira shuddered at the touch but did not dare look up.

"I forgive you for invading my land," Nobunaga said.

Another crack of thunder boomed in the evening sky. There was now no more sound in the camp, only Matsudaira's whimpers and Yoshimoto's blade rattling in his shaking hands.

"What have you done?" Yoshimoto asked through his teeth.

"You left me no choice," Nobunaga Oda replied, putting himself within striking distance of the defeated daimyō. "You came on my land, thinking to swallow us in your march to the capital. But Owari is mine, Yoshimoto, and now, with this new power, so is the rest of Japan."

"My head is so valuable to you that you would sully your soul with this... this abomination?"

"Your head?" Nobunaga asked, looking truly baffled. "Your head, you say?" he asked again before chuckling. The chuckle turned into laughter. Nobunaga's head shot backward, and soon, his laugh infected those around him and all the living men in the square shared it, though Yoshimoto could not see the humor in it. The rage building in the pit of his stomach made him tighten his grip on his katana, which he now held by the hip, ready to thrust. If he was to die, he told himself, he would do so after the fool. Sliding his back foot backward to give him a better stance, he pulled on his sword a little and made himself ready for his last action.

Nobunaga's hand struck the drum faster though, and cold fingers gripped Yoshimoto's wrists before he could thrust. More grabbed his shoulders, his legs, and the back of his hair. They forced him to his knees, and he screamed in a mixture of panic and rage. Yoshimoto was a strong man, but no matter his struggle he could not make any of his assailants budge. It was like fighting trees, and for the first time in his life, Yoshimoto Imagawa was powerless. He felt the teeth reaching the skin at the base of his neck, the young soldier from before ready to tear him apart, when the drum resonated once more, and everything stopped moving. A trickle of blood ran down his neck, where the teeth had just pierced the skin. Yoshimoto had not even realized how loud he had been screaming. His beating heart hurt in his chest, but he dared not move, not even when Nobunaga crouched right in front of him. This man, Yoshimoto realized, was no longer human. If he'd never really considered the existence of the soul before, he now had no doubt of its presence in every living thing, for Nobunaga Oda had lost his, and looking into his eyes was like staring down an empty well.

"Yoshimoto, Yoshimoto," Nobunaga said. "This was never about your head." The daimyō of Owari gently dropped the drum by Yoshimoto's hand, the one that still held his beloved katana. The dead surrounding him would not let him swing his sword, but it took Nobunaga some effort to pry it from his grasp. One by one, Nobunaga tenderly removed the fingers around the hilt, then moved toward the *saya* tucked inside Yoshimoto's belt, which he unslung with care. The katana found its sheath, and Nobunaga observed it with something like lust.

"All of this for a katana?" Yoshimoto spat. The teeth of the undead warrior sank deeper because he had moved.

"Oh, but this is much more than a sword," Oda Nobunaga replied, not even looking at his prisoner. "You held one of the most valuable treasures of Japan and didn't know it. And they call me a fool." The sword found his belt after he stood. He bent once more to retrieve the *kotsuzumi*, then turned and climbed on his mount.

The soldiers holding young Matsudaira dragged him away, and all the living warriors marched out of the square. Only Yoshimoto, Nobunaga, and the dead remained. They exchanged a look, but no word. As Yoshimoto cursed his victor in his heart, the fool grinned and pulled on the reins of his mare.

The once powerful daimyō struggled against the dead fingers' grip, but they refused to move, even a little. Then, just as the dark mare trampled the curtains of the square of command, Yoshimoto heard the drum once more.

Then followed pain, screams, and death.

CHAPTER 1
RONIN

Jokoji, Owari Province, sixty-five years later (1625)

From his bench, the rōnin observed the splendor of the mountains. Through his years on the road, he'd never spent too much time in Owari province, and when he had by chance crossed this new Tokugawa domain in the past, it wasn't so deep inland. Usually, he'd stick close to the sea or follow the main road connecting Kyōto to Edo. He presently regretted this habit of his. Jokoji Mountain, or any sight along the Shonai river since Nagoya, had been a wonder of nature. Momiji season had painted the trees yellow, orange, and red, with an occasional patch of green from stubborn hills.

Soon, the *kaede* trees would enlighten the gardens of the cities and temples with bright red five-pointed leaves signaling the coming of winter, a most difficult time for travelers. But until then, the rōnin would wander across Japan. Unless, of course, this current step in his lifelong journey proved fruitful for once.

"Sorry for making you wait," the jovial voice of a girl, barely a woman, said. She bowed in front of him, then wiped the sweat on her forehead as she straightened up.

Despite the freshness of the morning, her headcloth was drenched. Her face gleamed from her efforts, but she still managed an honest smile, which he returned with some embarrassment.

"Are you here for the challenge?" she asked, politely inquiring about his whereabouts even though she had more patrons waiting. The road near the junction leading to Jokoji Mountain was lined with benches on both sides of the small structure currently serving dozens of clients with food and drink. It was obviously not used to such activity, being so far from any town, yet the owner would end the day much richer than he had started it.

"You've heard about the challenge?" the rōnin asked.

"Of course," the girl replied, dropping her left arm akimbo. The rōnin understood she was using this conversation to catch her breath and was glad to oblige. "Haven't stopped serving samurai and the likes for three days. Coming!" The last was said to another bench, a little closer to the small structure, on which three traveling warriors waited. "Right," she went on. "What will it be?"

"Well..." he started saying, but shame kept the words in his throat.

"No coins, eh?" she asked, though not harshly.

The rōnin nodded, not even wondering how she had guessed it so fast. It was beyond obvious.

Ten years ago he had fought as a samurai, wore a set of armor made from lacquered iron plates laced together by rich leather cords, and served one of the greatest men who ever graced the land of Japan. The years had not been kind since his lord's death. One by one, he had exchanged the pieces of his armor, and when all of it was gone, sold anything of value down to the golden thread of his lord's crest on his *shitagi*. He now wore straw sandals patched up too many times with the rest of a fishing net he'd found on a beach near Ise, tied his hair with a piece of a flag he'd collected on an old battlefield, and offered his skills as a bodyguard whenever he had the chance. But few people needed bodyguards anymore, or warriors for that matter. Peace had offered much to the folks, and the Tokugawa's efficient administration obliterated banditry, but the thousands upon thousands of warriors who had survived the civil war now struggled to make ends meet. So when the rumor of a challenge set by the young daimyō of Owari echoed to the rōnin's ears, he rushed to Jokoji, nearly breaking his sandals for good.

"I've got a copper coin," he whispered. His last coin. An old coin minted in Kai at the time of the Takeda, before his birth, with a square hole so broken it now appeared round, and smooth, unreadable characters minted on four sides of it. "But I was hoping to pray at the temple on top of the mountain with it."

"You've got a nice sword though," the girl nonchalantly replied.

His hand went by reflex to the hilt of said sword lying on his right. He would offer his life before he abandoned this katana. Pneumonia had once taken him close to death, and he had sold the cord wrap of the katana's hilt for meds, but once recovered, the guilt of it had nearly pushed him to betray the last order of his master and commit seppuku. It took him a year of hard labor and privation before he could buy it back, and nothing would let him commit this kind of blasphemy again.

"It's not for sale," he replied protectively.

"All right," the girl said. "Swords aren't that valuable anymore, so I thought we could buy it from you. But it's your sword."

The rōnin let go of the katana, then fished the copper coin from his pocket. Opening his palm and looking at it, he realized once again how low he had fallen. In Kyōto, Edo, or even Nagoya, no one would accept such a currency. Maybe the gods would laugh at his gift. He might as well fill his belly before the challenge began. It was, he told himself, an investment.

"Tell you what," the girl then said, crouching so that their eyes stood at the same level. "We got some miso soup left from this morning's batch. It's a bit cold, but if you offer a prayer for a warm winter for us with that coin, on top of your own wish, of course, I'll get you a bowl. What do you say?"

"I would be eternally grateful," the rōnin replied, bowing his head to hide his shame.

"Just wait here a minute," she told him, and since he would not raise his head, all he saw were her bare feet leaving him alone.

From the corners of his eyes, he saw the girl taking the order from the other patrons, including the three warriors from before, then she hurried to the kitchen. A brave girl, he thought, like most people in this country, hard-working and generous in times of plenty. Truly, the worst kind in Japan was his own, he told himself.

He wondered if he'd meet anyone he knew at Jokoji. Maybe some old hands from the civil war, or men like him who had only experienced the end of it. He knew more dead warriors than living ones, and the latter category contained mostly his former enemies, though such a notion had gradually vanished over the years. They were mostly beggars and masterless warriors now, though some had managed profitable relationships with one lord or another.

His thoughts naturally drifted toward the challenge as

he waited for his soup. The echo of it had been vague. He knew it would happen today, and that Yoshinao Tokugawa, ninth son to Ieyasu Tokugawa and younger brother to the current shōgun, would be present as the lord of Owari province. There was a rumor of a great prize for the victor, though some people said the challenge would crown more than one person. It could have been a tournament, or a race maybe. Highborn sometimes had fancy ideas of entertainment, and vagabond warriors were only too eager to gain a few coins or even a hot meal. If this Yoshinao Tokugawa could be amused by his groveling, maybe he wouldn't spend winter hungry.

"Here you go," the girl said as she set a bowl of fuming soup next to him on the bench.

"Thank you," the rōnin replied with another bow.

"And if you strike the fancy of Lord Tokugawa, come back here with the change." She left him with a friendly wink, its nature unrecognizable to the rōnin. Even in his early thirties, he was still called handsome, though most of the time by women who thought they could get some coins out of him, but surely this girl wasn't thinking of him as such. There wasn't much to appreciate in his current state. Yet she had been generous, and even more than he had believed, he realized when he raised the bowl to his lips and noticed rice at the bottom. A full ladle of it, hidden under a generous layer of seaweed. He thanked the girl in his mind and let the salty-smelling soup warm his mouth and pass down his gullet. His respite was short-lived.

"Good morning, brother," a raspy voice called.

The rōnin lowered his bowl, and on the other side stood the three warriors from before, with the one at the center standing a step ahead of his comrades. The leader was of similar age as the rōnin, but taller, and obviously better fed.

He and the two others, who could have been his friends or his younger brothers, carried the double swords of the samurai, the katana and the wakizashi, though their quality was dubious.

They received no reply from the rōnin, who simply swallowed the contents of the bowl in one long gulp. From his experience, three brawlers never accosted a lone warrior for a friendly chat, and he'd rather finish this rare meal before they went on with their business.

"Not a chatter, I see," the leader of the trio went on just as the second sat on the rōnin's bench, on his right, by his katana. "Unless it means chatting with our waitress, that is. Pretty little thing, isn't she?"

"If you say so," the rōnin replied, holding the empty bowl on his lap like a monk hoping for some alms.

"Here for the challenge?" the one on the bench asked.

"I am. You too?"

"We are," the leader replied, his arms crossed in a way that would let him draw his katana easily. "Heard anything interesting about it?"

"Probably not more than you," the rōnin answered. "I was in Komaki when I first heard about it. Then more rumors in Nagoya. What did you hear?"

"Nothing much," the standing man replied, making a face and shaking his head.

"Besides the prizes," the younger one said, speaking for the first time and receiving a hard glare from his leader for speaking up.

"Prizes?" the rōnin asked. "As in, plural?"

The leader of the trio clicked his tongue and mouthed for the younger one to shut it.

"It seems there are to be several winners, yes," he still admitted. "And according to the rumors, the daimyō is ready to be *very* generous with them." The last sentence he uttered while holding his thumb and first finger in a circle representing the nationally known sign for money.

"Then, let me guess," the rōnin said. "You came here right now to recruit me into your merry band, with some offer to share the prize. An offer you will, of course, go back on the second you get your hands on it."

"Oy!" the sitting man spat, getting on his feet and immediately dropping his hand on his hilt.

"Unless," the rōnin went on, "you were thinking to thin the competition by taking a lone challenger out before it even began. Which one is it then?"

The leader's grin grew even wider, but the rōnin guessed the snarl in it.

"Bit of both," he replied, shrugging.

"Unfortunately for you," the rōnin said, turning his eyes to steel, "I work alone."

The unspoken signal that precedes any battle beat inside their hearts immediately, and the three men moved. They lowered their stance at once, and the two closest thugs went for the hilt of their katana. But the rōnin moved faster. He dropped the empty bowl on the hilt of the leader's sword and punched the wrist of the second man at the same time, then, hands free and in place, drew both their wakizashi, which he crossed in front of him until they met the skin of the two men's throats. They straightened up as one, and the leader swallowed hard. This had gone faster than his eyes could follow, or his mind could comprehend.

"Draw your blade and they both die," the rōnin told the younger thug who had barely moved and seemed stuck in his pre-drawing pose.

"All right, let's all calm down," the leader offered, hands raised in a show of submission.

"What's all this?" a voice rang over the eerie quiet of the resting place.

The rōnin dared a look on his right, from where a samurai dressed in black walked with heavy steps toward the troublemakers. The rōnin had seen enough of those men in the province to know they kept the peace in the name of the daimyō. Their reputation was formidable, and not all unkind. This man even displayed the air of capability shared by veterans of many battles. So when he reached the four swordsmen, the rōnin took a step back and put some distance between the wakizashi swords and their owners' throats.

"Just a misunderstanding," the trio's leader said as he massaged the thin red line on the side of his neck.

"Apologies for the ruckus," the rōnin said as he lowered the two short blades and pointed them downward, hilts toward the two men.

"You got some nerve," the samurai in black said, squinting at the three of them, "fighting like this with the daimyō being so close. If you're here for Tokugawa Yoshinao's event, I suggest you get going. It's about to begin and you wouldn't want to be disqualified, would you?"

While the men's words were neutral in tone, it fooled none of them. The three thugs shared a silent look, as if weighing their options, but they didn't have many. This was a proper samurai, working under the lord of those lands. They would gain nothing from his death and had everything to lose, including their spot in the challenge about to take place. What they failed to notice was the utter danger to their lives. The rōnin could feel the martial spirit of the samurai. Veterans carried the pain of their victims in their strides, and this man had claimed many lives, he could feel it at the tips of his fingers. A wrong turn of phrase and he would butcher those three amateurs.

"Apologies for the nuisance," the leader said as he readjusted the two blades of his *daishō* set, and in terms of apologies, this was all the samurai in black or the rōnin got. The trio left toward the red bridge crossing the Shonan River and Jokoji Mountain looming a little further down the road.

"I saw what happened here," the samurai said. "It wasn't your fault, rōnin, but don't you dare trouble the peace of Owari." The rōnin nodded but otherwise said nothing. "It was a nice bit, what you did with the bowl. I'll remember that one." A single chuckle passed the samurai's closed lips, and the tension vanished.

"It doesn't always end so well though, does it?"

"Aye," the samurai replied.

The rōnin's mind journeyed off, as it always did when the tension of a fight, no matter how brief, cleared. At least this time he had no blood to wash from his katana.

"Sekigahara or Osaka?" the samurai asked. "You're a bit young for Sekigahara, so I assume it was Osaka who gave you that scar."

"Osaka," the rōnin replied as his finger moved to the jagged line along his jaw. It hadn't been such a terrible blow, not his worst wound by a long shot, but somehow the mark proved tenacious.

"I fought at Sekigahara myself," the samurai replied, "and a little at Osaka, though not nearly as much."

The rōnin stiffened a little, and slowly rearranged the katana in his belt, dropping his hand on the pommel to cover the crest. The Tokugawa had been on the other side of the ramparts at Osaka, and bad blood stained longer than soot.

"No need for that," the samurai said, nodding at the

katana's covered pommel. "I recognized the six coins of the Sanada clan on your scabbard. Osaka was a lifetime ago, and the Sanada warriors' bravery is the stuff of legend, no reason to be ashamed."

"Will your lord allow me in his challenge knowing I stood with his father's enemies?" the rōnin asked.

"Yoshinao might be young, and unbloodied in war, but he's all right," the samurai answered. Coming from him, the rōnin thought, this was great praise. Men forged in war seldom complimented those virgin in it.

"Besides," the samurai went on, "old rancors might soon have no place in this country." The samurai looked distantly toward the mountain as he spoke, or, as the rōnin guessed, toward a bleak future. He'd seen that look on the faces of soldiers when rumors of war spread. "Never mind me," he said with a tap on the rōnin's shoulder, "but do move on. It's about to begin."

If the rōnin thought the road was brimming with travelers before, the last stretch to Jokoji was bursting with activity. More than a hundred weapon-carrying men and women waited at the base of Jokoji Mountain, many of them accompanied by non-fighting folks, wives, children, retainers, students, elderlies, and others. On top of them came people of various crafts, attracted by the presence of so many warriors and their patronage. Courtesans, obviously, but also traveling smiths, doctors, monks, sandal-weavers, and dozens of crooks selling amulets for luck or victory in the coming challenge. All faced the mountain, and the rōnin, never one to enjoy a crowd, circled around Jokoji with whatever time he had left.

The herd thinned as he moved away from the main road. He remained close enough to hear the confusion among his peers. No one seemed to know what exactly was about to happen, but everyone agreed it was to be a rare event.

Jokoji was not the highest peak in central Japan, nor even in Owari, but climbing it would still prove a challenge in itself. The forest grew thick all over it, with, as far as the rōnin could see, only a central, straight flight of stairs cutting through the southern flank of the mountain all the way to the top, where a temple of the Rinzai school of Zen blessed the pilgrims. Even those stairs would leave the traveler breathless, but from what he'd heard, the monks up there could lift any misfortune from a man's fate with their blessing. Yoshinao Tokugawa was also said to use the location as his hunting lodge, and the rōnin could easily believe those forests teeming with game.

Every hundred steps, facing the crowd, a Tokugawa soldier stood by a small table. They wore no armor, only the same black *hakama* and *shitagi* as the samurai from earlier. Even more surprising, some did not carry swords but the hooked staff called *jitte*, an instrument gaining more popularity by the day within the Tokugawa ranks. The rōnin was observing such a soldier when the bell from the temple rang. As one, all the soldiers he could spot took a step forward and brought their hands around their mouths to increase the volume of their voices.

"On behalf of Tokugawa Yoshinao, daimyō of the Tokugawa Owari domain, welcome to Jokoji," they all shouted. The rōnin stopped to face the closest soldier, who kept his gaze straight, looking at no one in particular. He was too young to have taken part in Osaka, so the rōnin relaxed a little.

"Warriors and adventurers," the soldiers went on, "you've come from far, the rumor of a great challenge and reward guiding you to this mountain. We are grateful for your presence, and will now explain both the said challenge, and the reward attached to it. First, the prize."

Even if the rōnin had found a location with less competition than the entrance of the mountain, he was still standing within a small group of peers, including, he regretfully observed, the three men from before.

"Ten of you, at most, will be declared victors, with no ranking among them. As such, there will be ten prizes."

"Spit it out already!" a vagabond warrior shouted.

"Should you be among the ten, the daimyō will grant you one wish. Anything in his power can be asked."

"What if I want all his money?" the leader of the trio asked, which made several others laugh.

"It will be yours," the soldier replied in all seriousness, which turned the laughter to impressed whistles. If the rōnin had his doubts regarding the nature of the event, he now believed something unique was afoot. The greatness of the prize probably meant a more dangerous challenge than he'd expected. Only those who did not laugh understood it.

"Now, for the competition itself," the soldier went on, squaring his shoulders. "You will race to the temple, where Tokugawa Yoshinao is waiting. The first ten will be declared victors."

"That's it?" an old warrior asked by the rōnin's side. "Just a race?"

"Jokoji Mountain is home to bandits, *yōkai*, and even four *Tengu*," the soldier replied, though it felt more like the next step of his explanation. "It is unlikely you will climb the mountain without meeting any of them, and each of them will try to kill you."

Only a couple of men laughed then, but even they quickly relented. If this was some kind of entertainment, the rōnin thought, it was truly twisted.

"If you are not ready to die or kill, please step away from the competition now," the soldier said, stretching his arm in the opposite direction to the mountain. No one in this group accepted the offer, but the rōnin saw a few men from other gatherings walking back toward the road.

Ready to die or kill wasn't an issue for him, but death in such a random place, in such a random event, would not suit his goal.

"If you wish to proceed," the soldier said, increasing the volume of his voice, "you will receive a thousand *mon*, either in copper coins or silver ingot, according to your preference." Even the rōnin tensed at this. One thousand *mon* was a sum he hadn't been near in a decade and would guarantee a year away from hunger.

"Even if we lose?" someone asked.

"If you lose," the old warrior from earlier replied, "it means you're dead."

Again some of the challengers laughed, but not the old warrior, nor the soldier.

"On the table, you will find a stack of *ema*," he said. The rōnin had failed to notice the wooden plaques before, but they were actually hard to miss. Probably fifty of those wishing tablets formed a neat pile on the small table, and by their side waited a few brushes and some ink. "Each participant will take one *ema*. On the front side, at the center, you will write your name. Under it, you will either write the name of a non-participating person who accompanied you here or your hometown address."

"It's for our corpses," the old warrior said, whispering the words to the rōnin, who had also guessed as much.

"If no name or address is written, the temple will take care of you, should you fall," the soldier said, confirming the old warrior's guess. "On the back, you will write your wish. Each *ema* has a cord. You can wear it on your chest, your back, or hanging on your belt. You may give up at any point of the ascension, in which case you will hand over your plaque and receive your participation prize. No one walking down the forest will be harmed, so feel free to give up if it gets too much for you."

Those are nice bandits and yōkai, the rōnin thought.

"Are there any questions?"

"If my comrades fall, should I bring their plaques?" the leader of the trio asked in a jesting tone. His second laughed and elbowed him in the ribs, but the rōnin guessed the question had been serious.

"No," the soldier simply replied.

"Are we allowed to kill those who attack us?" the rōnin asked. He did not specify if he meant the inhabitants of the mountain or the participants. In the end, it was all the same.

"Yes," the soldier replied.

He was about to say something else, but the bell of the temple rang once more, and the soldier in black took a step from the table.

"Now please form a line and fill the *ema* in good order."

A line would hardly describe what the warriors formed, but one by one they signed a plaque and inscribed their wish on the back, until it was the rōnin's turn. His mind was still reeling with the explanation of this challenge. Something felt off, but he could not put his finger on it yet.

He picked the last *ema* of a pile. A typical pentagonal tablet resembling a house the way a child would draw it.

The brush was quite dry and most of the ink gone, but he didn't need much, anyway. On the front side, he traced the two characters forming the title Rōnin. His identity had long stopped mattering. Since the end of the siege of Osaka, he was a masterless samurai, a wanderer. He left no indication for his body; they might as well just burn it. In fact, he considered himself lucky that a temple would take care of it. For years he had assumed when the day came, he would just rot in a field or feed the eels of some river.

"You sure?" the soldier asked, eyeing the tablet from the corners of his eyes.

"Certain," Rōnin replied.

He scribed the back of the plaque with more care, and more discreetly, then hung it on his chest, facing forward. The old warrior from before came after him and was the last. This all happened just before a third strike of the bell.

"Now get ready. The bell will ring once more in a few seconds, and the challenge starts with it," the soldier shouted. Some of the warriors disbanded from the group and walked a little away. Rōnin felt his heart beat faster in anticipation of the bell, and his palms turned wet, just like before a battle.

"Don't rush in," the old warrior said. He stood on Rōnin's left, and he wondered for a second if the old man was speaking to himself.

"You know it's a race, right?" Rōnin asked.

"It's not a race," the old man replied. "It's a battle. And in battle, do you really want to be on the frontline?"

"A battle?"

The bell on top of the mountain rang again for the last time, and from all around Jokoji, warriors rushed toward the edge of the forest. Rōnin did not rush, but neither did he walk as the old warrior did. He let the most enthusiastic dash ahead, knowing that no man would have the stamina to reach the temple at this speed. Rōnin thus proceeded at something like a jog and soon passed under the shadow of the first trees. Ahead, some warriors were already vanishing between the trees, leaving nothing more than the crushed leaves under their feet to mark their presence.

A bowl of soup and a ladle of rice would not sustain him running uphill for long, so Rōnin opted for a controlled speed, using the branches for support when the mountain gained in steepness, though never letting go of his sheathed katana for more than a breath.

After a minute, a scream echoed further up and on the left. It was answered by a gunshot on the other side of the mountain. Shrieks and shouts intensified, slowly at first, then almost without interruption. Rōnin emptied his mind, reminding himself that he was mostly dead, anyway. Screams, gunshots, fear, this had been this world for a while. He walked more than he ran then, not only because the slope was stealing his breath, but because he tried to locate the closest screams and correct his course accordingly. Blades clashed somewhere on his left, just once, and he thought he heard a gurgling sound, but his attention was stripped away.

"Watch out!" someone said on his back.

A man bolted from behind the tree Rōnin had been using for support, sword in hand. Rōnin only saw he was bare-chested, barefoot, and bearded. His mind thought *bandit*, and his right hand moved to the hilt of his katana, but the bandit was already slashing his blade down toward Rōnin's neck in a powerful strike.

All thought veered from Rōnin's mind, and he let instinct kick in. An instinct forged in the school of Master Tabiya, then under the guidance of Lord Sanada. His hands moved before his brain could. His left hand pulled on the *saya*, while the right drove the blade forward. Rōnin took half a step, then drew his blade completely, but the blade wasn't meant to strike, the pommel was. With the strength of an arrow leaving the bow, Rōnin punched his crested *kashira* right at the center of the bandit's forehead, and the bandit's sword fell harmlessly from his grasp. It all happened while the bandit's sword came down, and surely the man thought he had pushed his attack with perfect timing. He dropped unconscious to his knees, and Rōnin sheathed his sword before the rest of the bandit toppled. Then Rōnin breathed out.

"You didn't kill him?" the old warrior asked.

"He was too close for that," Rōnin lied. "Thanks for the warning."

"If you hadn't taken care of him," the old warrior said, bending a little over to catch his breath, "he would have come at me next. Do you believe me now, about this being a battle?"

"Aye, it's a battle all right," Rōnin replied as he crouched to turn his opponent on the back. He was breathing, and a bump was already forming where Rōnin had struck. If at first glance the man did look like a bandit, a closer inspection proved he was nothing as such. His body was that of a well-fed and well-trained warrior, who until recently had been well-trimmed too. A pretense, that's all it was. "How did you know?"

"They said there was no ranking," the old soldier replied as Rōnin dragged the unconscious body next to the tree he had emerged from.

"Ranking?" he asked, grunting with a last effort.

"If it was a race, there would be different prizes according to the order we reached the top, wouldn't there?"

"It makes sense," Rōnin replied as they naturally resumed the climb together.

"In fact," the old soldier went on, "the way this soldier spoke leads me to believe they don't even expect ten people to make it to the temple."

"I had the same impression," Rōnin agreed.

The old warrior started breathing harder through his nose. If it had been a race, he would have had no chance, but maybe the two swords at his hip were not for show, and he had, after all, spotted the "bandit" before Rōnin. His presence also soothed the lone warrior a little.

"I'm Tarō Daisuke, by the way," the old soldier said. "Nice to meet you... Rōnin." He said the last while squinting to decipher Rōnin's calligraphy. "Your parents have an odd sense of imagination."

Rōnin smiled in reply; the old man knew this could not be his real name.

"Nice to meet you Tarō-san," he replied.

"This technique you used earlier—"

"Battōjutsu," Rōnin replied, "though some call it Iaijutsu."

"Never heard of it, but it was impressive. Don't think I ever saw anyone reacting faster than that in all my years..." His words stretched as they both observed a warrior rush down the mountain on their right, running so fast he might hurt himself. They shrugged after he disappeared and went on.

"How about you Tarō-san, where did you learn?"

"Ah!" the old warrior barked. "I learned on the field of battle. Dōjō and proper masters are for noblemen's sons, no offense." Rōnin took none. He was actually the son of a nobody, but this was a story he would rather not delve into. "I was born the son of a very minor samurai, serving a barely more important samurai, under a minor lord of the Mori clan. They sent me to battle after battle since I could barely call myself a man, and through alliances, betrayals, defeats, and so on, served different lords. Then one day it all stopped, and I too could have written that on my *ema*," he said, pointing at Rōnin's plaque. "I've taken part in over thirty battles and never managed to get myself killed, though you could say I never achieved anything worth mentioning besides surviving. All I hope for now is not to die masterless. Will you help me, Rōnin?"

"You saved me earlier," Rōnin replied, "I should be the one asking for your help."

"I doubt he would have—"

A man running down, straight in their direction, stopped Tarō Daisuke mid-sentence. Both warriors lowered their stance and moved to their swords' hilt, but quickly realized they didn't need to. He was another runaway, and Rōnin recognized him; the youngest of the three thugs.

"Help me, help me," he pleaded, catching Rōnin by the edge of his worn-out shirt, breathless and eyes wide with fear. "Don't let them get me, please." His face was splattered with drops of blood, none his by the look of it.

"Where are your friends?" Rōnin asked.

"They...heaven's sake." The young thug blanched suddenly. Rōnin thought he was about to throw up, but he managed to keep it within. "They're dead. It happened so fast. One second they were standing there. We even got one of them bandits, we got him good. We were laughing, then they came, and, and..."

"More bandits?" Daisuke asked.

"No, not men, they were not men. They, they..." The young man swallowed hard, his eyes going back to his friends' deaths. "I ran. I just ran."

"You did well," the old warrior said, dropping his hand on the young man's shoulder. "The soldier said we should leave the mountain if we wanted safety."

"Where did it happen?" Rōnin asked, thinking to avoid the location of whatever killed the young thug's friends.

"Right there," he said, turning around and pointing in a straight line toward the top of the mountain. Rōnin heard the string of a bow releasing its tension, then the *thwack* of the arrow as it sunk into the young man's eye. He did not even have time to scream.

"Shit!" Daisuke barked as more missiles thumped into the young thug's body. He and Rōnin split to find cover behind two trees. A last bow shot its arrow, which smacked into the dead young man, sending him falling backward into a parterre of brown leaves.

"Rōnin, you're all right?" Tarō Daisuke asked.

"Better than him," Rōnin replied. "So much for being allowed to go down safely."

"He turned around," the old warrior shouted. He seemed to realize the sudden silence, for his next words came quieter. "They waited until he looked up, as if he was going upward again."

Rōnin peeked from the side of his tree to get a look at those *yōkai* who followed the rules of men and could shoot arrows with outstanding skills. They moved slowly, silently, in the shadows of the trees. Crouching more than standing, Rōnin saw creatures walking on two legs, with capes of feathers and ram horns sprouting from shaggy heads. They spoke using rattling sounds and grunts, coordinating their movements in their approach of the two hiding warriors. But for all their bestiality, they held samurai long bows or carried spears.

"Do you want to go back?" Rōnin asked Daisuke.

The old warrior shook his head, pouting.

"I'm too old. Going downhill would be hard on my knees."

Rōnin smiled in response. Daisuke had drawn his katana during the action, and now held it low, while he, of course, would keep his sheathed until it came time to strike.

"I counted three," Daisuke said.

"Same."

An arrow bounced off the tree Rōnin used for protection, forcing him back behind it completely. They were coming closer. He could now hear their breathing, nearly as ragged as his. Sounds of battles were still happening here and there, with the rare *teppo* being fired. Rōnin signed for Daisuke that he would take the two on the left, going around the tree first. The old warrior nodded and twisted on his heels to face the other way around. To deceive them, Rōnin took a look just like before, and this nearly won him an arrow in the mouth. He moved from the other side immediately, dashing out before the archer could ready his next shot. For a heartbeat, he wondered if maybe the old warrior was just using him as a decoy, but he heard the ruffle of Daisuke's feet as he too bolted from his cover.

"Oy!" one of the creatures called, pointing his long spear toward Rōnin as his comrade prepared another arrow.

Rōnin corrected his course to attack the archer and nearly slipped on dead leaves. The archer was already rearranging his stance, slowly, methodically lowering his bow, as any master of *kyūdō* would. By his side, the spear-wielding creature pointed his wicked polearm forward, ready to skewer the approaching warrior. Rōnin veered left, on the side of the spearman, recognizing that he would never reach the archer on time and that any step made him an easier target. He looked as if circling them while still getting closer, keeping his eyes on the spearman's, telling the creature he was coming for him. Both opponents were focused on him. They wanted his life, and one of them had killed the younger thug, so Rōnin would not hesitate this time. He heard the string reach its maximum tension and felt the arrow aimed at him. A split second before the archer released, the bow bumped into his comrade's spear, the two weapons conflicting because of their difference in reach. This was the moment Rōnin had been working for, and his time to act. He shifted on his ankles and resumed a direct course toward them.

"Shit," said the archer as he unwillingly released his arrow into the emptiness of the forest, over Rōnin's shoulder.

The katana left the sheath, fast as a lightning bolt, slicing through the spear and the creature's wrist in the upward strike, then across the archer's face on the way down. The second couldn't scream, the first couldn't stop. The spearman fell to his knees, holding his half-severed hand as blood flowed over Rōnin's left arm. The wandering warrior twisted on his right foot and thrust the tip of his blade into the man's mouth, for he now knew those two were no *yōkai* but people. They could wear masks, helmets, and capes. They could pretend to speak with grunts and move through the forest like spirits. But they died like men, with a lot of blood.

"Rōnin," Daisuke called as the lone warrior shook the blood from the blade.

Rōnin remembered the old man and switched his focus toward the last of the three creatures as it quietly nocked a new arrow on his bowstring, the previous one being deep into Tarō Daisuke's chest. The old samurai was struggling to remain on his feet, blade held upward near his wincing face.

The lone warrior did not waste time calling for Daisuke. Instead, he used his breath to rush at the archer. Battōjutsu did not have running techniques per se, but Rōnin had long rectified this flaw and timed his last step of a dash as if he'd been walking, stomping his foot a little harder. The monster's mask prevented him from seeing Rōnin coming his way and he kept pulling on his bowstring, though, at this distance, even a feeble arrow would have sufficed. Rōnin, feeling he would be too late for a perfect cut, struck before he usually would, aiming at the archer's ankle. He barely felt the graze of metal on bone and already the sword came through the leg. The archer screamed like a man and fell on his ass as blood splashed all the way to the old warrior. The shriek ended when Rōnin reversed his attack and cut through the creature's throat. Then everything became silent again, at least around him.

"Tarō-san!" Rōnin called after he shook the blood off his katana and sheathed it. But the old warrior would not reply. The arrow had lodged itself in the left lung, and Daisuke Tarō, veteran of more than thirty battles, died in a menacing *hassō-gamae* stance, stubborn to the point of breathing his last while standing. Rōnin, a lone warrior once more, closed his eyes and joined his hands in prayer, not for the old man's soul but for his bravery, and left him in the forest of Jokoji Mountain, standing at the feet of his fallen killer.

For a second, he wondered if he should go back down, but the shame of the thought put him back on the path to the temple right away.

He had already killed three warriors—for he now knew they were neither bandits nor *yōkai* demons—and seen two others die, not even counting the one he had knocked out and who might never regain his wits. A thousand *mon* was a worthy sum, and he had done more for less, but in this time of peace he wondered why the daimyō would go to such length for a challenge. If this was not entertainment, then it had to hide something deeper. Wandering and masterless warriors were a plague for Japan now that the empire was at peace, and maybe this was a twisted way to reduce their numbers. Yoshinao Tokugawa might have hired one bunch to fight another. It would be a cruel way to deal with this problem, but it certainly was efficient, and probably economically sound in the long run. And if it was just for entertainment, Rōnin thought, then it said a lot about the young daimyō of Owari.

Rōnin ran faster after the short fight with the archers. He did not do so on purpose and actually did not realize it. His blood was pumping faster, his breath controlled. This was his element, no matter how often he pretended otherwise. Bodies littered his path, some belonging to challengers, others to masked men and fake bandits. The forest was mostly silent when he reached the point where he could see the top, though the odd scream disturbed the forest once in a while.

On the ridge of the slope, where earth and sky met, a strange shape rose from the ground. Rōnin slowed his pace to a walk. His forehead was drenched in sweat, his mouth dry but his mind clear. The spirit stretching out in front of him was nearly as big as a bear, with a cape of feathers like the archers from before, but white. His face was dark red, drawn in a scowl, with a long white mustache and a straight protuberant nose. A Tengu, Rōnin understood, the guardian spirit of the mountain, and probably one of the best warriors the daimyō had hired for this event. There was a man under the mask, yet even this knowledge failed to reassure him as he stopped a dozen steps from the spirit. The Tengu wore only shoulder armor and held a massive *ōdachi* sword, the longest Rōnin had ever seen. It raised its arms and took a *jōdan* stance, sword held above its head with both hands, making the guardian spirit appear even bigger. Whether Tengu or samurai, this opponent was strong and skilled, Rōnin felt it in his stomach.

"Have ten people arrived already?" Rōnin asked the spirit as it shuffled a little closer. The Tengu shook its masked head slowly. "Then I'm sorry for what's about to happen."

Rōnin resumed his advance slowly but circled around the spirit instead of coming straight at it. Fighting on a slope was disadvantageous, especially with his opponent wielding such a long sword, so he had to put himself on the same level. The Tengu seemed content in letting him. They faced each other; the Tengu scowling down at Rōnin, sword above its head, and Rōnin, katana impatiently waiting in its sheath while the warrior slowed his breath. Four steps separated them, but none of them moved.

The lone warrior breathed out, almost completely closed his eyes, and let the voice of his master enter his mind, calling for the next move.

Juntō Sono Ni.

A high curtain forming a square on top of the mountain had drawn the limits of Jokoji temple, not unlike the curtain separating actors and spectators at a *kabuki* play. Rōnin stepped through it and came into sight of a most beautiful temple ground. The main building was a typical structure of wood, mounted with a massive copper-colored double roof reaching almost to the ground. Huge maple trees protected this sacred space with their shadow, and the sunlight filtered through in hues of red and orange, making it look like dusk even though it was barely noon. A small pond welcomed white and orange fish on the temple's left side, as Rōnin observed while he crossed the courtyard. He could only see one monk, the one who stood by a bell twice bigger than he was, and who had probably called for this whole battle to begin. The lone warrior would have expected the daimyō to wait in front of the temple's building, or at the center of the square, but, surprisingly, all the men Rōnin could see had gathered under a maple tree, near a small shrine barely bigger than a shed, resting on the highest point inside the square.

In front of the shrine, on a simple stool, sat a young man. He had to be the daimyō, Rōnin thought. From what he had gathered on his way to the mountain, Rōnin knew Yoshinao Tokugawa would be in his mid-twenties. He had seen no war, being only fourteen when the civil war ended for good, but people seemed to consider him a peerless martial artist. There were even talks of him receiving the title of fourth head of the *shinkage-ryū* school of *kenjutsu*. Rōnin could see from his posture, back straight as an arrow, and from his sharp eyes, that the young man indeed carried the soul of a true warrior, one with honor in his heart. Thus he knew this challenge had not been for entertainment. Rōnin faced the young Lord of Owari and bowed deeply.

Nine guards stood left and right of the daimyō, and when Rōnin recognized the one from this morning, he bowed to him as well, then a third time toward the shrine behind, though he did not know to which deity or person this small building had been dedicated.

Then he knelt and dropped the two halves of the Tengu

mask in front of Yoshinao Tokugawa. There was a small wave of murmurs, but no reaction from the daimyō.

"Welcome," Yoshinao said before trying to read the name on the wooden plaque. "Rōnin. You have done well in defeating a Tengu."

"He fought honorably," Rōnin replied.

"As did you," the daimyō said. "Please, take a seat while we wait for the other challengers." Yoshinao Tokugawa had a soft voice, used to being obeyed, yet humble. He stretched his hand toward the circular straw mats laid on both sides of the small path leading to him, six on the left, four on the right. Two were already taken.

On the left side, in the back corner, sat a monk. A *sōhei* warrior monk, dressed in two layers of robes, white under and saffron on top. The monk sat in a meditative pose, the bottom of his prayer beads stuck between his thumb and first finger. His eyes were closed, but Rōnin knew that even if he opened them, they would see nothing, for a wide, straight line cut through them. Despite his blindness, the monk had made it to the top before the lone warrior, in part thanks to the cross-shaped spear resting by his side. Rōnin knew of warrior monks specializing in their usage in the past, but since the previous *shōgun* had all but destroyed the religious schools of martial arts, their kind had mostly vanished. Rōnin would have gone on the other side of the path rather than disturb the man in his meditation if it wasn't for the other challenger.

On the right side, in the back corner as well, knelt a demon. Rōnin shuddered at the sight of him, then remembered that a few minutes ago he had fought a Tengu and three *yōkai*. The mask was perfect though. The lower part snarled in a mouth from which protruded four long canine teeth like tusks, and a wrinkled nose, while the upper part hid two dark eyes made darker by the man's makeup, and two horns the length of a thumb sprouting from his forehead. A hood covered the demon's scalp, with only a plaque of metal at the edge of it confirming what Rōnin thought: this man was a *shinobi*, a skilled assassin of the shadows, trained from childhood in the art of death. The wooden plaque hanging at his belt contained only one character, Kiba, the fang. The lone warrior could see no weapon whatsoever, but the smell of fresh blood was unmistakable. He thus chose the left side and sat on the front mat in the corner, the furthest one from the *shinobi*.

Rōnin sat in a cross-legged position, not liking the *kiza* form of kneeling with the feet flat under the ass that seemed to gain in popularity recently, and then waited in silence. He had barely let his shoulders relax when a young page appeared from nowhere and knelt by Rōnin to hand him a cup of hot water. He gulped it with pleasure, and probably less decorum than expected from a guest of a daimyō. Yoshinao did not seem to mind, and his attention was soon drawn to the curtain closest to them, from where three more warriors appeared as one. If no one reacted at Rōnin's arrival, those three appearing forced the daimyō to rebuke his guards with frowns as they gasped and grumbled almost unanimously. Rōnin too fought to keep his thoughts to himself, for the three warriors were not typical samurai.

The one walking in front was tall and muscular, with a powerful jaw and arms to shame a smith. A heavy *naginata* ending in a thick curved blade balanced with each of her steps, and the rattle of a black and red complete armor covered the deep voice of this warrior.

"You don't need to do that now," she told her companion who was biting the paper off of a cartridge of powder even as they walked the path leading to the daimyō.

The musketeer pushed the cartridge back into one of the leather bags at her belt and slung her long *teppo* matchlock gun on her back before she made a small series of gestures that Rōnin could not interpret. She was probably the oldest of the three, though not by much. Her hands were a misery of scars and burned skin, the price paid by many gunners, and the strap belt clicking with smaller pistols and bags of bullets showed her passion for those weapons. Rōnin had seen firsthand the efficiency of those long-distant fighters and heard tales of female units that could decimate ranks of soldiers before they reached the frontline.

"To be ready is one thing," the first one replied to the hand gestures, "but what will those fellas think if you load your gun right as we are about to meet their lord, huh?"

The silent musketeer sighed and nodded as they stopped in front of Yoshinao Tokugawa. Rōnin then observed the last and youngest of the trio. She could not have been over sixteen. Her bow rose much taller than her, but her quiver was half-empty. She was a thin girl, shy and discreet, and if not for her weapons, the warrior would never have guessed she too was one.

"Welcome to Jokoji," Yoshinao said as the three women bowed. "You've done well, Ikeda Yūkihime," he continued after reading the name of the *onna-musha*.

"With all due respect," she replied, a hint of anger in her voice, "the only *Lady* Ikeda here is my sister. I'm a samurai and would be treated as one." The guards of the daimyō shuffled and frowned, either displeased by her tone or because she fancied herself their equal.

"My apologies, Ikeda-dono," Yoshinao replied with an apologetic bow. "I did not mean any insult."

"None taken," Yūki replied.

"If you don't mind my question," the daimyō then asked, "are you the daughter of Ikeda Sen?"

"I am," the woman replied with pride. Rōnin understood from the reaction of the guards that the question had been asked for their benefit. He too knew of the fearsome reputation of Ikeda Sen, the greatest *onna-musha* of the civil war.

"Ame here is a captain in my mother's musketeers unit," Ikeda Yūki went on. "And this is my sister, Tsukihime."

"The Ikeda clan have been friends of mine for decades," Yoshinao Tokugawa replied as the two other women bowed once more. "I am feeling infinitely better for your presence. Please, take a seat. It shouldn't be long now."

Yūki, Tsuki, and Ame, Rōnin told himself as the three women turned around to sit. Tsuki and Yūki barely looked related, besides their turned-up nose. The lone warrior bowed his head when the younger one caught him staring, and she discreetly smiled in response. They filled the three mats on the right side, leaving the archer to sit next to the *shinobi*, something she did without even flinching.

The servant from earlier proceeded to give them a cup each as well, and on his path used this chance to refill the others'.

Rōnin wanted to ask what all of this had been about, but since no one else spoke, neither did he. Despite the remonstrance from earlier, the musketeer used the bit of time to clean the muzzle of her *teppo*, expertly emptying the bits of paper and powder into a square of fabric reserved for that purpose. The rattling of her rapid yet careful manipulation was soon replaced by the sound of steps coming from the center of the temple ground.

The curtains split once more right in front of the main building, just where the central stairs led, and two more warriors stepped through. Or more accurately, as Rōnin observed, a samurai and his student.

The boy, whom Rōnin aged around fourteen, was breathless, covered in blood and sweat, his hair sprouting in every direction despite the band originally keeping it in place. He held both his katana and wakizashi ready for action, though they had already seen plenty, judging by the red marring them.

His master walked behind peacefully, arms crossed under his chest, an impeccable white *shitagi* shirt over a red *hakama*. The samurai walked on a pair of *geta* sandals raised on two teeth each, making his steps loud inside the square, but his voice did not reach Rōnin. The two exchanged a few words, ending with the boy bowing respectfully to his master.

"We'll be right there!" the samurai shouted with a wave.

They moved toward the *temizuya* pavilion where purifying water flowed without interruption from the mountain's spring. The student was about to rinse his blades in the pouring water, but his master cuffed him behind the head. He then handed him a towel with which the boy cleaned the blades before sheathing them. Master and student then followed the purification protocol in a synchronized manner. Rōnin wondered if they were father and son, but everything set them apart in appearance. The master had a leather-like skin tanned by years traveling the road, while the boy's was still smooth. The latter's eyes were sharp and full of energy, the older man's tired and full of humor. His beard was scruffy, peppered in gray, and his hair reminded Rōnin of a wet raccoon, with no sense of aesthetic or etiquette. The boy, on his side, rearranged his unshaven *chonmage* topknot as soon as his hands were cleaned.

As they walked up to the daimyō, Rōnin noticed the

closest samurai to Yoshinao Tokugawa whispering into his master's ear. Yoshinao's eyes grew wide with surprise. It was the first time Rōnin saw a spontaneous emotion on the daimyō's face.

"I am told you are master Musashi Miyamoto," the daimyō said, resulting in a gasp from all the other guards, and Rōnin as well.

"Yagyū-dono is correct and has good eyes," Musashi replied with an amused smile passing over his lips. "How did you know?"

"Same as you recognized me," the bynamed Yagyū replied. "While we never met, we fought many times in my mind."

"I hope you don't treat me too harshly in there," Musashi said, tapping on the side of his head.

"I have yet to defeat you," the Yagyū samurai answered before both were taken by a bout of laughter.

This was simply astonishing to Rōnin's ears. The samurai on the daimyō's side, the lone warrior now understood, was Yagyū Hyōgonosuke, current head of the Shinkage-ryū school and one of the most respected swordsmen in the empire. Actually, one could say the only living swordsman with a greater reputation than his stood in front of him. Musashi Miyamoto, creator of the Niten Ichi-ryū form of kenjutsu using both blades at the same time, and legendary traveling warrior, graced Jokoji with his presence. Some people doubted his existence to the point of calling him a fable, and it was indeed remarkable that one man had managed to defeat so many masters in his youth. He had made himself more discreet since his famous duel on Ganryū island, but one look was enough to see he was a peerless master and a fearless one too, judging by his relaxed attitude.

"My apologies for arriving so late," Musashi told the daimyō with a bow. "It is my fault for waking too late."

"You honor us with your presence, Miyamoto-dono," Yoshinao replied. "And you are?"

"I'm Mikinosuke," the boy replied, pointing at his chest with his right thumb. The smack came to the back of his head with a great sound.

"Mind your manners," the master said without anger.

"My name is Mikinosuke, Lord Tokugawa," the boy said more politely, giving a deep bow with his head almost reaching his knees. "First student of Musashi-sensei."

"Only student," Musashi corrected as he dropped his hand on his student's shoulder.

"Welcome to you both," the daimyō said before stretching his hand toward the empty mats. "Please take a seat."

They moved to sit behind Rōnin, who used all his willpower not to glance at the most famous rōnin that ever lived and instead focused on his cup being refilled for the third time.

This time nothing happened for long minutes, maybe ten of them, and Rōnin heard the boy shuffling uncomfortably behind him. The samurai in black he had met in the morning stepped toward his lord and whispered something, to which Yoshinao replied with a curt nod. It seemed eight was going to be the final count, and Rōnin sighed at the idea that so many warriors had either perished or retreated. He gave a thought to Tarō Daisuke, wondering if the old man still stood defiantly under the rusty canopy of the forest. But then, just as Yoshinao Tokugawa seemed to agree with the result, a great shout echoed from outside of the square.

"Hey! Come back!" a voice called with a supremely angry tone.

A burst of cawing laughter was the only reply, and even from the distance, Rōnin could hear two pairs of feet running toward the temple. A samurai burst through the curtain like a cannonball, sword in hand and mouth wide open in delight. The flap did not even have time to close back before another Tengu jumped after the samurai.

"You... you cheat!" the Tengu shouted, pointing his blade at the laughing samurai, who was now bending over to regain his breath.

"What? Me? Cheating?" he asked between breaths. "Who said I had to fight with you? I just had to get past you, didn't I?"

"You bastard!" the Tengu said before he reached for his mask, which he threw in utter rage. He then raised his sword and took a fighting stance, forcing the samurai to do the same.

"Tanzaemon!" Yagyū Hyōgonosuke called from the bottom of his lungs, freezing the former Tengu into his place. "Get out of here!"

The bynamed Tanzaemon seemed to consider the order from his superior and winced in frustration, but ultimately pushed his blade back into its *saya* and left without a second look at the samurai, who then bent backward to let a long sigh of exhaustion into the air. He seemed to remember the reason for his presence and jogged toward the group. Halfway through, he raised his hand and waved at the daimyō.

"Yoshinao!" he called with extreme familiarity. "You've grown so much, boy."

"Uncle Tadatomo," the daimyō replied in a somewhat slightly tense tone. "I didn't expect to see you here."

"Here at Jokoji, or here at the top of the mountain?" the samurai asked as he came to stand in front of his nephew.

"Both," the young man replied honestly.

"Aye, well, I wasn't busy. So, here I am!" the samurai replied, stretching his arms wide.

"Please, take a seat," the daimyō said.

Tadatomo dropped on the mat next to Rōnin, still breathing like a bull and sweating like a pig. His first reflex was to untie the gourd from his belt and press it to his lips. As he drank large gulps of what Rōnin assumed to be sake, the samurai noticed the stare.

"Sorry," the samurai said, "I don't have much to share."

"It's all right," Rōnin replied, "they served us hot water."

The samurai made a guttural sound to show what he thought of the daimyō's gift, and Rōnin agreed to himself that this man was rather funny, if not polite. And he was, after all, the only proper samurai among the nine challengers. He wore a dark-blue *shitagi* shirt of noble quality, with a black *hakama*. The top of his head had been recently shaven, while the rest was tied into the same type of topknot as the boy, and a thick, black mustache covered his upper lip. Honda Tadatomo was the name scribed on his tablet. Rōnin stiffened when he read it. The two of them had found each other on the same battlefield once, on opposite sides.

This laughing samurai was the second son of Tadakatsu Honda, first general of the Tokugawa clan, and the greatest samurai of his time. Tadatomo should have followed in his father's footsteps, but his addiction to sake had led him to a great loss during the war at Osaka, and to an easy victory for Rōnin and his lord. Some people had claimed Tadatomo committed seppuku on the morrow of this battle since no one had heard much about him since. But here he was, grinning and drinking as the last challenger who made it to Jokoji temple, though partially by chance, it seemed.

Tadatomo Honda plugged his gourd when the young

page came to remove the last mat, the one next to the blind monk, for it seemed nine was the final count.

Tokugawa Yoshinao stood but held his hand down to let the nine warriors know they could remain at ease on their mats. He then turned to face the small shrine. Rōnin expected congratulations or a cheerful comment perhaps, so when the young lord spoke with sorrow in his voice, he felt bemused.

"This here is a temple to Bishamonten," he said, "god of war, punisher of evildoers, and protector of the nation." The latter part was said with a great sense of tiredness. "But today, Bishamonten will not be enough to save Japan."

The young daimyō looked over his shoulder, eyes heavy with tears—and guilt, Rōnin thought.

"I apologize for calling you here under false pretenses," he then told the nine, bowing at an angle usually reserved for nobles of the highest ranks.

"So there's no prize, huh?" Honda Tadatomo asked as a wave of murmurs passed through the small group. Rōnin felt sick to his stomach, thinking of the young thug and old Tarō Daisuke who had died for the lies of a nobleman.

"There will be rewards," the daimyō answered. "As promised, I will give you anything in my power. But not today."

"That's just great," Yūki Ikeda spat.

"You've all fought bravely today and showed me the depth of your skills. If you do not wish to listen to my plea and would rather leave, I will understand, and I have prepared a sum of ten thousand *mon* per individual, in golden ingots. There will be no resentment on my part, you have my word."

Ten thousand *mon*, Rōnin told himself. With such a fortune he could buy back anything he'd lost over the years and then some more. He could even learn a trade and leave the doomed path of the warrior behind.

"But if you stay," the daimyō went on, "you will have to swear never to speak of what I'm about to tell you to anyone. This is of the utmost importance. I am not playing with you when I say the fate of Japan, and maybe more, is at stake."

"Intriguing," Musashi said without warmth.

"Master, that's fantastic," the boy, Mikinosuke, said enthusiastically. "If you save Japan, surely—"

"Quiet, Mikinosuke," Musashi replied, gently interrupting the boy.

"I need your answers," Yoshinao Tokugawa asked. "Will you listen or leave?"

Rōnin dropped his gaze, wondering what he should do. Money would not fulfill the wish he had written on the back of his plaque, but this was a lot of it. This could change things.

Among the nine, some would not need the gold. Lords of all standards would sell their lands to retain the services of Musashi, even for an evening, and the Ikeda clan had its treasury full. Others among them might not even be allowed to receive it, the blind monk for one. Rōnin was ready to bet that none of the other eight had come with a buyable wish in mind.

Honda Tadatomo looked at the bottom of his gourd, and if his reputation was true, Rōnin guessed the samurai was calculating how many barrels of sake he could buy with such a sum. They exchanged an embarrassed look, then Tadatomo shrugged as if to say that they'd made it all the way here, anyway.

"We're all in, it seems," he said.

Yoshinao smiled, but again, Rōnin perceived some sorrow.

"Have any of you heard of Izanagi's curse?" Yoshinao asked.

"Izanagi?" Mikinosuke asked. "The god?"

"Yes," Yoshinao said. "The god who created life and Japan. He and his sister-wife, Izanami, as you all know, gave shape to the world and to our nation. They procreated and gave birth to many gods, Amaterasu of the sun, Tsukuyomi of the moon, and Susanō of the storms among them. My apologies for speaking of Shinto beliefs in such certain terms, Zenbō," the daimyō then said, looking toward the blind warrior-monk who would, of course, be Buddhist, just like the temple they stood in.

"No need to worry about me," the monk named Zenbō replied in a voice full of compassion.

"Izanami died giving birth to Kagutsuchi, the god of fire, which enraged Izanagi," the daimyō continued. "In his madness he went into Yomi, the land of the dead, to resuscitate his wife. But she had already become part of that cursed land, and her body had changed to that of a rotten corpse. Izanagi tried to flee, forgetting his love for her, and as he reached the border between the two worlds, Izanami, furious at her husband's abandonment, promised that she would kill a thousand people each day. Izanagi replied he would then give life to a thousand and five hundred each day." Yoshinao's voice trailed off there, and he got lost in his own thoughts. No one dared to interrupt him for a few seconds.

The musketeer made a small series of signs targeted at her leader, who harrumphed at the end.

"Ame would like to know why you're telling us a story every child in Japan knows," Yūki said.

"Because it's not a story," the daimyō replied heavily.

"Didn't you call it Izanagi's *curse*?" Musashi asked. "It

sounds to me that the curse in this tale came from Izanami. Without Izanagi, people would have long vanished from this good earth."

"That's because people misunderstand Izanagi's words," Yoshinao replied. He hesitated then. The words formed in his mind, Rōnin guessed, but refused to pass his lips.

"Please, enlighten us," Zenbō asked.

"Izanagi—" Yoshinao started before he swallowed a ball of saliva. "Izanagi never said he would give birth to one thousand and five hundred new people."

"What?" Tadatomo asked, as confused as Rōnin was.

"Let me be clearer. There's a curse on Japan. It's been going on for centuries. I do not know who created it, but it's here. For some time I doubted it, but I believe it with all my heart, and with your help, we will cure our nation from this curse."

"What curse?" Yūki asked bluntly. "What on earth are you blabbering about?"

"To make it simple, a curse to revive the dead," the daimyō answered.

Tadatomo and Yūki both snickered and chuckled at the words, and even Rōnin wondered for a second if this was all a jest. The mute musketeer asked her leader for confirmation.

"Yes," she replied with a smirk, "that's what he said." But the smirk vanished when she realized the young daimyō and his samurai were not smiling back. In fact, they looked even more sullen than before.

"Please," the daimyō said, "hear me out."

Rōnin heard his heartbeat in his chest, realizing the seriousness of the situation, or at least how the daimyō and his men saw it.

"This is what I've found," he went on. "Any man or

woman who died a warrior's death is marked by the curse of Izanagi, and can be recalled as a *kyonshī*."

"A *kyonshī*?" Tadatomo asked with a cough. "As in an animated corpse. You cannot be serious?"

"I am very serious, uncle," Yoshinao replied. "The curse is attached to four keys. The first is a *kotsuzumi* drum whose owner, upon writing the character for death on its skin with his own blood, can conjure the dead back to life by striking it. When he does so, any corpse in the vicinity, whether it died centuries or mere minutes ago, becomes his slave. They fight as they did in life, tapping into their instinct to kill anyone their master wishes."

"How do we stop them?" the shinobi asked practically, his voice muffled by his mask.

"Individually, my theory is that any blow to the spine should destroy them. Of course, if they are burned, crushed, or beheaded, it should do the trick." It was a weak attempt at humor, but it seemed to remind Yoshinao that all hope wasn't lost and he regained some strength in his voice. "I believe this is why we burn our dead as often as possible, why we have seconds to cut our heads when committing seppuku, or even why we collect the heads of samurai we have defeated. It's all a way to prevent the curse. But, as most of you will know, many warriors are left on the battlefield to rot, or die alone somewhere.."

"I still don't buy it," Tadatomo spat, waving his hand down. "No offense, Yoshinao, but it sounds a little too... fantastic. Has anyone ever seen this curse in action? How can you be so sure?"

"It was used not so long ago," the daimyō replied. "Sixty years ago to be exact, at Okehazama."

"Okehazama?" Tsuki, the archer, asked, hand over her mouth. "Where Nobunaga Oda defeated the mighty Yoshimoto Imagawa while being outnumbered ten to one?" Her voice trailed off by the end of the question, realizing what had truly happened then.

"Yes," Yoshinao replied. "As you can guess, he wasn't really outnumbered."

"Shit," Yūki said.

"As far as I know, he never used the curse after that battle, whether because he feared it or because he just didn't need to is unknown, but he was smart enough to avoid it. Many of the men on his side swore to keep it a secret, and since most died when Nobunaga was assassinated, it remained a rumor."

"How do you know then?" Rōnin asked.

"Because my father was there that day," the daimyō answered. "His name was Matsudaira Takechiyo back then, and he served as the second of Yoshimoto Imagawa. He saw the dead rising and killing. He surrendered in fear, and served Nobunaga Oda loyally from then on, keeping it a secret until his deathbed, where he told me the truth. For years he sent agents to collect information on the curse and trusted me with his findings. Unfortunately, the drum, which had been lost during the assassination of Nobunaga, was recently found by someone else, and in the wrong hands, it could mean another century of civil war or simply the annihilation of all living things in Japan. My father would never joke about this, and he died with all his wits."

"Yes," Tadatomo agreed, "the old Tanuki was never one for jokes, that's for sure."

"I had never seen my father so panicked before," the daimyō said. "He knew he was going to die in the next few days, but even that would not let him rest from what he had seen a lifetime ago. If Tokugawa Ieyasu feared the curse even as he stood at the door of his own demise, I beg you all to take it seriously."

"What else did you find about the curse?" Zenbō asked.

"The dead will rise as far as the drum can be heard, no more, and will remain *alive* only within this distance. The owner of the drum must then command them to move if he wants to lead them anywhere, and he must keep striking the *kotsuzumi* before they reach the limits of his power."

"They would move slowly," Musashi commented.

"Exactly," the daimyō replied, "and not discreetly. But there's worse."

"Is there?" Tadatomo asked with a scoff.

"No one has ever used it, otherwise we wouldn't be here, but the curse can be strengthened. There's a ritual that can grant the drum and its owner power beyond its regular reach, possibly all over Japan. It has to be performed on the altar at the center of a place called Onijima. This altar is the second key and the talisman activating it the third. I found nothing about the talisman, so I suggest assuming it is already in the hands of the drum master."

"Onijima?" Kiba, the shinobi, asked. "Demon Island?"

"Do you know of it?" Tsuki asked.

"Yes," the shinobi slowly replied. "It is a legendary place, where dark magic has been performed since before the first emperor. No one knows where it is, or even if it is real."

"My father believed Nobunaga built his last castle, Azuchi, as the gate to Onijima," Yoshinao explained. "I also believe it, but none of my agents found anything there to corroborate this theory."

"How do we stop *it*?" Yūki asked. "The curse, I mean."

"Two ways," the young daimyō said, holding up the first two fingers of his right hand. "We can destroy either the *kotsuzumi* or the altar."

"Do we know who has the drum?" Rōnin asked. "Or where it is?"

"I...I don't know where it is," Yoshinao answered, though it felt off to Rōnin, and, judging by his frown, to Tadatomo as well.

"So we go for the altar," Yūki said, translating the signs from her gunner.

"That is my suggestion, yes," the daimyō said. "And this is actually why I called for this challenge here today. I found a last piece of information recently, and am now entrusting it to you, noble warriors. The fourth and last key to the curse is actually the key to Onijima. It is a katana, to be more specific. A famous blade named Yoshimoto-Samonji, passed from the time of Master Samonji to Yoshimoto Imagawa, then taken by Nobunaga at Okehazama. From what I found, it can unlock access to Demon Island, where you will destroy the altar."

"Where is this Samonji sword?" Zenbō asked.

"I do not know," Yoshinao answered, then added, "and cannot know." His voice had turned to steel when he said the last, making them understand more by his silence than by his words.

Yoshinao Tokugawa feared spies in his entourage. It explained why he had issued such a random challenge, and why he had asked for ten strangers to save Japan rather than his skilled Yagyū samurai. Whoever possessed the drum could have worked on his dark plan for years and planted agents all over the islands.

"Why can't you—" Mikinosuke started asking before the elbow of his master cut the words in his ribs. Musashi shook his head, and the boy became silent.

"Today," Yoshinao said, "you have proven your skills, your resourcefulness, or your luck. You have fought my men and did not hesitate. You have also shown me that a wish in your heart was worth more than money, which makes you incorruptible. When you come back successful from this mission, I will do everything in my power to grant them to you, even if it means my own death. So, I am truly and pathetically sorry for asking you this, but please," the daimyō said before he got on his knees and kowtowed toward the nine warriors, "please, save Japan!"

Rōnin was without words, as were the others. By reflex he passed his thumb over the six-coined crest of the Sanada on his katana's pommel, thinking that his wish lay at the end of this mission, and he could not have asked for a better purpose. His mind still reeled with all that had been said, but he was certain of one thing: he would make his dead lord proud, or die trying.

CHAPTER 2
IKEDA TSUKI

Inuyama Castle, Ikeda domain, Owari province, 1620

The garden's castle was even quieter than usual, nothing disturbing the girl's concentration other than the mating call of a pheasant parading in the dry moat. She focused, stilled her breath to a trickle, and sharpened her sight to a single point. Her vision darkened into a tunnel at the end of which stood the target, a circular shape of straw tied to a thick piece of wood. Fifty steps separated the girl from the target. It was barely bigger than a samurai's helmet, and two black dots represented the eyes, but at this distance, she could barely distinguish them. It did not matter; she knew where they were and saw them in her mind's eye. The girl aimed between the two, carefully, slowly drawing the bow with an inward breath. She held the arrow as she breathed out, feeling the tension of the string down to her backbone, not rushing anything, not even when the fire pulsed through the veins in her arms. Then, when she ran out of air, just before she would breathe in again, she let go.

The string twanged, and just as the arrow thwacked into the

target, right between the eyes, she breathed in. Yūki, her lover, Ame, and all the last warriors of the Ikeda clan clapped with pleasure, but without enthusiasm.

"I'm sorry, Mother," the girl said, bowing her head to hide her tears. "I could not pierce the straw target."

Ikeda Sen, the greatest onna-musha of the civil war, terror of the battlefield with her unit of musketeers, shook her head disapprovingly. It had been going on for hours, and for days before that. From dawn to midday, Ikeda Sen would stand by her youngest daughter, patiently watching her progress in the art of archery.

"Tsuki," Sen called as she took her own stance, "your posture is perfect, your aim true, and your breathing impeccable. At twelve, you already shoot more accurately than anyone on this domain. Yet, I would not take you to war even if you were my only worthy archer. Do you know why?"

"I'm not strong enough," the girl guessed.

"I've seen you shoot at sixty steps. You're strong enough," her mother said as she too drew the bowstring, keeping the second arrow dangling from her drawing hand. "What you lack is purpose."

The sound of the arrow planting itself past the straw target and into the wood was akin to a thunderbolt. The aim wasn't nearly as precise, but the effect stole one of Tsuki's heartbeats.

"If you want to hit your target," she went on, nocking the second arrow, "you'll hit your target. But if you want to destroy your target—" Another clap of thunder followed the second release. "—you'll destroy them and their will to fight."

Tsuki had thought about this argument from her mother since the last time she heard it. In fact, she had thought of little else.

"Japan is at peace, though. We don't have enemies," she replied, keeping her head and her voice low.

"You're right. We have peace. But being at peace and having no enemies isn't the same."

"I don't understand."

"Why do you think I teach you the bow and not the arquebus?" That too was a question Tsuki had often wondered. Firearms had proved their efficiency during the civil war, and many saw their use at the tipping point of the conflict. Bows and arrows still had their purpose, but there was no denying their place in war was coming to an end.

Tsuki shook her head to tell her mother she could not find a suitable answer.

"Because with peace, traditions will come back," Ikeda Sen replied. "Music, prayers, arts of all kinds, even something as simple as observing nature will come back into our lives. People will resume their study of archery, not for its killing potential, but for its philosophy."

"Why should I seek to destroy my target then?" Tsuki asked honestly.

"Because tradition is our enemy too," her mother replied, her voice filling with quiet anger. "When war turned the country red, women were needed. We could fight, train, even own castles," she went on, nodding toward Inuyama's great keep. "Men tolerated such things because they needed us and quite frankly because we were better than them at most things. But with peace, they will seek to put us back into our place, reduce our responsibilities, and marry us and our castles to—" Sen seemed to notice her rising rage and breathed it out, opening her fist at last. She came closer to her beloved daughter and put her calloused hand on her cheek, offering Tsuki the soft gaze of a caring mother. "I need you to find your purpose before my hard-fought reputation is gone and can protect you no longer. And once you find it, Tsuki, your arrows will be unstoppable."

"All I'm saying is that maybe, just maybe, this is a pile of horseshit," Tadatomo Honda said.

"The daimyō sounded sincere," Tsuki replied in defense of Yoshinao Tokugawa. The young lord had left a good impression on her. She saw him as a humble man full of compassion and caring for his people.

"I'm not saying he's lying," Tadatomo said. "Just that he might be confused."

Following the gathering, the nine had departed the temple, climbed down the mountain, and made a first stop by the inn used by Tadatomo on the previous night, where he had left his armor during the challenge. The daimyō of Owari had offered each of them the one thousand *mon* sum given to all participants, but most asked the lord to keep it until their return, only taking what was necessary to prepare for the journey, and even then, few actually asked for anything. The sad-looking warrior who named himself Rōnin accepted a few coins, which he gave to a young girl serving food by the side of the road down the mountain, and before they had left the temple he had tossed one into the *saisen* box for worshippers. When she asked him on the way down what he had been praying for, he had simply said, "A fair winter."

The way out of Jokoji soured her jolly mood with the sight of many bodies being lined under white sheets. Knowing what she now knew, she guessed they would be cremated very soon. Folks were crying for their lost ones, she even saw a woman pulling handfuls of hair out of her scalp in sorrow, and Tsuki wondered if it was truly worth it.

She wanted it to be. Yoshinao Tokugawa had sacrificed his men, or at least some he had hired for the event, and many warriors had perished for those nine to be gathered. It had to be for something.

Now, as they sat in the main guest room of the inn, which had been cleared of any other patron, per Tadatomo's loud request, Tsuki found herself questioning her place among all those skilled warriors.

"Look," Tadatomo went on, "maybe the old Tanuki truly believed he saw the dead rise and passed his panic to his son on his deathbed. And maybe there have been rumors or legends of this Izanagi curse in the past. But come on, we have stories about everything in our mythology. If we start believing all of them, might as well take the first boat for the continent."

"What do you think is going on then?" Musashi Miyamoto asked.

"I think that Yoshinao's father was very young at Okehazama, and that Nobunaga was a crafty old bastard," Tadatomo answered, which received a few nods, even from Yūki. It might have been her imagination, but Tsuki felt the shinobi sitting by her side stiffening a little at the mention of Nobunaga.

"I wouldn't be surprised if Nobunaga tricked his opponent by masking his men to look like skeletons or something similar, and let fear destroy the Imagawa's camp," Tadatomo went on.

"It does sound like the Fool of Owari," Musashi said, striking a thoughtful pose.

Ame tapped on Yūki's arms as the *onna-musha* emptied a cup of sake, and signed her comment.

"She says that there has only been one sighting of those

kyonshī living corpses. Not enough to call it evidence," Yūki said.

"Exactly," Tadatomo replied, crossing his arms victoriously. "Thank you, sweetheart."

"Call her that again," the *onna-musha* said, slamming her empty cup on the table, "and this will be your last word."

"What?" Tadatomo asked, frowning. "Are you two…Oh, I see."

"Got a problem?" she then asked, turning on her bench to face the samurai.

"No problem at all," he answered. "We all find pleasure where we can. I have myself been known to play a bit of "sheath the katana" with my comrades, if you know what I mean. Though in my case it would be more like sheath the *ōdashi*, aye?" Tadatomo went on, poking Rōnin in the ribs with his elbow before struggling with a bout of laughter. The lone warrior did not partake but still smiled politely.

"Ugh," Yūki commented as she turned back to her table. Tsuki could not prevent a giggle from escaping her lips. She liked the middle-aged samurai, despite, or perhaps because of, his candor.

"What are you suggesting then?" Rōnin asked.

"All I'm saying is that it might be the easiest mission any of us might ever have to accomplish and a most lucrative one too," Tadatomo answered as he lifted his own gourd to his mouth. For some reason, he had refused the sake from the inn, which led Tsuki to believe the contents of his container must hold some expensive alcohol.

"You'd cheat money out of your nephew?" Zenbō, the blind monk, asked from the third table where he alone enjoyed some tea. He was handsome for a monk, Tsuki told herself, and what he'd lost with his eyes he had gained in a most charming grin.

"By Kannon and all the Bosatsu, no!" Tadatomo replied defensively. "Look, we all go to Azuchi—it's lovely at this time of the year anyway—we search for Onijima. If it exists, good, we destroy the damn altar, if not, well... we can always say we did. Who's gonna know? Right? Easy as picking beans from a plate," he said as he actually picked a pod of edamame from a plate and squeezed the beans straight into his mouth.

"As long as we actually go to Azuchi," Musashi said.

"Master!" Mikinosuke barked. "That would be cheating."

"Not if all of this is a farce," the master swordsman replied.

"Kid," Tadatomo said, tapping Mikinosuke's elbow to get his attention. "Look around you, will you? What do you see?"

"Nine peerless warriors," the boy replied, puffing his chest with pride.

"What you see is a joke," the samurai said. "Yoshinao has the best-trained samurai of Japan under his command. I know he kind of suggested he could not trust them entirely, but why should he trust us, huh? He trusted those nine by his side enough, and I don't know you, but they didn't give me the feeling of being any less skilled than us. Instead, he 'entrusted' the future of Japan to two kids, a blind monk, an assassin, a mute musketeer, and the shabbiest-looking wandering warrior of the land, no offense, mate, but you're supposed to wear your clothes, not the other way around."

Rōnin sniffed the left pang of his *shitagi* and made a face that agreed with Tadatomo's comment.

"Not forgetting the most famous drunkard of the nation," Zenbō replied, flashing his charming smirk.

"Exactly," the samurai agreed. "Thank the gods we have Musashi-dono and a Takeda *onna-musha*, otherwise I would think Yoshinao was trying to turn us into a troop of comedians or something."

"She's not mute, you know," Tsuki said, her voice barely more than a whisper.

"Excuse me?" the samurai asked.

"Ame, you called her a mute musketeer. But she isn't mute, she's deaf."

"How does she—"

"She reads your lips, dingus," Yūki interrupted him, and to prove the point, Ame held her fingers in an obscene gesture in his direction.

"Fine," Tadatomo sighed. "But you can't argue that it's all very strange."

"No argument here," Musashi replied.

"If there really was some bastard out there willing to raise an army of... *kyonshī*, this," Tadatomo said in a whisper after checking left and right that no one stood within earshot, even though the guestroom had been empty since they came in, "then Yoshinao should send an army, not just us nine. Something tells me my nephew is hiding something."

"And wants to keep the Tokugawa name out of it," Rōnin continued, which received a nod of approval from most of the others. Tsuki had not gone so far in her reasoning. She wanted to trust the daimyō, but now that they spoke out loud what they had understood from the gathering at Jokoji, there was no denying the situation was murkier than Yoshinao made it sound.

"Nevertheless," Zenbō said after a few seconds of thoughtful silence, "we've been hired to accomplish a mission, we might as well give it a shot. And if this curse does exist, then we can decide what to do then."

"I concur," the shinobi replied, his first words since the

temple. He might have been sitting right next to her, but Tsuki was startled to hear him. She had forgotten about his presence.

"Again," Tadatomo said in a defensive tone, "I didn't say we shouldn't try, just that we should set low expectations. As I said, I have no problem with a quick trip to Azuchi. Could be there in a week's time on foot."

Ame signed a short series of words after knocking on the table for Yūki's attention.

"Right," the *onna-musha* said, "Azuchi isn't our first destination. We are supposed to get the blade first. Yoshimoto-Samonji, is that right?"

"The blade taken by Nobunaga from the dead hand of Yoshimoto Imagawa," Musashi said in an ominous tone. "Forged by the great swordsmith Samonji then passed down from warlord to warlord for the past centuries."

"Where do we find it?" Mikinosuke asked his master, but Musashi found nothing to say and shook his head.

"If we assume it hasn't been stolen after the assassination of Nobunaga, then not sold on some black market, and that's a big if—" Tadatomo said.

"It hasn't," Kiba, the shinobi, commented.

"Right, so *if* it hasn't, we have to believe it is still within one of Nobunaga's castles, right?" No one corrected the Honda samurai; this was a sound theory.

"It won't be in Azuchi," Rōnin said. "Yoshinao said his agents searched the place top to bottom, what's left of it at least."

"It leaves us with, what, three castles?" Yūki asked.

"Not really," Tadatomo answered. "We can scratch Nagoya castle, which was completely rebuilt when Yoshinao became daimyō of the province. It would have been found then."

"Kiyosu and Komakiya castles are also within the Owari domain," Tsuki then said, speaking Ame's signs. "Yoshinao would already have had them searched."

"Back to square one," Rōnin said, lowering his head as most of them did.

"Where else could the fool have stored it?" Musashi asked but received no reply as they thought about it.

Not all of them though. Tsuki dared not speak at first, for she assumed they would laugh at her. The idea even came that she might have been confused, yet she had been certain that Nobunaga Oda had controlled five great castles, not four. She timidly raised her hand and coughed in the other.

"What is it, Tsuki?" her big sister asked.

"What about Gifu castle?" the archer asked.

"Gifu?" Rōnin repeated, shaking his head in confusion.

"Gifu was the domain of his wife's family, the Saitō clan," Tsuki explained. "Nōhime was from there, and when her father died, after she married Nobunaga Oda, the domain passed to him. He barely lived there, but it was his, wasn't it?" Her voice had faded away at the end, for everyone looked at her with something like wonder. She wasn't used to this kind of staring.

"Shit," Tadatomo finally said. "You're right."

Yūki smiled at her little sister, and from the corner of her eye, Tsuki saw the blind monk grinning in her direction. The girl blushed and looked at the floor, hoping with all her heart that Gifu, the castle of the famous Lady Nō, was the right destination and that within they would find the key to Onijima, Demon Island.

CHAPTER 3
MIKINOSUKE

Settsu province, 1617

In the evening, shortly before the sun vanished into the sea, Mikinosuke dropped a clam shell into the offering box of the small temple he had called home for the past months. He joined his hands silently, closed his eyes, and asked for help. The statue of the Bosatsu in the temple might listen this time. Its role, Mikinosuke knew, was to watch over the men lost at sea. The boy was not lost, nor was he sailing or fishing, but he needed help. The first flakes of snow had timidly fallen on the ground of the hill facing the sea, and he knew it was only a matter of days before they came back stronger and thicker. He would not make it through another winter like that; even at seven years of age, he could feel it in his bones. So Mikinosuke prayed for a sign or a gesture from the Bosatsu or some other savior.

The boy had not used a coin for two reasons. First, there was a gash at the bottom of the box, near the corner, chiseled by his father, from where they grabbed the coins offered by the visitors of the temple. Second, his father had just taken all of them before climbing down the slope leading to the local watering hole.

Mikinosuke would not get beaten for dropping a shell in the box. His father, for all his many faults, wasn't a violent man. He was too weak for that. Sometimes, Mikinosuke wished his father would show anger or any manly emotion, for that matter. Anything to prove to the boy he had not been given life by a lowly crook. Yet time and again his father had shown the colors of a coward and a cheat.

He barely remembered the day, two years before, when his father stripped him from their hometown, to follow the rumors of war near Osaka. At first, things had gone well. The fields of battle were easy pickings. Warriors always missed a hidden coin on a corpse or chose to leave a pendant given by a wife or a mother on the body of its owner. Sometimes, when too many vultures—as they were called—gathered where a fight had just happened, Mikinosuke had to drag bodies through blood and mud to be stripped away from the crowd. It had taken less than a day to get used to dead people.

They spent evenings removing the fletching from arrows or the bullets from torn flesh to sell them back to either of the two armies and for months they had not gone hungry. But the war ended. Not just the siege of Osaka; the whole civil war ended. Suddenly, a country that had lived at war for sixty years woke not knowing what to do with itself, and Mikinosuke discovered misery.

They should have gone back home, but his father said it was impossible, though he never said why. The money dried up fast, their tent did not survive the winter, and they found refuge in the small temple over the sea. For more than a year, Mikinosuke learned tricks from his father, how to snatch purses from people in crowded streets, how to bring tears to the eyes of widows for some scraps of food, and how to dig holes in offering boxes for hollowed coins. This was never enough, though. His father would go down with the sun, almost daily now, and climb back staggering, dropping on the floor of the temple mere seconds before snoring like a bull, smelling like rice wine and smoke.

Mikinosuke was tired of feeling cold, hungry, and sorry for his poor excuse of a fatherly figure. So he gave a shell for a sign.

In the morning, when he woke, his father was cold and blue. A pool of drying vomit trickled from his mouth, and Mikinosuke was alone. He didn't scream, but he cried a little. Not for his father, no, but for himself. At seven, he was now an orphan, and could not remember where his people's town lay. He wiped his tears and tore a plank from the back of the temple, then started digging a hole. Somehow, despite his hunger, he thought burying his father was the right thing to do. The last thing he would do for him. After that... he didn't know.

The ground was hard, and his arms soon tired. At this rhythm, it would take the whole morning to dig the hole.

He paused and heard a noise. Geta sandals, stepping on the path leading to the temple. Just one person. The boy stopped and crouched. The temple having been built on stilts, he observed the approaching person from under it. It was a man, a samurai, judging by the hakama. Mikinosuke thought he would wait for the man to offer a coin, then take it for his travel, but the samurai offered nothing, not even a prayer. When he reached the temple, the man simply turned around and sat on the stairs leading to the sansei box. Mikinosuke heard the sound of a katana slowly leaving its scabbard, then a long sigh, then nothing but the man's breathing and the rolling of the waves downhill.

Mikinosuke was going to wait for the man to leave, but all he could think about was this samurai's swords. With them, he could defend himself, or sell them, or find himself some work, maybe. Those two swords were the response from the Bosatsu, he told *himself. All it would take was a smack on the head of the sighing samurai with the plank in his hands, and he would leave.*

He crouched his way around the temple, quiet as a mouse, then paused at the corner of the building. The samurai was still mostly hidden to him, but he could see the man's legs, and the sword resting naked on his lap. If the man was right-handed, as all samurai were supposed to be, he would not be able to defend himself from his attack, even with the sword drawn. Mikinosuke knew he would probably not kill a grown man with his boy's strength, but maybe daze him enough to snatch the sword and finish the work with it. It didn't take a man to plunge a katana into someone's neck.

He swallowed hard, adjusted his grip on the plank, then ran to his victim. He hadn't meant to, but he shouted, the plank over his head preventing him from seeing his victim's face. There were less than four steps between them, and all Mikinosuke cared for was the katana on the man's lap. It was there, shining with the morning sun, waiting for him. Then, suddenly, it wasn't there.

Mikinosuke felt the wind of the sword passing an inch over his scalp, cutting through the plank as if it was a piece of paper, and he stopped in his tracks just as he was about to hammer it down. The upper half of the plank fell and Mikinosuke saw the samurai, sword in his left hand, looking at him the way a hawk would a sparrow. He was feral, Mikinosuke thought with a sudden surge of fear. His unkempt beard, his full head of shaggy hair, and the white scars crossing over his arm and face spoke of a beast, not an educated noble warrior. If Mikinosuke had been a little taller, his head would have been split in two, and the man had struck with his left hand.

The samurai understood the boy would try nothing else and sheathed his katana back into the scabbard. Mikinosuke dropped the useless plank and fell to his knees. Not to beg, but because all hope was now gone. The samurai was in his own right if he wanted to take the boy's head, and maybe it wouldn't be such a bad thing, Mikinosuke thought. Then the samurai spoke.

"You look hungry," Musashi Miyamoto said.

For seven years, Mikinosuke had never left his master's side for more than a night, and only when Musashi visited the red-light district of some town. Even then, the swordsman made sure his student lacked nothing, and hunger became a distant memory. He learned to love his master's voice, even when it preceded a strike on the arms or legs to correct his posture as they trained, or even when it came in admonishment for the boy's candor in front of their hosts. Musashi wasn't only the most famous swordsman in Japan, he was also an artist and philosopher whose company was sought after by anyone of note, be they samurai, monks, or wealthy merchants. He regaled his hosts with stories of his training years and the masters he had defeated in his youth. Then, when they asked for the chance to observe his famous Niten Ichi-ryū techniques with two swords, the master would ask the student to oblige them. If any of them felt cheated by having the boy perform the demonstration, all admitted he had the bearing of a future master. Mikinosuke trusted his skills but could see the immense gap separating him from his master. Yet this gap suited him, because it meant his path would remain by Musashi's side for many years still, and he could not wish for anything better. In fact, the only thing he wanted more than his master's presence was for the name of Miyamoto Musashi to shine brighter still and be recognized as the greatest swordsman not only of their time but of history, for surely the man was it.

There was just one thing Mikinosuke wished his master could be better at though: humility. No one had ever accused Musashi Miyamoto of being humble, or quiet.

"You should have seen your master's face," Musashi boasted, "when I grabbed his best student's spear and pulled him on my fist. That was worth the trip to Nara." Musashi laughed to his heart's content, then suddenly stopped, realizing what he had just said. "Heavens, I'm so sorry."

"No need to apologize," Zenbō replied honestly. "People often forget I am blind."

"Me and my big mouth," Musashi said, scratching the back of his head, while Mikinosuke shook his.

"I was a little younger than your student when you came to our school," the monk said, "and still had my eyes then. I vividly remember your skills, Miyamoto-dono."

"So does your master," Musashi replied before roaring with laughter again.

"Sadly, master Hōzōin passed away seventeen years ago," the monk said without animosity. "He didn't survive long after the dojo was forced to close."

Mikinosuke slapped his forehead in embarrassment at his master's blunder and slowed his walk to put some distance from them. He liked the monk and looked forward to seeing him in action. Musashi had often told the boy that of all the schools he had challenged, he remembered the Hōzōin spear fighters as a most fearsome bunch, and here was one of their last representatives in the flesh. He was still young, but Mikinosuke had learned to trust his instinct when it came to judging other warriors, and this Zenbō gave him the impression of a peerless fighter. All the others too, even the loud Tadatomo Honda or the sullen Rōnin.

"So, how does it feel to be the only student of a great

master?" Rōnin asked the boy when Mikinosuke slowed to his level.

"It's an honor," the boy replied, "but it's exhausting."

"I can imagine, yes," Rōnin vaguely replied.

"Have you met him before?" the boy asked, more to keep the conversation than with genuine curiosity. They had been on the road for two days already, and besides the first diner, when Mikinosuke sat by the archer girl's side, it had so far been quite boring. They had reached Mino province in the morning, and thus no longer traveled inside Tokugawa Yoshinao's territory. Musashi had warned the boy to be more alert after they crossed the border, but so far the warning had proven uncalled for.

"We both were at Osaka, I believe," Rōnin answered.

"Miyamoto-dono was serving the Tokugawa, but we never faced each other on the battlefield, or I wouldn't be here to tell the tale."

"I am certain my master is also grateful you didn't cross paths on the field," Mikinosuke politely said. He didn't believe those words but knew they were expected of him. No one could hold a candle to his master, even though Rōnin hid some bestial strength as well, the boy believed. For all his downcast appearance, Mikinosuke saw the lone warrior as a dependable man. And he too he could not wait to see in action.

"What do you think of all this?" Rōnin asked. "This curse story, I mean."

"I think once we break it, my master's fame will reach heaven," the boy answered matter of fact.

Rōnin snickered at the boy's enthusiasm, not scornfully though.

"That is your wish? To make your master's fame soar?"

"It is!" the boy confirmed.

"That's good," Rōnin said. "Nothing feels better than serving someone we truly love."

Mikinosuke agreed, but could not find the words to reply to the sudden drop in Rōnin's tone. There was an intense sadness in the man's behavior, and the boy could not guess its origin. Neither did he want to. So he went back to the former topic.

"I'm just wondering…"

"Yes?" Rōnin asked, inviting the boy to open up.

"Well, there's this sword we are going after, right? Yoshimoto-Samonji?"

"Correct."

"And it is the key to Demon Island where the altar to strengthen the curse of Izanagi can be found. We are supposed to destroy this altar because we don't know where the drum that calls the dead back to life is or the nature of the talisman."

"That is also correct," Rōnin said, nodding as if to say he didn't know where the boy was going with that.

"Well, why don't we just destroy the sword then?" the boy asked. "I mean, if we break the key, no one can get to the altar. It wouldn't matter then, would it?"

"Ah!" Tadatomo Honda barked. The samurai had been walking a little behind, but Mikinosuke had failed to realize how much closer he had come during his conversation with Rōnin. Of all the members of his party, he was the one Mikinosuke appreciated the least, though his feelings for the shinobi weren't clear either. Tadatomo Honda was as loud as his master, though he had not earned the right to be so. Musashi based his behavior on years of victories and skills forged on the road, while Tadatomo's reputation was that of a losing drunkard. If he had been the man, the boy would have committed seppuku a while back or at least distanced himself.

"That's because you didn't think it through," Tadatomo said as he stepped to the boy's right.

"What do you mean?" Mikinosuke asked coldly.

"Think, boy, think," Tadatomo replied, tapping on the side of his head. "When was this curse created?"

"The daimyō just said it must be many centuries ago," the boy replied.

"Exactly, but when did the swordsmith Samonji live?" the samurai asked.

Mikinosuke did not know and shook his head.

"About three hundred years ago?" Tadatomo asked Rōnin.

"More like four hundred," the lone warrior confirmed.

"What does it say about this key?" the samurai then asked the boy.

"That it was forged after the creation of the curse," Mikinosuke answered unhappily.

"And thus that the key to Onijima might be forged again," Tadatomo Honda said. For all his lack of belief in their mission, and for all the loudness of his mouth, the boy had to admit the drunkard could think. "Though, mark my words, we are chasing a fable. Don't you think, Rōnin?"

The lone warrior seemed uncomfortable, stuck between the samurai's practical views on the question and the boy's passion.

"Let's just say if there is smoke, there's probably a fire," he finally answered, looking at no one.

"Exactly," Mikinosuke said triumphantly. "So let's follow the smoke to where it leads."

"Well, seeing where it leads right now, I truly hope it's not for nothing," Tadatomo replied before pointing over the horizon, and just as Mikinosuke turned his attention in that direction, Gifu castle appeared behind the closest hill.

It was still quite far, but they could easily see it, a black-and-white three-story castle, perched on top of a steep mountain known as Mount Kinka. The castle looked small and lonely, surrounded by a thick forest still green despite the season. A cloud loomed a little under the castle, making it appear even higher than it already was. They would probably not ascend the mountain today, but Mikinosuke already felt tired just thinking about it. Jokoji was a breathy hike compared to Kinka.

From what Tsuki had told them, the town of Gifu, at the bottom of the mountain, had been razed to the ground following the assassination of Nobunaga Oda, and some claimed his wife had taken her own life inside the castle when she saw the flames devouring her people's houses in the valley. The enemy, mostly soldiers of the traitor Akechi Mitsuhide, were said to have fought Oda's men bitterly to reach the castle, but the defenses held, at a great cost of lives. They could not yet see any of it, and would need to cross the Nagara River first anyway, but the castle loomed like a corpse-eating crow on the mountain, even at a distance.

Mikinosuke observed Mount Kinka stretching a little on their right as the road bent left to avoid the nearest hill, but something caught his eye in the trees lining the path. A branch shuffled against the wind. He squinted to get a better look, thinking he might spot a bird or a squirrel, maybe. Instead, a glint reflected the sunlight through the leaves. His hands went by reflex to the hilts of his swords.

"Watch out!" he shouted. His two swords were leaving their scabbards when he heard the whistle of the arrow flying from the tree. A sudden wind passed by his cheek from behind, then a flash. The arrow, which had been coming straight at him, broke in half a mere hand from his eyes, split in two by Rōnin's katana. Never since his meeting with Musashi had the boy seen a sword striking that fast.

Then all hell broke loose.

From both sides of the road sprang men covered in dark colors from head to toe. Leaving the cover of vegetation, they came in silence, not a shout among them, except when an arrow darted into the tree from earlier and a man fell with a shriek. Mikinosuke would thank Tsuki later, for the battle was coming his way, and now his swords were out.

Don't let the enemy dictate the pace, Musashi had taught him many times over, so the boy bolted toward the threat. Three men came at him. Shinobi, he understood, though none looked like Kiba. As one they removed the black blouse covering them. Under it they wore some kind of lacquered fabric that shone as they moved, gleaming from purple to dark blue depending on the angle of the light. Their movements were serpentine, not straight, and their clothes made them look both slow and fast at the same time, like the light of a candle passing in front of the eyes. The three came with short, straight ninjatō swords, but the fluidity of their movements, added to those camouflage-like garments, made focusing on any of them difficult. Mikinosuke blinked as they crisscrossed as one, then reappeared as three.

Look past the enemy. Misdirection only works on focused eyes, his master said, so the boy looked beyond the shinobi, letting his peripheral vision and his instinct drive his blades. He noticed the difference in size between the three, the interval between their steps, the perfect coordination, and the moment one stepped up to come after his neck.

We use two swords to attack and defend at the same time.

Mikinosuke stepped up to put himself inside his opponent's reach, then raised the wakizashi in his left hand to block the shinobi's blade before it could descend. At the same time, he stabbed his katana upward, right into the enemy's guts. A short grunt passed through the fabric covering the man's lower face, but Mikinosuke did not miss the look of utter shock in his eyes. They had thought him the easy target, and the realization made him boil inside.

He cut through the man's abdomen to pull the blade free, spraying blood on the dying man's companion as he stepped to the side to pursue the attack. The blood forced the second shinobi to raise his arm to shield his eyes. Mikinosuke shot his left arm upward, cut through the shinobi's wrist, and in the same movement cleaved the man's face in half. He did not even have time to scream for his severed hand.

The two dead men fell together, but the third jumped over the first, slashing his ninjatō downward with speed.

Nothing breaks past two swords.

Mikinosuke crossed his swords above his head, receiving the full force of the enemy's attack. He dropped to one knee, and his arms bent, but the ninjatō stopped long before his head. The shinobi lifted his knee and sent it into the boy's chin. Blips of light exploded in his eyes as Mikinosuke fell on his back. He remained conscious and quickly leaned on his elbows, just in time to see the shinobi stand over him, the tip of his blade pointed toward the boy's throat. Then the shinobi froze, and from his chest, near the heart, a curved blade appeared. His arms dropped as he looked in confusion as the blade made its way through his chest, then the blade shot upward, cutting through neck and head in a single, fluid motion. The shinobi fell in a curtain of blood, and through it, the boy saw Kiba, the fanged demon, standing unperturbed, his mask dripping with gore.

"Thank you," the boy managed to say. The demon nodded back at him, then ran to his next victim, his *kusarigama* sickle twirling at the end of the chain by his side.

"Mikinosuke, you're all right?" Musashi asked as he knelt by his student's side.

The swordsman had not even drawn his blades, and Mikinosuke felt ashamed that Musashi had thought of him with such alarm that he ran to him swordless.

"I'm fine, sensei," the boy answered, accepting his master's hand to get up.

He shook the blood from his two swords and remembered to breathe.

"We need to help the others," the boy shouted.

"Do we?" Musashi asked smugly.

A rapid observation of the road sufficed to understand that they didn't. The ambush had failed. Two bodies rested by Rōnin's side, and as he blocked a third shinobi's attack, Tadatomo sliced through their opponent's neck with a backstep cut as perfect as any the boy had seen. Behind, the three women had handled the fight just as well. Ikeda Yūki had left her *naginata* inside some big man's chest and now held another ambusher by the throat, two feet from the ground. The musketeer put her short gun against the shinobi's heart and pulled the trigger, spraying a muffled mess of gore from his back. Not even bothering to check the two women, Tsuki released an arrow toward the front of the group, and, following the missile's direction, Mikinosuke saw a shinobi tumble by Zenbō's feet, the arrow lodged in his neck. The monk had faced the brunt of the attack, especially after Musashi left him, and five bodies lay in the dirt around him. Two more faced him, but their lives neared their ends. They hesitated, the monk didn't. His spear seemed to dart by itself, ending its course in the closest opponent's throat. The second thought to use this chance and swung his blade, but he barely raised his hand before Kiba's chain curled around his wrist. The chain tensed, preventing any movement from the purple shinobi, and Zenbō simply slashed his spear free and through his last opponent's neck in the same movement. Then it was all over.

As the nine gathered in front, the monk bowed respectfully toward the dead, and the demon shinobi uncurled the chain from his last victim's wrist. Mikinosuke had yet to regain control of his breathing or his heartbeat.

"Zenbō, my apologies for leaving you alone," Musashi told the blind monk with a hint of embarrassment.

"None needed," the monk replied, not a single drop of sweat on his bald head. "I am glad your student came out unscathed."

Mikinosuke dropped his head in shame.

"Who were they, and what the hell did they want?" Tadatomo asked after he let some of his precious sake down his throat.

"Shinobi," Kiba said.

"No shit," the samurai replied.

"From which clan?" Tsuki asked. She was trying to pry the arrow from her target's neck, but it took her sister to pull it free.

Kiba knelt by the last dead and removed the mask of fabric covering his face, then the hood, and finally searched inside the man's tunic. He had been a young one, Mikinosuke observed. Five years older than him at most.

"Fūma," Kiba said as he unveiled a tattoo of the character for *wind* at the base of the young shinobi's neck.

"Fūma?" Yūki asked. "Never heard of them."

"They used to be simple criminals, near Edo," Tadatomo told her, looking suddenly all serious.

"The samurai is right," Kiba said as he stood back up. "They were small, and acted against the law, but recently they have grown fast."

"So you can speak in sentences," Tadatomo joked.

"Those were few," the shinobi continued, ignoring the jeer. "I don't think they were supposed to attack, just watch. If the boy hadn't spotted them, we would never have seen them."

"Well done, Mikinosuke," Musashi said, patting his student's back. The boy blushed, but a part of him thought the shinobi had exaggerated the compliment on purpose.

"Why were they watching us?" Yūki asked.

"Do you really need to ask?" Tadatomo replied. "It means someone is after us, or at least our goal."

"Someone with the means to hire shinobi," Rōnin said.

"It seems," Tadatomo went on, "that Yoshinao has been betrayed, and things have just become more complicated for us."

CHAPTER 4
TADATOMO HONDA

Osaka, 1615

The mud in his mouth tasted like wet copper. His brother kept him struggling inside the puddle for a few seconds before pulling him out by his unbound hair. Tadatomo gasped for air. If the battle hadn't completely sobered him, this was quickly doing the trick.

"Bowing in the dirt isn't enough! How dare you show your face here?" *Ieyasu Tokugawa, retired shōgun of Japan, asked through his teeth.*

"I came to take responsibility for our losses," *Tadatomo replied, repeating the words drilled in his drunken mind by his older brother as he accompanied him toward their great leader. Tadamasa had tied Tadatomo's hands behind his back, unknotted his hair, even applied dirt on his armor, and punched him in the face, anything to make Tadatomo look more pitiful than he already was. Anything to gain some sympathy. But he had failed in his mission; Ieyasu had no sympathy for his friend's son.*

"Responsibility?" *the true ruler of Japan asked.* "Don't make me laugh, dog! You do not know the meaning of the word. You *have no sense of it, no sense of honor. You... pathetic excuse of a son!"*

"General," Tadamasa called, kowtowing in the mud by his little brother's side. "I am begging—"

"Silence!" Ieyasu barked.

The retired shōgun was not famed for the volume of his voice, usually preferring hurtful remarks over remonstrances. But that morning's battle was a stain on his name and that of the Honda. It should have been an easy victory. They outnumbered the Sanada defending Osaka castle three to one, and the three-pronged formation should have left the enemy surrounded. Tadatomo had been given the honor of commanding the battle, with direct orders to keep the central column a little behind to attract the enemy within.

All his life as a grown man, Tadatomo had dreamed of the day he would assume command on the battlefield. He would finally show his father, his brother, and Japan that he was the worthy son of Tadakatsu Honda, "The samurai among samurai." People said that Tadatomo had his father's skill, and Tadamasa his unwavering soul, but at Osaka, Tadatomo would show them he wasn't just a blade and could prevail under pressure.

Then, at dawn, feeling the weight of his name, and the judging eyes of his ruler on his back, Tadatomo drank a cup of sake to calm his nerves. When that failed, he took a second, and a third. The next thing he remembered was the screams of his soldiers as Sanada and his crimson warriors punched through his forces. Reeling on his saddle, he unsheathed his katana, intending to rally his men, but puked all over himself, and when he regained control of his stomach at last, ready to order a counterattack, the battle had all but been lost.

"Five hundred men," Ieyasu, shaking with rage, said. "Five hundred brave men lost because their commander was drunk. Shame on you, Tadatomo."

The drunk samurai found no words, and his brother trembling by his side did not help. He knew he had lost his only chance to leave his mark on the history of the nation. Or a brilliant one, at least. Now, if anyone remembered Tadatomo Honda, it would be as a shameful drunkard. Years of hard training with the sword, the bow, the spear, and the horse had just gone down a hole of shame. For the first time in his life, Tadatomo regretted being born a samurai. If he'd been born a peasant, no one would have expected much of him, and life would have been simpler, if not easier.

"Your father," Ieyasu went on when he understood the defeated samurai would not reply, "was my greatest retainer, and my friend. He stood by my side in more than fifty battles, never receiving a single wound despite fighting in the thick of it every time. If he could see you right now, he would die of shame."

But the great samurai would not see his son's disgrace, for he had been gone for five years. One day, ashamed of his own sickness, the samurai among samurai had taken his spear, his armor, and his deer antler–mounted helmet and left. No one had seen him since, making it all the harder for his son to match him in anything.

"I should have you beaten to death like a dog," Ieyasu Tokugawa spat. "But in your father's name, I'm giving you a choice." With those words, the general picked a tantō sword from the platter by his side and threw it in the mud at Tadatomo's knees. "You may take your own life, without assistance, to regain what little honor you had, or go, and live your life in shame."

"Brother—" Tadamasa called, not looking up from his kowtow. Tadatomo knew what his brother was thinking; he should accept Lord Tokugawa's request and stab himself in the abdomen, to preserve the family's honor if nothing else.

"Uncle," Tadatomo called, making all the men in the assistance gasp for this insolence. "I'm afraid I can't commit *seppuku, because I haven't prepared my death poem. Let me think about it, and then I'll come back on your offer."*

For years, the look on the old Tanuki's face, and the curses passing through his brother's teeth, accompanied his exile, warming his nights with a few giggles, even when shame took his feet at the edge of many cliffs.

Tadatomo was puffing and huffing shortly after they penetrated the green forest of Mount Kinka. He told himself the short night in the ruins of Gifu's village was to blame for his lack of breath, or maybe the absence of a proper meal to start the day, but the truth hurt more. He was simply no longer the fit young samurai who had accompanied his father on campaigns, and this mountain was thick and oppressive.

Among the nine, only he and the *onna-musha* wore armor. He would not get caught unprepared this time, so he left the ruins ready for war. The samurai clad himself in chest armor, supported by square lamellar shoulder plaques, greaves, and armored sleeves to complete the set, the ensemble colored in a mix of black and blue. All Tadatomo had left in the bag hanging on his back was his *kabuto* helmet, and only because he felt silly wearing it next to all his companions dressed with kimonos, robes, and hakama. He knew they were right, this would only slow his advance up the mountain, but arrows and darts would bounce off of him, and that was worth the extra sweat.

"Wait," he said, hailing the girl Tsuki, who, while walking in front, seemed to hang back a little for his benefit. "Just wait a second, please." He dropped his elbow against a pine tree for support, but the girl, when she turned around, looked as fresh as the morning dew.

"We just started climbing, Honda-san," she said. "Are you sure you want to wear all of this?"

"It's not a race," Tadatomo replied, pushing himself from the tree to keep moving. "This cursed katana will still be up there if we take our time, you know?"

"Ah!" the big sister scoffed. "So you admit it's cursed."

"For making me climb another mountain, yes," the samurai replied.

"Don't be a spoiled brat," she said. "It's not that steep, and we are not even moving that fast."

He was about to unsheathe his katana and use it as a cane, but the image of his father shaking his head reproachfully prevented him from doing so. The old bastard would never have let him shame a sacred blade like this.

"Spoiled brat my ass," Tadatomo said after a grunt of effort to step over a sprouting root. "You'd struggle too if…" He had been about to blame his difficulties on his armor, but the *onna-musha*'s looked even heavier.

"If I was old too?" she replied, smirking like a fiend, arms crossed under her imposing chest. The musketeer by her side laughed at the jibe, though her cackle sounded off.

"I'm not that old," Tadatomo said.

"Yes, you are," Mikinosuke replied, passing by his side in effortless leaps, like a goat kid.

"So is your master then," the samurai said. Musashi walked by his side at that moment, looking as easy climbing the mountain on his high *geta* sandals as if he'd been strolling around a lake. "Wait, how old are you, Musashi?"

"I was born in the eleventh year of Tenshō era," the swordsman answered.

"You're two years younger than me?" Tadatomo scoffed

with honest surprise. In his eyes, Musashi Miyamoto looked much older, but such was the prize of the wandering swordsman's life. The great master was lean, and hard, and tanned like old leather, while *he* had ridden horses, and eaten and drunk more than necessary all his life. Tadatomo felt suddenly soft. And it wasn't just the physical differences that embarrassed him. Musashi was close in age to him, but their reputation could not be more different. One had soared from below, the other fallen from the highest peak.

"Rōnin," Tadatomo called in a shout, "how about you?"

"I'm just thirty-four," the lone warrior answered back, before adding an easy, "old man."

Even the sullen Rōnin was making fun of him, Tadatomo realized as the others laughed.

"Can't believe I'm the oldest in this group," he said, shaking his head.

Kiba jumped down the tree he was about to use for support then, landing like a cat and straightening up right away. Tadatomo could not see through the demon mask, but the way the shinobi tilted his head led him to believe he was also judging him.

"Go ahead," Tadatomo said, "tell me you're in your early twenties and I'm just a withered old turtle."

"I'm sixty-five," the shinobi replied.

"Ha, ha," Tadatomo said in a fake laughter. "Wait, are you serious?"

The demon shinobi did not reply. Instead, he performed an unnecessary backflip and pulled himself up the closest branch, then vanished within the trees.

The samurai resumed his march painfully, watching the back of his comrades who did not seem to realize how steep the mountain rose. He saw the moon-shaped tip of Zenbō's spear passing on his right, just as he heard the monk's steps crunching the dead leaves under his feet. The monk breathed easily as well and seemed happy with himself.

"What?" Tadatomo barked nervously. "Are you going to tell me that age is an illusion and I'm merely a reflection of my tainted soul or something?"

Zenbō's grin only widened at his words.

"You are not old, Honda-san," the blind monk replied. "You are just as you see yourself."

"Give me a break. I'm just tired. Didn't sleep well in this ghastly village."

"It's never your fault, is it?" the monk asked after his genial smile faded.

Tadatomo boiled inside. Who was he to reprimand him like a child?

"I'm going to kick your blind ass, you know that?" the samurai asked between two loud breaths.

"You'd have to catch me first," the monk replied, and before the samurai knew it, Zenbō reversed his grip on the spear and used the butt end to check the path ahead. His stride increased, both in length and speed, and the blind monk seemed almost to float on the forest's surface, while Tadatomo could barely walk.

He passed his hand over the shaven part of his scalp and shook the sweat from it. Zenbō's words, for some reason, would not leave his mind. They came back and formed a loop. *You are just as you see yourself. It's never your fault, is it?* What did he know of his life? Growing up in a monastery, following the same rituals every day of every month, never thinking for yourself, the blind monk had it easy compared to him. Tadatomo, on the other hand, was the son of Tadakatsu Honda, the samurai amongst samurai, and every living minute had been a struggle against his father's shadow. The pressure of the family name, the constant retelling of his ancestors' fame, he had lived with them over his head since childhood. He deserved a little sympathy here, and he was tired, damn it! *Screw this monk,* Tadatomo told himself, *and screw all of them!*

He raised his head to curse his traveling companions, but none stood nearby. They had gone ahead, and even as he silently focused, Tadatomo could not hear a single footstep. He looked above, trying to catch a glimpse of the shinobi, but saw nothing. Frowning, he stepped up a little, choosing his path to avoid roots and fallen trees.

His calves felt like marble, and the fire in his lungs brought the taste of copper into his mouth, but he kept on moving. The forest's silence made him nervous, and when he slowed his steps to locate his comrades, all he heard was the wind and his own heart drumming against his temples. A mist crept from the ground, a sign that he approached the low-hanging cloud circling up the mountain. Feeling suddenly cold, he pulled his helmet on his head to get some warmth. Soon, his neck got sore from the added weight, and the line of sweat running down his back cooled and made him feel even more uncomfortable. *Screw this mountain too,* Tadatomo thought. *Stupid mountain, stupid Yoshinao, and stupid sword. All of this because an old man shat his death bed with made-up memories—*

A sharp sound interrupted his thoughts, like two swords clashing once, but softer. The sound echoed between the trees, so Tadatomo could not pinpoint its origin. He turned on himself several times, squinting to see through the mist and the vegetation, but the forest remained as empty as before, and he as lonely.

The mist rose to his knees in just a few steps, and the samurai bumped his foot on the stump of a broken tree. He cursed, spat, then kicked the dead piece of wood, hurting himself even more in the process. Then, the same sound as before echoed through the forest, and this time he recognized it—a drum.

His chest seemed to compress on itself, his heart beat faster. Tadatomo was still sweating, but it was a cold sweat now. A *kotsuzumi*; he had just heard a *kotsuzumi*. Just as Yoshinao had claimed. First, some Fūma shinobi had attacked them, now a drum. Hands shaking, he checked his surroundings with more urgency.

"Calm down," Tadatomo told himself, breathing slowly through his lips. "Calm down. They're just pulling a prank on you. Very funny!" he then shouted. They were teasing him for being so vocal about the curse. He was angry at them, but knew that should the roles be reversed, he would also childishly mock them.

"Come on, mates, you've made your point," he went on.

He got a reply, something between a sigh and a grunt, and his blood chilled. The grunt echoed around him, then faded away. Tadatomo swallowed the bitter chunk of saliva stuck in his mouth and pushed through the mist slowly.

"Oye!" he shouted, drawing his katana with a loud scrape. "I seriously don't like it. Show yourselves, or I'm gone. I'm a Honda, I don't need the money. I can just go back to my people and live a life of comfort."

The same grunt replied. From closer this time. His bowels slowly twisted on themselves, threatening the samurai with a coming bout of loose stool.

"You guys are thick, you know that? I don't need this! Screw you all, and screw Yoshinao with his fairytale!" Tadatomo shouted from the depth of his lungs, before turning on his heels, ready to climb down Mount Kinka and head back to whichever castle would welcome him. But a few steps from him stood someone. The silhouette was shrouded in the mist, face covered by the shadow of the forest's rich canopy.

"Shit, you scared me," Tadatomo said with a sigh, bringing his right hand over his drumming heart. "All right, I admit it," he went on as he twisted his hips to push his sword back into its scabbard. "You got me good, but you owe me some clean *fundoshi*." The samurai managed to put the tip of his sword into the scabbard despite his shaking hands, but something stopped him from going further.

The silhouette moved toward him, but his movements were off. It was a man, walking on two legs, though they seemed to barely hold him, and the man looked as if about to stumble with each step. He could barely lift his feet at first and dragged them noisily through the dead leaves. A sword hung from his hand. Tadatomo wasn't sure, but it seemed to him the katana was short, maybe broken. None of his companions had a broken blade as far as he remembered. And if the blade was too short, the arm it dangled from was too long, with his hand nearly reaching his knees. Tadatomo took an involuntary step back, letting go of the idea of sheathing his katana.

The man coming toward him walked more steadily and grunted. His steps quickened, though he seemed to walk sideways.

"Who's that?" Tadatomo called as he lifted his sword toward the threat. "Answer me, damn it."

The man increased his pace, his armor, now appearing in more detail through the fog, rattling with each step. The grunts turned to moans. Tadatomo looked behind, but he was so deep inside the cloud that he could not even see the ground. The man with the broken sword was but a dozen steps from him.

"Back off, or I'll gut you," the samurai said. His breathing came in rasps, the sweat under his helmet ran down his neck in fat drops, and Tadatomo felt the urge to shit more and more pressing by the second. Five steps between them.

"Last warning!"

The man ignored it and swung his blade at the samurai with a hoarse shriek that made the hairs on Tadatomo's arms stand. He took a step back, on purpose this time, and cut straight through the man's elongated arm, letting it jump away from the body with the broken blade. But the man did not stop, nor did he slow, or scream, or bleed. Both his arms shot forward, the one good hand emerging from the fog a mere few inches from Tadatomo's eyes, and then the monster's face appeared as well. The samurai screamed like never before.

Tadatomo shielded himself with his left arm, shoving it by luck inside the monster's mouth as both fell. He landed on his back, though the back of his head bumped into the stump of a tree fallen by the wind. He did not care a second for the pain of it, his panicking attention was all for the monster, and Tadatomo knew in his heart that Yoshinao had spoken the truth.

If it had been a man, it was a long time ago. All that remained of the dead soldier was a rotten corpse smelling like putrefied raw meat, broken skin like an old boat sail, colored in hues stretching from brown to gray, and holes crawling with maggots wriggling through a canvas of ligaments, dried veins, and bones.

"Help!" the Honda samurai screamed as the severed arm of the dead one kept swinging at him.

In his fall, Tadatomo had pushed his left knee between them, but the pressure was so intense that he thought his thigh might explode. The monster could not care less that its victim lay on the ground, it kept pushing with all its weight, using its last hand to try to claw at Tadatomo's face. The samurai caught its wrist with his right hand, the katana having fallen from his grasp as he landed on his back, while his armored left arm suffered between the jaws of the monster.

Tadatomo remembered Yoshinao's words, all of them. He did not want to become one of them. This was the ugliest, filthiest, most twisted thing he'd ever seen. Its teeth were breaking on the armored sleeve, yet it did not relent. Its jaws worked on his arm the way a rabid dog would. Tadatomo heard the plaques of the armor crack between the teeth and felt the added pressure on his arm. It was a matter of seconds before the monster chewed through it and tore his arm off, bit by bit.

"Help!" Tadatomo called again, never daring to leave the monster from his sight.

Its nose had vanished a while back, giving the samurai a gruesome view of his insides. Thick liquid poured from the hole and dripped on Tadatomo's face, and a long-legged spider emerged from the cavity where the nose had been, disturbed by the sudden activity of its habitat. It climbed on the dead warrior's skull and vanished behind it, leaving the living and the dead samurai to their struggle.

The monster's severed hand kept tapping on the side of Tadatomo's chest armor as if its blade was still stuck in its hand. The samurai glanced toward the arm he had cut off, worried that somehow it might be crawling back to the body, but thankfully it looked as dead as it should be. In doing so, Tadatomo saw the edge of the stump he had bumped into, crowned with splinters as long as a knife. The nearest of the splinters was so close to his face that he had cut himself on it in his fall.

"Suit yourself, you ugly bastard," Tadatomo said through

gritted teeth as he let the dead one fall on him while lifting his leg as much as possible. The monster stumbled forward. Its head, driven by the arm stuck between its teeth, collapsed onto one of the splinters, which pierced one of the glassy eyes and stabbed deep inside its brain, if it still had one.

Tadatomo rolled from under the monster, kicking the ground to put some distance while still on his ass. It now just looked like the body of some poor bastard who had fallen on the wrong tree during a battle. The samurai stood on weak legs and quickly bent over to grab his katana. He remembered the gluey liquid on his face and wiped it with the back of his hand urgently. Then, and only then, he threw up.

Tadatomo purged himself of anything his body had eaten or drunk over the last couple of days and then some more. It hurt like hell, as if every fiber of his body wanted to cleanse itself, remove any trace of this encounter. As he dropped on his knee, watching the line of bile descending from his lips to the forest ground, he heard something shuffle.

Slowly twisting his head, the samurai witnessed the moment the body seemed to reanimate itself. The *kyonshī* pulled its knees closer to the tree, then dropped its hand against the stump and pulled its head from the splinter.

"You must be shitting me," Tadatomo spat.

The dead warrior rose to its feet once more, then turned its head toward the samurai, offering a view of the gaping hole in its face. It grunted a raucous shriek when it noticed the living man, and hobbled toward Tadatomo in its uncoordinated way.

Not this time, Tadatomo thought. He spat, slashed his

katana, and struck. The monster's head fell, bounced a few steps downhill, and the body finally dropped.

Tadatomo looked at the decapitated body for a few seconds, not daring to hope much. Yet nothing happened, and he managed to peel his eyes off the corpse as his breath slowed back under his control.

I need to tell the others, he thought as his feet moved by themselves toward the castle and through the cloud hanging over the mountain.

CHAPTER 5
RONIN

Jōshū, 1601

"Again!" the old teacher barked.

"Hai, sensei!" the boy replied, fighting his tears and returning to the neutral position.

Not looking, he sheathed the iaitō sword for practice back into its scabbard. The skin between his thumb and first fingers had hardened to the point of callousness during his first year inside the dōjō. Even if he were to miss the saya, he wouldn't prick the skin to the blood anymore. And he didn't miss anyway. The same could not be said about his legwork.

"Shatō!" the teacher called.

The boy was the last of the students standing on the planks of the dōjō, all the others watched from the sides, where they sat in silence. They had mastered the waza, at least enough to meet their teacher's expectations. Only the youngest boy remained and now faced his patient teacher holding his precious katana out of the saya.

The boy drew the sword from the scabbard, as if to cut

through an opponent's raised arms, then followed with a diagonal cut that would shatter his right shoulder. The boy had been slow enough to measure his movement so far, but he knew the third cut was his weakness. He stepped with the right foot, then brought the sword down diagonally, aiming across the left side of his opponent's chest, while swiping his left foot behind to complete the five-step waza. He knew he had failed and blinked even before the tip of the teacher's sword pierced the skin of his right knee.

It wasn't much, certainly not more pain than a needle would inflict, and at least this time he had bandaged his knee in preparation so he would not have to spend his evening hunched over the wooden floor to clear the blood, but it still hurt.

"You always step too far," the teacher said as the other boys grunted in frustration. If not for their youngest comrade, they would be out and getting ready for dinner by now.

"Yes, sensei," the boy obediently replied.

"Why do you always step too far?"

"I don't do it on purpose, sensei," he said, sniffing tears back.

"So why don't you stop then?"

"I...I don't know," the boy said. His bottom lip quivered, but he kept the pose, sword pointing forward, his weight on the wounded knee.

"You've been with us for three years, Nagakatsu, and you have yet to understand your reach. You know why?" the teacher asked, straightening up and finally sheathing his katana back in its saya. The boy shook his head. "Because, you, think, too, much," the teacher went on, slapping the top of Nagakatsu's head with his hardened fingers with each word. "I can hear your brain counting the breaths, picturing the spots for your feet, and remembering the angle for each strike. You need to stop thinking, Nagakatsu. We are battōjutsu swordsmen. Thoughts are too slow for us. We move before the thought, thus it is useless. Stop thinking and let your instinct drive your blade. And *what makes instinct strong?"* the teacher asked the whole dōjō this time.

"Practice!" Nagakatsu and his comrades answered in unison.

"Practice," Shigemasa-sensei agreed. "And for heaven's sake, do not let me stab your knee so easily," he went on, dropping a loving hand on his student's shoulder. Tears fell from the boy's eyes then, but the teacher pretended not to notice.

"Again!" he barked.

"Hai, sensei!" Nagakatsu replied as he resumed the neutral stance.

His instinct had been ferocious on that day as the nine warriors chosen at Jokoji climbed Mount Kinka. Eight of them had gotten into the cloud circling around the mountain, where Rōnin could not see a step ahead of him. The forest had disappeared as they approached the castle grounds, and the climb went on with no interruption. He had been following the inclination of the slope, knowing that at the end of it stood Gifu castle, when he heard the strike of a drum. One of them asked if the others had heard. They all had. None moved then. The quiet anticipation of what was to come pulled Rōnin into his warrior's focus. He shut his eyes, just like in meditation, and felt the world around him. His comrades had spread after they penetrated the cloud, but he could hear some of them breathing or shuffling. Then he heard a scream. Tsuki.

Rōnin dashed toward the scream, its origin muffled by her sister's distressed calls. He all but stumbled on her and her aggressor, a tall soldier wearing some old armor that Rōnin did not recognize. The soldier had grabbed the girl's hair, pulled her head backward, and as Rōnin took the first of the five steps, he thought the aggressor was about to bite her neck. Rōnin's beloved katana flashed out of its scabbard as he took the second step and cut through the soldier's neck with the third. He could have stopped there but tens of thousands of repetitions of the *Shatō* waza drove his blade and his feet. The second cut dragged across the soldier's spine diagonally, and the last, which he aimed higher than usual, severed the hand grabbing the girl's hair from his arm. The soldier dropped on the floor in three pieces, and the girl on her knees. But Rōnin felt as if something was missing, as if his form wasn't complete.

"Tsuki!" Yūki called when she reached them, dropping on the ground too with so much verve that the cloud parted away from them a little. "Are you all right?" she asked her sister, pulling a strand of hair behind the girl's ears and checking her face for any trace of wounds.

"I'm fine," the archer replied, though her rapidly rising shoulders said otherwise. She was shaken and would need a few seconds to get over the attack.

"What happened?" Mikinosuke asked when he and his master arrived.

Ame put her scarred hand on Rōnin's arm, probably sensing the doubt creeping on his face. He meant to smile reassuringly, but he couldn't budge the impression of discomfort from his chest.

"Thank you, Rōnin," Tsuki said as she used her sister for support to get back on her feet. "What's wrong?"

"I don't know," the lone warrior replied. He revisited the memory of this short fight and tried to decide which part felt off, but nothing struck him as a mistake on his part. In fact, nothing bothered him until the very last movement of his *waza*, the *kochiburi* shaking of the blood. Rōnin did something his master usually prevented outside of the *dōjō*, if not fighting, but he had to be sure, so he drew his katana from its scabbard. There was no blood.

Musashi came to stand by Rōnin's side and saw the katana too. It was stained and would need a good scrubbing, but none of it was red. The two swordsmen shared an understanding gaze.

"What is it, sensei?" Mikinosuke asked.

"Oye!" Tadatomo's voice called from somewhere below. Rōnin had forgotten about him in all of this.

"We're here!" Yūki called back.

"I've seen one!" Tadatomo shouted before they could see him. He was running at last. "I've seen—" His words stopped when he bumped and nearly tumbled on the head Rōnin had just cut off. The samurai did not seem to realize what he had just kicked and thanked Kiba for keeping him on his feet, though he stiffened at the sight of the demon mask.

"What have you seen?" Musashi asked the samurai.

"The dead!" he said. "It's all true. Yoshinao spoke true. He came at me, all snarling and smelling like a dead mouse, or a shitload of them, and tried to bite my arm off. Even after I killed it again, it came back." Tadatomo's voice was quickly rising in panic and his sight went nowhere in particular. The cloud was floating back around them, and Rōnin suddenly felt the urge to leave this place. Tadatomo might be a drunk and a bit of a coward, but he had fought in enough battles to strengthen his spirit against panic.

"Did it bleed?" Rōnin asked.

"I wouldn't call it blood," Tadatomo replied. "It was more like a mix of pus and sap and shit if you ask me, but it wasn't blood. Why?"

Rōnin touched the side of his katana, and when he lifted his finger, a slimy substance stuck between the blade and him. It fit Tadatomo's description perfectly, and then the lone warrior remembered the body he had split in three.

Kiba seemed to follow his thoughts. The shinobi peeled his outer shirt from his back and swung it in the air as he twisted on his heel, blowing a powerful gust of wind around them. The fog retreated and they could finally see each other clearly, as they did the bits of corpse on the ground.

"Shit," Yūki said as she crouched, while her sister, Mikinosuke, and, for some reason, Tadatomo gasped.

"Can anyone tell me what we are gasping about?" Zenbō asked.

"The man Rōnin cut down," Yūki replied. "He's dead."

"I had guessed as much," the monk said.

"No," the *onna-musha* replied. "He's been dead for a while."

Tadatomo had kicked the head somewhere else, but what remained could not have belonged to a man who had just perished. Rōnin had seen fresher corpses in the mass grave of Osaka. Parts of it had bloated out of its armor, like swollen abscesses that had burst ages ago. Maggots and bugs were squirming out of the wounds inflicted by Rōnin, and they had obviously called the corpse home until that morning. The monster's legs were bare bone under the knees, and strips of skin above, as if it had been wearing short pants made of its own skin. The lone warrior was glad the head had disappeared.

"Whose crest is that?" Mikinosuke, surprisingly stoic for the situation, asked.

The twice-dead man wore a set of armor that must have been his pride in life. Rōnin guessed the plaques of iron protecting him had been blue once, though now it had faded toward the green of old copper, and a white flower had been drawn over his back. Rōnin's sword has split the flower in two, but he counted five petals, like the symbol of the Oda clan, but not exactly the same.

"The bellflower of the Akechi clan," Kiba answered.

"Akechi?" Tadatomo blurted out. "As in, the clan who destroyed the Oda?"

"I thought the Akechi had been whipped out too," Tsuki said.

"They were," the shinobi replied. "After they killed Nobunaga, the Akechi clan waged war against any Oda bastion, but most retainers of the Oda joined forces to destroy the traitor. The Akechi clan died entirely a few weeks after Nobunaga, forty-three years ago."

"So did he," Musashi said, nodding toward the twice-dead samurai. The fog was returning and soon covered the rotten corpse. Yūki rose before the cloud would envelop her.

"I still can't believe it's real," she said, though her tone conveyed the opposite feeling. "If those things have been here all along, shouldn't we have heard about it?"

"Those things were dead until that bastard hit his drum," Tadatomo spat. "What? You didn't hear it?" he asked when everyone seemed to stare at him. They had heard it, but with all the commotion, the drum had slipped from their mind. They heard it better the second time, loud and clear, coming from below, from within the forest.

"He's here," Kiba said ominously. "Whoever is calling the dead is close by—with his drum. It's our chance to end it."

"The shinobi is right," Rōnin replied. "If we move fast en—"

His voice ended abruptly, cut by a low wave of murmurs slowly turning to echoing grunts and moans. They heard the dead as they returned to life; the corpses leaving their peaceful resting places. They stripped themselves from tree trunks, emerged from the ground, and picked up their nearby rusty blades, and while Rōnin could see none of it in the fog, it felt as if the forest was moving on him.

Ame, who stood a little above him, made a series of tapping sounds between two stones from which jutted some sparks. Rōnin saw them through the thickening fog, then the tip of a match turning red. The glow told him of her presence, and the metallic rattle of her matchlock assured him she was ready. But the musketeer had nothing to shoot at for now. The dead were gathering from below, cutting their escape route and protecting their master.

"How many are there?" Mikinosuke whispered.

"Too many," Musashi answered.

"What do we do?" Tsuki asked. But no one answered.

There was a sudden silence. Rōnin stopped breathing, but his heart beat so intensely that surely all the others could hear it. Kiba moved past the lone warrior in silent steps, stretched his piece of cloth, and waved it in front to blow the cloud away. The first of them jutted at him arms stretched, and they all resumed their grunts as one, their thirst for death giving volume to their moans. The shinobi grabbed the wrists of the *kyonshī* and managed to stay on his feet, though the way he bent backward spoke of the monster's strength.

Rōnin rushed to his aid, sword ready to be drawn, but an explosive sound behind preceded his attack, and the monster's head popped into tiny pieces. When he looked behind, Rōnin saw Ame's face through a fresh hole in the cloud, already working on a new cartridge of powder to fill her arquebus with. Kiba's *kusarigama*'s chained sickle twirling noisily caught Rōnin's attention back in front. The shinobi did not need any time to recover, and threw the sickle in an arc above his head, making wider and wider circles with each rotation. The blade gained in speed and cut through the fog, creating just enough space for the lone warrior to see the swarm of dead coming from the forest. Kiba grunted with a sudden effort and pulled on his chain. It straightened for a moment, tensing against something. The shinobi pulled with both hands, like a fisherman fighting his catch. A *kyonshī* soon fell at his feet, one wearing the Oda armor, but whoever he had been in life, Kiba ended his resurrection with a mean kick to the neck.

"What do we do?" Yūki asked when she stepped next to Rōnin.

So far it seemed the dead moved slowly enough to be fought. Whoever controlled them could probably not see them in the fog, but each noise, each gunshot, and each shout would attract the dead closer and closer. They could go back to the base of the mountain, using the slope and the surprise to punch through the swarm, but their grunts increased by the second. Not everyone would make it if they retreated.

"We should leave this damn cloud," Tadatomo said.

"Let's go to the castle," Rōnin replied.

"We'll be trapped," Yūki said.

"But at least we'll get some visibility," the lone warrior said. The drum rang again, and all the grunts seemed to twist in their direction.

"To the castle!" Yūki shouted just as the closest of the dead seemed to get within a few steps.

Rōnin waited for her to take the first step back, then darted up the mountain, feeling the wind of Kiba passing him by. He was the last among them, but the sounds of the dead seemed to gain in distance. The living could outrun them. However, new sounds emerged in front, warriors shouting and blades clashing. Rōnin heard the distinctive sound of flesh being crushed and armor deflecting blades, followed by a resonating *bang*. He burst from the cloud and came into view of the castle, just a few steps ahead, but between him and the gates, the battle raged on.

The dead were coming from both sides, surrounding the nine before they could enter the castle. Musashi, Mikinosuke, and Tadatomo were working on the doors, trying to push them open despite their thickness and the bar locking them from the other side. On their left, Zenbō was keeping the dead at bay by himself, and in other circumstances, Rōnin would have taken the time to marvel at the monk's skills. He was remarkable. Tilting his head to hear his opponents, he thrust his spear through a *kyonshī*'s face and pulled it toward him, letting the body fall by his feet before he reversed his grip and smashed the butt end of the polearm into a second's face, creating an explosion of long-dead brain matter.

"The spine!" Rōnin shouted when he saw the corpse at Zenbō's feet wriggle. "Aim for the spine."

Zenbō twirled the spear vertically around himself, twisted on his heel, and slammed the pole down on the back of his first victim, crunching it with a loud smacking sound despite the dead one being armored. It stopped moving, and the monk returned to the second, who, despite missing most of its head, kept coming at him. The blind monk thrust his spear again, driving the straight blade into his opponent's chest, and with apparent ease lifted him off the ground. Twisting his torso, Zenbō threw the dead warrior against a stone of the castle's wall. Something must have broken in the *kyonshī*'s body, because it did not move anymore.

"Will you open, you bitch," Tadatomo grunted.

"Tsuki, help them!" Yūki shouted as she cleaved a corpse

in half with a huge swing of her *naginata*. The archer let a last arrow fly somewhere into the group of dead samurai approaching the blind monk, but all it did was plant itself into his throat, barely slowing the monster down. Her arrows would not help against those reanimated corpses.

"More are coming on their side," Zenbō told Rōnin, meaning the *onna-musha* and the musketeer. "I can deal with them here." Trusting him, the lone warrior rushed to the right side of the gates just as Ame pulled the trigger of her *teppo*. The explosion rang in Rōnin's ears, but he had to admit, the effect of her bullets was more convincing than the arrows. The closest *kyonshī* to Yūki exploded in two halves, and even the one behind fell backward.

The lone warrior put himself on the *onna-musha*'s left, right in time to block a dead samurai's sword. The monster's skill was terrible, but the strength behind the attack was full of power. Rōnin diverted the rusty katana rather than just stopping it, and the corpse got caught in its momentum. It impaled itself on Yūki's *naginata*, which she had angled for this purpose. The blade jutted from the dead's back but had missed the spine, so Rōnin slashed his sword across the lower back. The *onna-musha* then let it slide lifelessly from her polearm and resumed a fighting stance. Already five more were coming within reach. Zenbō held himself well, but more bodies came his way, and a few others already stepped through the cloud from where the group had come from. They had to move, and fast.

"Yūki, Ame," Rōnin called, "take care of those at the center."

"You sure?" the *onna-musha* asked.

"Go!" he said as he sheathed his sword back for the next attack.

Ame moved right as she closed the lock of her arquebus,

and her lover followed a heartbeat later. As Rōnin turned to focus on the five incoming *kyonshī*, he heard the gun fire, then the grunts of the *onna-musha* as she reaped second deaths in the enemy's ranks.

Rōnin ignored the look of horror from those monsters walking toward him, three of them holding swords, and the last two coming with spears gripped between their rotten hands. The closest still wore a samurai mask with a long, white mustache and a scowling mouth. Rōnin focused on him, locking his stare in the dead gray eyes. This man had been an officer, and his katana had kept its sharpness. More surprising even, he held it with both hands. So far, the *kyonshī* he had observed seemed to barely hold their blades, but this dead samurai, if not for his decayed skin and the long gash across his neck, could have passed for a living one.

They regain their skills, Rōnin told himself. *The longer they come back to life, the more they remember.* Yoshinao either had not told them or did not know about it, but it made things so much worse.

Rōnin shook his head to come back to the now, crouched a little to strengthen his stance, and started checking the distance between the five monsters coming at him.

"*Shihoto Sono Ni!*" The voice of Master Shigemasa came like a crack of thunder, and Rōnin moved before he could think about it.

The katana darted, pommel first, toward the masked samurai, landing with so much strength on its forehead that it staggered backward. Rōnin, twisting the blade to readjust the angle, thrust it on his left, punching the tip through a dead *ashigaru* foot soldier's throat and breaking his spine. Coming back to the first threat, Rōnin applied more strength than usual with his downward strike, cleaving the masked *kyonshī* from neck to armpit. He pushed his attack, taking the next step, cutting down again, felling the third, then again with the fourth monster. Both fell at his feet, leaving a last spearman to face him. The *kyonshī* pulled on its spear as if about to thrust it into Rōnin's belly, but the lone warrior moved before it could happen, applying an extra step to the *shihoto sono ni* technique in the form of an extended horizontal cut. For a moment, Rōnin wondered if he had made a mistake by modifying his master's teaching, but Shigemasa-sensei laughed in his mind when the head of the last dead bounced on the ground. He then shook the nonexistent blood from his katana and put it back home.

More were coming already; he had only gained a brief respite. He could see them through the fog, hear their guttural calls, and smell the rot. And with each step, they seemed to walk better.

A double explosion caught his attention, and Rōnin saw Ame, a smoking gun in each hand and a glowing match stuck between her teeth. She sheathed them back inside the leather sash strapped from her shoulder, then pulled two more while Yūki Ikeda lopped a head with a backstroke of her *naginata*. Further along the castle's wall, Zenbō seemed to breathe with more difficulty, but a small heap of corpses had formed at his feet.

Tsuki screamed as the gates finally opened, worrying Rōnin that more dead were coming from inside. Then he realized she had reacted to the appearance of the demon shinobi, who, it seemed, had managed to sneak inside the castle and open the gates from within.

"Into the castle!" Tadatomo shouted, waving for the four warriors to join him.

The lone warrior was the first through the gates, though he slowed his pace until he made sure Zenbō had gotten rid of his closest aggressor. The monk, once he felt the cold of the castle's stones above his head, bent over to regain his breath. Even Zenbō had been pushed hard in this battle.

Yūki and Ame all but bolted between the gates as Musashi and Mikinosuke closed them.

"Wait!" the *onna-musha* said.

The moment of hesitation from master and student was all Ame needed to throw a pouch through the interstice. Rōnin saw it arching in the air above the closest *kyonshī*, the glowing match she had kept in her mouth now planted inside the pouch.

"Now, close!" Yūki shouted.

The gates closed loudly, squashing a few daring fingers in the process, and both Musashi and his student pushed with their shoulders against the doors. A loud bang thundered outside and was followed by a dozen arrow-like thumps into the gates.

"Nail bomb," the *onna-musha* explained, translating her musketeer's signs.

"Move!" Tadatomo said as he and the shinobi carried the thick bar of metal that had kept the doors shut before and placed it across, just as Kiba had found it.

"I told you I would open it," the shinobi said, standing at an arm's length from Musashi Miyamoto. "You should have helped the others." Rōnin felt the shinobi's bloodlust but thought he was playing with fire, talking so rashly to Musashi.

"I didn't know if I could trust you," the swordsman replied, accepting the challenge and stepping even closer to the demon shinobi. "You could have found yourself facing the undead inside too."

"The dead of the castle are just dead," Kiba replied.

The door banged and shook under the impact of *kyonshī*

ramming it, pulling another high-pitched shout from Tadatomo, who then walked away from the gates.

"It won't hold for long," Rōnin said.

"There are closets and heavy pieces of furniture in the next rooms," Kiba replied.

"On it," Yūki said, waving at Ame and Tadatomo to follow her.

Rōnin put his shoulder against the doors when another blow made it bounce. The dead were grunting and moaning on the other side as if communicating. Their blades broke against the thick gates, and some bones snapped under the pressure of the swarm, but the lone warrior knew that more and more were coming. Zenbō dropped against the right slab of the gates, his uncaring smirk back in place.

"Not sure how much I can help carry things around," he said to explain his presence here. Rōnin smiled back, glad for the monk's presence by his side. There was something profoundly reassuring about Zenbō, as if the world could crumble and he would still find a reason to smile.

They bounced off a little when another hard blow rammed the doors.

"I know it will sound weird," Rōnin said, "but didn't you feel like—"

"—They were improving?"

"So it wasn't just an impression," Rōnin replied, mostly to himself.

"At first they could barely walk," the monk went on, as, from the end of the hallway, Yūki and Tadatomo dragged a heavy wardrobe across the floor. "But by the end, they seemed to remember their training. One even parried my thrust."

Rōnin raised an eyebrow in shock. This was worse than expected.

"Admittedly, it had been a feint, but still, it takes good reflexes," the monk went on.

Tsuki came first, arms filled with two chairs. She dropped them at the base of the doors, then left her spot for the wardrobe. Within a couple of minutes, the hallway was filled with anything that could be carried from the first floor of Gifu castle, and finally, Rōnin let go of the door.

"They won't come from here," Musashi said, clapping the dust from his hands.

"Neither will we leave from here," Yūki said.

"Let's check the situation from above," Rōnin offered.

The hallway and the rest of the first floor were empty, especially now that the furniture had been used to barricade the only doors. Spiders and rats had been using the castle since its fall, their presence marked by networks of webs and a layer of droppings in the corners, but they had scampered away when nine warriors started battling an army of dead people.

The second floor was another story altogether. It told the fierceness of the battle that had happened over the mountain some forty years ago. Soldiers in armor lay here and there in great numbers, arrows sprouting from their decaying bodies. Some carried the crest of the Oda clan, others the wave crest of the Saitō clan of Lady Nō. They had perished defending their leader's wife, and Gifu castle became their grave.

"Why do you think they didn't rise?" Mikinosuke asked. The boy had both his swords in hand, but his master walked confidently among the fallen samurai, arms crossed over his belly.

"Maybe the castle prevents whatever power the drum holds. Or maybe the drummer is too far away," the swordsman replied. He slid a panel from the closest room, opening it for the first time in four decades. The smell flooded Rōnin's senses and forced him to hide his nose in his elbow.

Inside the room, three bodies lay face up, two children and a woman, the marks left by the knife across their throats barely visible after the skin had dried and shrunk. The only other body in the room belonged to a bare-chested samurai, bending over the knife he had plunged into his bowels. His head was nowhere to be seen, proof that he had had some assistance in his seppuku ritual. The old mats under him were stained brown where the blood had flowed. At least they didn't need to worry about him.

"Is that Nōhime?" Mikinosuke asked, pointing at the woman.

"Probably not," his master answered. "The lady never had children."

Rōnin crossed the room to stare through the loopholes in the wall and immediately understood the beheaded samurai. The day he took his and his family's lives, Gifu had not been surrounded by an army of *kyonshī*, but the effect must have been more or less the same. They swarmed the castles from every direction, a sea of moving corpses, spreading from the cloud wherever space allowed them to. Their grunts twisted his bowels. It was like listening to an angry beehive, if the bees had vocal cords to moan or teeth to chatter and tear your skin with.

From the other side of the floor, Rōnin heard the mechanism of Ame's matchlock. She stood like him, in front of a series of loopholes, her arquebus barely passing through the slits and aimed at one of the monsters. Yūki dropped her hand on the cannon of the firearm and gently pushed it down.

"Keep your bullets, love," she said.

Because of the upturned roof between the first and second floors, Rōnin could not see the closest *kyonshī*. He spotted a few decaying hands trying to grab the edge of the roof, but so far they lacked the ability to pull themselves up. So far.

He stepped back into the corridor and heard a sudden crunch of bones. Kiba was kneeling by a body wearing the mark of the Oda clan, hands on both sides of the long-dead head and letting it dangle after snapping its neck.

"One can never be too prudent," the shinobi said before he moved to a second body.

"Fair enough," Tadatomo replied as he followed the shinobi's example and knelt next to some poor warrior whose life ended with an arrow stuck in his guts. He must have suffered for a long time then, but, thanks to Tadatomo Honda, he would not suffer a second time, if those things even suffered.

"Zenbō?" Rōnin asked, observing the blind monk who stood like a guardian statue on top of the stairs they had come from, spear standing by his side.

"I think I'll stay here a bit," the monk replied.

The fight at the gates, and the ascension of the mountain before that, had been more than any of them had first imagined. Fighting the Fūma shinobi the day before had been one thing, but this, another completely, and maybe the monk needed some time to recover despite his usual nonchalance. Rōnin was happy to give him said time and only wished he could allow himself to rest a bit, but until they found a way out of Gifu and Mount Kinka, there would be none.

He crossed the corridor, opening the various rooms to more miserable scenes. In the last one, two men faced each other on the floor, naked. Rōnin could not see the face of the one on the left, for it was buried against the chest of the other. They had died in each other's arms, but Rōnin shuddered at the thought that one of them had to kill the other before joining him. This could have been his fate, ten years ago.

"Rōnin," Mikinosuke called from the third floor, his head popping down from the staircase. "We found something."

There was no urgency in the boy's voice, so Rōnin climbed the stairs slowly. The third and last floor consisted of a single, square room, with a balustrade on the four sides. In usual circumstances, it would be the chamber of the castellan, but when the siege occurred, the room had turned into a platform for the archers. More than thirty lined the balustrade, and some had crawled back into the room, the blood trailing behind proof of their last effort in life. But they were not the reason for Mikinosuke's call.

At the center of the room, surrounded by Mikinosuke, Tsuki, and Musashi, on her knees and bending over like the headless samurai from before, rested the body of a woman. She had kept her head, and Rōnin guessed she had been amongst the last to perish. Her kimono had been black and pink, with petals of sakura dancing in the wind on her back. Her hair remained black, even after forty years, and her socks white. She had not used a short *tantō* to take her own life, but a full-length katana, and when Rōnin put his hands on her shoulders to sit her up, he already guessed what they would find in her belly.

"Yoshimoto-Samonji," Musashi confirmed.

The lady still gripped the hilt of the cursed blade. Contrary to what most samurai did, she had pierced her heart with it, not her guts, making her end a little quicker.

"Is she—" Mikinosuke asked.

"Nōhime," Tsuki answered.

Musashi brought his hands together as Zenbō would have and closed his eyes before mumbling a prayer for the lady. She must have been a great beauty, but now her face was wrinkled like a dry frog. The powerful Nobunaga Oda had loved her, cherished her, and whispered words of comfort into her ears. They had been young, and powerful.

"What is that?" Tsuki asked as she knelt by Rōnin's side.

A paper was stuck against the lady, the blade pinning it into her chest. The blood had rendered it mostly red and brown, but the characters remained mostly readable. Even her calligraphy had been elegant.

"Her death poem," Rōnin answered. "She must have written it just before she..."

Though my corpse rots,
On the upper floor
Of Gifu castle,
My heart remains forever
With my lord.

The pain in Tsuki's voice as she recited the last verses ever written by the finger of Nōhime gripped at Rōnin's heart. She had more compassion than most young people, even for a lady who died a generation before her birth. It was time to leave Nōhime to rest, Rōnin thought as he gently worked on the lady's fingers. They had found the cursed blade at least. All that remained was for a way out to magically appear for them.

He pulled a finger from the hilt of the four-hundred-year-old katana, and when it cracked, the sound of a drum echoed in the distance.

Rōnin shared an anxious look with the archer, then a high-pitched moan came from the lady's throat as she straightened her head. Her dead eyes fell on Rōnin, who still had his hand around her fingers in an intimate pose. For a second no one moved. Then the lady shrieked and shoved herself against the lone warrior, who screamed with utter fear.

Rōnin grabbed Nōhime by the throat and pushed on the hilt of the Samonji sword at the same time, anything to keep those gnarly teeth and thin fingers from his face. She was frantic, as terrible in death as she must have been sweet in life.

"Shit," Rōnin cursed as his strength failed him. Those things were stronger than the living, especially when they had the advantage of being above.

Her mouth smelled like death, and not the poetical kind she had suffered, but that of a rat killed by a cat and left for days because it had gotten bored with it. She snapped her teeth so close to his nose that Rōnin had to turn his face from her. He tried to put his leg between them, but she had him pinned down completely.

Musashi's hands fell on her shoulders and the master swordsman pulled with all his strength, lifting her from the lone warrior with a loud grunt. She tumbled backward and crashed against the wall. Mikinosuke was on her next, crossing his two blades through her neck to bring her some deserved peace.

"Thank you," Rōnin said as he accepted Musashi's hand.

"At least we got the sword now," the swordsman replied, nodding toward the Samonji which had remained in Rōnin's hand.

"We've got more problems too," Mikinosuke said.

Around them, more dead rose from their peace. The archers came back to life, slower than their lady, but with just as much passion for death.

"Help!" Tsuki screamed.

CHAPTER 6
YUKI IKEDA

Inuyama Castle, Ikeda domain, Owari province, 1623

"I forbid you from taking another step!" Ikeda Sen shouted with all her feeble strength.

"Or what?" Yūki barked, though she did stop in her tracks, an arm's length from the gate of the castle she had known all her life. "You'll keep me away from the world for another twenty years?"

"The castle is safe," Sen replied before a bout of coughing caught her. "This is all I care about, your and your sister's safety."

"Safety?" Yūki spat. "Safety from what? From experiencing life?" This argument had been going on for years between mother and daughter. Inuyama Castle had long lost its splendor in the young woman's eyes. She craved more. A pit had dug in her chest whenever she heard news of the country. A new era was shaping up in Japan, and she was missing it. It was already bad enough that no war had taken place for eight years, but now, almost on a weekly basis, came offers of marriage for her and her sister. Yūki could feel it, her mother was weakening, and soon, she would have to hand her daughters over to some greedy samurai, "for *your safety."* Yūki did not want safety or a husband, she wanted to see the land and fight for her own fame. She wanted to spend her days with Ame, and see Tsuki grow to be whatever she wanted to be. Inuyama was a prison.

"You're not ready for the world," her mother replied.

"Mother," Tsuki called as Sen suffered another bout. She supported her mother, but when Sen realized her youngest daughter also carried a bundle on her back, she must have understood things had gone further than anticipated.

"Why did we practice every day from dawn to dusk?" Yūki asked.

"Yūki-nē," Tsuki intervened. "Stop it, she isn't feeling well." But her sister would not listen. The day had come for her to speak her mind and lighten her heart from all those thoughts she had kept caged in it since teenagehood.

"Why did I train until my hands became hard like rock, if not to fight? Why did you make Tsuki shoot arrows until her fingers bled?"

"I wanted you to be ready, in case," Sen replied.

"Ready for what?" the onna-musha barked. "The world is moving on without us. You molded us into warriors, but there are no wars! You are wasting us here. Don't you understand, Mother?" she asked, looking into her mother's eyes with all the love she had for the woman. "I just want to be like you."

Sen trembled because of the wind but did not reply. She heard the resolve in her daughter's voice, and maybe a part of her remembered a young woman who had defied her husband's orders and volunteered a unit of women musketeers to the cause of Ieyasu Tokugawa. She stood straighter and met her daughter's resolve with her old strength.

"You want to leave?" she asked.

"But I will come back," Yūki replied. "Once my name is

engraved into the annals of our nation's history next to yours, I will come back."

There was a moment of doubt. Sen fought the urge to plead for her daughter to stay, but the warrior overcame the mother, and she embraced Yūki to let her know she understood.

"War is not what you think," she told her daughter as they shared this last embrace.

"It doesn't matter," Yūki replied. "This is what you trained me for."

They separated, Sen nodded, and the doors of Inuyama opened. The castellan wasn't surprised to see her deaf musketeer standing on the other side, travel-ready as well. They both nodded to each other, and Ame bowed in gratitude.

"I will miss you, Mother," Tsuki said, her lips quivering with emotion.

"Me too, Tsuki," Sen replied as she embraced her second daughter. Her grip was stronger with Tsuki. "War took two husbands and one son from me. Do not let it take my daughters."

"We will come back," Tsuki promised.

"Take care of your sister," Sen said as she pushed Tsuki at arm's length. "She thinks she's strong, but she needs you, more than she knows."

When she heard her sister's scream, Yūki's heart skipped a beat. In no time she bolted up the stairs leading to the last floor of Gifu castle, which the dead had already swarmed. Musashi Miyamoto was pushing a dead archer across the room and over the balustrade, while his student leaped like a tornado and cut through a *kyonshī*'s head with ease. Rōnin moved with extreme efficiency, his sword barely visible as it cut through a *kyonshī* who had just woken up.

"Tsuki!" the *onna-musha* called when she reached the top of the stairs. Her vision blurred as she searched for her little sister, and a high-pitched ringing bounced between her ears. Tsuki was nowhere in sight. She had lost her sister. Her breathing came with difficulty and her legs got weak.

"Yūki-nē!" the archer screamed from the corner of the room, behind Yūki.

The girl was on her back, pinned down by a bloodthirsty dead archer. She kept it away using the back of her bow, pushing it inside its mouth. Her arms would fail her, or the monster's hands would reach her face and claw it raw. Yūki moved toward her sister, just as another of the dead archers seemed to notice the girl and stumbled toward them.

Time slowed to a trickle. Yūki could barely move. Sounds muffled around her, except for her breathing, which came in loud rasps. Her sister needed her and called for her, but Yūki Ikeda remained in her spot, petrified. The second of the two monsters coming after Tsuki knelt near the girl's face, its hands empty, but viciously stretched toward the girl's eyes. Yūki's heartbeat banged rhythmically but faster, and she called for her sister but did not hear her own voice.

Rōnin appeared in her peripheral vision, like a ball of fire. Even with the sluggishness of the world in her mind, the lone warrior was moving fast. He chopped his sword once, a head fell, he reversed his grip and sliced upward, and a second head tumbled. Tsuki pushed the inert body with her bow and used his hand to stand back up. The warrior handed her a naked katana, not his, which she accepted readily, throwing her bow in the room's corner. Yūki could not comprehend what she was seeing. Her sister, sword in hand, came to her and spoke words she could not hear. Yūki nodded, or at least she thought she did, and Tsuki left, brandishing her blade as if she knew how to use it. How come she was still alive? Yūki wondered as she tried to follow the flurry of movements.

Her instinct told her to look to the left, so she did, just in time to see a *kyonshī* about to grab her throat. She gasped, but could not pull herself to raise her *naginata*. It was so heavy, and she would be too late. The monster snarled green teeth and one of its eyes, which had miraculously survived all those decades, observed her with a horrifying hunger.

The monster vanished, and when Yūki followed the blur, she found it on the floor, Tadatomo on top, using the tip of his helmet to bash the *kyonshī*'s face to a pulp. The samurai lowered himself a little, and above his head passed the weighted end of Kiba's chained sickle. A body fell by Tadatomo's side, and the samurai nodded his thanks to the shinobi. As the chain retracted toward its owner, the *onna-musha* spotted the moment Kiba left the main room to kick an archer over the balustrade and sent him down with its brethren. The shinobi stepped outside, but Yūki could barely follow his rapid movements as he sliced through air and bones with his sickle.

Kiba blurred outside and passed behind Rōnin and Tsuki, who fought in front of her very eyes, coordinating naturally despite her lack of training with a katana. She could barely swing the damn thing, but the lone warrior compensated for her poor skills with expert cuts, his left hand always on her back to guide her movements through the melee.

A hand fell on her shoulder, and Yūki startled in panic. When she turned, she saw Ame holstering one of her short guns. The love of her life looked tired, but focused and tense, as usual. The musketeer dropped both her scarred hands over Yūki's face, then on her ears, putting her in the same silence she herself lived in. It was amazingly quiet.

Ame moved her hand on her chest, then on Yūki's.

I'm with you, she meant.

She tapped on both chests again, but the other way around, and then lifted her little finger.

Are you with me?

Yūki nodded. Her lover gathered the five fingers of her left hand toward her mouth and lowered the hand all the way to her belly in a slow, straight line, her lips pursed as if she was breathing out.

Breathe, just breathe.

Yūki closed her eyes and followed the advice. She breathed in, then out, until all air had left her lungs. Slowly, she reopened her eyes, and the world came back. Every sound of battle around her, every movement in the periphery of her vision, they all got to her clearly.

"Thank you," Yūki said before kissing her lover on the forehead. Then she yelled. The shame and the rage of her panic attack poured lava into her veins. She brushed past Ame and grabbed the monster who was coming at Tadatomo, then threw it against the pole of the balustrade with a loud grunt. Since it was not enough, she pressed the attack with a vicious knee in its chin. She broke the monster's jaw, and its mouth would no longer close. It wouldn't need it for long, anyway. With an ire-filled arm, she chopped its head, getting her *naginata* stuck in the pole. A *kyonshī* came on her left, so she lowered her stance to use her shoulder armor and pushed against it with all her might. The monster bumped against the rail of the balustrade. She caught its ankle and lifted the cursed being over, letting it fall into the army of undead warriors.

Checking the noisy swarm, Yūki realized that through sheer mass, they had managed to reach the roof of the second floor, at least on this side.

"Yūki-nē, you're all right?" Tsuki asked as she joined her sister. They had finally gotten rid of the undead inside the castle.

"I'm fine, Tsuki," she replied, shaking her head to chase the last of her confusion. "I don't know what happened. I saw you there and, and..."

"It's all right, it's all right," Tsuki said, patting her sister's biceps with love. "I'm fine, you see?"

"For now," Yūki replied.

"They are about to breach the gates!" Zenbō said as he reached the upper floor.

The two sisters rejoined the others at the center of the room.

"What do we do?" Tadatomo asked as he wiped the gore from his katana in the crook of his elbow. He had changed completely over the morning's event, Yūki told herself, again, with a pang of shame. If even the drunkard could fight bravely, what the hell had just happened to her?

"We need to split," Rōnin said.

"Split?" Yūki asked. "Are you crazy?"

A tremor shook the castle, forcing the nine to wave their arms to keep their balance.

"Was that an earthquake?" Mikinosuke asked.

"No," Zenbō answered. "It's them."

The drummer had gathered the attack on one side, and now the entire army of the dead pressed on Gifu castle, pushing the building westward with the weight of their bodies. The poles creaked here and there, and the castle seemed to moan. Yūki felt her balance shift. Gifu would not hold long.

"We split," Musashi agreed. "When the castle goes down, we hang on to whatever we can, and we rush down the mountain. Do not look back for the others, just go."

"Why should we split?" Yūki asked, hating the idea.

"From what we saw, I think the drummer cannot give specific commands to the dead," Rōnin explained. "If we split, he cannot tell them to pursue each of us. We have a better chance for some of us to make it this way."

"I concur," Kiba replied.

"Wait," Zenbō called. "What about the Yoshimoto-Samonji?"

"I have it," Tsuki replied, holding the blade in front of her until she remembered the monk could not see it.

"Do you want me to take it?" the blind monk asked.

"My arrows don't do much damage on the dead, I will use the blade," she replied. Zenbō flashed his charming smile at her.

"In that case, let's all gather at Azuchi," the monk went on.

The castle creaked and swayed dangerously. The angle of the wall would make the ascension easier for the *kyonshī* on the outside, while those prying the gates open would be here any second. It was a race between the castle and the dead, which would break through first.

"On the roof," Rōnin said, probably sensing that Gifu had still too much life in it and they needed to put more distance between them and the dead.

Yūki used the balustrade to jump on the upper roof, then extended her arm for Tsuki to climb after her. The swarm of monsters was now so high that they could almost reach the girl's feet as Yūki dragged her on top. One by one, the nine made it to the relative safety of the roof, just in time to hear the dead swarming the third floor.

"Remember," Musashi said. "Don't look back, don't call anyone, just run straight ahead, and we'll meet at Azuchi."

"I still don't like your stupid plan," Yūki barked as the castle lunged a little more.

Some beam or some pole would soon snap, and the rest would naturally follow. The *onna-musha* crouched as low as possible, following the example of Kiba. She grabbed one of the black, rounded tiles, tested it, and found it strong enough.

It's gonna be all right, Ame signed.

Yūki was about to sign back that after this ordeal, they would go back to Inuyama and never leave it again, but the castle gave up before she could say any of it.

There was a loud moan from Gifu as its supporting poles cracked, and like a hunted whale, the castle toppled, slowly at first, then fast. For a second, the view of the collapsing roof filled Yūki with wonder. Surely no one had ever appreciated Mino province from such a vantage point. It was as if she was about to fly off. Then it all went down. She screamed, others did too, and the roof crashed on the side of the mountain, with enough speed and at such an angle that great planks of it slid like luges. Yūki was on one of them. She held on to the tile, screaming until her balance crumbled and she tumbled on the side, rolling over and over again on her shoulder, nearly killing herself against a pine tree. She finally stopped moving, and for a moment wondered if she should even get up. The forest ground was comfy, her head spinning, and she was pretty sure to have a couple of broken fingers. At least she had kept a hold of her *naginata*.

When she stood—much faster than she should have—Yūki realized she was back inside the cloud from before. The hundreds of dead who had come this way had raised so much dust that it had turned yellow and floated even thicker than before. She resisted the urge to call for her sister. Already the dead seemed to adapt to the situation and their grunts changed to her direction.

The *onna-musha* was about to leave, but a hand grabbed her wrist, and, before she could scream, another covered her mouth. She recognized the touch and the smell of her lover.

"Let's go," the musketeer said in her hoarse, hesitant voice.

Tsuki? Yūki asked, writing the character for her sister's name in her lover's palm.

"Trust her," Ame replied.

The *onna-musha* understood how her mother felt the day they left. She understood everything her mother had said too. She made a promise in her heart not only to go back home when the journey ended but to beg for forgiveness. War was ugly. The thought of losing someone was heartbreaking. And the world wasn't safe. Her mother had been right all along, but now she had to trust her sister and whoever she found herself with.

Bursting through the cloud hand in hand, Ame and Yūki rushed down Mount Kinka and headed west through the countryside of Mino, toward Azuchi, and toward Demon Island.

CHAPTER 7
RONIN

Osaka, 1614

"Ei! Ei!" the warlord shouted from his wobbly position.

"Ōh!" the soldiers replied with a heartwarming pleasure, ending the victory cry for the hundredth time that day, at least.

All afternoon, and deep into the evening, soldiers and samurai had cheered their leader and celebrated their first victory of the war. Not a single man within the Sanada ward stood sober, and many actually couldn't stand still anymore. Least of all their general, Sanada Nobushige, so close to collapsing from the empty barrel he stood on that men started betting on the timing of his eventual fall.

Nobushige was as resplendent in victory as he had been fearsome in battle. The events of the day were only a few hours old, but the tale had already been told so many times that they had taken a near mythologic tone. Nobushige had ridden his horse through the central prong of the Tokugawa army, cutting heads left and right with each swing of his spear. They claimed he had reaped a hundred heads, and his crimson demon samurai more than a thousand.

Nagakatsu knew those tales to be grossly exaggerated, but also guessed how important they were for the morale of the men. He had fought in the thick of it, experiencing his first battle at the center of a unit of foot soldiers. Nobushige had offered a horse for the young swordsman to ride into battle, but because of his poor riding skills, Nagakatsu chose to fight on foot. The battle took place near the castle's fortifications, and the lack of horse did not leave him winded as the fighting began. He saw the moment the general rammed into the Honda ranks, a few seconds before his own unit joined the melee. Nagakatsu focused on following the six-coined crest of Sanada and assured himself to widen the wedge started by the man he had come to serve. He discovered that morning that killing was easy, even trained men, and that his talent with the sword was nothing to be ashamed of. In the dōjō, he used to practice with other dedicated students and had always assumed to be of average skills. In reality, he was a lethal beast, and once unchained on the field, he not only widened the wedge but even punctured through the enemy lines, motivating the other ashigaru foot soldiers of his unit who fought like the demons they titled themselves to be. So few of them died that the ambience around the fires was just cheerful. They had won the first battle and were undefeatable.

"Did you see—" Nobushige asked before burping in his fist. "Did you see how they shat themselves when Nagakatsu cut their officer's sword arm as if it was made of paper?"

Nagakatsu blushed at the sudden attention of his new comrades and dropped his eyes in the cup of sake that seemed to magically refill anytime he emptied it. The mentioned strike, according to all who had stood by Nagakatsu's side, tipped the scale of the fight, and losing this officer made the rest of the

Honda forces rout, especially since their commander was drunk as a tanuki.

"For Nagakatsu! Ei! Ei!"

"Ōh!"

"Thank you, Sanada-sama," the young warrior said. "I was just lucky to be at the right place, at the right time."

Nobushige shook his drunken head, then opened his eyes suddenly because the barrel had been shifting.

"Victorious warriors are entitled to boast," he said. "I will have no humility in my camp tonight. Nagakatsu," the general called, looking all serious, "if you don't brag right now, I'm calling it a night for all of us."

All the soldiers around the fire turned their pleading eyes toward the young swordsman, murmuring for him to say something that would let the wine flow. He'd never been trained for that in the dōjō of Shigemasa-sensei, and the words came painfully to his blurred mind.

"I think you're mistaken, Sanada-sama," the young man said, earning himself a few disapproving grumbles. "When I sliced through that samurai's arm, he didn't shit himself. All the soldiers of his unit did though."

The following laughter drowned his embarrassment, and men twice his age came to pat his back and shoulders. Sanada Nobushige was bending backward in his guffaw, and Nagakatsu was invited to down his cup by his closest comrade. He had never felt so good before. It wasn't just the wine or the victory. It was the camaraderie, the joy of survival, and the eyes of his warlord on him.

The general imitated the strike of the young warrior from his precarious position, and finally fell onto the trampled ground of the camp, turning the soldiers' laughter into pure euphoria.

Nagakatsu came to help him up, but Nobushige laughed so

hard that it took a couple of tries to get him on his feet. Even then he could hardly control himself, and Nagakatsu used all his fading strength to keep the general standing against him.

"You fought bravely today," Nobushige said, hand on Nagakatsu's shoulder for balance.

"You honor me, my lord."

"But your armor, and your sword..."

"My lord?" Nagakatsu asked, sobering really fast because of his general disapproving tone. He had rarely practiced with armor before and knew some of his techniques had been slightly stiff during the battle. As for his sword, it had seen better days, being the one he acquired when starting his seventh year at the dōjō.

"They'll have to be replaced," Nobushige confirmed. "It won't do to have one of my best men fighting without my crest on him."

Nagakatsu felt warmth in his chest. He'd never realized before that the one thing his life lacked was a lord to serve, and a man to love.

Yoshimoto-Samonji reflected the flames as any other blade would. The pattern of the waves by the edge was unique and elegant, and a blacksmith could probably see in it the hand of a master, but to Rōnin, who judged blades by their aptitude for bringing death and their resistance, the katana seemed like most. From across the evening fire, Musashi claimed he could feel the vibration of the blade as if it was calling for blood, but the lone warrior could only see a fine piece of steel. He put it in front of his eyes again, curve up and forward to check the quality of the edge. Even after forty years inside Lady Nō, it had kept a razor-like sharpness, which in itself was remarkable, but Rōnin could not see what made it the key to Demon Island. He told himself some curse would have been sealed inside the blade, and he would not be able to "see" it. The tsuba guarding the hand looked even older. It was a magnificent piece, with a complex design reminding Rōnin of a butterfly. It wasn't rare for owners of great swords to change such a part of the katana, especially if they possessed a tsuba with historical value. This one could have belonged to the Taira clan of old. Of the Yoshimoto-Samonji, the tsuba was the part Rōnin found the most interesting.

His inspection finished, he offered it to the master swordsman, who simply shook his head to show his lack of interest.

"Once you've held a proper Masamune in your hands," he explained, "the others all feel the same."

So the lone warrior handed it back to Tsuki, who sat on the grass next to him. Reverently, she slid it back into her *obi*, the absence of a scabbard forcing her to tie it with care. Once it was back at her hip, the archer did not seem to know what to do with her left arm.

"You can shift its curve down," Rōnin said with a smile. "This way you won't cut yourself on it."

"Isn't it...unethical?" she asked.

"Not really," the lone warrior answered. "And I don't think anyone here would care. People used to carry them like that, you know?"

"They did?" Mikinosuke asked, his mouth full of roasted fish. His gaze moved to his master for confirmation.

"It is true," Musashi Miyamoto replied after swallowing a bite of the same fish. Tsuki had shot three in the nearby river before sunset, the last one being big enough for master and student to share. Her arrows having no effect on the dead had made her feel useless. At least, Rōnin thought, they could eat thanks to her, and knowing this would improve her mood. "Back when this blade was forged," the swordsman went on, "it wasn't a *katana*, but probably a *tachi*. Those blades are longer, and meant to be used by horse riders, which is why they wore them face down."

"Doesn't seem shorter to me," Tsuki said timidly.

"It isn't," Rōnin confirmed. "Warlords nowadays don't really need *tachi*. One of its most recent owners would have had it shortened. Either Yoshimoto Imagawa or Nobunaga Oda,"

"My money is on Nobunaga," Musashi replied as he threw the now useless skewer back into the fire. "Yoshimoto was more of a traditionalist."

"Can you fight on a horse?" Tsuki asked.

"Never liked them much," Musashi replied, making a face.

"Same," Rōnin answered as well.

"Oh, really?" Musashi said, looking truly surprised. "I assumed you were amongst Sanada's famed riders."

"I fought with his foot soldiers," Rōnin replied. "The Crimson Demons."

"You fought under Sanada Nobushige?" Mikinosuke all but shouted.

"I did," Rōnin replied with a nod.

"What was he like?" the boy asked, eyes filled with stars. "I heard he was the greatest samurai of Japan."

"I thought Tadatomo's father was the greatest," Tsuki said, moving her gaze from Mikinosuke to Rōnin.

Musashi grated his throat gravely, giving himself the look of a master about to lecture his students.

"Tadakatsu Honda was the most powerful warrior of his time. A beast on the battlefield, capable of unmatched prowess with his famed Tonbokiri spear. Nobushige Sanada, on the other side, is considered the greatest for his sense of honor and loyalty. Am I correct in my assessment, Rōnin?"

"You could not have spoken truer words, Miyamoto-dono," Rōnin replied. "Nobushige was..." he started, looking at the boy, but the words remained stuck in the lump blocking his throat. "My lord was radiant, indomitable, you could say. Even when we knew the war was all but lost, his example was enough for us to keep fighting without a second of hesitation. When he was riding to battle, death, pain, defeat, all those things were nonexistent in his mind, only honor mattered. There's never been a more honest samurai in Japan."

"He sounds remarkable," Tsuki replied. "I wish I could have met him." The sorrow in her voice was genuine and seemed to match Rōnin's sadness. The water in her eyes reflected his, and the lone warrior told himself that the girl had guessed more than her youth suggested. From the way she looked at him since Gifu, Rōnin knew Tsuki liked him, but now, she must have understood that no matter what, no one would ever fill the hole in his heart.

"Me too, Tsuki. He would have loved you."

Mikinosuke was about to speak but Musashi put his hand on the boy's wrist to keep him quiet. Rōnin didn't mind talking about Nobushige. If anything, it kept him alive a little longer, but this evening wasn't the right moment for it. When their journey ended and the threat was over, he would tell them everything about Nobushige Sanada and the Crimson Demons. Until then, he had to focus.

Azuchi was four to five days ahead. They could be there faster if they used the main road, as Musashi had first offered after they found each other, or some boat to sail over the sacred Lake Biwa, as Tsuki suggested. But neither option satisfied Rōnin. The road would be used by regular travelers, and words might get out of their position. Whoever controlled the dead would be sure to have it watched. As for the lake, after Kiba told them during their last night together that the Fūma shinobi specialized in amphibious missions, Rōnin found Biwa more menacing than practical. The lake was still a day ahead anyway, and before that, they had to remain alert. Who knew if either the drum master or his hired shinobi weren't already on their scent, or worse, if they had captured one of their companions and made them talk?

"Do you think everyone is fine?" Tsuki asked, following the same train of thought as Rōnin.

"Worried about your sister?" Musashi asked plainly.

"Not really," the girl replied. "I'm sure she's with Ame, and as long as those two are together, nothing can happen to either of them. But Tadatomo-san..."

"I wouldn't worry about him either," the swordsman replied with a knowing chuckle. "I know he didn't look his best when climbing Gifu, and his reputation took a hit at Osaka. But Tadatomo is a strong man, much stronger than even he knows. I'm good friends with his older brother, and let me tell you, even after everything that happened between them, he speaks of Tadatomo with pride. Did you know that at Sekigahara, he forced the Shimazu soldiers to a retreat with a mere regiment of cavalry?"

"I didn't," Tsuki replied, eyes as big as sake cups.

"Really?" Mikinosuke asked, clearly not believing what he'd just heard.

"Yes, really," the master said, slapping the back of his student's head. "I even heard he cut two men in one stroke and broke his katana doing so. Do you know how strong you must be to go through two men and their armor?" Musashi whistled, impressed at his own tale.

"You were there, weren't you?" Rōnin asked, meaning Sekigahara.

"Aye," the master replied, dropping his gaze into the popping fire. Rōnin had fought at Osaka, the last great battle, but veterans all claimed it had been a skirmish compared to Sekigahara. "I was there on the day the future of Japan was decided. Back then I fought against Tokugawa, simply because I had grown on the other side. I was sixteen, barely a man, and not a day has passed since without me remembering this butchery. Imagine that, Mikinosuke, two hundred thousand fighting men!" Mikinosuke had probably heard it all dozens of times, but his eyes still gleamed as if it was the first. "The battle lasted six or seven hours, but it felt as if it took days. By the end of it, Tokugawa Ieyasu was the sole master of Japan, and thirty thousand men had lost their lives. Thirty thousand men…" His voice trailed off, losing itself in the memory of Japan's bloodiest battle in history. "…in six hours." After a few seconds, Musashi resurfaced from his own mind and realized how the three others stared at him. He faked a cough and became himself again.

"I wouldn't worry about the other two either," he went on. "Kiba is probably going after the drum master by himself, and I doubt anything can get to Zenbō. Mark my words, he'll be there at Azuchi, waiting for us with that stupid grin of his."

"What do you think awaits us there?" Rōnin asked after a few chuckles warmed the group. The night had settled in during their meal, and even with the fire, he felt the freshness coming with the darkness. They would soon take turns keeping watch, and Rōnin had volunteered to be the first.

But until then, he didn't mind getting the conversation going. He had truly missed sharing some time with comrades.

"If you had asked me a couple of days ago, I would have said that nothing awaits us but ruins," Musashi replied. "Now... let's say that seeing the dead rise opens one's mind to new possibilities."

"Onijima..." Tsuki said to herself. "It has to be an island, right? How can there be an island inland?"

"Maybe on the lake," Mikinosuke said, though it sounded more like a question.

"Maybe," she replied, not feeling it.

"And how can a sword be a key to it?" Rōnin asked. He didn't expect any response. Some questions can only find their answers in experience, and this was one.

"Do you think Nobunaga ever used it, this altar I mean?" Tsuki asked.

"If he had," Musashi replied, hands extended toward the fire, "we would probably not be here to talk about it. I might be wrong, but I believe even the Fool of Owari knew this power was too dangerous. He gathered the keys, had all the cards in his hands, but never used them, either because he didn't need this power or because he died first."

"It says a lot about the bastard we are dealing with this time," Mikinosuke said.

"Watch your language," the master said, looking at the boy sideways. "You have a point though. If Nobunaga Oda, the most power-thirsty warlord that ever lived in Japan, chose not to use the curse of Izanagi, who could be this man who got his hands on the drum?"

"Any clue?" Rōnin asked the swordsman.

"At first, I wondered if it could be Yoshinao himself," Musashi Miyamoto replied after a loud harrumph.

"What?" Tsuki asked in a high-pitched tone. "Surely not."

"I don't think so anymore," the swordsman replied. "But it wouldn't have been the most twisted plan ever. You have to know, young Ikeda, that the Tokugawa face their own curse. Not like the one *we* are dealing with but a curse nonetheless. Ieyasu had more than ten sons, but less than nine years after his death, only two remain, Yoshinao and Hidetada, the current shōgun. Yoshinao was the ninth son, but he is now the second most powerful man in the nation. With a little more power in his camp, he could overthrow his brother and start his very own line."

"Why don't you think it's him anymore?" Mikinosuke asked his master.

"To be honest, just my instinct," the swordsman replied. "I quite like the young daimyō, and if he has managed to retain the loyalty of the Yagyū samurai, he can't really be half bad."

"Who then?" the boy asked.

"No clue," Musashi answered matter of fact, throwing his hands in the air. "Could be anyone. Someone still bitter about Osaka, a sympathizer of the emperor, some foreign forces, who knows? Before the civil war started, I doubt anyone would have given a chance to the Fool of Owari, or even considered him. Yet he unified Japan and brushed all the old, powerful clans from the map."

"Now we know how," Rōnin said.

"True, but maybe we are just dealing with another Nobunaga," Musashi said before stretching and yawning loudly. "In any case, we don't need to stir our noodles thinking about it. All the answers will be given to us at Azuchi."

With that Musashi Miyamoto let himself lie in the grass,

using his outer shirt as a pillow, and within twenty seconds snored without a worry in the world. Rōnin envied him, and when his two other companions followed the swordsman's example, the lone warrior envied them too.

Rōnin doubled his guard duty in the morning when Musashi Miyamoto proved impossible to wake. Mikinosuke assured them it was a common issue with his master. Tsuki got some more fish, Mikinosuke rekindled the fire, and Rōnin patrolled the area. It was a quiet place, not far from a snow-covered mountain called Ibuki. Not a strand of grass moved, oddly, and Rōnin went back to the fire just as the smell of roasting fish seemed to pull Musashi from his slumber.

The day passed quietly, their march lolled by Musashi's voice regaling them with tales of his adventures. A spat of rain threatened the afternoon, but it was soon gone. The master swordsman believed a typhoon was hitting the southern coast but would not bother them. He made the journey easier, and Rōnin walked better knowing the greatest wandering warrior of Japan stood by his side.

By common accord, they avoided forests and groves but also tried to stay clear of houses and roads. When Lake Biwa appeared on the horizon, they veered a little south to travel with the lake's edge on their right, knowing that Azuchi would be on the other side of the southern shore. At first, avoiding signs of habitation took a few detours, but in the afternoon, they found the land less and less used. Shortly before dusk, they crossed a valley between small forest-covered hills, and Rōnin wondered if they should call it a day there.

"Oh, I must have been thirteen then," Musashi said, answering Tsuki's question. She had listened to him patiently all day long, and still found the grace to ask for more. "His name was Arima Kihei. A big brute, ugly as a monkey's ass, and just as hairy." Tsuki giggled at this. "He was passing through my village in his journey to hone his skills and issued a challenge to whoever dared. I did, and I must admit he laughed when I came to the challenge's location, armed with a staff and thinking myself a man. So I charged him as he roared in laughter with his head backward, and—"

The story ended abruptly, and the tension rose at once. Musashi stopped walking, removed the hands from his sleeves, and scanned the plain with a thick frown.

"What is it, sensei?" the boy asked.

"I know this place," the master replied.

"Not fond memories it seems," Rōnin replied.

"Where are we?" Tsuki asked.

Musashi Miyamoto did not reply right away. His mind worked to retrieve the memory disturbing him. In it, he filled the plain with absent features to make it look different. A house maybe, a hunting party, or a religious procession perhaps. He shook his head; that wasn't it.

"People," he said to himself, "there were so many people here. And...shouts. Shouts and screams. And it smelled like..." The swordsman sniffed the air as if it was that day. "It smelled like gunpowder and iron." His eyes grew wide. He pointed toward the closest grove. "They came from there. We knew they were waiting for us, but our leader sent my unit to cross the valley to lure them. They attacked, came at us with spears, swords, and arquebuses. When our lines clashed, our comrades came from the sides. A volley of arrows flew from there," he went on, pointing at the opposite grove. "It killed a bunch of enemies but many of our men too. It was chaos. And not just here. All over this place. Cannons boomed every other minute, further south, but we could hear them crash nearby. I killed men barely older than I was but received a bad blow to the head and found myself under the corpse of a foe. The battle raged on for long minutes, and when enough of us died, the enemy moved to their next target, not even finishing the wounded or helping their comrades."

Rōnin heard the tremor in Musashi's voice as he recounted what must have been a horrendous battle. He could not begrudge his reaction. Battles live fresh in veterans' minds, they never go away, Rōnin knew it all too well.

"Master?" Mikinosuke asked, putting himself next to Musashi and gently pulling on his sleeve.

"I think we should go," the swordsman replied, "we're in Sekigahara. This land belongs to ghosts."

The *kotsuzumi* rang and echoed throughout the valley, feeble as it reached the four warriors perhaps, but strong enough to fill their chests with dread.

"No," Musashi said as he found the origin of the sound.

At the edge of the forest he had first pointed at, there was a horse, standing quietly. And on the horse sat a man. A samurai, judging by the two horns of his *kabuto* helmet. They could not see him clearly at a distance and under the shadow of the trees, but they saw the drum dangling in his hand. The drummer lifted it and let it drop on his right shoulder.

Tsuki raised her bow and methodically drew the string until the fletching caressed her cheek. The horse rider then hit the drum once more, and the grunts soon followed.

Mikinosuke unsheathed his blades, just as the first wobbly silhouettes appeared behind the drummer. He remained on his horse, unafraid of the cursed warriors he had just woken up. The drum left his shoulder, and he gathered his reins. Tsuki let her arrow fly, and even at such a distance, she would have hit true if the man hadn't kicked his mount quickly enough. They saw him gallop toward the next grove, the one they should have brushed if their path hadn't been interrupted.

"We need to go," Rōnin said, not waiting for an answer before he started at a dead run.

There was another strike of the drum when the horned samurai got inside the second grove, but this time they did not wait to find out if the dead had risen. They knew they had. The empty land between the two groves still glistened with the morning's rain. It looked impossibly long to Rōnin, as if running made no difference to the distance. Reanimated corpses were pouring from the woods on their right, and some appeared on the left. The drum was used again somewhere further. Whoever this drummer was, he clearly did not want them to get out of Sekigahara, and, as the path steepened to a slope, Rōnin feared he might get his wish.

"Sensei," Mikinosuke called between two breaths. "We'll never get through on time."

He was right, Rōnin realized. The path was already darkening with the victims of Sekigahara who had been left to rot. The two groups would meet before the four warriors could get through.

"To the forest!" the lone warrior shouted, pointing toward the grove where they had first seen the drummer.

"What?" Musashi barked. "Are you crazy?"

"It's the furthest place from *him*," Rōnin replied. "If we

get in there and lose him, he won't be able to direct the *kyonshī* at us."

"Shit," Musashi replied, though he too changed the direction of his run and followed Rōnin's lead.

There were two more strikes of the *kotsuzumi*, now from their backs. The grove drew near, but the dead came even closer. They now looked at ease on their two legs, though few seemed to go any faster than a walk. Tsuki shot at twenty paces from the closest and got him in the knee. It did not destroy the leg, but the undead warrior tumbled helplessly, nonetheless. In life, it had been an archer, and as they approached it, its arms flailed to grab them. Mikinosuke, who ran a little ahead, broke its neck with the back of his katana.

"What are you doing?" Rōnin asked when Tsuki knelt by the now still body.

"Refilling," she explained, expertly pulling arrows from the dead archer's quiver.

"Hurry up!" Rōnin shouted, for the dead came ever closer.

The flow of *kyonshī* pouring out of the forest continued without interruption. They came with any form of weapon used in the civil war, or empty-handed but just as menacing. Their armor had aged and rusted in the forest for the past twenty-five years, and many stumbled on broken legs and decaying bodies, but their obedience to the drum was absolute.

Rōnin adjusted his run to meet an eager corpse whose lower abdomen had been picked raw by the animals of the forest. Bits of skin and flesh dangled under its ribs, but somehow it did not prevent the monster from raising its spear as if about to harpoon the lone warrior. He crouched with his last step, then lunged, shooting the katana out of its scabbard and cutting through the naked spine of the dead in one motion. The katana was sheathed before the dead fell on the ground in two pieces, and Rōnin resumed his run without losing a second.

Mikinosuke seemed to run even faster as he swung his two swords, bashing skulls and breaking limbs in a flurry of movement. The boy was in his element on the field of battle, and each of those quick, endless slashes was applied meticulously. The dead fell in front of him as surely as the grass under his feet.

His master did not even bother drawing his swords. On his *geta* sandals, Musashi contented himself in tripping and shoving the dead from his path, grabbing their thin arms and pulling them forward. He was right, Rōnin thought, it wasn't like they could kill them all, and there was no use damaging their blades on opponents that did not feel. Musashi's sense of timing was perfect, and the way he used the enemy's momentum against them left Rōnin amazed.

An arrow fizzed by his ear, and for a second he worried that the dead could use their bows after enough time, but when the head of a *kyonshī* in front of him erupted from its neck, Rōnin turned and found Tsuki readjusting a second missile. Her arrows were not the same as before though. The one she was about to let loose had a head split in two like a snake's tongue. In the hands of an expert, these arrows could sever an arm, a leg, or, a head. The missile whistled so close to Rōnin that he felt its wind, then passed through another corpse's neck before embedding itself into the next's face.

"Save them," Rōnin told the girl. They might need those arrows later, and it was pointless to waste time on the coming *kyonshī*. Better to pass through and disappear.

He ran a little faster to help Mikinosuke, who parried

the strike of a man who must have been huge in life. The boy slipped and dropped on one knee, but held his block. Before Rōnin could intervene, Musashi rammed into the tall *kyonshī*, shoulder first, and sent it flying against a tree. Another moving corpse lunged at the master, who twisted on his heel and accompanied the lunge with the flat of his hands. Rōnin slashed his katana right above the lunge of the dead soldier and sliced through its rotten neck. The three swordsmen then moved on, Tsuki and the Yoshimoto-Samonji right behind them.

As soon as they stepped inside the forest, the temperature dropped. The ground looked fresh and naked where bodies had been resting until a few minutes ago. This place hadn't seen so much activity since the battle of Sekigahara but now teemed with dozens upon dozens of reanimated corpses and four living people running for their lives. Hundreds more would be coming from behind as well. The drummer must have awakened every dead soldier in Sekigahara and sent them on their track, or, more accurately, toward the Samonji katana. This was the reason for this chase, and Rōnin promised himself that no matter what, he would not let the girl be taken.

He backed down all of a sudden when a corpse came almost within an arm's length of Tsuki. She hadn't seen it and gasped when Rōnin unsheathed right by her hip. The lone warrior first cut the corpse's arm, which then twirled in the air, before he cleaved it from shoulder to hip with a loud *kiai*. He did not even take the time to sheathe his blade and pulled the girl by the wrist.

The boy jumped from one body to the next, landing nimbly before their heads kissed the ground. He took longer to stand back up, and his shoulders rose higher than usual as he fought for his breath.

"Mikinosuke," Musashi called.

"I'm fine, sensei," the boy lied.

"Just a little further," Rōnin said, pointing his katana toward the light he could spot through the trees ahead. Hope gave them a surge of energy and allowed them to run faster. They were almost on the other side of the grove. With some luck, they had lost the drummer, and without its guidance, the dead would wander aimlessly.

The four burst through the trees, and Rōnin realized his mistake. This was not the end of the forest, just a large clearing, and from all sides, more *kyonshī*, and a certain death. They were surrounded.

"Rōnin?" Tsuki asked, an unmistakable tone of desperation in her voice.

The lone warrior found nothing to reply. He'd rather save his breath and gain a few more seconds of fighting.

An old cannon covered in moss rested at the center of the clearing. This would be the place of their last stand. They jogged to it and backed themselves against the relic of Sekigahara. It had remained as such, pointing at the sky with its mouth shattered by a bad explosion, for twenty-five years. When they reached it, Rōnin pulled the Samonji from Tsuki's belt and let it slide down the cannon's barrel. She did not even fight it. She understood. They were about to die, but first they should prevent the drummer from getting his hand on the key to Onijima.

"I'm sorry for leading us here," Rōnin said as he tried to regain control of his breathing.

"It's an honor to die a warrior's death," Mikinosuke replied after he shook the fluids from his blades. Musashi nodded and grunted in approval.

"Can I shoot now?" the girl asked.

"As much as you want," Rōnin replied.

The dead wobbled a few steps away, showing no sign of hesitation. Some held their blades with both hands, just like at Gifu. How long would it take them to remember how to parry, counterattack, or even shoot? How long could they resist? Rōnin wondered. With the shrinking distance, Tsuki's arrows became devastating. A head popped from its body, and when it fell, Rōnin attacked.

Tsuigekito!

His blade sliced through a face, but it wasn't enough. Rōnin applied more strength in the downward slash and severed the corpse's spine.

Juntō Sono Ichi!

The blade went back to its scabbard, then out immediately. Rōnin cut a former spearman's belly but did not manage to reach the backbone, so he went for the head next.

Shato!

A body fell with the first two cuts.

Watch your leg, Nagakatsu!

A dead samurai came from a perfect stance and slashed his rusty sword downward. It would have passed through Rōnin's leg if he hadn't backed off in time. His next cut was filled with the rage of having nearly been wounded, and cleaved the *kyonshī* in half diagonally, completing the *Shato* waza. Rōnin removed the slime with a large wipe of the wrist and pushed the blade back home.

Shihoto Sono Ni! His master's voice called again.

Rōnin moved by instinct. He was in his warrior trance. Each movement was precise, economical, and deadly. Rōnin created a path of rotten bodies that took him further from the cannon and the others. Three more fell, then the next received an arrow at the base of the neck, shattering it completely.

"Rōnin!" Tsuki called with panic.

The lone warrior remembered to breathe and realized how far he had gone. He let go of his next intended victim just as the dead lunged into emptiness. A grunt accompanied his retreat.

By the cannon, the others were hard-pressed.

Mikinosuke was struggling, losing his energy with each stroke. He stood like a mountain, and bodies had piled at his feet, but the next just walked over them, and the boy was forced to step back. Tsuki was shooting faster than her art demanded, but at this distance, her loss in strength did not matter. She had exhausted her forked arrows and was back to using the regular ones, though her quiver was almost empty anyway. But the most worrisome, to the lone warrior's eyes, was Musashi. The master had yet to draw his swords and instead stood helplessly, his back against the cannon, a blank expression on his face.

"Sensei!" Mikinosuke shouted as his wakizashi got stuck in the bone of a *kyonshī*'s forearm. The boy kicked the knee of his aggressor, breaking it with a loud crack, but did not manage to remove his shorter blade and had to let go. Rōnin punched the dead samurai's spine with the pommel of his sword, and finally, Mikinosuke could recover his wakizashi.

"Miyamoto-dono," Rōnin said as he turned back to face the swarm of dead.

The swordsman nodded. The knot in his throat bobbed down and up as he swallowed. Rōnin noticed how the master's hands shook when he moved them to the hilts of his two swords, and the sudden fear in his eyes when he scanned the field of battle.

"Behind you!" Rōnin shouted, pointing above Miyamoto Musashi.

The master looked over his shoulder, where a nimble

kyonshī appeared. Its arms were wrapped around the cannon's barrel and he had one foot over it too. Either by luck or sheer bloodlust, the monster grabbed a corner of Musashi's shirt's collar. Its mouth opened wide, flashing brown teeth gleaming with filthy slobber. The *kyonshī* moaned with something like pleasure when about to close its maw on living flesh, and the sound drowned even the shriek of the swordsman.

"Help!" the master screamed in a high-pitched tone.

Mikinosuke was on the *kyonshī* even faster than Rōnin, cutting both an arm and the head with his two swords. The body fell like a bag of grain at the side of Master Musashi Miyamoto, who curled up in a ball, with both hands protecting his neck.

The greatest swordsman in the nation was trembling like a wet puppy, and whimpering as a child would.

"Sensei," Mikinosuke called, confusion weakening his voice. He was about to crouch and check on his teacher, but Rōnin did not let him.

"Leave him!" he said. "He won't fight."

Pushing the thought of the frightened Musashi from his mind, Rōnin came back to the present just in time to see Tsuki about to release an arrow at point-blank to a dead samurai. Rōnin's instinct tingled at the sight of this once-trained man, a hint of intelligence maybe, or the way his putrefied thighs seemed to contract. He pulled Tsuki by the belt just as she released her arrow. The dead samurai crouched with perfect timing, avoiding the missile, and pursued with an upward slash that would have cleaved her face in half. The distance was too great for anything else, so Rōnin shattered its shin to pieces. It fell, but without a second thought started crawling. Out of nowhere, Mikinosuke jumped on its back and crossed his swords through its neck. Rōnin saw tears in the boy's eyes, and rage, a lot of rage.

Mikinosuke leaped back and swung his katana toward another body, dislodging its lower jaw. He lunged, parried, lunged again. His martial *kiai* became shouts of anger. He cleaved and destroyed his enemies, but few were truly defeated. Rōnin meant to stop the boy, but since they were about to die, he might as well let him fight with the honor his master had lost. So the lone warrior followed the boy and finished those corpses that could still move, becoming nothing more than a death reaper. In the back of his mind, he could hear Tsuki calling for Musashi to snap out of it in her gentle yet urgent tone, but Musashi was truly gone.

"I can't," he said through his sobbing. "I just can't."

The hand from a crawling corpse grabbed Mikinosuke's ankle. The boy dropped at the feet of another, while the one on the ground found the ankle a worthy spot for its teeth. Rōnin slammed his foot on the back of its skull just as he was about to close its mouth on the boy's leg and squashed it like a melon. Mikinosuke rolled to the side and cut his opponent's ankles in the same movement. He climbed on the back of the helpless *kyonshī* and pulled on the dead's head until it snapped backward. The boy then fell on his ass, breathless and exhausted.

"I think..." he said through his ragged breath. "I think that's it, Rōnin."

Mikinosuke spat and staggered back to his feet. Already more dead were coming at them. Naturally, the two of them stepped back toward the cannon. Tsuki had no more arrows.

"Take his sword," Mikinosuke told her. "He won't need it anymore." There wasn't just rage in his voice, but pure disgust. Tsuki followed his advice and unsheathed the shorter wakizashi from Musashi's belt.

"Remember what I told you," Rōnin said. "You cut in two directions at the same time. Back or forth, and—"

"Up or down," she finished.

"Exactly," the lone warrior said. At least, he told himself, he would die in good company, and his lord waited on the other side.

On the horizon, through the trees, Rōnin spotted the horned helmet of the drummer. He sat still on his horse, waiting for this lost battle to be over. Rōnin wondered if the man would hit his drum then, and add his own body to the army of the dead.

Mikinosuke shouted in challenge. Tsuki followed his example, then Rōnin. Let death come, he thought, at least we fought.

Something landed somewhere behind the first line of *kyonshī*. Rōnin didn't see where it came from, but smoke fumed suddenly from what he now understood was a bomb. More landed here and there in the clearing.

"What is that?" Tsuki asked.

Rōnin coughed when the smoke reached his mouth. Soon he could see nothing further than his nose. But he heard the rattle of a chain twirling with speed, flesh being cut, and the hooves of the rider going away in a hurry. Bodies dropped. There were a few grunts of effort. Then a face appeared through the smoke, a demonic face with fangs sprouting at a wide angle from a scowling mouth.

"Kiba?" Rōnin asked.

"Follow me. Quick!" the shinobi replied.

Kiba jumped over the cannon, his body piercing through the smoke with barely a sound.

"Let's go!" the lone warrior shouted as he followed the shinobi. He heard rapid footsteps behind him and hoped all of them had understood the situation. Kiba was gaining ground, and the smoke surrounded him. Rōnin stripped any thought of fighting from his mind and focused on fleeing.

When they pushed through the smoke, there were no more corpses in their path. All his companions had followed, even Musashi, who, face down, looked as if he would have preferred all of this to have ended there.

CHAPTER 8
MIYAMOTO MUSASHI

Ganryū Island, 1612

A piercing ringing whistled in his brain as he observed his adversary. The duel had lasted the length of a breath. They now stood motionless again. The gentle tide of the Kanmon Strait was as slow and steady as his heart was racing. Blood trickled from Musashi's forehead, then parted around his nose before it plopped into the sea. A scratch, nothing more, while at the end of his weapon, Kojirō Sasaki had suffered a mortal wound. The spectators on the beach, unable to see the result from where they stood, unanimously held their breath. From their point of view, it must have looked like the two men struck and missed. But it could not be further from the truth.

Two reasons explained Sasaki still standing. First, the end of Musashi's bokken was so deeply embedded in the skull that he kept him upright using the strength of his arms. One of his eyes had popped under the impact, blood drooled from every hole and orbit, and a few teeth had bounced from his mouth like fleas from a dog's back. Second, Sasaki had not believed for one second the scruffy, wandering swordsman would defeat him, and his body had yet to realize it was dead. Musashi had also joined the island of the duel with no thought of defeat in his heart. The idea had been foreign to him.

Since Sekigahara, and before as well, Musashi had known only victory. His natural strength and skills had taken him out of hopeless situations against true masters of kenjutsu, and his fame had grown beyond his expectations. He had become accustomed to victory and turned into a boastful man in the blink of an eye. Arrogance became second nature, but he had earned the right to it.

Sasaki Kojirō should have been another simple stepping stone on his path to eternal fame. He was a short-tempered swordsman with above-average skills and used a nodachi long sword rather than a katana. Some called him the best in the West, but Musashi had scoffed at the challenge.

On the morning of the duel, he took his time, ate well, and did everything he could to anger his opponent before the fight even began. During the crossing of the strait, he carved himself a wooden sword out of a spare oar. This would not only be taken as an insult by Kojirō, but would also give him an advantage. His opponent was used to fighting men armed with a katana and would know this weapon and its reach like the back of his hand. But this time came a swordsman wielding a bokken of random length. His strike would be an enigma, to either of them, yet Musashi wasn't worried.

Then the duel happened. They both struck once. Only once.

At the end of the wooden sword, from the one eye still in place, Musashi felt all the cold judgment of his opponent. He'd been lucky, that was all. If he'd applied a couple more cuts to the oar, or if the tide had been against him, or even if the wind had been on Kojirō's side, their situation would be reversed. Just pure, dumb luck.

Musashi dislodged his temporary weapon from Kojirō's forehead, and the man dropped into the sea. The crowd's cheer was deafening, but Musashi barely reacted to it. Kojirō Sasaki floated closer to him, his scabbard bobbing with the tide by his side until his students came to drag him away. The people ignored the defeated swordsman as he was taken behind a screen; all they cared for was the victor. In flocks, they surrounded and praised him. In a matter of hours, the tale of this duel would spread, and within days Japan would be abuzz with exaggerated versions of it.

Yet, in his heart of heart, something had broken.

He let go of the bokken, for his fingers could no longer hold it. He made fists with them to hide the shaking and let people congratulate him.

But from that day on, Musashi could never hold a sword without the cold grasp of his mortality gripping his heart.

The rain pounded the walls of the abandoned house deep into the night, and wide puddles had formed where the roof had collapsed. They could not build a fire, not only because it might alert the enemy of their location, but also because nothing would burn here. It was to be a miserable night, but Musashi had stronger worries to face.

The day had finally come. He had known it for thirteen years. He could only keep the pretense going for so long and had managed well, all things considered. But now that it was in the open, all his natural bravado had deserted him. His shoulders had slumped, he dared not look at anyone in the eyes, and he even seemed to have forgotten how to fall asleep carelessly.

Tsuki had managed to close her eyes, though she had repeatedly apologized for leaving the Samonji. It wasn't her fault at all, and Musashi hoped she knew that. She was an archer and a damn good one. Hiding the cursed blade was the best they could have done under the circumstances. Even Kiba said so.

The shinobi was coming and going from the house every other hour to make sure they had not been followed. It seemed unlikely that the horned samurai would find them here. The house was so thickly covered in leaves and moss that without Kiba's help, they would have missed it. In the night, neither the dead nor the Fūma, whom they had not seen since before Gifu, would find them. Yet Kiba did his thing and kept them safe.

Everyone kept the others safe, except him. He was a hindrance.

Mikinosuke would not speak or even look at him. The boy had found a corner to sulk and care for his swords as he had been trained to do, keeping the sharpening sounds to a minimum, and Musashi knew better than to bother him. He had betrayed the boy since they had met.

Rōnin was looking from a hole in the wall and suddenly moved toward the broken door. With a couple of pulls, he dragged it open to let the shinobi in. Kiba was soaked and fat drops of rainwater followed his entrance. He and Rōnin sat on moldy tatamis at the back of the room, ignoring the swordsman completely.

"Still nothing?" Rōnin asked.

"Thankfully," the shinobi replied.

"How about the cannon?"

"Too many of them, and I did not see their master," Kiba replied. "In the morning, I will be able to spot him if he is nearby."

"I'll go with you," Rōnin offered.

Kiba shook his head. "I'll do better by myself."

The lone warrior seemed to consider it for a second and accepted the idea. Rōnin was a good man, Musashi knew it. A true samurai at heart, and not one to let fear still his hands. Maybe he could take care of Mikinosuke from then on.

"How about him?" Kiba asked. Musashi didn't need to watch to know he was the target of the question.

"To be honest, I don't know," Rōnin replied. "I can't believe I never realized he hadn't drawn his swords so far. He fought well without them, so I thought he just didn't need them. Barely a scuffle for the master, I told myself."

"I think he was mostly reacting," the shinobi whispered. "At Gifu, he was just pushing them from him, though he did it skillfully."

"I don't know what to think of it, to be honest," Rōnin said. "I mean, I practiced from my younger years with his name in my chest. Boys trained to be the next Musashi Miyamoto. Every news of his victories made us vibrate with excitement."

"Imagine how *he* feels," the shinobi replied, though Musashi didn't know if *he* meant him or the boy.

"I should check on him," Rōnin said as he stood from the mat.

"Rōnin," Kiba whispered, "if he becomes a liability—"

"I know," the lone warrior sadly replied.

If he became a liability, the shinobi would have to make sure the drummer didn't get his hands on him. Musashi could trust the demon shinobi to protect both the group and their patron, and could also trust him to make it quick. He imagined Kiba appearing out of nowhere, then the sensation of his sharp *kusarigama* sickle passing across his throat, and shivered.

"Miyamoto-dono," Rōnin said as he sat to face him.

"You can drop the *dono*," Musashi replied.

He raised his head to look at the lone warrior and saw a hundred questions in those sullen eyes.

"What happened?" was the question he chose. Musashi didn't know if he spoke of the battle at the clearing or simply *what happened* to him, but he chose to answer the latter.

"You've heard about my duel with Sasaki Kojirō at Ganryū?" the swordsman asked.

"The whole of Japan has," Rōnin replied.

"That day, I killed Kojirō, but he took something even more precious from me."

"What is it?"

"My confidence," Musashi replied. He hadn't meant to whine, but this was how it came out. "We train and hone our skills, but truly it is our spirit that we strengthen with each swing of the blade. Every drop of sweat, every blister, every cramp, we suffer them to build the confidence that no matter who we face, we will come out on top. And often, the victor is the one who had the most faith in himself, not the most skilled one. The stories you've heard of me are all true, at least in essence, and all those masters I defeated, I did because I faced them without a single hint of fear in me. But when Kojirō slashed his *nodachi* and cut me here," the swordsman said, pulling his hair apart to show the scar on his skull, "he took it from me, my confidence. I haven't fought once since."

"But Ganryū was, what, eleven years ago?"

"Thirteen," the swordsman replied.

"You've been hiding your fear for thirteen years, Miyamoto...san?"

Musashi nodded.

"At first, I thought it might pass, and I actually enjoyed a time of rest, away from duels and challenges, but eventually I had to accept invitations from warlords. They all wanted me to demonstrate, so I found excuses to refuse. I'd claim with an air of authority that *a true swordsman does not unsheathe his sword lest he means to kill his opponent* or something of the sort. They said I had become a well of wisdom, not just a sword, but a mind as well. I should have gone in hiding, but I was still young and hoped that my hands would stop trembling, eventually. Then came Osaka..."

"Did you fight at Osaka?" Rōnin asked, though he probably knew the answer.

"I was suffocating simply by wearing my armor," Musashi answered with a scoff. In the corner of the room, Mikinosuke was applying himself to the sharpening of his wakizashi with more vigor, it seemed to his master. "I gave strategy advice to my lord, and they weren't half bad, but every morning I woke with a ball in my stomach, thinking that I might be expected to draw my sword and fight."

"This is how most soldiers feel, you know?" Rōnin said, trying his best not to sound judgmental, and failing.

"I am not proud of myself," Musashi replied. "When the war ended, I seriously thought to give up the sword and become a monk, but in my travels, people offered me food, lodging, and gifts, simply for my presence. All I had to do was pretend and never let my swords out of their scabbards. I chose comfort over honesty."

"So you cheated?" Mikinosuke's voice cut through the rain like a crack of thunder. The boy stood and crossed the room, wakizashi still in hand. "All those years you cheated?"

he asked with obvious disdain. "Whenever you trained me, whenever you scolded me, or told me the same stories, over and over again, it was just a pretense?"

"I did train you, and I am still your master," Musashi replied with more strength, though not enough to threaten the ire in the boy's glare.

"I thank you for your teaching," Mikinosuke said, "but it seems I have repaid you well enough, either as your bodyguard or as your puppet. I cannot believe all those times you made me demonstrate in front of our hosts, it was to cover for your angst. And I thought you were just proud of me," the boy said, hardening his grip on the wakizashi's hilt. "I was so stupid."

"I am proud of you—" Musashi replied.

"Stop the bullshit, old man!" Mikinosuke shouted, slashing his sword in the air and pulling a pitiful yelp from his master. "You're just a coward."

Tears of rage filled the boy's eyes. Rōnin put his hand on his wrist to ask him to be quiet, but there was no calming this storm. It was the second time a fatherly figure had disappointed the boy, and Musashi knew Mikinosuke would never trust again. The boy turned around, having said his piece, though there was much more to say.

"You know," Musashi said, "when you found me, I had my sword out to put it through my guts. I was tired of living a lie, and it was a good spot to end it. Then you attacked me and I reacted. I felt hope when I looked at you, a chance for redemption. It was the last time I swung my blade at anyone."

Musashi choked up at the memory, thinking that the Mikinosuke of then looked very much like the one from now.

"So you didn't even have the guts to kill yourself?" the boy asked. Musashi bristled at the words and at the tone.

"You needed me," he replied.

"I don't anymore," Mikinosuke said. "Feel free to resume where we met," he went on, dropping his wakizashi.

"Mikinosuke!" Tsuki called in horror. She had been listening all along, Musashi realized.

"Don't worry," the boy told her, "he won't do it."

He walked back to his corner and slumped on the floor, keeping his back to his former master. Rōnin shared a sorry look with Musashi, but eventually, he went back to observing the exterior. Kiba was the last to check on the swordsman, though nothing filtered through his mask. Musashi easily imagined the disgust on the shinobi's face as well; after all, he hated himself, so why wouldn't the others?

The wakizashi was peacefully resting on the floor, moonlight bouncing on its blade. For most of the night, Musashi Miyamoto thought of grabbing it and calling an end to his torments. No more pretending, no more lying to the world. One quick stab, a bit of pain, and all fear would be gone.

But when the sun rose and enlightened the abandoned house, the blade was still clean, and Musashi found himself pathetic beyond words. Then came sounds of explosions.

"Ame!" Tsuki called as she sat up in a panic.

Musashi had dozed off in his contemplation of the short sword, but his heartbeat shot up with the gunshots.

"They aren't far," Rōnin said. He had been up and was trying to see signs of the battle, peering through the wall.

The house came alive with activity. Mikinosuke was on his feet next, then picked up his short sword, which he sheathed without a second look at his teacher. Tsuki was tying up her hair and then checked the tension of her bowstring. She had four arrows left, just the regular kind.

"What do we do?" she asked Rōnin.

"The sound will draw them," the lone warrior replied, looking at Kiba.

"The clearing will be accessible," the shinobi then said, following Rōnin's thoughts. "I'll go get the Samonji."

"Take Musashi with you," Mikinosuke said as he readjusted his two swords inside his belt. "Away from the fighting."

"I concur," the shinobi replied, sending a shiver down the spine of the master swordsman.

CHAPTER 9
AME SUZUKI

Inuyama Castle, Ikeda domain, 1615

The clouds were bouncing left and right in a ragged rhythm above Inuyama Castle. Her body felt the impact of Ikeda Sen's running footsteps, her master's face a misery of fear and effort. Ame could not understand that face at first. What could possibly make the fiercest onna-musha *of Japan look so desperate? And why was she in her arms, looking up? Why was Sen running? And what was that sound? What was that pain?*

Sen looked down at the girl and spoke, but her voice did not pass through the loud ringing. It was akin to the sound of a heavy piece of metal being dragged across a floor of marble. Ame shook her head, but the ringing wouldn't stop. Soon, it was joined by a series of popping sounds from inside her head. They started small and far within, then closer and closer, like gunshots. And when one painfully burst in her left ear, the pain grew in intensity. All at once she felt it coming back.

She shrieked from the bottom of her lungs, though that too she did not hear through the ringing and the popping. Something was stabbing the inside of her ears, and her hands felt like they'd been stacked with thick needles. Ame could barely open her eyes anymore, so strong was the pain, but when she did, she saw Ikeda Sen shouting something at her. A new wave of pain hit her, and Ame arched uncontrollably. Both she and Sen fell on the path of pebbles leading to the castle, and the girl landed on her side.

She saw her hands, raw, bloody, ruined. Were they really her hands? Why was this happening to her? she asked herself as her vision darkened, and, finally, the pain vanished.

A feeble light passed through her eyelids and called her away from soft dreams. She blinked, but it took a few seconds for shapes to form again. Her confusion was such that she failed to recognize her master's bedroom at first. She wondered why she was lying on Ikeda Sen's futon, and how long she had been sleeping.

The pain was mostly gone, and the ringing completely. In fact, she felt an incredible sense of peace, tucked as she was under a thick blanket of silk. It was so soft and refreshingly cold. She slowly felt the pulling pain on her hands and lifted her arms. They had been tightly bandaged, so she could not see how bad it was. It had to be bad, she thought as she remembered the pitying look she had seen before passing out. She smelled the aroma of the cream that had been applied on her hands, something like pine sap. Her own breath smelled terrible, she suddenly realized. She must have been in bed for days.

What went wrong? she asked herself as she lowered her arms slowly.

She had been standing on the training ground, lined up with all the girls training to join Ikeda Sen's famous musketeers unit. They had been laughing and sharing stories of the boys they liked in the castle, a topic Ame could not care less about, but the camaraderie was good. Mechanically, they went through the process of shooting and reloading the arquebus. Then, what went wrong? Had she forgotten to close the lock before she filled the barrel with some powder? Had she put too much of it? Surely she could not have been so careless as to let the serpentine match drop before she finished reloading the teppo?

Whatever the reason, the damn thing had exploded in her hands just as she lowered it to take aim, and now she lay on Ikeda Sen's futon.

She felt something through the floor, just a small tremor, and looked up. Yūki was there, sitting cross-legged on the tatami, by her feet. Sweet Yūki, her best friend. The young girl, though being only fifteen and as such one year younger, could beat any grown woman or man on the domain in practice bouts, yet, looking at her sleeping with her head down, you could not guess her to be so fearsome. Ame smiled and felt her heart swell for her friend's presence by her side.

Leaning on her elbows, she called her name, but no sound came out of her mouth. Ame harrumphed to clear her throat, then called again, louder, but still no sound came out. Something must have disturbed Yūki's sleep at the same moment for she got startled and woke at once. She rubbed her eyes and looked at Ame, pure joy drawing her features. On her knees, Yūki came closer and held her gently by the shoulders.

Yūki's lips were moving as tears of relief filled her eyes, but Ame heard none of it. She called her friend's name but still could not hear her own voice.

Panic slowly came back, and Yūki's face morphed from pleasure to worry in a few heartbeats. Ame recognized her name on her friend's lips, but not the sound of it.

"What's happening?" Ame asked silently. At least silently to her.

Yūki reacted by extending her arm as if to say not to worry, though her face said otherwise. The young onna-musha *looked toward the door panels of the room and shouted, or so Ame thought. She shouted again, and this time Ame reacted by shedding tears and feeling the pain burn in her chest. She could not even hear her own sobbing.*

Ikeda Sen burst into the room, accompanied by the healer of the castle.

"What's happening? What's happening to me?" *Ame asked, though no one seemed able to answer.*

The healer examined the left side of her head while Ame struggled to even keep breathing. The room started to spin and shrink around her. She was losing her wits and wanted to scream. She did scream, but not for her own benefit. She felt Sen caress her forearm as the healer went across the room to check the other side of her head. There was blood at the tip of the healer's fingers.

Ame closed her eyes and prayed for all of this to end. She had lost her hearing. She wanted to die.

Then a hand fell on her chest, just above the heart.

When she opened her eyes again, Yūki was looking at her with a bright, warm smile on her lips. Yūki pressed the hand on her own chest, then moved the hand to Ame's heart again.

"I'm with you," *she meant without words.*

Ame focused on her friend's eyes and let her breathing slow down.

Yūki then made the same gesture the other way around, first Ame's chest, then hers, and this time she raised her eyebrows questioningly.

"Are you with me?"

Ame nodded.

Ame raised her *teppo* when the Fūma shinobi jumped above a walking dead and pulled the trigger just before he would descend. He had clearly thought to take them by surprise but received a bullet between the eyes for his poor judgment. The dead shinobi landed on the back of the *kyonshī*, which then tumbled face first. Yūki's naginata slashed through both their necks before the dead could rise again, and before the shinobi might come back to life. Though it might not have happened, because there had been no drum, or at least none that Yūki heard. Those *kyonshī* had been there before, and so had been the drummer at some point recently. But the dead were not alone. The Fūma shinobi had launched the attack, or at least had tried to. Using the dead as cover, they had approached seemingly undetected while she, Yūki, and Tadatomo got ready for the otherwise small crowd of *kyonshī*. The Fūma thought to have trapped the three, but it was without counting on Ame's presence. To the deaf musketeer, their quiet stepping felt all the more discerning when mixed with the clumsy march of the dead. She understood the presence of the assassins a couple of seconds before the first stepped out of a *kyonshī*'s shadow, a glowing bomb in hand. She shot him in the wrist. The bomb exploded from within the dead's group, and the battle began.

For some reason that only he found funny, Tadatomo grabbed the head Yūki had just cut and threw it with all his strength into a walking corpse's face. It fell under the impact and the samurai bent backward, apparently laughing. He turned and said something while looking at Ame, then seemed to remember she would not hear him, so he mouthed his words slower.

"I can only trust them as far as I can throw them," he said, then went back to laughing at his own joke.

By her side, Yūki shook her head and made a gesture that only Ame would understand.

Idiot.

Ame smiled at the insult. She knew Yūki enjoyed Tadatomo's presence, at least after Gifu. He had come down from the mountain a changed man, strong, reliable, stupidly brave. It was he who had suggested that they head straight to Lake Biwa and use a boat all the way to Azuchi. And they had almost reached their destination when Ame felt the ground shaking under dozens and dozens of staggering feet.

The dead were slowed by the light slope at the top of which they stood, so she fished a paper cartridge from the pouch hanging at her belt and bit its end off. As she spat the piece of paper, she expertly filled the pan with some powder, locked it, then poured the rest down the muzzle, then the useless paper she had clenched into a ball. Without looking, she took one of her custom-made bullets from a second pouch, the one on her back, and let it slide down the barrel. The ramrod was in her hand next and pushed the contents of the barrel all the way to the end. Soldiers using *teppo* learned to refill their arquebuses in under thirty seconds, the musketeers of Ikeda Sen in twenty. *She* could do so in fifteen seconds.

Ame adjusted her aim, using this chance to figure out how to make a difference. Reloading faster didn't mean hurrying, Sen would say, it meant more time to find the perfect shot.

Those dead were moving more nimbly than at Gifu. Tadatomo had claimed that they seemed to get better as time went from their reanimation, and she was inclined to believe him. Yet they remained clumsy, especially those rotting archers and musketeers who seemed incapable of using their weapons and just wielded them like clubs or blunt swords. She discarded those from her sight. Half of the others had been spearmen and swordsmen. Among them, some wore strong armor, but her *teppo* would shatter through those with ease. She scanned among the closest dead samurai. The one coming at Tadatomo had had half of his torso blown off by a cannonball, and the samurai would deal with him. But two foot soldiers stumbled toward her lover. She picked the one on the left, blew on the match to reignite it, aimed for the base of the neck, and put her finger on the trigger. She was about to shoot, but a shadow moved right behind her target. Instinctively she adjusted her aim and shot. The flash of the shot made her blink, but she saw the impact tearing through the dead, and imploding inside the shinobi's shoulder.

His disguise had been perfect; he looked just like the dead, with moss covering his clothes and mud his face. But his movements were too perfect, even in his imitation of the *kyonshī*. Ame did not, of course, hear his screaming, but she saw him wriggling on the ground, then something astonishing happened. The dead she had meant to shoot at first turned around slowly, its attention drawn by the wounded shinobi. It raised its broken sword and thrust it into the shinobi's belly. Ame could not believe what she was seeing. The dead samurai let go of the sword in the shinobi's guts, then knelt and dug its teeth into his throat. She could imagine the shrieks and the gurgling as two more *kyonshī* joined the feast and pulled long strips of red flesh through their teeth.

Tadatomo was busy with a dead archer, shattering its

knees with sheer brutality, and Yūki was thrusting her naginata into a soldier who had died barely a man. Ame went to her lover and tapped on her shoulder to get her attention once she had dealt with the young soldier. Yūki was sweating as if it was noon in the middle of summer but seemed otherwise unbothered. If not for the shinobi, there was no doubt they could overcome this rabble of *kyonshī*.

What? Yuki asked.

They can't differentiate the living. The shinobi are hiding among the dead. If we force them to show themselves... Rather than finish her thought, she pointed toward the carcass the corpses were ripping apart.

"Oh, shit," Ame read on Yūki's smiling lips.

Her lover turned her attention toward Tadatomo, and the samurai brightened when Yūki repeated what Ame had just said. He turned just in time to cleave through a spearman's pole, then chop its head off, but Ame could see his eyes scanning the field for a sign of living to offer to the dead. She did the same. It was only a matter of time before the noise attracted more, and they had to keep moving. They had chosen to stay and fight because they stood on higher ground, and because of the shinobi, whom they'd rather deal with than have on their backs.

Ame reloaded while checking the swarm. They were coming closer, and soon she wouldn't have the luxury of picking her targets unless they retreated again and again, but this could go on for a while. She took a knee, blew almost religiously on the match to make it glow, shot, and saw a cloud of red where a man lost his foot to her bullet. Like before, the dead around pressed on him and turned him into their next victim.

The next cartridge was in her hand, but she felt something through the bottom of her feet. A rumble, coming from their left, from the dark forest they had chosen to avoid on the way here. Ame tapped on Yūki's arm again when she saw the trees moving.

We need to go, Ame said. *More dead people.*

They could still try to leave, running away from the swarm, and maybe the shinobi would not pursue now that some of them had perished.

*Let me grab that fool and—*Yūki did not sign the last word. Instead, her head shot toward the original threat with alarm.

What?

A sound, Yūki replied. *A whistle.*

Then, right in front of her eyes, the shinobi warriors stripped away from the original crowd of dead and rushed toward them. If the swarm didn't help, they might as well fight like living men.

"Shit," Yūki said.

Ame counted seven. They removed their disguise to reveal those color-changing garments that turned them into mirages, then drew their straight *ninjatō* blades. They ran up the slope, snaking in what first looked like uncoordinated courses, but when Ame struggled to pick her target, she understood it was all on purpose. Those shinobi had revealed themselves because of her.

And Ame would accept their challenge.

She plucked the glowing match from her arquebus and put it between her teeth, then looked briefly at her lover.

I'm on it, you watch my back.

Yūki nodded, and Ame went to show those assassins how she had gained the respect of Ikeda Sen.

She took a couple of steps forward, then kicked a few strands of grass to see where the wind took them, and at what speed. The seven shinobi seemed to pick up the pace.

They were halfway up the slope. She lifted her *teppo* to her shoulder and took aim. Those men had been trained to confuse the eyes, and the afterimage of their movements trailed long after them. Ame focused on their feet. She waited for the moment between two breaths and pulled the trigger. The one in the middle flipped forward, his left leg torn at the knee. He landed pitifully on his back. None of his comrades reacted to his loss. The dead wobbling from behind would take care of him though.

Ame wouldn't have time to reload, so she let go of her arquebus and pulled two of the five pistols hanging on her shoulder strap. She had designed them with passion and cared for them with something like love. Now they would kill for her.

Fifteen steps away, she used the burning match in her mouth to ignite her left pistol, and shot, catching a shinobi in the chest just as he was about to change direction. This was the way to get them, the tiny break in their tempo when they stepped the other way. A second later she shot the second pistol. Her aim had been slightly off, and the bullet just got into the next shinobi's hip. It slowed him down but did not stop him.

Her empty pistols went back on her chest and she took two more. The four assassins were almost on her. She leaped backward and fired both pistols at once. The heads of the two shinobi on the sides burst like ripe fruits, but the last two were too close for her to draw her last pistol. The tallest of them jumped and raised his sword, the other crouched and lunged from the ground. Ame lowered her stance and felt the naginata brush her back right before it impaled the shinobi above midair. She could not hope to stop the expert strike of a trained assassin, so she didn't. She raised her hand and received the blade right through the palm, then grabbed the shinobi's wrist with her free hand. The assassin looked at her, eyes round with shock.

She grinned back at him, the glowing match still stuck between her teeth, and it was a malicious grin. Her hands had not felt a thing since the explosion. Once again, she had drawn strength from her accident, and as she twisted the shinobi's wrist and forced him onto his knees, she thanked the gods for her past ordeal. He let go of the blade as she crushed his arm with an iron grip, and Ame pulled her last pistol. At point-blank, when she pulled the trigger, nothing remained of the upper part of the shinobi's head.

Ame laughed silently to herself. The smell of powder surrounded her; the sight of her skills as well. Without Yūki's polearm it could have gone really bad, but what would life be without her, anyway? The last living shinobi stood motionless a few steps ahead, defeated, his clothes soaked near the hip wound. He knew death was near, no matter what, and was quickly fading away. The dead were a few seconds behind him. Ame walked to him while Yūki removed her naginata from her last victim.

When she got within the shinobi's reach, he swung his blade, but too weakly to threaten her. Ame grabbed his arm long before the blade could harm her and looked into his eyes. The mask of fabric over the shinobi's mouth moved when he spoke, but her lip reading could not help her understand. She chose to believe he was cursing her. His skin was paling already.

The musketeer took one of the premade pouches of powder from one of her bags. There were two left, and none had nails within, just regular explosive bombs. She chose the smallest, which she slid inside the shinobi's shirt. He did not seem to understand, and his eyes were closing by themselves. She then plucked the match from her mouth and planted it inside the pouch's shut hole. Now the shinobi understood, and he seemed to regain some desperate energy. He meant to reach the pouch inside his shirt, but Ame kicked him in the chest with so much strength that he started rolling down the slope. He did not stop until he bumped into some *kyonshī's* legs. Immediately *they* lowered themselves to his level, and Ame turned back just as one of them jammed its spear into the shinobi's cheek. She walked back, picked up her *teppo*, and felt the wind of the explosion. Judging by the look on Tadatomo's face, it was a thing of beauty. The samurai, who had remained on top of the slope, raised a thumb of approval.

She was about to return the gesture, but just then, from behind her new friend appeared the helmeted head of a *kyonshī*. The bigger swarm coming from the forest had advanced much faster than expected. This one was moving so fast that she wondered for a second if it was another Fūma, but the lack of skin over its teeth assured her it had been dead. Ame pointed her finger at the dead in alarm.

"Ah!" she shouted, not finding the words.

Tadatomo twisted his head, opened his mouth, probably gasped, and meant to raise his katana, but would be too late. The monster was thrusting its own blade with conviction, and already Ame could picture the tip puncturing through her friend's chest. Her scream hurt her throat, but suddenly the dead's arm broke from its body and the sword dropped. Tadatomo did not let this chance go and finished the *kyonshī* once and for good. A projectile had shattered the arm at the elbow, and when Ame followed the direction of the missile, she saw Tsuki running through the swarm, Rōnin and Mikinosuke a couple of steps ahead.

"Yūki!" Ame called, pointing at her lover's sister.

The *onna-musha* saw her sister as well but also noticed

the way the dead seemed to give up the slope to surround their companions.

Cover us, Yūki told her lover, then shouted something at Tadatomo and left. The samurai came to stand by Ame's side, his face dripping in sweat, but his natural smile still in place.

"I protect you," he mouthed slowly.

Thank you, she signed back.

"You're welcome," he replied.

Yūki slid down the slope, naginata at the ready, probably shouting her lungs out. Ame was ready to shoot a few seconds before her lover reached the first of the dead about to surround her sister's group. She fired at the one behind Tsuki, then reloaded. Yūki was now in the thick of it, cleaving a *kyonshī* who had been threatening Mikinosuke through the back. The boy twisted on his left and felled another instead. Tsuki lowered herself and picked the arrows from the corpse's quiver, so Ame shot again above the girl, punching a large bullet through the chest of a moving corpse with long white hair. Tadatomo tapped on her shoulder and she felt him leaving. Their side of the slope would still be under attack, even after the explosion from before, but she could count on him.

The group emerged from the swarm just before Ame shot a third time, so she twisted on her knee to check the samurai. Tadatomo was parrying the massive blow of a katana-wielding *kyonshī*. She shot it in the face. Her friend bent forward to catch his breath. He was exhausted, but his first reflex was to untie the gourd at his belt and push it to his mouth as he stepped back toward her. As the gourd found his belt again, he nodded toward the coming group.

The joyful reunion would have to wait, they had a swarm of dead to lose.

A conversation happened between Rōnin, Yūki, and Tsuki, too fast for Ame to follow. She read the words *boat*, *Fūma*, and *water*, then Yūki pointed toward the slope where a dozen shinobi bodies lay. This seemed to convince Rōnin, who then nodded in approval.

They left the slope a few seconds before the next wave of undead reached them, and rushed toward the lake.

As they descended the hill and were about to climb the next, Ame turned to Tsuki. The girl seemed in good shape; in fact, she even looked like she had grown. Maybe, Ame thought, after this whole horror-filled adventure, she would do better to find her own path, away from her big sister.

Other friends? Ame signed when the girl looked at her with smiling eyes. Tsuki did not use their sign language very well, so Ame made it as simple as possible.

Coming, Tsuki replied. *Find us.* She then pointed at Mikinosuke and signed the word *teacher*, and hesitated on the next word. Not finding it, she put hooked two fingers under her upper lips and looked all menacing.

Kiba? The shinobi? Ame signed.

"Yes!" Tsuki said.

So only Zenbō was missing, the musketeer told herself, though something told her not to worry about the blind monk. They who had climbed back from a loss were hard to kill, she told herself.

As they reached the next hill, Ame turned around to check the swarm and immediately stopped running.

"Look!" she tried to shout.

Her companions followed her example. There was nothing to worry about anymore. The swarm had simply stopped moving halfway through the hill, and now formed a perfect line of unmoving corpses, standing still and looking in their direction. The ones at the back were still gathering, and the swarm kept filling above the hill.

The drum? Ame asked her lover.

Heard nothing, Yūki replied.

A few *kyonshī* tumbled forward and just fell face-first. Those no longer moved and remained on the ground helplessly, dead again. They had reached the limit of the drum calling.

At least we don't need to run, Ame signed. The *onna-musha* then grabbed her behind the head and kissed her on the forehead.

Let's treat your hand, then we go, Yūki said.

Two minutes later, having found their breath again, the group moved toward Lake Biwa, leaving a crowd of dead spectators to grunt on their backs.

The group reached the lake within a few minutes, slow-moving minutes, for they wanted to give Kiba and Musashi ample time to catch up. Two rowing boats floated peacefully by the shore, attached to a narrow pier. A couple of huts stood right at the beginning of the pier, their southern sides covered in drying fish hanging from hooked threads. Some still had water dripping from their mouths. The fishermen and their families had left a few minutes ago, either because of the sound of battle or because they spotted six wandering warriors coming this way. The path leading to the huts had been used regularly over many generations and was now hard and naked. No vegetation protected it, and Ame hoped this would help Kiba and Musashi spot them, though it might also help the Fūma.

Tadatomo, grinning like a fiend, picked some of the fish, but when he saw Yūki's reproving features, he left a small stack of coins at the corner of the hut's door.

While the samurai started building a fireplace, Tsuki took Mikinosuke to check the boats. Ame could see from the boy's gait that something was off with him.

He found out his master is a coward, Yūki explained, translating Rōnin's words.

Musashi? Ame asked, using the sign for the swordsman's name they had made up after Jokoji, two swords crossing.

Yūki nodded, making a face.

Will he be all right, the boy?

Don't know, the *onna-musha* replied. She turned to Rōnin and started asking the question with signs as well, then shook her head when she remembered she had to speak. Rōnin shrugged. He traced the character *Tsuki* on his left palm, then the one for *help*. *Tsuki is helping him*, was what he meant. Typical Tsuki, Ame thought with pride.

Yūki called for the musketeer's attention and signed the words Rōnin had just spoken, unbeknownst to her.

He asks if you can shoot every couple of minutes to help Kiba find us.

What about the Fūma? she asked.

It's a risk we have to take, Yūki replied.

Don't tell Tadatomo, he's going to freak out when I shoot, Ame said as she stepped a little away, leaving Yūki to explain the joke to the lone warrior.

When she fired her first blank round, Tadatomo ended up on his ass, almost burning his face as he had been blowing life to his fire. She giggled at his reaction and read some foul curses on his lips, then worked on the next round.

She spaced her shots to every five minutes, when she

emptied the first of her two gunpowder bags. Azuchi was still far away; powder had to be preserved.

After half an hour of shooting in the sky, Ame got bored. The taste of fish lingered in the back of her mouth, and she would have killed for some green tea or even some sake, but she knew Tadatomo would never share his. Her five pistols were ready for the next battle. She had filled more cartridges and cleaned every piece of equipment that she did not currently use, down to the buckle of her belt, but she was getting bored. Tadatomo and Tsuki were snoring against the hut, while Rōnin and Yūki seemed in the middle of a serious conversation. The boy stood at the end of the pier like a guardian statue, arms crossed in the exact manner his master usually adopted.

She prepared a new bullet-free shot, but just as she was about to remove the ramrod from the arquebus, she spotted the two men they had been waiting for rolling down the hill in an extreme hurry.

"Hey, hey," Ame called, waving toward Yūki and Rōnin.

Ame squinted and saw that Musashi was holding onto Kiba, then realized it was the other way around; the swordsman was keeping the shinobi up but was also checking behind every few steps.

Prepare the boats, Ame signed to Yūki just before she picked a bullet from her belt. *Something's coming.*

CHAPTER 10
KIBA

Iga Village, 1581

The screams echoed throughout the village even after most houses had burned down to the ground. The soldiers of Oda Nobunaga were stripping children from their mothers, killing the former and shaming the latter. People the shinobi had known all his life were being pierced by spears and dismembered in front of his very eyes, turning the streets he had walked for as long as he could remember to puddles of blood and mud. The magnificent horse in front of him kicked the ground and splashed some of it on the defeated shinobi's face.

"It's the last one?" *the horse rider asked.*

"All the others are dead," *the samurai standing behind the shinobi replied.*

The horse rider dismounted and landed in the same puddle his horse had kicked, spreading even more of the bloodied water on the shinobi. He wore dark boots, protected with dark greaves on which the flames devouring the village shined bright. On each of them, a five-petaled flower had been painted in gold.

"Look up," the rider said. He didn't ask, he ordered. Yet the young shinobi kept his head low.

"I said—" the warlord went on just as he wiped the sole of his boot on top of the shinobi's head "—look up!"

The shinobi gathered his fuming rage in his eyes and stared back at Oda Nobunaga, the man who had ordered the destruction of his village for no other reason than to increase his already humongous domain. He prayed for all the spirits of his dead comrades to fill his glare with their thirst for vengeance and strike the Fool of Owari down from the afterlife. But nothing happened. If anything, the shinobi got scared by the sight of his enemy. Nobunaga was a monster through and through. A lean man, with eyes as dark as his soul. Cunning vibrated from him, but the worst, the shinobi thought, was this loathsome smirk. The warlord took pleasure in the destruction of the shinobi village and in the pain of so many people.

"What's your name?" he asked.

"I have no name," the young shinobi replied.

"Ah," Nobunaga said. "I had forgotten you people are no one and all the same at once. Well, you are all stupid."

A house collapsed on itself somewhere behind the warlord, spraying firefly-like sparks in the night sky.

"Had you accepted my offer, your people would have survived."

"We would never serve a demon," the shinobi replied. "We are proud shinobi, not mercenaries."

"You're mistaken," Nobunaga Oda said, tilting his head like a rooster would to observe a worm. "You 'were' proud shinobi. Now, you are nothing."

The warlord crouched to put himself at the shinobi's level and kept studying him. They had lost to this man, not just because he had greater numbers, but because they had underestimated him. Nobunaga had brought a lot more *teppo* than the leaders had assumed, and with it, he tore through their defense in a mere day. When the line had crumbled, the shinobi of the Iga clan gathered at the citadel to protect their master, offering their bodies and the death of many enemies to honor their land, but a last volley killed all but one shadow warrior. A bullet was still lodged in his shoulder.

"You want to kill me?" the warlord asked.

"I will kill you," the shinobi replied, snarling.

"Get in line," Nobunaga said. He was about to stand, but the shinobi had one last act of defiance up his sleeve, or rather in his mouth.

He cracked the capsule stuck at the back of his teeth, the one he had placed there after the last volley of bullets. It was meant for him to kill himself rather than face interrogation and spill the village's secret. But the village had no more secrets to reveal anyway, so the poison could be used otherwise.

He spat it out with rage, and a green gob of saliva mixed with poison landed on Nobunaga's cheek. He'd missed. If it had gotten into the eye, the warlord would have died within a few hours. All he had to fear now was the acid burning his skin.

The samurai behind kicked the shinobi in the back of the head, sending him flat in the puddle, cursing him for his insolence, while Nobunaga screamed in utter pain. The shinobi smiled. He would have preferred to kill the monster, but Nobunaga would now live with a reminder of the Iga defiance.

Nobunaga grabbed him by the back of the neck and squeezed until he thought it would break, then dragged the shinobi a little further and pushed his face into the tainted water. He struggled for air.

"I curse you!" Nobunaga shouted as he kept the young shinobi's mouth and nose under the water. "I curse you to live and see me rise, powerless, useless, as you have shown yourself to be for your pathetic village. You want to see a real demon? Then come *at me with all your rage, pissant, for you will not die until you've bathed in the demon's blood, this I curse you with."*

He received a blow to the side of the head and immediately lost consciousness. In his dream, the curse repeated itself in Nobunaga's voice.

When he woke, the shinobi was in the middle of a scene of carnage. Everything was ash, bones, and red. But he wasn't dead. Alone, he took care of his people's remains, mended his wounds, recovered, and built himself a mask to become the very thing he was hunting. He became Kiba, the fangs of vengeance.

But by the time he left the ruins of Iga, Nobunaga Oda had already been assassinated, and Kiba spent the rest of his life looking for a real demon to bleed.

The clearing looked peaceful. Not a single movement disturbed its awakening. The cannon sat in the middle, covered in moss, its wheels broken and useless. The ground had been trashed by hundreds of feet the day before, and corpses lay here and there, but those were not moving.

From a distance, Kiba and Musashi had observed the undead leaving the forest, attracted by the sound of battle somewhere north. Then they had waited for the one-legged and crawling *kyonshī* to follow their comrades. Only then had the two men sneaked toward the clearing.

"If *kyonshī* were around," Musashi whispered, "we'd see them."

"It's not the dead I'm worried about," the shinobi replied.

"The Fūma then," the swordsman guessed. "Do you mind me asking..." Musashi then said, and since he received no reply whatsoever, he went on, "What's the difference between your clan and theirs?"

"The Fūma are mercenaries," Kiba replied. "*We* were a proper clan, with land of our own, a code, allies, and enemies. My comrades and I specialized in guerrilla, spying, and sometimes assassination, but never for the benefit of the highest bidder. Our leaders and teachers were samurai, and our land was rich. The Fūma are just killers, very skilled ones, and their leader, Kotarō, the one they call the Wind Demon, is said to be an expert in the art of murder. His victims never see him coming until the last second, just before he plunges his claws into their guts and pulls them out. When I kill, I kill fast, and without a sound, Kotarō Fūma lives for his victims' shrieks. That's the difference between them and me. Does that satisfy your curiosity?"

"A bit too much," Musashi replied. The swordsman had blanched a little, and hopefully could not guess the smirk behind the demon mask.

Kiba stood without warning but also without alarm and walked across the peaceful clearing. If the Fūma were around, they would have heard their whispering, he told himself. Besides, if they had set an ambush, it meant the sword wasn't here anymore, and their whole mission had failed. Musashi followed promptly, his *geta* sandals hanging around his neck after Kiba complained of their noise.

The swordsman had aged over the night. The veil of confidence he had worn over the last thirteen years had been shredded during the previous day's fight, but Mikinosuke had pulled the last thread of it. Now only remained the husk of what Musashi Miyamoto had been. Kiba pitied him. *He* had been trained to push fear away before he could even run. Too young to remember the details of it, he knew his first years in the Iga village had been spent measuring his potential as a shinobi, and he'd been found good enough. When Nobunaga Oda came to Iga, Kiba had been a little over twenty. Not a master of ninjutsu yet, but a decent shinobi still. Most of his skills, though, he gained in the following decades. He honed them like he would have a sword, with passion, with experience, and with a thirst for vengeance that would never be satisfied. He never even neared death, and after thirty years of challenging it, understood that Nobunaga's curse held strong. It would take the blood of a demon so that he could die in peace. This, and all his childhood's training, made fear a foreign concept to him, but not to Musashi, and Kiba truly pitied him, though he would not hesitate to take his life if he proved a liability.

"Take it," Kiba told the swordsman when they reached the exploded mouth of the cannon.

"Why me?" Musashi asked in a whining tone.

"Do you want to stand watch while I do?" the shinobi asked rhetorically. "I'm not asking you to wield it, just get it and we go."

Musashi swallowed hard when he moved his gaze to the muzzle of the cannon but proved smart enough not to risk the shinobi's anger. He slipped his sandals on his feet to gain a bit of height, then put his right arm inside the barrel, all the way to the shoulder.

"It's not there."

"Are you reaching the end?" Kiba asked.

"No," Musashi admitted.

"Then use one of your swords and fiddle through the damn cannon."

Musashi removed his arm from the cannon and dropped his right hand on the hilt of his wakizashi. It was shaking. Kiba could see the man wanted to do it, but fear would not let him. He was helpless.

Kiba removed the short sickle from his lower back discreetly while Musashi fought himself in his heart, then, with all his shinobi's speed, he grabbed the swordsman's wrist and piqued the sickle in the man's palm, just the tip.

"Hey!" Musashi shouted, removing his hand right away. "What did you do that for?"

"Does it hurt?"

"Of course, it does, you moronic murderer."

"Are you angry at me?"

"I would punch you in the face if you didn't wear that stupid mask," Musashi replied, his own face adorned with the scowl of a brawler.

"And are you afraid of your sword right now?"

Musashi did not reply this time and seemed incapable of any words. His mouth hung open, bottom lip red where he had licked the blood from his palm.

"You are covered in scars, Musashi," Kiba went on with as much gentleness as he could muster. "You fought a long time before fear paralyzed you, and you got cut, stabbed, and punched. You often spilled blood, yours and theirs. Pain used to be your ally. Remember all the pain you suffered from training, the pain that pushed you to fight for a better life, and, of course, the pain from your opponent's blades, they will bring you back to being the greatest swordsman Japan has ever seen. Until then, you just have to be more angry than afraid, for those two emotions cannot cohabit in one person's heart."

"Damn," Musashi said, "you are actually quite understanding. I didn't expect that."

"I'm also not very patient, young man, so get me that sword before I give up on you," Kiba replied.

"No need to be so irritable, for heaven's sake," Musashi

said as he unsheathed his sword without hesitation and shoved it into the cannon.

The swordsman's blade grated the inside of the barrel, then there was a sound of steel on steel. Further away, the battle raged on. A loud explosion followed what sounded like a barrage of bullets, then nothing for some time. Kiba would have preferred to be there as well, with the girl who didn't seem afraid of his presence.

"Got it," Musashi said a second before the Yoshimoto-Samonji exited the cannon.

"Good," Kiba replied.

In all those years searching for demons that did not exist, Kiba had developed a sense for anything resembling dark magic. Being a shinobi, he didn't believe in any of it, for his people were experts in the art of illusion. But he could spot the intent of a curse, the malevolence imbued in some item, like the rope used by a man to hang himself, or the cup from which poison had been drunk. The Samonji was vibrating with such evilness. Musashi held it for the shinobi to take it.

"A sword without its *saya*," Kiba said with a smirk Musashi could not see. "You keep it. Maybe it will cure you."

"You're a terrible healer, you know that?" Musashi replied though he lowered the sword. His hand still trembled, but not as much as before. Maybe, Kiba thought, he wouldn't have to end the man's life after all.

Two more shots marked the continuation of the battle.

"We have to go," Kiba said.

Leaving the way they came from, they walked toward the battle. There hadn't been any shots for a while now, but the growing mass of grunts led them, and soon they came into view of a hill swarming with the *kyonshī* from Sekigahara, former enemies now moving as one. They had gathered on the northern side of the hill and formed an arching front line. The dead were looking ahead, as if they expected the return of someone, but some still milled around helplessly and a handful returned toward the forest they had emerged from.

"Do you see any of them?" Musashi asked as they observed the army of the dead from a distance.

"There are some fresh bodies," Kiba answered coldly, "but I don't think they were our companions." The shinobi moved, again, without warning Musashi, and decided to go in the direction those *kyonshī* were looking at. Lake Biwa would be this way, and maybe Rōnin had changed his mind and chose to face the risk of the Fūma amphibious units. Kiba didn't approve of the lake, but sometimes decisions have to be made in the moment, and Rōnin was a warrior with a good head on his shoulders. He could trust him.

"What do you think of those undead?" Musashi asked after some time strolling the peaceful countryside.

"What do you mean?"

"Well, you called me young man earlier, and at Gifu you said you were in your sixties. I thought you were joking then, but I'm not so sure now. You also knew about Onijima. And you have this *I was born into the depths of hell* attitude," Musashi said, perfectly imitating the tone and voice of the shinobi. "So I think if one of us knows something about them or this Izanagi curse, it would be you."

"I don't sound like that," Kiba lied. "And I'm sorry to say that I don't know more than you. Onijima, until we met, was a legend. I still don't completely believe in it. I learned about it as I searched for details regarding demons, but besides the island's name and some vague information on a source of power hidden on it, I found nothing."

"Not much then," Musashi said, sounding disappointed.

"Despite its name," the shinobi went on, deciding to share his theory with the swordsman, "I don't think this curse was made in Japan."

"You don't?"

"Most of the weapons we use come from somewhere else. We modify them, improve them, and master them, but we did not invent them. I believe it is the same with this Izanagi curse. Whoever is searching for it right now is playing with something none of us understand completely, like a child toying with an arquebus. I wouldn't worry too much about the nature of the curse though."

"Why not?" Musashi asked. "It's a power beyond anything I've ever seen. It could help to understand it."

"Our goal is to destroy it," the shinobi replied. "Curiosity might be based on a good sentiment, but understanding too much of some things can also be dangerous. Tempting, one could say. And we already know enough."

"I don't feel like we do," Musashi said.

"We know that the use of the drum is limited," Kiba explained. "The drummer can call the dead back to life, and give them simple orders, like *kill them*, *go this way,* maybe an indication to stop or go faster. Gifu was a mess, but yesterday, the drummer was right in front of you. If he could direct them to individual targets, he would have sent the dead after the girl since she carried the Samonji."

Musashi nodded, chin resting between his thumb and first finger.

"We also know that their reach is limited," Kiba went on.

"Like Yoshinao said."

"But we have a better understanding of it now," Kibe replied. "It's mostly assumption, but I think anywhere the sound reaches, the dead rise, but no further. And the *kyonshī* cannot move beyond that. So we can also assume the strike of the drum creates a 'zone' of power that keeps the dead alive. How long those zones stay active is another problem." The shinobi said the last almost in a whisper to himself. He hadn't thought about it so far before, and he found himself getting curious, despite his previous comment.

"But the drummer moved around yesterday to call more dead and send them to us," Musashi observed. "Does that mean that he could lead further if he keeps striking the *kotsuzumi*?"

"Possibly," Kiba admitted.

"Which means he could march a whole army of dead people across Japan," the swordsman said with alarm.

"In theory. Yoshinao also hinted at it. But it sounds like a bothersome process. Those things aren't what you could call fast walkers."

"Unless," Musashi went on as if Kiba hadn't spoken. "Unless he can stop them from...living again. Then all he'd have to do is get them transported somewhere and just recall them, again and again."

"I hadn't thought about it," Kiba admitted. "It sounds... perilous."

"It sounds like an unstoppable power, yes."

As they discussed, the hand carrying the Samonji had stopped trembling. Musashi, Kiba realized, needed to keep his head busy.

"That wouldn't work with their waking time though," Musashi said, continuing his own theory.

"Their what?"

"Oh, it's how I call this thing Rōnin mentioned. The dead seem to get better after some time coming back to life. I'm the same when I wake, I can't function properly for half an hour. Those *kyonshī* seem to improve, or regain their skills you could say, as time passes from their revival. If the drummer keeps putting them back to sleep, then reviving them, they would be slow to get useful every time, whereas if he marches them, they are already at their best by the time he needs them."

"Interesting," Kiba said honestly. Musashi had a lot more to him than his cowardice suggested. "I hadn't thought it through."

"I think it goes deeper though," the swordsman said. "It might be my imagination, but I think the dead from Sekigahara moved better than those at Gifu, even from the beginning."

"So?"

"So the former had been dead for twenty-five years, the latter for forty and some. Fresh corpses would require no time to resume the fight for their new master if I'm correct."

"That would be troublesome," the shinobi replied.

"*I concur*," Musashi said in another imitation of the shinobi, before he giggled heartily.

If he could follow Kiba's thought, Musashi would not find the heart to laugh. Kiba understood the danger *he* now faced. He was alone with the greatest swordsman that ever lived in Japan, though said swordsman could barely hold a sword at the moment. If anything happened and Musashi died, he could be called back and swing his blades at the full extent of his skills, but without the paralyzing fear. If it came to that, if the situation seemed desperate, Kiba told himself, killing Musashi wouldn't be enough, he would have to destroy him beyond any chance of revival.

Kiba's instinct kicked in and he had to stop himself from reaching for his sickle. It might have been a shadow stretching too far, or the timid sun reflecting on a blade, but something had moved nearby, and not in a natural way. The ground had turned rocky, with boulders half the size of a man sprouting from the hills. A good spot for an ambush. Sixty years on the lookout had tuned the shinobi to read his surroundings, and he trusted his gut more than anything else. They were being followed.

"Musashi," he said quietly, "are you faster on your feet or on your *geta*?"

"On my feet. Why?"

"Then nonchalantly remove your *geta*," Kiba said, trying his best not to make the swordsman nervous. The way Musashi's hands trembled told him he had failed in this, but he obeyed nonetheless and hung his sandals on his chest with a thin cord like before. Gradually, Kiba changed their course and veered slightly east.

"What is it?" Musashi asked. His gait was so stiff that Kiba worried this would betray them.

"Don't look, but we are being followed. I said don't look!" Kiba grunted through his teeth. "Trust me, and everything will be all right."

"What do we do?" Musashi asked, his crackling voice betraying his growing panic. "Can we lose them?"

"If they are the Fūma, we can't," Kiba replied. He did not want to tell the swordsman that by himself he might escape them but Musashi stood no chance. "We need you to get back to the others with that sword."

"Shouldn't you take it to them?" the swordsman asked. "You're probably faster than me."

"But maybe not than them," Kiba replied. "I can stall them for you, could you do the same for me?"

Musashi opened his mouth but did not reply, shame keeping his words in his throat.

"When we pass the ridge, right after that oak, you run

north for as long as you can see the tree, then you veer west. It should put you back on the track to our people."

"What about you?"

"Don't worry about me," Kiba said. "Worry about that sword."

"I'll get it to them. You have my word," Musashi replied, an echo of his old strength back into his voice. For some reason he could not explain, Kiba believed him at this instant.

"Thank you," Kiba said as they passed under the shadow of the great oak standing atop the ridge.

"It was an honor knowing you, master shinobi," Musashi said, hand clutched around the hilt of the Samonji.

"The honor was mine, Miyamoto-dono," Kiba replied.

Musashi waited until he walked under the sun again, and darted north in a heartbeat. Kiba twisted on his heel to face their pursuers, the weight of his loyal *kusarigama* chained sickle twirling by his side. Just by feeling them against his thighs and lower back, he checked the presence of his freshly sharpened *shuriken*. He was ready.

"No need to hide any longer," he shouted.

A shape quietly peeled from a large tree further down and planted itself on the path Kiba and Musashi had just climbed. Kiba knew upon seeing him that the time had come to test the limits of his own curse and get rid of it. He had finally found his demon. It could only be Kotarō Fūma, head of the Fūma clan, the Wind Demon.

He was tall, taller than any man Kiba had ever met, with long, thin, spider-like limbs. Both his gloved arms ended with four straight claws, each as long as his forearm. They could almost reach the ground without the man bending his knees. Contrary to his men, Kotarō stood bare-chested, flashing the character for the word *wind* carved onto his chest. He still wore a dark purple cloak over his naked back ending in a hood, which he slowly pulled back as Kiba trod down the slope. The absence of a hood revealed a white-painted face with furious lines of black and red stretching over it, like a furious warrior in a kabuki play.

There were no demons in this world. Kiba knew it. But this man, whether by reputation or by his nickname, was the closest thing to it, and Kiba found himself looking to the coming battle with anticipation. Sixty years he'd lived for this very moment. He walked slowly, fighting his own bloodlust to give Musashi as much time as possible. Kiba knew he might die, Kotarō wasn't alone. But he'd make sure to kill the demon first. He sped up the twirling rhythm of the weighted chain but kept his feet light. Fifty steps. The Wind Demon picked a thin tube from his belt. Thinking it was a blowgun, Kiba prepared himself for the dart, but when it found Kotarō's lips, only a whistle came out.

Two Fūma shinobi darted from the left and right of the path, dashing toward Kiba with their swords held low. He should have known the right to fight a demon had to be earned. Some sacrifices were needed.

They moved well, in the typical Fūma pattern Kiba had seen before, but their footwork seemed almost stiff compared to those he had fought last time. Students, Kiba understood, probably not even out of their teen years. He was either being tested or being used for training, and both ideas infuriated him. He leaped back twice, forcing them to almost meet before they came to him.

When the one on the right reached the place where he had stood, Kiba crouched and pulled on the chain with strength. The young shinobi did not even notice the sickle Kiba had left on the ground. It sliced right through his leg as it returned to its master, and Kiba thrust it upward into the young man's chin before he could even scream, carving his face in half to get the blade out. The other reacted by shifting his weight and raising his short sword to prevent Kiba from charging at him, but the Iga shinobi shouldered his victim into the second's blade. The corpse dragged the sword down, leaving the second young man defenseless. He should have let his sword go and stepped away, but his inexperience proved his downfall. Kiba slit his throat before he could pull his blade out of his comrade's chest, and he fell with a loud gurgle.

Kiba had no energy to waste on boys. He'd need to keep as much as possible until Kotarō agreed to fight. While watching his demon, he wiped the blood on the uniform of the dying shinobi, then stood up for the next challengers.

Kotarō whistled three short times, and three more shinobi darted from the cover of rocks and trees. Kunoichi, Kiba realized from their silhouettes, and much more skilled than the previous two. The fight had put him a little further from the demon. He would have preferred to get closer, but he still waited on his spot. The three kunoichi formed a line, their movements so perfectly synchronized that Kiba could only see the first.

He reached for a shuriken in his belt and threw it spinning right at them. The kunoichi raised her hand and intercepted the shuriken in the middle of her palm. There was no blood, and from the sound it made Kiba knew some padding had been lined into her glove. Kiba had not meant to harm her with the throwing star, anyway. He pulled on the string connected to the shuriken, the one the kunoichi had failed to notice because of its thinness, and she stumbled forward.

The second leaped above her but lost her tempo. Kiba was on her in the blink of an eye, kicking her in the chin with a backflip. Her head shot backward with a yelp. He'd hoped to destabilize the third as well, but she had good reflexes and jumped above both of them, pirouetting upside down and trying to cut him in the process. Kiba flattened himself on the ground to avoid the tornado, then rolled on his shoulder when the first kunoichi came back with a vengeful thrust. He slashed his sickle as he stood back up, severing her arm halfway through the forearm. She screamed, but this time he did not have the luxury to end his victim's torments.

Somersaulting forward to avoid the third kunoichi's attack, Kiba found himself pinned to the ground by the second. She straddled him, blocking his sword arm with her knee. Hers was free, and she aimed for his throat with a thrust. He deflected her attack with the flat of his hand, pushing the blade into the hard ground. It broke in two upon impact. The tip spun into the air until Kiba grabbed it and jabbed it into the kunoichi's eye. She remained motionless for a second, then tumbled on him.

The third, and best of the trio, aimed for his skull this time. Kiba could feel her wrath from the way she hammered her blade down. He pulled the lifeless body of the second kunoichi up and slightly slid under her at the same time, then felt the blow meant for him passing through her shoulder. Shoving the corpse to the side, and trapping the blade in the process, he then shot his feet upward to stand on his hands. He kicked down with all his weight and broke the third kunoichi's humerus with a loud cracking sound. She shrieked for a second before he found himself on her back and coiled around her like a snake. Her left arm dangled uselessly, so he put more pressure on the other with his right arm. His legs were compressing her chest, constricting a little more every time she breathed out, and with his left arm, he held her in a headlock. She struggled for air but still fought him.

In front of them, the first kunoichi was tying her severed arm with the string from his shuriken. Kiba watched her while he finished the third, and she watched him kill her comrade without trying anything. She tightened the string and blood stopped flowing immediately. Then she checked him, murder in the eyes. Kiba snapped the third one's neck when she stopped moving. He wasn't done, but his kusarigama now lay on the ground, between them, out of his grasp.

Pushing the lifeless body from him and getting back on his feet, he then flicked two more shuriken from his belt. She might have just lost an arm, but she still meant to fight to the death, and Kiba found her resolve admirable.

Pain came before he understood why.

Something hit him in the leg as he crouched to get some spring. When he lowered his gaze, he saw a dart. A short, dark missile ending with green feathers. He had not even seen its thrower, but he almost swore for his mistake. When he lifted his gaze back, the one-armed kunoichi was almost on him. Sixty years of experience told him to jump forward, not backward as most people would. It got her by surprise, but her blade still connected with his left shoulder and cut deep into the muscle.

Kiba clenched his teeth against the pain, and wrapped his hand around her throat. This time he heard the dart flying from a bush, and put himself behind the second kunoichi. He tripped her, coiled his arm around hers, crouched to retrieve his sickle, and stabbed three times into her heart before she could react. He let her go from his mind and threw the weighted end of his kusarigama into the bush from where the darts had been thrown. There was an impact, and when he retrieved it, the weight was bloodied and covered in brain matter. Whoever he'd just killed, she had not been a fighter, just a marksman.

The Iga shinobi cursed himself as he returned his gaze to the Wind Demon. He'd been fooled. There had been three whistles, so when three kunoichi came forward, he had not assumed there would be more. Such a simple yet cunning tactic. Worse, the dart was poisoned. He could feel it running through his veins. Using one of his stringed shuriken, he slowed the blood flow around his thigh but knew he was already too late. This would just give him some more time. Across the path, the Wind Demon was grinning in a most malevolent way.

"Children and poison, that's your way?" Kiba asked Kotarō when the distance shrunk to thirty steps.

The Wind Demon's grin slowly turned into a smirk. The whistle came back between his lips, almost indistinguishable inside his clawed hand. Kiba heard nothing and wasn't sure if Kotarō had even used it even when he removed it. Then there was a sound like a howl and a bellow, something between a wolf and a bear, but more threatening than either. It came from behind a tree on his right. As soon as his gaze went toward this bestial shout, he felt a presence rise behind him, on his left. This time he had guessed something like this would happen and crouched right as a massive blow cut through the air above him. From the wind of the blow on his neck, he thought whoever had snuck behind him used a whip or club maybe, but when Kiba front-flipped and threw the weight of his chain at him, he realized his opponent had come empty-handed. Though a *hand* would hardly describe what this man used.

He was nearly as tall as Kotarō, but made of pure muscle. Wide of chest, of shoulders, of everything else, and hairy as a boar, this massive shinobi could have passed for a *yōkai*, and the way he snarled his pointy teeth made Kiba wonder if he was truly one. Yet, despite his great size, he had managed to sneak upon him. He was dangerous, Kiba understood as he retracted his chain right before the beast could catch it.

Kiba landed on his feet but barely felt the ground. He was losing his sensations. Kotarō now stood fifteen steps away, and Kiba thought he might as well charge the Wind Demon rather than waste time on this Fūma beast. But what mattered was giving time to Musashi, and playing this game a little longer served that purpose.

Far away, in the direction he had sent Musashi toward, Kiba heard a faint gunshot. He smiled behind his mask, knowing that through his sacrifice, the Samonji would reach its destination. *Just a bit more time*, he thought, *let's give him a bit more time.*

The beast's shoulders rose widely with each breath, yet Kiba heard none of it. Was the poison affecting his hearing? He thought not. The beast was just a great shinobi and used his size to mislead his opponents.

No need to overthink at this point, Kiba told himself. He leaped forward, giving no sign of it beforehand, and aimed at the beast's neck with the tip of his sickle. But the Fūma shinobi simply raised his hand and let the blade plant itself in his palm with no reaction to pain. The beast closed his hand on the blade and shot the other around Kiba's throat, keeping him in the air with ease. Before the Iga could react, he then stretched his wounded arm to the side, pulled on Kiba, and head-butted him right in the face.

Kiba had been hit many times in his life, but never like this. His world rocked into a confused mix of flashing lights and pain. Even through the mask, he felt the beast's forehead like a battering ram. The taste of blood came next. He had bitten the inside of his cheek. The pain kept him focused enough to see the second headbutt coming, but not enough to react. This time he heard the mask crack under the impact, and then the beast howled. And still, the poison flowed through him and numbed his senses.

He tried to pry the sickle back, but the beast held onto it tight, even if it was destroying his hand. Kiba looked into his eyes and saw wide and dark pupils. The beast had been drugged up to kill pain and fear. He crunched Kiba's throat a little harder. The Iga shinobi could no longer breathe. Out of desperation, Kiba threw the weighted end of his chain toward the beast's neck. It coiled around three times, and Kiba pulled with all his fading strength.

Kiba's vision started spinning and funneling; he would soon lose consciousness. He focused on the chain and saw how it seemed to dig into the beast's skin. There was no way his opponent could keep at it for too long, but the drugs would make him oblivious to it. All the Iga shinobi had to do was endure longer, and if there was one thing Kiba excelled at, it was outliving his enemies.

He pulled gradually stronger, hearing the chain's links tense to their limit, and applied still more tension. The poison was numbing his own pain, but air refused to pass his throat. The beast seemed to understand his end was coming first if he did nothing, and he tried to grab the chain with his wounded hand. Kiba did not let him. He twisted the blade to get a better grip and put his foot in the crook of the beast's elbow to keep the arm away. From the outside, this duel would appear dull and unmoving, but the intensity of the struggle made Kiba shiver with the effort. He pushed with his foot and coiled his arm around his side of the chain. No need to be subtle anymore. Kiba grunted with the effort, the beast as well. His vision darkened, and the taste of blood flooded his mouth. His legs got weaker first, and his eyes closed by themselves. *Keep pulling,* Kiba told himself as his mind buzzed like an angry beehive.

The shinobi did not feel the moment his head kissed the ground, nor the grip loosening around his throat, but that first breath of fresh air was like a stab through his lungs. He gasped painfully, and the world came back at once. He was still pulling on the chain, and the beast's face looked extremely purple in contrast to the lush grass.

Finally letting it go, Kiba coughed hard as he got on his knees, then, legs trembling, on his feet. He could hear nothing over the buzz still ringing inside his brain but saw Kotarō, so impossibly close, raise his arms, and all around him came his shinobi. He shook his head to regain some senses and counted twelve of them. *Not done by a long shot,* Kiba told himself.

"Too scared to finish an old man by yourself?" Kiba asked. He thought of making himself appear weak to attract his opponent but didn't need to. He was weak. His wounded leg buckled and Kiba dropped on his knee. The sickle did not leave the ground when he meant to lift it; the weight was just too heavy. Kiba checked his thigh for any sign of worsening, and when he raised his eyes in alarm, all he saw was Kotarō's foot about to slam the side of his head. Kiba fell like a toppled tree, smacking into the ground with such strength that his mask split in half down the middle. The pieces still held on his face, as if he'd infused his own stubbornness into the mask over the decades.

Kiba was on his back, incapable of finding the strength to sit up. He would have loved to take this last foe, but even his beloved mask had broken. He had nothing left to give.

Kotarō shoved the tips of his left claw in the mask's

interstice and peeled the two halves away from Kiba's face. The Wind Demon, Kiba thought now that his senses were no longer obstructed by anything, smelled like rotten wood.

"You've had a long run," Kotarō said in an ashy, gravelly voice. His first and last words to Kiba. He raised his right claw, bringing it next to his grinning, deranged face, ready to thrust it into Kiba's eyes, which he closed. He did have a long run.

"Kotarō!" a voice shouted, cutting through the solemnity of the moment.

The Wind Demon flickered a glimpse further up the path, his arm still at the ready. His painted face turned to a scowl.

When Kiba checked behind, he saw Musashi under the great oak and meant to curse, but no words passed the mess of blood in his mouth. All of this for nothing, the shinobi told himself. If there was one thing he hated, it was waste.

"Is this what you want?" Musashi shouted, holding the sword above his head. A kind of growl passed through Kotarō's throat. "Step back, or I break it to pieces!" Musashi knelt and put the sword against a sharp boulder while in his right hand, he lifted a rock as big as a fist. If he hammered it on the Samonji's flat, the katana would shatter. *Not bad*, Kiba thought before unwillingly scoffing. It did not please Kotarō Fūma, who pulled his claw a little more.

"Don't you dare!" Musashi shouted. "I'll do it! What will your master say, huh?"

"What do you want, Miyamoto?" the Wind Demon asked. There was another single gunshot in the distance, and Kiba wondered again if it was for them.

"Step back," Musashi replied. "Step back all the way to the ridgeline over there, you and your murderers. I'll come get my friend and leave the sword under this tree instead. When we are gone, you can take it."

"Why would I trust you?"

"I don't care why," Musashi said.

"I'll come after you," Kotarō replied menacingly. "You know that, right? I'll come and gut you with my bare hands. You will beg, and cry, and bleed, but I'll make sure—"

"Please," Musashi said as he raised the rock in his hand, "keep talking, go ahead." Kiba enjoyed the look of pure hatred painting itself on the Wind Demon's face. If they made it out alive, he would have to tell Mikinosuke how his master made a demon back down.

"You better run fast," Kotarō said as he straightened up.

"Don't worry about me," Musashi replied, "I excel at running away."

Slowly at first, Kotarō stepped back, then invited his warriors to do as much. Kiba leaned on his elbows to watch the demon walking away. His curse once again proved true; he would not die.

"Damn," Musashi said as he reached the shinobi, "you *are* old."

"A little older than the last time we saw each other," Kiba replied as Musashi helped him off the ground. "Why did you come back?"

"If I came back without you, what would my pupil think?" the swordsman said.

"But you were supposed to get the Samonji to the others, not barter it for my life."

"The Samonji?" Musashi asked in a fake, confused tone. "I'm not giving them the Samonji." And indeed, the sword in his hand wasn't the cursed one, but his own katana. The Samonji was quietly resting inside Musashi's *saya*, next to his *wakizashi*. "I thought they wanted *my* sword. Do you know how much the katana of Miyamoto Musashi is worth on the market? A small fortune, let me tell you that."

"Idiot," Kiba replied with pride, an amused smile crawling on his old lips. "They'll come running like the wind once they understand they've been duped," he went on, checking over his shoulders, seeing Kotarō pacing like an animal in a cage on the other side of the valley.

"They would have come after us no matter what," Musashi said.

"True."

They stopped under the shadow of the oak just as another shot resounded northwest of their location. Musashi, holding both the shinobi and his sword, turned around to face their foes. More of them had gathered around their leaders. The swordsman raised his katana above his head, then jammed it into the soft ground.

"Can you run?" he asked the shinobi.

"Will have to," Kiba replied. "Just tell me when."

Musashi took a deep breath as Kiba removed his arm from the swordsman's shoulders. He could no longer feel his leg, but could still move it at will. When he removed the string around his thigh, it would hurt like hell, but that would be a good problem to have. The side of his face was bruising, the cut on his shoulder still bled, and his crushed windpipe would feel like a chimney for days, but he thought he could still run.

"Now!" Musashi shouted.

Both men rushed north, as Musashi had before. Kiba fought the urge to check behind, knowing the Fūma would be on their track. He let the swordsman run a couple of steps ahead, using his back as a target to focus on. His tired legs would do the rest. A few seconds later, they heard a shout full of hot-blooded wrath from their back.

They veered slightly west to follow the edge of a grove, which put them in the direction of the gunshots. Kiba's lungs seemed to fill with lava. He coughed and spat every few steps, but still focused all his will on following Musashi's back. The swordsman ran well, better than he had expected. Musashi may not have wielded a sword in years, but he kept at his training seriously, this much was certain.

When the swordsman leaped over a rivulet, Kiba imitated him, but he tumbled in his landing.

"Up," Musashi said as he grabbed him under the armpit again.

"I...I..." Kiba said, not finding the strength to speak more. *I can't keep going*, he thought. Yet his legs kept running with Musashi's support. No need to worry about balance, just keep running.

He heard some ruffling on their back but did not trust his ears anymore. Everything was spinning and buzzing. Nature passed by in blurry flashes, yet he felt as if he moved with extreme slowness. Another gunshot. Then an arrow planted itself right by his foot. Musashi yelped and seemed to pick up the pace, his breathing ragged, and his face drenched in fat pearls of sweat. Musashi by himself would make it, Kiba thought with guilt.

"Thank you," Kiba whispered. Was he even moving his legs anymore?

"Not yet," Musashi replied. "They're there!" he then said, beaming.

Right ahead, down a last slope, Lake Biwa stretched far and wide, and right by its closest shore, a group of six people. As his vision darkened, Kiba recognized the deaf musketeer, who shouted something while she reloaded her arquebus. The others moved at once, running toward two small boats at the end of a flimsy-looking pier. A shadow stretched past him, so Kiba checked over his shoulder to see a Fūma shinobi gain ground on them. Another few steps and they would be within his reach.

A bullet crashed into the Fūma shinobi's forehead shortly before that, and he fell backward just as Musashi and Kiba reached the flat ground. He was no longer running. Musashi was doing all the work. He heard the planks of the pier under the swordsman's feet.

"Get in!" Rōnin shouted a second before Kiba felt the swaying boat under his back. The oars hit the water frantically, the girl's bow twanged, and a little further the musketeer shot her firearm.

Kiba managed to open his eyes and lift his head, seeing the shore getting further slowly. The Fūma were gathering, more than he had seen before. Kotarō was waving his arms at his warriors, hurling orders Kiba could not hear. Some of them plucked something from their backs.

"*Mizugumo*," Kiba whispered.

The Fūma's domain of predilection was the water. They were said to walk on it faster than on the ground, and now Kiba knew how. The members of their amphibious unit slid the flat *mizugumo* platforms under their feet and just as soon came to the pursuit.

"Heaven's sake," Musashi spat. "They never give up."

Kiba had learned the trick of water-walking, but these shinobi had mastered it. The *mizugumo* would give them a wider surface to stand on, and pockets of air under the feet would keep them afloat better, but how many years did it take to move so nimbly? Kiba counted eight of them, sliding over the lake as if it was frozen. The boats had not gained enough distance, and with the poor balance they offered, the warriors were at a serious disadvantage.

Tsuki shot from the prow but failed three times in a row.

The water shinobi moved like snakes and avoided the missiles with ease. From the other boat, Ame wasn't doing much better. At least she had Tadatomo to reload her arquebus for her while Yūki rowed with all her great strength.

Kiba looked at the archer, her face crisping with frustration at her missed shots.

"Damn it," she said when her fifth arrow plopped into the water harmlessly.

"Wait," Kiba told her in a weak voice. "Wait for Ame to shoot first," he went on. "When they shift their weight to avoid her bullet—" He did not manage to finish his advice. All went dark. He heard a gunshot, a twang, and a scream. His mind became silent, though he could still feel the world moving around him. Then there was a whistle, and Kiba passed out.

CHAPTER II
THE NINE

They kept the boats at a gunshot distance from the shore, but no more. Their destination was most likely known by the enemy, so they might as well sail straight toward it. Boats would be slower than running shinobi, but even the Fūma could not run all the way to Azuchi, and their path would not be a straight line. If they did not tarry, the eight would reach their destination with time to spare, at least compared to the Fūma. The horned samurai was another problem. They had not seen him since the previous day, before it all went to shit, and he had been riding a horse.

"How long to Azuchi, you reckon?" Musashi asked when it was his turn to row.

Rōnin's arms were sore from hours of pushing their small vessel on the water, but Musashi had needed the rest. They all did, but the three on this boat needed more. Kiba had yet to regain consciousness, though he breathed better now. Seeing his face had been a shock. No one had expected him to look so old. His skin had remained white because of his now broken mask, but his wrinkles were deep, and his stubbly beard silver. Looking at him sleeping the poison off, it was hard to remember him vaulting in the air and felling enemies a third his age. Tsuki had taken care of his shoulder, but only time would heal the rest. Now she lay down in the boat, exhausted to the point of not caring if she was soaked or not.

"At this rate," Rōnin replied, "maybe by tomorrow evening."

The night was on them, but they would need to keep going. The moon shined bright enough to lighten their path, but not strong enough to prevent sleepiness. Rōnin nodded despite his will to keep up and converse with the swordsman. Musashi needed help to stay focused. Just like everyone else, he'd had a long, trying day.

"Will you miss your sword?" Rōnin asked.

"It's just a sword," Musashi replied between two pulls. Rōnin heard the lie. "It was given to me by Lord Hosokawa Tadaoki when... you know what, never mind."

Musashi's famed bravado had yet to catch up with him, especially because they sat within earshot of the boy. His actions of the day were commendable, but he had not fought per se.

"I'm sure Yoshinao will give you another one," Rōnin offered.

"He'd better," Musashi replied.

The oars came in and out of the water a few times, disturbing little more than the reflection of the moon on the surface. In the other boat, they had Yūki Ikeda, Tadatomo, and Ame to row. Even Mikinosuke would manage for a short time, but here only he and the master swordsman had the strength for it. They might need to shift some people at some point, but no matter what, Musashi and Mikinosuke would not find themselves on the same vessel. At least not willingly.

"You should rest, Rōnin."

"I'm fine."

"I will be all right," Musashi replied.

"No offense, Miyamoto-dono," Rōnin said with a hint of sarcasm in his voice. "But your ability to sleep is nearly as legendary as your sword skills."

"But not as much as my cowardice," Musashi said without taking offense. "And if I have to keep rowing to keep us from a clan of vicious shinobi, I'll do it until my arms fall off, believe me."

"Are you sure?" Rōnin asked more seriously.

"We will need all the energy we can get," the swordsman replied. "I can't imagine things will go easy at Azuchi, no matter how much I hope for this altar to be just there, waiting for us to smash it to pieces. There will be more fighting, and I'd rather you have rested than me. Let me do this for us, please."

"All right," Rōnin said as he allowed himself to curl down on his narrow bench. "In that case wake me up in a couple of hours."

"Will do," Musashi replied.

The rhythmical bobbing of the boat and the sound of the oars dipping into the water put Rōnin in a pre-slumber spirit. His thoughts gently drifted away. He wondered what they would find on Demon Island, what kind of altar they had to destroy, and if they would manage to do so before the enemy caught up.

Tadatomo finally gave up and tapped on Yūki's shoulder to stir her. She yawned loudly and stretched, probably enjoying this brief moment before reality kicked in. It vanished in the blink of an eye.

"For shit's sake!" she barked when she noticed the sun flirting with the horizon.

"Calm down," Tadatomo replied after shushing her. "You'll wake the others up."

"You rowed all night?" she hissed.

"I'm all right," he said.

"We agreed to take turns," Yūki went on.

"What do you want me to say?" Tadatomo replied. "You girls were too cute, holding hands in your sleep. I didn't have the heart to wake you."

She punched him in the shoulder, making the boat sway. He laughed at her reaction, but he had spoken the truth. He liked both Yūki and Ame; they were good people, but he liked them together even more, and if he could give them a few precious hours of peace, it was worth the fatigue of a night rowing.

"Besides," he went on, "I couldn't let him row all night and not me."

He had observed the back of Miyamoto Musashi throughout the night, wondering if he could endure the rhythm of the master swordsman. A few times he saw Musashi nodding off, but eventually, he would shake his head and get back to it.

"I'm up now," Yūki Ikeda said, "so give me the oars."

"Gladly," he replied. "Couldn't feel my fingers for the past three hours, so I hope you enjoyed your nap."

"You're an ass," she said.

Tadatomo giggled when he left the rowing bench and took her spot against the hull. Ame was lying across from him, her eyes slightly open, and her smirk telling him she had guessed what he had done.

Thank you, she said.
You're welcome, he replied.

"Come on! Pull harder!" Yūki shouted from the other boat. "Show him the might of the Ikeda!"

Tsuki put all her back into it, rowing despite the fire in her arms. She grunted, clenched her teeth, and flashed cheeks as red as Mikinosuke's. The sun was getting hot, its reflection on the water doing nothing to the intensity of the effort.

"Come on, boy!" Tadatomo shouted, cheering for his champion. "Are you gonna let a girl beat you? Where is your pride?"

"Screw... you..." Mikinosuke replied with each pull.

"Give up, Mikinosuke," Rōnin cheerfully commented. "She's an archer. A back like marble, these. There's no shame in losing to her."

The lone warrior winked at her after teasing the boy, who predictably reacted by putting even more verve into the challenge. She exchanged a look with Mikinosuke, hoping he'd understand she meant him no ill will, this was just for sport. But the way the boy looked back at her, with zeal, forced her to recognize how serious it was to him. She responded in kind. Her boat seemed to surge forward when she allowed herself to shout with the pulls, and soon she spotted the prow of her sister's boat next to her. She was winning.

"No, no, no," Tadatomo barked, "give it your all, Mikinosuke! I bet coins on you, boy!"

"Shut... up!" he replied.

He now sat at the same level as his master, who had remained strangely quiet since he woke from his morning sleep, and this, even more than the competition, angered Mikinosuke. He was positively screaming in his effort and soon started catching up with the other boat.

"Almost there," Rōnin called, looking toward the small island that marked the end of the race.

"Go, Tsuki!" Yūki cheered.

"Come on, boy," Tadatomo called, clapping his hands.

Tsuki was starting to feel light-headed, and her fingers hurt from the grip, but she wasn't about to give up. She was a daughter of Sen Ikeda and would make her clan proud, even if it meant pulling a muscle for a stupid, stupid race.

"And—" Rōnin said, raising his hand. "Done!"

His arm went down, and the two contestants stopped rowing and leaned backward, huffing and puffing. Mikinosuke leaned over the wale, and dropped his head in the cool water of the lake, while Rōnin waved a handkerchief to wind Tsuki's face.

"Thank you," she said as she struggled to regain her breath.

Mikinosuke's head shot back from the water, spreading water all the way to the girl. She was certain he had done it on purpose.

"So?" he asked. "Who won?"

"Sorry, Mikinosuke," Rōnin said, "she did."

"No!" he barked, slapping the water. "I'm sure I did."

"Don't be a sore loser," Yūki cheerfully said, "you did well against an Ikeda warrior."

"I only lost because my boat is carrying two cows," Mikinosuke replied.

"Hey!" Yūki and Tadatomo replied in unison.

"What? It's true! I was rowing for the two of you, while

Tsuki has a scrawny shinobi on board and Rōnin, who weighs as much as his clothes."

"Will you all quiet down," Kiba mumbled as he leaned on his elbows, supporting his painful head.

"Kiba!" Tsuki called. She left her bench to take the old man in her arms. "You're alive."

"Only if you let me breathe," the old shinobi replied, though he did nothing to push her away.

When she peeled away from him, eyes teary and throat knotted, Kiba was smiling. His bruise would need days to fade away, and she still had to get used to his grandfatherly appearance, but she was glad beyond words that he seemed better.

"Welcome back," Musashi said, just as relieved-looking as the girl. Kiba nodded back to the swordsman. There was a new sense of respect between the two men. Musashi had been surprisingly humble in his retelling of the whole deal with the Fūma, but Tsuki could feel it had been a lethal situation from beginning to end, and she did not doubt Musashi had acquitted himself well. She just hoped Mikinosuke would see it that way.

"Thank you all," Kiba said, bowing deeply. "For waiting for us."

"Come on, old man. We were just waiting for the sword," Tadatomo teased. "Besides, if you died, I'd be the older one again."

Kiba chuckled at that and suddenly coughed painfully.

"I'm all right, I'm all right," he told the girl who caught him by the shoulder. "I heard you just kicked the boy's ass?"

"Oh, come on!" Mikinosuke said.

"See? Told you," Musashi said, winking at Tsuki when the boats were about to dock against the bare shore near Azuchi.

The sun would still shine for a good hour, but the end of the sailing had been getting fresher. On the horizon, Azuchi had been visible for twenty minutes or so. At least its ruins had been. Nothing remained of the once glorious domain of Nobunaga Oda; the last he had built. Heaps of carved stones marked the basement of the castle and of all the great buildings gathered around the hill. There must have been dozens upon dozens of them. Mansions, gates, streets, temples, Azuchi had been a wonder of architecture, but following Nobunaga's death, a year before the swordsman's birth, Azuchi was reduced to what they now came upon.

However, Azuchi wasn't what Musashi had just commented about. The tall, handsome man clad in saffron robes was.

Zenbō stood precisely where they aimed to dock the boats. Fresh as dew, and grinning his signature smile, it seemed the monk had faced no hardship on his journey here.

"How on earth did you get here before us?" Musashi asked when he accepted the monk's hand.

"Travelers can be very generous with a poor, blind monk on his pilgrimage," he replied, making the pitiful face that seemed to have gotten him all the way to Azuchi.

"You used the main road?" Rōnin asked, baffled.

"I did," Zenbō cheerfully replied. "Two carts and I was

dropped right at the bottom of the hill. The last group even fed me some peaches."

"Peaches?" Yūki asked, sounding pissed at the monk for his nonchalance.

Zenbō tilted his head to listen better, and when Kiba, the last of them, landed from the boat, the monk resumed his smile.

"How was your journey?" he asked.

"Eventful," Musashi replied. "But we're all here."

"That we are," Zenbō replied. "By the grace of—"

"—our blades, mostly," Tadatomo interrupted.

"Did you find anything?" Rōnin asked.

The smile made itself more discreet.

"It may surprise you, but finding secret entrances to legendary cursed islands isn't my specialty," Zenbō replied, sounding genuinely sorry. "I searched the castle grounds but found nothing. Of course, you are welcome to try there again."

"It could be anywhere in the domain," Yūki said, giving voice to Ame's signs.

"And that's a big domain," Musashi commented with dread.

Zenbō tapped the butt end of his spear against the closest stone. The sensation of a very large piece of rock reverberated through the pole, to his hand, and left him sighing. This was going nowhere. The heat from the sun was no longer caressing his skin, and while the lack of light meant little to him, he would rather not be the only one searching the domain. Clouds had amassed in the sky during the afternoon, and they who had eyes would not be able to use them at night. Whatever ruin he had just been searching through right now would be the last for the day.

The others had spoken of swarms of dead and lethal shinobi on their tracks, but all the monk could reply was that since he arrived here, there had been no one else. They agreed that the Fūma at least would need an extra day to reach Azuchi, and since they could not wander the ruins for the next few hours, they might as well rest. Some still walked the hill, while the others prepared a fire and a meal. It would be so much easier, Zenbō told himself, if they knew what they were looking for.

The best he could offer was to check for any sign of irregularity in the remains of Azuchi. Cracks, holes, echoes, anything small the others might miss because they relied on their sight. Zenbō was about to hit the base of what must have been a gate, but the musky scent of sweat came to his nostrils. Everyone smelled like sweat to him, but in various ways. He had learned to make each smell unique in his mind by associating them with other ideas. Some people smelled like the color green, the sound of pebbles under the foot, or the rugged feeling of tree bark. This scent was that of a fresh kaki and carried the sound of metal on wood.

"Found anything, Rōnin?" he asked.

"How on earth do you do that?" the lone warrior replied. He had been trying to make himself discreet, but with Zenbō it was futile.

"You always step a little further with your right foot," the monk explained.

"My master used to warn me about it," Rōnin replied after a sigh. "And to answer your question, no, I found nothing."

"Not even with that?" Zenbō asked, pointing toward the

blade in Rōnin's hand. The monk didn't need any trick to feel the blade, it was painfully there. The Samonji vibrated, this was how he had worded it. An evil, dark, wretched vibration that made him feel uneasy. Rōnin had thought that maybe the blade would react somehow to the location of Onijima, being its key and all, but that too did not seem to have worked.

"I know it sounds silly," Rōnin replied after a heavy sigh, "but I thought it might magically make the door to Onijima appear if it got close enough."

"It was worth a shot," Zenbō replied as they naturally started walking back toward the fireplace. "Even Kiba said he could feel the blade's curse."

"Can you believe how easily we speak of curses and magic?" Rōnin asked, scoffing. "Until a few days ago, I thought a caterpillar changing into a butterfly was the closest thing to it, and even that I knew was not magic."

"Seeing the dead rising to the sound of a drum changes one's perspective, doesn't it?" the warrior monk said.

"That it does."

Ahead, the chitchat around the popping fire and the smell of fish informed Zenbō of all he needed to know. His companions were hungry, but the mood was almost jolly.

"I'm sorry to ask you this," Rōnin said as he grabbed Zenbō by the elbow to make him stop. "But could you please take the first watch? Many of us haven't slept well since before Gifu. And we didn't sustain ourselves on peaches, let me tell you that." He had spoken gently, and Zenbō found himself chuckling with the lone warrior.

"You would trust a blind monk to keep watch?" he asked, tilting his head with curiosity.

"Not any blind monk, though," Rōnin replied. "I've seen you fight. You handle yourself better without eyes than most warriors with two. Hell, even if I had four I wouldn't like my chances against you. So, yes, I trust you. Plus, I'm exhausted."

Zenbō could hear the lone warrior's smile. It hadn't been there when they departed Jokoji. Sometimes, the monk told himself, hardship improves people.

"I'm honored by your trust, Rōnin. I'll keep...watch."

"Then she shoved the damn pouch in the poor guy's shirt, planted the burning match in it, kicked him down the slope, and five seconds later, boom!" Tadatomo shouted, opening his arms wide and nearly falling backward. "An explosion of red, gore, and pieces of *kyonshī* flying over like fireworks at *tanabata*. Beautiful. And then, looking as fresh as a summer peach, not even bothering to look back at her work," Tadatomo went on, moving his shoulders in an exaggerated way, "Ame, her hair floating in the explosion's wind, and already on the lookout for poor old me, pointing toward a mean corpse coming for my head. Here," he said, raising his gourd toward the musketeer. "To Ame, the greatest musketeer of Japan."

"To Ame," the others replied.

Besides the samurai, none had anything but water to drink, but all accepted the toast and drank to her name. Tadatomo smacked his lips with pleasure.

Ame had trouble following the conversation from Tadatomo's lips. He spoke fast, enthusiastically, and not always looking her way, but she still found herself blushing and smiling. She wished she could hear her new friends call her name. Voices were such a distant memory. She could hardly recall any but Yūki's, and since they had been teenagers then, her voice must have changed.

The *onna-musha* was looking at her with obvious love. The light of the fire danced in her big, black eyes, and Ame found her more beautiful than ever. They had barely exchanged a word since Sekigahara, but the musketeer knew her lover was nervous. They could all feel it. Onijima, if they made it that far, would be an ordeal, and Yūki would be worried about freezing as she had in Gifu castle. Ame put her head on Yūki's shoulder just as Tadatomo gestured for her attention.

Clumsily but with ardor, the samurai spoke her language to her.

Do you have more... he said, his signs slow but as generous as the man himself. He hesitated with the next one, then gave up and made an explosion with his hands and his mouth.

Bomb, she said, showing him the sign she and Yūki had invented all those years ago.

Bomb, he repeated.

Just one, she answered, *but bigger.*

"Bigger?" Tadatomo shouted in his typical manner. "You got to keep it for the altar. Here, my money is on Ame destroying the damn thing and being the savior of Japan."

"Thank you, Tadatomo," she pushed herself to say. For a while after her accident, Ame had spoken, but the confused faces of her interlocutors had driven her into silence. Now, after years without uttering a word to anyone besides Yūki and Tsuki, she had lost her confidence in speaking. She knew her words came wrong and people usually laughed at her when she tried to speak, but not these people. Tadatomo looked as if he'd been slapped and could not find the words. She noticed the water accumulating in his eyes and felt hers reacting the same.

"Shit," he said, wiping the burgeoning tears with the back of his hand.

Her attention was taken away by Yūki, who squeezed her hand to call for her. The *onna-musha* stood without any warning and did not let go of her hand.

"Come with me," she said with her lips and a sign.

Ame followed Yūki away from the group, though someone must have said something because she turned back and offered an obscene gesture. Then they disappeared behind the broken wall of an old mansion further still.

They had barely hidden from the others before Yūki embraced Ame with both arms. Ame had expected something of the sort, but when the warrior started trembling, Ame understood her lover's needs were different than she had thought. She hugged Yūki tenderly and caressed her back. The warrior just needed the musketeer to be with her at the moment. When some time passed like this, Ame pulled from the embrace just enough to look her lover in the eyes. They were red and glistening.

What is it?

Tomorrow, Yūki responded, *if we find this island—*

Tomorrow will be fine, Ame said after interrupting Yūki's signs. *I protect you; you protect me; we protect Tsuki.* This had been their promise to one another since the day they had left Inuyama, but as she signed it this time, Ame realized their word for "we" wasn't exclusive, and she had used it thinking about the whole group, not just the two of them.

We kick the ass of the drum bastard, Ame went on with more verve, *then we go back home and live our lives together. That's the plan.*

"That's the plan," Yūki repeated as she finally smiled.

Besides, Ame said as she went on the tip of her toes to get closer to Yūki's lips, *tomorrow is tomorrow. Tonight, I am with you. Are you with me?*

"Always," Yūki answered before she kissed Ame, first tenderly, then with passion.

"Hey, boy, don't you dare look their way," Tadatomo said after the two warriors left the group. "I know what it's like to be your age, but keep your filthy eyes from them, all right?"

"Not everyone is as big a perve as you," the boy replied from his vantage position. Mikinosuke had insisted on keeping watch while the others dined, and sat on top of the tallest stone from the ruined wall forming their camp. It fooled no one; the boy only offered to do so to keep some distance from his teacher. *After Onijima,* Rōnin thought, *something would have to be done about these two.*

After Onijima, he repeated in his head, wondering why it sounded so strange. Just like the last moment he had shared with Nobushige Sanada, there would be a before and an after, he could feel it in his gut.

"Musashi, help me out here," Tadatomo said. "You've been with the brat for years. Don't tell me you never caught him, you know…" The samurai made a gesture resembling the unsheathing and sheathing of a katana.

"Hey!" Mikinosuke snapped. "Don't you dare answer, old man."

His first words to his teacher since Sekigahara, Rōnin told himself, shaking his head. *Sometimes, nothing is better than something.* Musashi reacted by lowering his head. This "old man," coming from his beloved student, would hurt deeply.

"Boy," Kiba said, ending his usual silence with a voice like daggers, "you have your problem with your teacher, that's one thing. But don't you dare disrespect him as you just did." The mood around the fire changed radically. Rōnin checked Tsuki, whose mouth hung open, about to bite into a skewer of roasted fish. She looked transfixed by the tone of the shinobi.

"No one asked you—"

"How old are you?" the shinobi interrupted.

"Fourteen," Mikinosuke proudly replied. "I think."

"Fourteen," Kiba repeated, nodding. "Do you know this is the age your master left his home, alone, with no one to teach him the rudiments of the sword while on the road? Two years later he fought at Sekigahara and survived when many didn't. He made a name for himself through sheer guts and self-taught skills, taking ancient, respected dōjō down one after the other, showing Japan what a man can accomplish when he puts his heart into it."

"That was before," Mikinosuke replied, though Rōnin could already hear his defiance weakening.

"Before?" the old shinobi scoffed. "Before he fought to the death against masters dozens of times? Or before he trusted his own *kenjutsu* against tried and proven techniques? Miyamoto-dono was thirty when his courage failed him. Think about that for a second, you brat, he was more than twice your age before fear finally got to him. Why don't we have this conversation when you turn thirty, Mikinosuke-kun?"

The silence around the fire was deafening. Tsuki slowly pushed her skewer into her mouth and the sound of her chewing drowned the rest. Zenbō smiled happily, but the others, including Rōnin, remained dumbfounded.

"And don't speak of such things in front of a young girl, Tadatomo," the shinobi went on.

"It's fine," Tsuki replied, coming to the rescue of the samurai who probably felt like it was his turn to get a spanking. "I've been traveling with these two for a couple of years. And they are not discreet." And just as she said so, a moan echoed from the location she pointed her thumb toward.

Rōnin tried to stifle a chuckle, but a look at Tadatomo, who was trying the same, undid both. The discreet laughter soon turned into a guffaw, and even Zenbō and Kiba could not remain stoic. The only one who did not partake in the humor of the situation was Mikinosuke, whose frown would not rest.

The night had become as quiet as a night could be in the early days of winter. No insects disturbed it, there was neither strong wind nor rain, and since no one lived nearby, it was just peaceful. Even the rhythmical snoring of Yūki or the cautious sharpening Kiba applied on his many weapons should have helped Tadatomo remain in his slumber. But there was no denying it, he could not sleep. And he wasn't the only one. Opening his well-awakened eyes to a sound nearby, he observed Musashi sitting up. The swordsman stared into the dying fire and sighed.

"Can't sleep either?" Tadatomo asked as he too gave up the fight.

"I'm afraid not," Musashi replied. Even through the dark,

Tadatomo could read the fear creeping onto the swordsman's face.

"You know, nothing might happen tomorrow," Tadatomo said as he worked on the string of his gourd. "There's no guarantee we'll find that entrance to Onijima."

"Even if we don't," Musashi replied, "we will eventually have to face the Fūma or the *kyonshī*."

Tadatomo tilted his head agreeingly as the gourd found his lips. For some reason, he could not be bothered with what might come toward them; only what stood in front worried him. His father had taught him to look forward, never backward, but this time it might have been a wise idea, he told himself. Forward was a mystery, behind a certainty, and it got the swordsman all riled up.

"How can I help you, Miyamoto-dono?" the samurai asked with sympathy.

"If it's not too much to ask," the swordsman replied without a second of hesitation, "I think a sip of that might go a long way."

"I doubt it," Tadatomo replied, his gourd of sake still in hand. "But we'll never know if we don't try."

With that, he tossed the bottle to the swordsman, who looked as if he could not believe what had just happened. Tadatomo chuckled at the sight of the famous Musashi Miyamoto staring at a simple gourd the way a monk might a sacred sutra. The cork left the tip and Musashi reverently brought it to his lips, then frowned.

"Honda-dono," he called as he lowered the gourd. "It's empty." He sounded almost disenchanted.

"I'm afraid so," Tadatomo replied. His sorrow for the swordsman was honest.

"How long has it been so? It doesn't even smell like sake anymore."

"Eight years," Tadatomo said.

"Eight years," Musashi repeated, shaking his head in admiration as he passed the empty bottle back to its owner.

"Alcohol destroyed my life, and shattered my family's honor," Tadatomo went on. "I lost my brother's respect, and what little I had for myself because of it. Eight years ago I stood by a cliff and emptied this gourd into the sea. It was either that or jumping." The samurai remembered the sound of the waves crashing and the laughter of the gulls flying over challenging him to become their next meal. It felt like another life ago. "At first, the smell was enough to overcome my thirst, but when it too disappeared, I had to make do with the sensation of the gourd on my lips. I think soon I won't need that anymore."

"Then you will go back to your brother?" Musashi asked. "Tadamasa is a friend," the swordsman explained in reply to Tadatomo's confusion. "And he misses you."

"Unfortunately, my brother will have to wait," Tadatomo said, the knot in his throat turning his voice a little coarse. "There's something I have to find before I can show my face to him."

"Fair enough," Musashi replied.

"My apologies for the sake," Tadatomo said in his attempt to change the subject.

"None needed. Conversing with you, Honda-dono, is worth a good bottle of wine."

"Hardly," Tadatomo replied with a scoff. "But it's as good as you're gonna get tonight, I guess. And I wouldn't worry about the enemy showing up tomorrow if I were you."

"Oh? Why not?" Musashi asked.

"Because they might very well show up tonight," the samurai replied in all seriousness before the mask peeled off his face and he went with a wide, victorious grin following Musashi's desperate sigh.

"I'm curious," Rōnin said as he observed the floor of what must have been a small pond in the backyard of a mansion. Now it was nothing but a dried patch of land covered in weed and fish bones. "What exactly did you write on the back of your *ema*?"

Mikinosuke was taken aback by the question. He had not given any thought to the *ema* since Jokoji. The world had changed so much for the boy since. The dead could come back to life, he knew his limits better, and his teacher was a coward.

"It doesn't matter anymore," he replied.

Two hours after sunrise, they had found nothing that could pass for a gate to a cursed island. By groups of three, they had split across Azuchi's ruins, using the three roads leading to the broken castle and behind. If something were to happen, they would gather there, but so far, their morning was nothing but ruins and weed.

"If it doesn't matter," Zenbō said, "then there's no harm in telling us."

Mikinosuke found nothing to reply to that. Zenbō always had this fascinating yet annoying capacity to get the last word. The monk stood motionless in the middle of a Zen garden that had once made this mansion's owner proud, but Mikinosuke knew he was actively searching in his own way.

"I wanted Musashi's *kenjutsu* to become a powerful clan's official school," the boy said.

"A noble wish," Zenbō replied.

"A useless one," Mikinosuke said. "I'm ready to bet Musashi had several excellent offers over the years, which he refused, and now we know why."

The boy's anger had abated during the night. Kiba had spoken harsh words, but Mikinosuke found himself feeling guilty upon receiving them. Musashi had lied to him for years, but he had also given him everything. Not once had the boy known hunger or loneliness since they had met, and he had received the techniques of the Niten Ichi-ryū; an invaluable gift in itself. His teacher might not use it anymore, but the boy's future was all set with his two blades.

"I just wanted his art to live on forever," he went on, shame tugging at his heart once more. "No matter what, the Niten Ichi-ryū deserves to shine." Mikinosuke stared at the hilts of his two swords with something like love. His feelings for Musashi might have become confused, but his passion for the two-sword techniques remained intact, and if anything, he would need to thank his master for his teaching. Musashi had, after all, trusted no one else with his life's work.

"No offense, Rōnin," the boy said with a sudden energy, "but the Niten would crush your battōjutsu in every fight."

"Oh? Big words from a small mouth," Rōnin replied with good humor. "Is this a challenge?" The lone warrior stood from his inspection of the dry pond and dropped his left hand behind the *tsuba* of his katana, ready to draw.

"Once we've saved Japan," the boy answered, "with pleasure."

"Deal," Rōnin replied.

"How about you?" Rōnin asked Zenbō, who had just moved a few steps closer.

"I'm afraid I don't usually accept challenges," the monk replied.

"No, I meant about your *ema*? What did you write on it?" Rōnin asked.

"The same thing I have lived for since I lost my eyes," Zenbō replied, his expression neutral for once, almost sad, Mikinosuke thought. "I wish for my school to be reinstated."

"What happened to it?" the boy asked. "If you don't mind my asking."

"Not at all," Zenbō replied, flashing his charming smile again. "Like many other schools of *sōhei* monk warriors, the Hōzōin-ryū was forbidden by Ieyasu Tokugawa when he gained control of all of Japan."

"Why?" Mikinosuke asked, baffled that such a wide genre of martial arts could be closed at once.

"Locally, some sōhei groups held more power than samurai, sometimes even more than the province daimyō," Zenbō explained. "Most of my kind were peaceful and willing to serve, but others rose and formed *Ikkō-ikki* rebellious groups. During the civil war, they were used by one warlord or another, but when it all ended, they became a threat. Not willing to risk the fragile peace of the nation, the shōgun simply forbade their existence, no matter if they actually harbored seditious thoughts or not."

"Do you really think Yoshinao can do something about that?" Rōnin asked. "That was a shogunal decree. Even he might not be powerful enough to reverse it."

"I still have to try," Zenbō replied. "I would try anything to bring my master's dream back to life."

"It sounds... excessive," Mikinosuke said, not finding a better word to describe the shōgun's decision.

"While I can understand his reasoning," Zenbō replied, "I agree with you. Master In'ei was never interested in war or politics. All he wanted was to grow his art and teach people to defend themselves with a spear. He dedicated his life to the Hōzōin-ryū and saw it snuffed with a wave of the hand. He deserved better."

As he said so, Mikinosuke guessed a certain anger coming from the monk. He slightly raised his spear and tapped the end of the pole against the Zen garden's ground. This was as far as he would let his emotions speak. Then he did it again, but this time more consciously. The third time he tilted his head, then knelt and dropped the flat of his hand on the hard ground.

"What is it?" Rōnin asked.

"I'm not sure," the monk replied. "There's something under."

Mikinosuke and Rōnin exchanged an expectant gaze and knelt by the monk's side. With their hands, they started digging. It didn't take long to feel some hard wood under their dirty fingers. Within a few minutes, they managed to excavate a trunk as big as a child.

"Doesn't look like a gate to me," Mikinosuke said.

"What's inside?" Zenbō asked when Rōnin forced the rusted lock open.

"Rice," Rōnin answered after a sigh of defeat. "It's just rice."

"Why would people burry rice under a Zen garden?" Mikinosuke asked.

"They wouldn't," Zenbō replied before he thrust his free hand into the pile of rice. He shuffled the grains, then his head tilted again, like a fox who had found a fish in a traveler's bag. When he pulled his hand from the coffer, spraying grains of white rice in all directions, he held a sword. A katana, sheathed into a dark *saya*, as beautiful as any Mikinosuke had seen. Its owner must have hidden it when the

Akechi army destroyed Azuchi some forty years ago, and the boy could understand why he would not want such a treasure taken by a traitor.

"It's not even rusted," Rōnin said when Zenbō pulled the blade from the scabbard.

"The rice kept it dry," the monk explained. He then brought the sword close to his face and sniffed it. "And its owner used some fine oil to keep it from rusting. Whoever it was, he valued this sword dearly."

"It's a beauty," Mikinosuke whispered despite himself.

Zenbō, still kneeling, handed the sword to the boy.

"Do you know anyone who needs a sword?"

"This is going nowhere," Tadatomo finally spat. He'd been grumbling since dawn, claiming that the sun had cheated them of some much-needed minutes of sleep. His mood only worsened with each building inspected. "We've been going at it all morning, and still don't have a clue what we are looking for."

"No use complaining," Kiba replied. The shinobi had climbed the hill the previous evening, hoping that his acute senses might detect the entrance to Onijima somehow. Nothing had come of it, but he had been tired then and still recovering from the poison. A good night of sleep had done wonders, and he now climbed every vantage point he could while his two companions searched from the ground. "It has to be done, anyway."

"Why?" Tadatomo asked, kicking a loose piece of stone from his path.

"What do you mean, why?" Kiba asked. He landed from

the tree he had used for observation, right in front of Tadatomo. Without his mask, he felt less threatening, a point Tadatomo seemed to disagree with judging by the step back he took.

"I mean, Yoshinao said his agents already searched Azuchi and found nothing. We're doing nothing more than they have."

The shinobi crossed his arms over his chest, wanting for words.

"I'm sorry to say I quite agree with Honda-dono," Musashi said as he joined the two others. "We don't have time to lose in repeating what others have done."

"I conc—I agree," Kiba replied after a long guttural sound. "Any ideas?"

"We've got to be smarter," Musashi replied.

"We've got to be lazier," Tadatomo corrected. "How can we search this whole hill faster and with less effort?" The samurai sounded as if he had an answer to his own question, so Kiba invited him to continue with a nod. "We have to think like the creator of Azuchi," Tadatomo went on. "Nobunaga Oda would not have just randomly built the entrance to Onijima. There has to be a logic behind all of this. Even if he had actually randomly chosen the location, this randomness would have a logic behind it."

"Somehow, this too makes sense," Musashi replied. "But I don't think any of us can think like the Fool of Owari. He *was* famous for his unique, cunning mind after all."

"He *was* a sick bastard all right," Kiba said without thinking.

He usually refrained from sharing his opinion as such. Emotions were flaws to be scrapped from the shinobi's arsenal, as his teachers would have said. But the mention of

Nobunaga had this indomitable power to make him boil within. And the two others picked up on it.

"Kiba," Musashi said, "you sound like you knew the man."

"I met him," Kiba replied. "I am the last shinobi from Iga, and I was there the day Nobunaga destroyed my people. We fought through our eventual defeat and gave much more than we took, but I was the last of us. The fool cursed me with a shameful life that would only end when I bathed in the blood of a demon. Back then, I thought he was the one, but he died, and I have wandered throughout Japan since. So far, the curse holds true."

"I'm sorry for your people," Musashi said.

"We'll have time to be sorry later," Tadatomo interrupted. "What can we use from your brief encounter with Nobunaga? Can it help us here?"

Kiba lowered his gaze and went on to remember the worst day of his long life. How could it be of service now, forty-three years later? What clue had the Fool of Owari left in the floating ashes of Iga? He felt the foot on his head, the bloody mud dripping on his face, the heat of the fire, and the screams of the villagers. He didn't require much focus for this; those details had never left him. Nobunaga's smile pictured itself in his mind. A victorious smirk. A man enjoying his victory through the pain of his victims. Kiba dug deeper. The golden flower on the warlord's greaves, the incredible darkness of his armor, the rhythm of his stallion's stomping. There had to be something.

"Found anything?" the young voice of Mikinosuke asked, disturbing the shinobi's focus.

"Nothing," Tadatomo answered. "What's that?"

"That's a..." The boy did not finish his sentence and looked away, blushing. "Zenbō found a katana hidden behind a mansion. He thought Musashi might need it, since he lost his at Sekigahara."

"That's very thoughtful of him," Musashi replied, playing along with his student's lie. "Will you thank him for me?"

"I will," the boy replied.

As far as Kiba could remember, it was the first time since the boy had offered for the swordsman to take his own life that they looked at each other.

"Actually," the shinobi said, "I need to check something. Why don't you stay with those two while I'm gone?"

If there was a reply, Kiba did not hear it. He left with a backflip that put him back on the tree from before, then he pushed toward the higher part of the hill, where the castle had been built. Using his shinobi skills, he vaulted from ruin to ruin, leaving the beaten path to those stuck on the ground. The sky was his realm, and Kiba soared all the way to the summit, landing at last on the southern rampart of Azuchi.

The once great town stretched in front of him as one broken landscape of stones and earth. A lifetime ago, he had learned the technique of the Falcon Eye, which allowed one to observe a vast land as if flying over it. It helped to notice the flaws in the enemy camp or the path for an infiltration. Azuchi had been well built. Not so much for defense but to impress, and when alive, the town would have been a marvel. Kiba tried to imagine it in all its splendor, with tall buildings and people milling around. He saw the patrols, the coming and going of carts filled with grain, and the religious ceremonies proceeding up and down the hill.

Where would Nobunaga have hidden his secret gate? What was the monster thinking?

No, Kiba thought, he could not see his old enemy as

such. He had to think of him as a man. A man with dreams, friends, and flaws. *What was his flaw?*

The sun was getting high. Kiba's shadow crouched almost all the way under him. He went deeper inside himself, letting the sight of Azuchi flood his quiet mind. From where he had come from, he could spot Musashi tying his new sword into his *obi*, and could guess his friend's smile. Mikinosuke was still there as well, his lack of social experience keeping his head low. Zenbō and Rōnin were walking up the central road to the castle, the blind monk tapping his spear against every protuberance of the land. On the other side, even closer to him, the three women inspected a square structure.

He spotted a cloud of dust an hour east. It seemed too big to be the Fūma, but too small and too fast to be a swarm of *kyonshī*. He would have to warn the others, but not yet.

It was there, at the back of his eyes. He could feel it. Something with Azuchi did not sit well. Something was flawed in its design. Something Nobunaga Oda would not have left for no reason. The warlord, despite his moniker, was no fool. But he was playful. Nobunaga's smirk had not been for the pain of his people, Kiba understood, it was just the sign of a man pleased with himself. He had played and won.

Did he flash the same smirk when climbing toward his castle? Kiba asked himself. *Which path would he have chosen? The central one, of course. No, not the central one. Why not the central one? Because it's not as wide. Why not? Central roads are always wider. This one isn't. How come?*

Kiba opened his eyes. He had found the flaw in Azuchi and knew where to find the gate to Onijima.

"Here?" Yūki asked, her voice full of doubt.

"Yes," the shinobi replied. "That's my best bet."

"Can you explain to us why?" the *onna-musha* asked.

Kiba was about to tell her that Musashi, Tadatomo, and Mikinosuke would soon be here, and the explanation would have to wait, but they arrived just then, to the ruins of a gate from the eastern path.

"This gate," he said, dropping his hand on the closest stone of the structure's basement, "was wider than all the others."

"Are you sure?" Rōnin asked.

"Yes," Kiba replied.

Zenbō took a series of steps leading from one end of the gate frame's base to the other.

"Barely, but yes," the monk said.

"So?" Yūki asked.

"Nobunaga would never have left such a blatant flaw in the outline of his town," the shinobi explained. "It had to be done on purpose."

"That's a bit light," Tadatomo said as he passed a finger under his helmet to remove the sweat.

"There's more," Kiba went on. "This gate, if I'm correct, would be the gate of the Ninomaru, the second district. But it is bigger than the others." As he spoke, the shinobi traced the characters in the dirt with his finger. "If we add the character for *big* in front of Ninomaru, what does it sound like?"

"*Ōninomaru,*" Mikinosuke read.

"Heavens," Rōnin called. "It sounds like *Oni no Maru*, the demon's district."

"Still think it's light?" Kiba asked Tadatomo.

"No," Tadatomo replied, scratching his head. "It sounds good, but it doesn't look great."

"No argument here," Kiba said, for the samurai was right. Ōninomaru might well be their best bet, but nothing else seemed out of place. It was just as broken down as the rest of Azuchi. The gate itself had turned to ashes decades ago, and only the stones marking the basement of the structure lay left and right of it. They would have welcomed a tall palisade, two towers for archers, and maybe a parapet, but anything of wood was long gone.

"We have to inspect every inch of the structure," Rōnin said.

"And fast," Kiba replied. "I spotted a cloud of dust coming this way. We don't have much time."

Tsuki could not believe what she was looking at. In her hand, a piece of stone, barely bigger than her thumb. She had found it odd-looking at the center of a majestic slab, facing the sky. At the time of Azuchi, this part of the structure would have been covered by the palisade, but years under the sun had worn the surrounding mortar, and all it took was a few taps from the pommel of her knife to dislodge it. In its place remained a gap. A perfectly shaped gap, like that of a scabbard.

"I think I found it," she called. "I found it!"

Her eight companions gathered in the blink of an eye and stood on top of the gate's base, looking down the small hole in the stone. No one dared speak for a time.

"Rōnin," Zenbō said, "would you do us the honor?"

Rōnin knelt by the hole, visibly shaken. With care, he unsheathed the Yoshimoto-Samonji from Musashi's old scabbard, and religiously let it slide down the stone. And nothing happened.

The blade went as far as it could, all the way to the *tsuba*. He removed it a couple of times and tried with more verve, but every time the guard bumped into the rock, and yet nothing happened.

"Do you think this is just the mechanism, but the door is somewhere else? Maybe you opened it already," Tadatomo asked.

"I think I'm not reaching the end," the lone warrior said.

"Is the mechanism busted?" Mikinosuke asked.

"I don't think so," Rōnin went on. Sweat was pearling on his forehead as if the whole situation was his fault. "I don't know why, it just doesn't—"

His head shot up with a revelation, and he searched for Musashi's eyes. The swordsman seemed to realize what the lone warrior meant, as did Tsuki.

"It has been shortened," she said, remembering the conversation she had with them before Sekigahara. "It was a *tachi*, right?"

"It was," Musashi agreed.

"Let me," Zenbō said before he all but snatched the sword from Rōnin's hands.

With dexterity, the monk dismantled the sword piece by piece. The archer had never seen anyone remove a blade from its hilt with such speed, but within a minute, the blind monk was sliding the guard from the sword and handed it back to Rōnin.

"This might do," Zenbō said.

Everyone held their breath as Rōnin let the naked Samonji katana slide down the hole. There was a click when the blade almost entirely fit, leaving only an inch of the hilt jute out of the stone. Rōnin let it go then, and more clicks followed until it sounded like a mill working at full speed.

The earth shook under them. Tsuki had to grab Tadatomo's hand to keep him on top with them. The ground seemed to grumble painfully as they struggled to keep their balance, and suddenly, further down, the stones started shrinking one by one.

"Jump," Kiba shouted.

Tsuki obeyed and jumped down the structure when she understood what was happening. The stones were shrinking *into* the ground, raising a cloud of dust around them. She coughed hard, even after the dust settled, and stopped when she saw the gaping hole marring the ground where the gate's base had been. Not just a hole though, she realized, stairs. The stones had been swallowed at different depths so that they naturally formed a staircase diving into the earth. The air coming up smelled foul and sent a shiver down her spine. The Samonji had vanished inside the mechanism, but none of them seemed to even care about it; they were solely focused on the stairs.

She could not see the end of it, but the staircase was without a doubt the path to Onijima.

CHAPTER 12
RONIN

If time had not been an issue, Rōnin would have spent some trying to understand how a sword could open a path to the underworld. Not that he cared for the mechanism itself, this kind of thing was never part of his curiosity, and he never thought of himself as a particularly clever craftsman. What he would have liked was to close the path back behind them. If they could take the Samonji with them as they entered the entrails of Azuchi, no one would be able to follow them, and they would have all the time in the world to find this altar and break this curse forever, though the idea of cutting their path to the light was not an appealing one either. Time was an issue anyway. Kiba had spotted people on their way to Azuchi; they had to be the enemy. For a second he thought of making a stand here or setting an ambush maybe, but if it failed, there would be nothing between the drummer and the altar. The only advantage they had was the Samonji, and some advance on their pursuers. The Samonji was gone; speed was thus of the essence.

"I didn't expect a path of sakura petals," Tadatomo said, "but that's not looking good."

"No argument there," Rōnin replied.

The sound of fabric being torn apart drew the lone warrior's attention. Kiba was shredding his outer shirt to pieces. Soon, he twisted four balls of hemp around as many sticks and applied some foul-smelling, thick oil onto the fabric. It quickly caught fire when he flicked a flintstone by the first of the torches, and when the others were also lit, he passed them around.

"Sorry about the smell," he said as he handed a torch to Musashi. "It's mostly made of fish and eggs." The second torch went to Tsuki, and the third to Tadatomo.

"Should we leave anyone behind?" Yūki asked.

"No," Rōnin replied. "We do this together." It felt like the right thing to do. Nine of them had journeyed from Jokoji and miraculously survived, and nine of them would come back from the depths of the underworld, the lone warrior promised himself.

"Judging by the tone of the conversation," Zenbō said, "I guess I'm glad not to have eyes."

"Lucky bastard," Tadatomo replied with a chuckle.

Kiba went down first, his torch flickering in a trail of harmless sparks. Rōnin stepped right after him and behind came Tsuki.

"Here goes nothing," Tadatomo said a few seconds later.

Within a dozen steps, the sun no longer helped them. It took a few seconds for Rōnin's eyes to adjust to the change of light, and soon Kiba's torch shined brightly, almost blinding him. The steps were made of the same stones as above and went straight, but the walls were nothing but earth and beams of rotten wood. How they still supported the passage was a mystery, but Rōnin prayed they would continue to act as such until their return.

"Do you see anything?" Musashi's voice asked, bouncing several times in the path.

"Nothing," Kiba replied after he stretched his torch-holding arm a little further. "Nothing but darkness."

"Remind me to thank Yoshinao," Tadatomo said.

The echo of their voices traveled down for much longer. Rōnin was tempted to ask Kiba to throw the torch and see how far it went, or maybe Tsuki to shoot a flamed arrow. But this was his fear speaking, and he knew fear was a poor advisor. The flame held by the archer kept his neck hot, but even that did not stop a cold shiver running up his spine.

They went down for long minutes like that, quiet mostly, making slow but regular progress. No roots came out of the sides now; they would not reach so far below. And there was not much earth either. Water dripped from above more often, and the irregular plops made the lone warrior nervous.

"What kind of happier thoughts can deal with this?" Yūki asked, probably in response to Ame's advice.

"What did she say?" Mikinosuke asked.

"She said we should focus on happy thoughts," Yūki replied, her voice like a shout in this environment.

"Like food?" the boy asked.

"Sure, like food. If that's what makes you happy," the *onna-musha* replied.

"Works for me," Mikinosuke said. "We had this amazing eel once, by a bridge near, uh…"

"Ise," Musashi replied.

"Ise," the boy repeated excitedly. "Even one year later I can still taste it."

"I'd kill for some good company," Tadatomo said as

Tsuki giggled at the boy's comment. "The girls from Edo's red-light district are remarkable but those from Kyushu are unique. How about you, Musashi?"

"Give me a quiet pond and a piece of wood to carve and I'll be happy as a sparrow in spring," the swordsman replied.

"No, I meant—"

"—I know what you meant," Musashi said. "But there are some things I would rather not teach my student. He'll have to find out by himself."

"As usual," Kiba suddenly said, "Tadatomo speaks from his ass. The women from Mutsu are the most agreeable."

This was so unexpected that the others chuckled as one. Even an old shinobi knew a thing or two about pleasure.

"As soft as their weather is harsh," Kiba went on as if speaking to himself. "I'll take you there, Tadatomo, and you'll see for yourself how wrong you've been all your life."

"I'll take you up on that," the samurai replied cheerfully. "Yesterday we also heard what makes Yūki and Ame happy," he went on.

"Yes, you did," Yūki replied proudly.

"So how about you, Zenbō?" Tadatomo asked.

"*Mizuame*," the monk replied matter of fact. His voice was distant, so Rōnin assumed he walked at the rear, which made sense considering he didn't need the light in the first place.

"Candies? Really?" Tadatomo asked with surprise.

"Well, I'm not allowed meat, alcohol, music, or sex," the monk explained. "The list of pleasures available to me is quite limited. So, yes, candies."

"I mean, sure, if candies lift your mood in this kind of place, why not."

"What is it, Tsuki?" Rōnin asked, feeling the girl tense a little.

"Candies was going to be my answer too," she timidly replied.

Another wave of laughter passed through the group. This place, no matter who had used it in the past, had probably never heard this sound before.

"Which kind do you prefer?" she asked the monk.

"I only know those from Kyōto," he replied.

"The ones from Inuyama, where I grew up, are very good," the girl said. "Would you like to visit it with us after all of this? I could show you my favorite candy shop."

"I... I would like that very much," the monk replied.

"It leaves us with Rōnin," Tadatomo observed. "What's your happy place?"

"My happy place is a person," Rōnin replied. "Or *was* a person, I should say." He hadn't meant to sadden the mood, but thinking of Nobushige never failed to sullen his heart. Ten years later, he still could not get over his lord's death.

"I'm sorry," Tadatomo said. "I shouldn't have asked."

"No need to be sorry," Rōnin replied. "Thinking of him makes this place lighter." Nobushige was gone, but the memory remained as vibrant as ever. He thought of the first time he helped his lord out of his armor because he had bruised his elbow, their second night together when they had snuck out of the camp to observe the enemy lines just the two of them, and their last embrace. Nobushige had been part of his life for less than a year, but his imprint would never leave, and as the walls of the stairs swallowed Rōnin deeper and deeper, he felt his lord's presence, and fear vanished from his heart.

Kiba almost tripped on the last step, surprised to have reached the end of the stairs after climbing down for so long.

"We've reached the bottom," Rōnin said over his shoulder.

"Finally," Yūki replied.

The stairs made way for something else entirely. The floor was paved with a different kind of stone and the walls were covered with it as well. Limestone, Rōnin thought. As Kiba waved his torch left and right into what appeared to be a corridor, shapes appeared on the walls. Carvings in a style that Rōnin had never seen before, squares within squares, with lines fleeting from their regular shapes into more squares. He passed his fingers over simplistic flowers trapped inside four-pointed stars and marveled at the sight of intricate waving patterns forming demonic faces. These carvings had at some point been adorned with colors, he assumed, but now only hues of brown and gray remained.

"Who made these?" Tsuki asked with pure curiosity.

"It doesn't look Japanese," Musashi replied.

"At least not our Japan," Zenbō said as he read the walls with the tips of his fingers.

"You mean the people before?" Tsuki asked, though Rōnin did not know who she was talking about.

"Or those who now live at the edges," the monk replied.

"It does look slightly Ainu," Tadatomo said. Rōnin had rarely encountered anything coming from those northern folks, but the image he had of their art resembled what he now saw on these walls.

"I don't know," Kiba said, "it looks foreign to me. And I don't mean it in a cultural way. It feels as if coming from another land. Even this rock is unfamiliar to me." He rubbed the tips of his fingers as he said so, letting some dust from the limestone pepper the ground.

"Kiba, wait," Rōnin called, stopping the shinobi a step before the wall ended. In his focus, the shinobi had not even noticed that the corridor branched out perpendicularly on both sides.

"Wait here," the shinobi said as he stepped into the right hallway, the flame of his torch trailing like a phoenix's tail. He was so light on his feet that when he came back, half a minute later, he startled Rōnin out of his skin.

"So?"

"It goes on like this for a while," the shinobi explained. "The other side as well, I assume."

"What do we do?" Tsuki asked.

"Let's split," Mikinosuke replied.

"Again? Are you crazy?" his master asked. "I say we stay together."

"We don't have time to check them one by one," Kiba said.

He had hammered the nail on the head; they did not have time to play it safe. This had been true since Jokoji, but it was even more urgent now.

"We split," Rōnin said. "But if the path branches even more, you come back on the central one and join the others. No need to lose everyone in a maze."

"I concur," Kiba replied.

"Kiba, Tadatomo, and I go front," the lone warrior went on. "The Ikeda on the left, and the others on the right, all right?"

They all agreed and resumed their different ways. Rōnin did not like it one bit, but what was there to like about journeying toward a place called Demon Island, anyway?

"Where are we going, you reckon?" Tadatomo asked a minute later.

"North," Kiba replied.

"Wouldn't that put us—"

"—Right under the lake," the shinobi said. "I assume we've been walking under it since the ground flattened."

The information seemed to agitate Tadatomo, who waved his torch above his head for any sign of water. Rōnin could no longer judge the distance or the time. He wouldn't have been surprised if outside the sun had already set, yet it could just have been less than an hour since they got in. Those walls, the stairs before, and those designs had a way of blurring the mind. Everything just looked like a long, unending hallway. It felt as if walking toward a mountain, except that they barely saw further than their noses.

"It smells different," Kiba said.

Rōnin sniffed the air and agreed that the smell was worsening. He knew this odor. He'd smelled it not so long ago.

"I don't smell anything," Tadatomo replied.

Rōnin searched through his memory for the nature of this stench. Usually, he could remember this kind of thing easily, but this time the veil was too thick. There was an earthy tone to the stench, but also an iron feeling.

The torch in Kiba's hand weakened, and within three heartbeats turned to little more than glowing fabric. The shinobi vanished from Rōnin's sight, but he heard nothing besides the man working on his small bottle of oil.

"Give me your torch," Rōnin asked Tadatomo, who relinquished his light with a grumble.

Rōnin meant to use the flame to help the shinobi pour some oil over his torch, but when the light passed next to Kiba's shoulder, it suddenly revealed the decayed face of a *kyonshī* standing at a hand's length from the old man.

"Shit!" Rōnin shouted as he dropped the torch and leaped back a step.

Kiba reacted similarly and went for the handle of the

sickle on his lower back, his torch still useless and on the floor as well. None of them moved any further. Nothing moved at all. The last torch was burning by the skeletal feet of the monster, but the corpse was not coming after them. It was shuffling on its white legs, its arms dangling uselessly, and a rusty long katana stuck into one of them. The monster did not even seem to care about the flame or about them.

"What on earth?" Tadatomo asked when he came to stand by the two others' side. Rōnin had not even realized they no longer stood in the hallway. It had opened to a room whose entrance the three of them now blocked, and a couple of steps from them stood the *kyonshī*.

"It's not attacking," Rōnin said.

"It's barely moving," the samurai replied.

The corpse was old, much older than those they had faced at Gifu or Sekigahara, with just a few layers of dry skin to cover its bones. Patches of white hair hung on both sides of its skull, and its armor was falling to pieces, its laces being the only reason it still held onto the frame of bones. Dead-eyed, the *kyonshī* stared into the emptiness of the floor like a child waiting to be scolded. Rōnin almost pitied it. No matter who he had been in life, no one deserved to be trapped as such for centuries, for this thing had been here for hundreds of years, this much was certain.

Kiba took a slow step toward the monster and picked up the burning torch while never leaving the dead from his sight.

"This armor," Tadatomo said, "I don't even recognize it."

"It's old, very old," Rōnin replied. "And so is he."

Kiba sniffed something on his left and turned his back on the *kyonshī*. His hand moved to the wall, and his fingers found a straight, man-made groove running parallel to the ground at chest level, a couple of inches high and deep.

When Kiba pulled his fingers from the groove and sniffed them, he frowned.

"It smells like my oil," he said.

He brought the torch toward it, and immediately the groove caught the flame. The fire spread along the wall, then turned at an angle with the room and ran all the way to the other side, changing direction twice on both sides and once at the end to climb over more entrances. The fire finished its course by Tadatomo's shoulder. The room was now bathed in a low light, but Rōnin wondered if that was such a good thing. It was three to four times bigger than his old dōjō, but only just as high. There had been carvings on the wall too, but they had smoothed to almost nothing. However, what almost made him turn on his heel was something else. The room, from corner to corner, was filled with corpses. They stood without purpose, hundreds of them, not leaving more than an arm's length between each other.

"Heavens," Kiba said.

A yelp caught their attention from the closest of the two entrances on the left, from where the three Ikeda women now joined the room. Tsuki was covering her mouth with her free hand, and Ame held one pistol in each hand. Guessing as much as Rōnin, they entered the room but did not move further than the closest *kyonshī*. Yūki waved her hand in front of an ancient warrior but received no reaction whatsoever. She then grabbed her *naginata* with both hands, ready to strike.

"Don't!" Musashi shouted from the other side of the room. His voice echoed a few times, and the *kyonshī* by his side slowly turned their heads in his direction before ultimately going back to their observation of the floor. "We don't know how they will react if we attack them."

The swordsman then hugged the wall until he joined the

first group, Mikinosuke right behind tugging at the monk's robe to help him move without touching any of the monsters.

"We saw the light," Musashi explained as he dropped his now useless torch.

"That was us," Rōnin said.

"It seems to go that way," Tsuki said when they too joined the first group. She was pointing toward the entrance at the opposite side of the room, where the light indeed seemed to line both walls of the exiting corridor.

"Then that's where we go," Rōnin said.

"Which way?" Tadatomo asked.

"The left wall has a bit more space," Kiba replied, though Rōnin could not really see the difference. The whole room was infested with living dead, and he assumed that as long as no one touched them, nothing would happen. He was actually tempted to go through the swarm. There might be clues as to those ancient warriors' identity. This knowledge would not bring them much, but his curiosity would not relent. So much was unknown about this curse, maybe figuring the age of those *kyonshī* would help understand when the curse had been created.

"When do you think they died?" Tsuki asked as they walked with their back as close to the wall as possible, proving that her thirst for answers was at least as strong as Rōnin's.

"They don't even look like samurai," Yūki said. "Look at those swords, they're straight."

"I've never seen armor like this," Rōnin replied when passing near an undead warrior who seemed to meet his gaze for a couple of seconds.

They walked by the entrance the three women had come from, then Rōnin, seventh of the group, passed in front of the second entrance on the left. This time he would not advise splitting. The light went from the entrance at the back of the room, and now that he knew the underground was swarming with undead warriors, nothing would make a split worthy. He stared into the darkness of this second entrance and shivered. Whatever existed this way would have to remain a mystery.

"Easy does it," Tadatomo said just in front.

A hand fell gently on Rōnin's shoulder, stealing a heartbeat from him. When he checked behind him he sighed with relief upon the sight of Ame, her glowing match stuck between her teeth. Her frown quickly extinguished his relief. She put her finger on top of her lips and dropped her left palm against the wall.

"What is it?" Yūki, who was closing the march, asked.

People, Ame signed. "People," she then said to Rōnin.

Just then, in the tranquility of the *kyonshī* room, the sound of the cursed drum rang true, its echo pulsing through the six corridors and freezing Rōnin's blood in his veins. Ame did not hear it, so Rōnin thought of mimicking the sound, but something moved in the corners of his eyes. A lot of things. He, Ame, and all the others, none of whom dared move or speak, observed the room coming to life.

Hundreds of corpses slowly twisted, forcing stiff joints and porous bones to shuffle. The sounds of knees rubbing and armor creaking made for an eerie racket as the dead turned to see their prey. Their grunts and moans came as one. The drum rang once more, and the dead took a first step, hundreds of years making it painfully slow.

"Move!" Yūki shouted from the rear.

"Ah!" Ame screamed when she looked at her lover.

From the darkness of the second entrance, right behind Yūki, jutted a pair of bony arms. She had not seen them.

The fingers dropped on her armored shoulders and a face came into the light, jaws extended at a ridiculous angle. The *kyonshī* bit into Yūki's skin, right at the base of her neck, ripping a strip of flesh as it pulled its head backward.

"Yūki-nē!" Tsuki screamed with dread, so loud that even her sister's shriek of pain was drowned. Blood splashed from her neck and covered the *kyonshī*, whose teeth gleamed in red.

Ame reacted before Rōnin, shooting the *kyonshī* through the side of the head before it could do more damage. She knelt to support her lover in her fall, then turned toward Rōnin, a face marred with deep wrinkles of terror.

"Run!" Ame shouted.

The dead rushed, their thirst for blood becoming more urgent now that one of them had claimed some. Rōnin drew his sword and cut the closest, then kicked it in the chest.

"Go!" he told Ame, who passed behind him, supporting a bleeding Yūki. The *onna-musha* could still stand, walk, and hold her polearm, but the blood pouring through her fingers left no doubt about the gravity of her wound. She still wielded her heavy weapon and toppled an upcoming *kyonshī*, though she did not hurt it enough. Rōnin finished the job with a backstroke.

Tadatomo shouldered a dead warrior coming too close to the wounded warrior and remained on her right to keep the others at bay. As he did, Kiba and Mikinosuke carved a path of bodies with unrelenting attacks, while Zenbō drove a wedge through the thin mass of moving corpses blocking the back entrance.

"Rōnin!" Tsuki shouted, her bow at the ready. Too many people stood between her and her target, which Rōnin understood was coming close to him. At random he knelt and slashed his katana behind, hoping to cut the *kyonshī* through the abdomen. The dead warrior had been a little too far, and the blade only grated against the exposed spine, but kneeling had at least saved him from a lunge. As he stood, he flicked his sword as if to remove the blood from the blade, thus cutting through both arms of the moving corpse. Far from stopping it, the monster came back with a shriek, teeth forward.

The arrow fizzed by Rōnin's ear and ended its course in the back of the *kyonshī*'s skull, punching with such strength that the head exploded in two halves.

The press of dead warriors was crushing the nine into the corner of the room, but the relentless efforts of Kiba, Zenbō, and Mikinosuke kept them at a distance long enough for the others to catch up.

"Keep going!" Rōnin shouted once he was close enough.

Musashi went first, Mikinosuke right behind him.

"Move!" Tadatomo barked. Zenbō and Kiba obeyed his command, Tsuki on their heels. Tadatomo went next, the corridor being too narrow for him to remain at the *onna-musha*'s side. Ame still held her and the two of them left the room side by side. When Rōnin exited it as well, he gave a wide slash of his sword that would have left his teacher pale with anger. Two heads fell to it, and he hoped the falling bodies would obstruct the others.

It didn't work. Those dead, while they had just received a purpose, had been reanimated for many, many years, and already their instincts seemed to kick in. They stepped over the obstacles—one even jumped—and clumsily but surely jogged after the lone warrior.

Rōnin ran, checking behind him every few steps while in front he could see how much slower Yūki moved, and how much harder a task it was proving to be for Ame. Yūki was already a big woman, but with her armor on, she would weigh a lot more than the musketeer. Love might have given the woman strength, but there was only so much she could do.

Sounds of fighting echoed from the front, and when Rōnin stepped by another crossing of corridors, he noticed headless bodies on the ground. The sounds coming from left and right left no doubt that more were coming. The *tap tap* of Zenbō's spear against the walls accompanied the shouts of Tadatomo calling for those in front to keep running.

"Yūki," Ame called, shaking her shoulder. "Yūki!"

"I'm... still here," the *onna-musha* replied. Her naginata was trailing behind her, barely held between her fingers.

"Watch out!" Rōnin shouted when he saw the stretched hand of a *kyonshī* jutting from the darkness of the hallway on the left. Ame would not hear him, and her sight was all focused ahead.

Mae!

Rōnin lunged forward, faster than ever, pushing on the tsuba of his katana with his thumb with so much strength that he barely needed to pull it out of the scabbard. The katana flashed, his eyes barely registering the movement he had not even commanded. It sliced through armored arms as if they were made of paper. Refusing to take a breath, the lone warrior twisted his hips and slashed through shoulder, neck, and chest, cleaving a dead warrior in half. He now stood at the entrance of the left corridor. Ame nodded her thanks, but from the other opposite side, Rōnin saw in alarm another of those monsters.

The scene unfolded slowly in his mind. The dead had no hands to wield weapons with and waved half-fallen arms toward Yūki. The *onna-musha* twisted her head and saw it coming. She meant to raise her *naginata*, but Rōnin could see she would be too late. Ame noticed the fear in Rōnin's eyes and moved in a heartbeat. With her right arm, she pulled Yūki backward, and with her left, she shielded her lover from the monster. The *kyonshī* dug its teeth into her forearm just as Yūki bumped into Rōnin. The unnatural shriek of Ame called for time to resume its course.

The monster shook its head viciously, ripping flesh from the bone the way a hound would. Ame drew one of her pistols with her free hand and dropped it under its chin. Its head exploded upward and showered the three of them in a mush of slime and bones.

"Ame?" Yūki called from Rōnin's arm. "Ame!" she called again, some of her strength coming back at the sight of her wounded lover.

The musketeer stared at her ruined arm in shock. The match between her teeth shook. Tears poured at once.

"Oh, Ame," Yūki said, her voice trembling. "No, no, no."

The army of the dead coming from the main room called Rōnin's attention. They would be on them in a matter of seconds. Ame followed his gaze, then looked at the lone warrior, and no words were needed between them. The musketeer dropped her empty pistol, drew another, and while she did, Rōnin passed Yūki's arm over his shoulder.

"What are you doing?" the *onna-musha* asked.

"We're going," Rōnin replied as he pushed his katana back into its saya.

The lone warrior did not look behind; he knew how far the dead were from the breathing of Ame. She shot once, and a *kyonshī* fell. Tadatomo and Mikinosuke were guarding the next hallway's crossing and resumed the march just before Rōnin got to their level. Another shot. The distance from Ame had widened.

"Rōnin," Yūki whimpered. "Stop. Please."

But he did not stop, nor did he slow down. He trusted his back to Ame entirely. Nothing would pass the captain of the Ikeda musketeers, and nothing would go anywhere near Yūki for as long as Ame's blood flowed through her veins.

"Ame!" Yūki shouted when she looked behind her.

"Go!" Ame replied.

The dead were swarming through the corridor, their feet stomping at a run now. The space was no longer widening between them and the *kyonshī*. Further down the hallway, the fire lining the walls abruptly stopped. This was the end of the path. His friends would be there to fight the dead, using the narrowness of the exit to block them. Only a little further and they could mount a defense. Rōnin thought to warn the musketeer, but when he checked behind, she wasn't looking at him. Ame had drawn her arquebus and blasted a flaming shot through the mass of *kyonshī*, toppling two of them with one bullet and making more of them stumble on the lifeless corpses.

She tossed the firearm into the mass and meant to resume her escape, but a hand grabbed her ankle. Bony fingers wrapped around her leg and prevented Ame from moving. She found one of her pistols and shot the arm off with speed. The musketeer limped from the swarm, her left arm dripping with blood. She might make it, Rōnin thought with hope, though the sight of her had little to offer.

The lone warrior pushed further and nearly reached the exit, from where he could see his comrades forming a crude semicircle to welcome the army of the dead, but a sudden resistance stopped him in his tracks. Yūki was grabbing the flaming grooves right before it ended, using all her great strength to prevent a single step from him.

"We wait for her," she said through her teeth. Her lips were blue and her skin pale, but her resolve was full of fire.

Rōnin looked back in alarm. Ame was barely jogging. Her eyes were losing their focus, and she was in immense pain. The dead were so close that if one fell, they would tumble on her. So many arms and blades jutted on her back, willing to shred every piece of her. Only one thing kept her moving, the woman waiting for her at the exit. But Ame, Rōnin read from her face, knew what was going to happen if she did nothing.

"Tadatomo!" she screamed, though the sound was lessened because she kept the match between her teeth.

The samurai appeared right next to Rōnin and hugged the *onna-musha* by the waist. With a grunt he pulled, and Rōnin pushed, and the two warriors managed to strip Yūki away from the wall just as her lover reached for it. Ame turned around and raised her one good arm, then shot through the mass of moving corpses. The shot echoed and the grunt of the fallen dead followed. She dropped the pistol and went for another. Ame tilted her head to bring the burning end of the match by the serpentine mechanism and pulled the trigger. She then dropped it too. When she went for another firearm, her shoulder-strapped belt carried none. Rōnin saw her shoulders fall. She turned around and stretched her arms to block the passage. A last, desperate attempt to give the others some time.

"Ame," Yūki whimpered, struggling against Rōnin and Tadatomo's grip.

"Rōnin, we can help her," Tadatomo said.

But there was no helping her. Rōnin knew it, and Ame knew it.

Ame dropped her head and saw the bag of powder hanging at her belt. Arms came from behind and grabbed her by the wrists. A sword pierced through her ribs, and teeth dug into her thigh. But Ame did not even scream. She kept looking down and opened her jaws. The burning match dropped from her lips, spreading sparks in its fall. It touched the rim of the bag, but a tremor moved her hips the wrong way and the match bounced on the floor. She'd failed, and tears of regret poured down from those eyes that missed nothing. Ame looked up, not hearing the grunts of all those undead warriors on her back. She felt the terrible and many pains of her tortured body but ignored them. All she saw was Yūki, raging against her two captors, gathering enough strength to shake them from her, and running in her direction. Yūki fell just before she could reach her, or at least that was what Ame assumed. Another blade pierced through her leg, but the musketeer would let none of them get close to the woman she loved. Yūki stood back up, the match in her hand.

"No," Ame said. "No, Yūki."

There was not a shadow of doubt on Yūki's face, nor even any anger. She was paler than ever, and her lips had cracked, but she was beautiful.

Yūki put her hand on her own chest, then on that of her lover.

I'm with you.

Then she dipped the match into the pouch of powder.

The explosion sent Rōnin and all the others on their backs. He heard it, then nothing but a loud ringing and the echo of Tsuki's scream bouncing inside his head. He searched for the ceiling and the ground, the spinning making it impossible to recognize up from down and left from right. Rōnin thought he had lost his sense of reality for some time, but when he got it back, debris from the corridor was still falling from the sky.

Tsuki was screaming, her head lost against the chest of Kiba, who had prevented her from going to her sister. She had just lost everything.

Tadatomo was on his ass next to Rōnin, his face disfigured by two furrows of tears.

"No," he whispered, his mouth agape and his eyes refusing to blink. He still held his katana, but a child could take it from him. Rōnin had seen this look before, on the faces of soldiers who had lost their closest comrades in battle and could not believe they were truly gone. When Rōnin put his hand on Tadatomo's shoulder, the samurai did not even react. He just stared at the corridor, as if the two women would miraculously step out of the rubble. But no one would ever hear Yūki Ikeda's great laughter, or witness Ame's genius marksmanship. They were gone.

"Tadatomo," Rōnin said, shaking the man with compassion. "We will mourn them. I promise we will mourn them. But right now, we have to honor their sacrifice. We've got to use their last gift."

The samurai nodded, though Rōnin could not feel his heart in it. Ame and Yūki had given them time, but not enough to let their tears stall them. The fallen hallway would slow the dead and the living, but it would not be enough.

Zenbō was leaning on his spear, the weight of their losses sapping him of his optimism. Being a monk, he had never known war, Rōnin thought, and had probably never lost people in such a brutal manner.

Mikinosuke stood like a statue, his two loyal swords hanging by his side. He looked at his master with uncomprehending eyes. He had known loss in his life, but never one like this. Musashi took his student's face between his hands and whispered words Rōnin could not hear. The boy nodded and sheathed his swords.

He did not realize he was doing so, but Rōnin was stepping toward the girl. Her sobs were constricting his heart, but before he knew it, Kiba gently led Tsuki into the lone warrior's arms. She trembled in spasms. Rōnin could feel her tears through his worn-out shirt. He held her a little closer and used this time to observe the place they had landed in.

The fire they had lit in the central room had spread further than just the hallway and now illuminated a massive place. A dome, perfect in shape, higher than the highest structure Rōnin had ever seen. The corridor they had emerged from was the sole entrance he could see, and since the dome was mostly empty, he could not imagine there was another. The fire traced its contours, but other lines of it crisscrossed geometrically over the floor, giving a warm light to the place.

"Onijima," Kiba said.

Their side of the "island" was flat and bare, save for the drops of water dripping from this ceiling that seemed as far as the sky. When he observed the wall of the dome, Rōnin realized it was lined with human bones. It made him shiver, but at this point, it almost seemed to fit. The part of the dome they stood in was crescent-shaped, the tips of the crescent stretching thin and far probably to the other end of the gigantic room, though he could not see all the way there, for a massive structure stood in between. A three-story pyramid, as tall as a hill, with a central staircase leading from the bottom to the flat top in three sections. A narrow bridge separated the crescent part of the room from the round-shaped one at the end of which stood the pyramid. He could not see how deep the fall on both sides of the bridge would be, but if this was truly the underworld, Rōnin assumed it would lead to nothing but death. But no matter what, they would have to cross that bridge and climb that pyramid, because, without a doubt, the altar waited at the top.

"They're gone," Tsuki whimpered in his chest. "I can't believe they're gone."

The lone warrior took her face between his calloused hands and forced her to look at him. She was broken. And who wouldn't be? But he could not let her be that way, not yet.

"They lived their lives together," Rōnin told her. "It ended too soon, but they spent their days, down to the last, together."

"What about me?" she asked with a deeper sob. Tsuki was not the kind to think selflessly, Rōnin knew it. This was sorrow speaking. "They left me."

"I'm sorry," Rōnin said before kissing her on the forehead. "I'm so sorry." He didn't know what he was apologizing for. Even as the rush from the main room reeled back in his memory, Rōnin could not find anything he could have done differently, but just like all the others, he knew in his heart things could have gone otherwise.

"Tsuki," Kiba said, dropping his hand on the girl's shoulder. "Yūki and Ame were brave warriors. Ikeda to the bone. They're gone, but their courage now lives in your heart. Can you be strong for them, and for us?"

The old man's words immediately quieted the archer's sobbing. She seemed to breathe deeper against Rōnin's chest. Her grip tightened on his arms, and she pushed herself from him.

"Let's go," she said in a tone that reminded the lone warrior of the *onna-musha*.

Painfully, Tadatomo got back on his feet and cleaned his blade in the crook of his elbow. The dust had begun to settle from the blocked corridor. Probably aware of what he might see, he looked away and toward their destination.

Musashi moved first, Mikinosuke walking in his footsteps. Rōnin was about to follow them, but the sight of Zenbō standing like a stubborn tree got his attention. He thought the monk might still be processing the loss of their two friends and needed some encouragement too.

"Zenbō, are you—"

The monk put his finger on his lips to ask for Rōnin's silence. He hadn't been in shock; he had been listening.

"The drum?" Rōnin asked in a whisper.

"Not only," the monk replied.

"We need to move, now!" Rōnin shouted to the others.

One step was how far he went before he too heard it. The drum was beating frantically from the other side of the blocked path, but this time it was accompanied by some other instruments and the grunts of hundreds of corpses pushing against the rubble. The *kyonshī* answered their master's eagerness, and the press increased. Small rocks fell from the blockage, then heavier ones rolled. A decrepit hand jabbed through, then pushed the debris from its path, then soon more appeared, as if the wall of broken stone was sprouting arms.

The drum rang louder now that holes had been punched through, and Rōnin recognized the plaintive notes of *shō* pipes. He turned his attention back in front, just in time to see shapes rising from the ground, right by the ridge of the crescent. They stood as one, dozens of dead warriors wearing similar helmets, thick armor, and straight swords. Whether by reflex or upon the request of their new master, those guardians of the island moved toward the bridge.

They ran faster than any other of those monsters had so far and would reach it before Musashi or Mikinosuke.

Behind, the rubble cleared at once, raising another cloud of dust from which charged the hundreds of dead from the previous room. The seven could make it to the bridge and maybe fight the guardians off in time. But then what? Rōnin wondered. Could they outrun the untirable dead to the altar and destroy it before the drummer claimed the pyramid? Rōnin did not think so.

"Back!" he shouted, breaking his run at a dead stop.

"What?" Tadatomo asked, though he followed the lone warrior's example.

"We don't need to destroy the altar! We only need to kill *him*," Rōnin said.

"Rōnin's right," Tsuki replied as she picked up an arrow from her bow. "We can end it here."

The seven gathered around Rōnin, forming a line facing the upcoming monsters.

"When he shows himself," Rōnin said, "we charge. Don't think about helping each other. Just kill the bastard."

He saw only resolve on his comrades' faces, even as an army of moving dead poured from the settling dust, swords held high, shrieking and moaning like a herd of enraged beasts.

"Keep your arrows," Rōnin told Tsuki just as she was about to shoot.

The *shō* pipes did not cover the stampede, but the drum resonated through the island with vigor. The drummer stuck a different note than usual and followed suit with a few more. The charging army split under his command, and without slowing down, milled around the seven.

"They're flanking us!" Tadatomo said.

"No," Musashi replied. "They're surrounding us."

The dead ran around the seven, dead eyes still locked on the group, and soon completed a thick circle of macabre monsters. The warriors formed their own circle, puny in comparison. When the first of the dead reached their companions by the bridge, they all turned to face the seven, and the drum rang once more, but this time their master had hit the center of the *kotsuzumi* in the lowest note. Everything became quiet at once. The dead no longer moved or groaned. They just stood there, thirty steps from the seven, like good hounds waiting to be unleashed for the kill.

Rōnin had kept facing the corridor and now could hear the pipes again. The *kotsuzumi* was no longer being used like a war drum; the drummer used it in harmony with the *shō*. Everyone in the small circle turned to face the music. The monsters parted, walking sideways while never losing their focus, and in their stead came the enemy.

A Shintō priest clad in white and wearing a high black hat appeared. He waved an *ōnusa* wand streaming with long bands of white paper, almost ironically warding off evil spirits from their paths. Next came the two pipe players, also priests, the *shō* connected to their lips raised in front of their faces preventing Rōnin from seeing if they felt the terror of their situation. The perfectness of their music led him to believe they had come willingly and knowingly. Behind them, a bright red umbrella bobbed up and down with each of their slow steps. The priest holding it kept the umbrella low enough to cover the face of the drummer walking before him, but the drum was plain for all to see. The character for death painted in blood looked both fresh and old and when the hand of their enemy struck it once more, Rōnin's heart was about to burst with anger.

They stopped walking right after they emerged from the swarm, and from behind them came the shinobi. The tall one with a face painted in black and red lines stood on his master's left, while undistinguishable shinobi spread left and right of the procession.

"Kotarō," Kiba whispered through his teeth.

The pipe players lowered their instruments at the end of a long note and took a step to the side. The wand waver did as much. Only the drummer and the umbrella carrier moved, just a couple of steps. Then the umbrella rose, revealing the face of the man who sought absolute control of Izanagi's curse.

"No," Tadatomo said. "Impossible." The samurai looked as if he'd seen a ghost.

"Who's that?" Mikinosuke asked.

Rōnin had never met this man, but could just as easily guess his identity. And when Musashi spoke, he confirmed what the lone warrior had assumed.

"Hidetada Tokugawa," the swordsman replied. "Brother of Yoshinao, and current shōgun of Japan."

CHAPTER 13
TOKUGAWA CLAN

Tokugawa Ieyasu's bedroom, 1616

"Such is my final request to you, my sons." Ieyasu spoke with pain, every breath sounding like his last.

Yoshinao looked again at the folded piece of paper in his hand. His mind reeled from everything he'd heard in the past few minutes. Never in his young life had he heard his father joke, and never had he seen the man tremble. His death was near, the healers had claimed so, and a quick glance sufficed to know Ieyasu now stood at the doorstep of his demise, but this was not what upset him. He had spoken of fighting corpses and a great curse, of Japan's doom, of a drum, and of Nobunaga Oda.

"Father," Hidetada called, kowtowing toward their illustrious lord, "with all due respect, if what you say is true, we should learn more about it. We could—"

"No!" Ieyasu barked, slapping the tatami mat with more strength than any of them thought he still possessed. "You will leave this curse alone. I am not entrusting my knowledge of it so *that you can claim it. I am trusting you to leave the dead alone, and the living from calling them ever again."*

As he spoke, Tokugawa Ieyasu scanned the room, barely able to lift his head from his pillow. Five sons had made it to his castle on time, and each had received a part of said knowledge. None knew more than the others; just enough to keep their eyes on any sign that the curse would be searched for.

"We will do as you asked, Father," Yoshinao said, kowtowing as well. When he looked up, Hidetada was hiding his snarl from him. His oldest brother was Ieyasu's heir, but Yoshinao was the favorite, and there was little love lost between the two, though Yoshinao never really understood why.

"I have spent my life trying to unite the living," Ieyasu said between ragged breaths. "Now, my sons, you have to make sure the dead do not spoil it."

Ieyasu died in the evening, leaving five sons to mourn him, but none stayed any longer than necessary, for they all knew what kind of danger they faced: each other. Ieyasu had been a most astute man, capable of guessing his enemies' moves and motives, and brilliant enough to lead Japan from war to peace. But he was also a flawed father who overestimated his sons. Yoshinao knew he would never see his brothers again unless one came for his knowledge of the curse.

He looked up at the information on the paper, then burned it.

There were four items, each necessary to claim the curse: a sword, a drum, an altar, and a talisman. None was named in his document, but this was now his own personal knowledge. The others, he guessed, would know of the nature of one item each, but none would know how many others there were. Yoshinao was now the guardian of a heavy secret.

When he arrived at Nagoya, he immediately sent spies to infiltrate his four brothers' domains. Not to find out about their secret, for Yoshinao truly intended to follow his father's instruc-

tions, but to inform him of their health. If one of them died under suspicious terms, he would have to make his move to secure the secrets of the others. He did not once wonder which of them would act first, for in his mind it was painfully clear only Hidetada had the ambition, the guile, and the callousness to kill his own brothers.

He looked just like his brother, but twenty years older, a face adorned with the scars of a man who had spent his life on the battlefield. Hidetada wore a complete set of dark and red armor, topped by the horned helmet they had spotted at Sekigahara. There was no symbol linking him to his clan on his person, but the resemblance with his brother was too strong to leave any doubt, with one big difference—Hidetada's eyes were full of malice where his brother's flashed compassion.

"So this is Onijima," the shōgun said, twisting his head left and right to get a good look at the dome. "I thought it would be bigger." The last he said with a smile that Rōnin would have loved to punch in.

"Hidetada, why?" Tadatomo asked.

The two men were of similar age, and since Tadatomo's father had been Hidetada's father's greatest retainer, they had surely shared many years of proximity in their youth.

"Tadatomo," Hidetada called, stretching his arms as if welcoming an old friend. "I'm glad you're here. Well, not *here* here, but here in Onijima. You're about to witness the greatest moment of Japan's history." The shōgun sounded as if about to burst with enthusiasm. "You just need to ask and I'd be happy to welcome you on this side, you know?"

"You just killed my friends," the samurai spat.

"That was unfortunate," Hidetada replied, shaking his head with feigned sorrow. "Though, to be fair, they killed themselves. Now, now, drop that bow!" he shouted, pointing a mean finger at Tsuki, whose bow was ready to release. "Here me out. There's a way for all of us to leave this place and get what we want."

"Oh, I know what I want," the girl replied, lips trembling with rage.

"You're Tsuki Ikeda, right?" he asked. "Well, Tsuki, it'd be a shame for your clan if I never made it out of here. There's a letter waiting on my desk in Edo, with clear instructions as to what will happen to the Ikeda if I do not return from my pilgrimage. And, of course, there's another with the name Honda on it."

"Bastard," Tadatomo said as the tension of Tsuki's bow lessened.

"Listen," Hidetada went on, dropping his arm and straightening up. "I'm not your enemy here. I have no quarrel with any of you. If you step down right now, whatever my brother promised you, I'll give it to you, and then more. You don't have to fight the inevitable."

"Why are you doing this?" Rōnin asked.

"Right. You," Hidetada said, shaking his finger toward the lone warrior and grinning with curiosity. "Despite my best efforts, I didn't quite catch your name."

"I'm just a rōnin."

"Sure. Well, Rōnin, right now I just want to get there, on top of that pyramid, and gain more power than anyone else has ever had."

"Why?" Tadatomo asked, baffled. "You're the shōgun. You're the most powerful man in the nation. You have everything."

"Japan…" Hidetada replied, shaking his head. "Japan is small. Too small to defend itself."

"What on earth are you talking about?" Rōnin asked.

"We'd been fighting for sixty years," the shōgun said. "And even longer than that, truthfully. Japanese against Japanese, gaining nothing more than what we already had. Such a stupid war."

There was actual sadness in his voice, and this exact feeling had been shared by Rōnin many times over.

"But what allowed it to come to an end?" Hidetada asked.

"Guns," Musashi replied matter of fact.

"Guns," Hidetada agreed. "Guns, cannons, explosives. Those things coming from afar first shifted the balance of power in our nation, then made Japan tremble with red-hot war, and finally allowed peace to settle. Guns, from foreign countries." The last word he said with undisguised hatred. "Foreigners have weapons and ships we can barely understand, and knowledge we've never even dreamt of. One day, they will crush us, enslave us like they did the rest of the world. Unless we crush them first." He tightened his fist and shook it as if the heart of every foreigner rested inside.

"Conquest?" Rōnin asked. "That's your objective?"

"Look," Hidetada replied, going back to his jovial self. "We've tried in Korea, and failed, despite greater numbers and more experience in warfare. My own son believes we should just close the country; prevent it from any foreign intervention. But with that," he went on, pointing toward the altar, "I could conquer any country I step foot on."

"This is madness," Mikinosuke spat.

"This is the future," Hidetada replied. "No matter what my brother told you, you are not saving Japan. I would never harm our nation. I will march the dead across the sea, and spread our influence further than any other man before, and Japan will become the center of a world without war. Think about it. One wave of conquest, using the dead to defeat our enemies, and that's it. They will resist at first, and their dead will fill the ranks of my armies, but then, when their neighbors fall, how many nations will willingly submit? I'm not a monster, I will welcome anyone who submits to me with open arms. Just like I would welcome you and make you all esteemed members of my court. You've all proven your worth."

"If we let you go unopposed?" Rōnin asked.

"And once you've given me the talisman," Hidetada said.

"The talisman? We don't have it."

"Yes you do," the shōgun replied with a wink. "*You* just didn't know you had it."

From the line of warriors, one stepped out. His saffron robes appeared almost red in the warm light of the dome, and his steps were long and quiet. When he reached the shōgun, Zenbō fished something from inside his robe and placed it in Hidetada's open hand.

"Zenbō?" Tsuki asked, her frown of confusion finding its match on all the others' faces.

"I am sorry," the monk replied as he let go of the Samonji's guard.

CHAPTER 14
ZENBO

Nara, Hōzōin temple, 1607

Hōzōin In'ei had strictly and lovingly trained each student in his dōjō to keep his emotions in check and mask them under a veil of silence when they ran too strong. But, after the latest announcement, his dōjō vibrated with indignation. The old man sat at the end of the training ground, his spear lying across in front of him, seemingly unperturbed by the reactions of his hundred students. Zenbō knew this was just a show of self-control. There was no way his beloved master could take the news so easily and casually announce their lives had just been wasted under his care. The samurai standing behind him, a sullen warrior with a dark kimono and the symbol of the Tokugawa clan on his chest, was the reason for In'ei's apparent obedience.

"Shishō!" Okuzōin called. Being In'ei's number-one student for decades, the others had gotten used to the big man raising his voice. Even after his defeat against Musashi Miyamoto, few considered him anything else than a genius with a spear, and he, more than anyone else, would lose from the morning's announcement. His anger was legitimate, though Zenbō's had reached heights he hadn't discovered before. "Surely we can do something about it. Not once have we picked up our spears against the Tokugawa, or any other warlord. The spears of Hōzōin remained peaceful throughout the civil war. It has to count for something?"

The old man raised his hand to ask for silence. At eighty-six years of age, he could no longer address a room full of students if they did not let him.

"I understand your pain, Okuzōin—"

"With all due respect, you don't," Okuzōin said, interrupting the old master in a way that would have earned him a thrashing a few years ago.

"What do you mean by that?" In'ei asked, raising his bushy eyebrows high enough for the first rank of students to understand he would not tolerate another insult.

Cowered by many years of such threats, Okuzōin lowered his head. Zenbō, who sat next to him, would not relent so easily. While still considered a novice, he had spent ten years under In'ei. He had bled from blisters and fought pain, tears, and cramps winter after winter, without once complaining about the hardship of the training. In'ei had called him his best novice and favored him with private lessons. He was the future of the school, they all thought so. It would first be Okuzōin, then him. At least this is how it was supposed to go until the shōgun decided to forbid any school for warrior monks. He'd just lost a future he had barely glimpsed, but already adored.

"He means that you are old, sensei," Zenbō replied, stirring a loud gasp from his comrades. "And don't have much to lose."

In'ei's shoulders rose and his bald, hairless head seemed to bristle like an angry cat.

"Do you think that is what I wanted?" he asked, shaming all his students to silence at last. The samurai by his side stiffened as well but otherwise remained quiet. "Do you think I wanted to *give my life to the spear, just to have it taken away at the last minute? I wanted Hōzōin-ryū to survive me by centuries. I wanted all of you to spread its teaching, and help folks remain safe in their own houses with a staff if that's all they had. But nothing lasts, not even dreams. Let this be a lesson to you all. Japan is now at peace. Martial arts will have to evolve or disappear. There is no other way."*

"But there is!" Zenbō shouted, standing with passion.

"Sit down, Zenbō!" his master shouted back.

"Zenbō," Okuzōin whispered, tugging at the bottom of the young monk's robes to make him stand down.

"No!" Zenbō replied. The word echoed throughout the hall and all kept their eyes lowered. "We are the spears of Hōzōin, warrior monks, and lifelong students of In'ei. This is not how we go." As he spoke, he saw the samurai bringing his left hand by the hilt of his katana. Zenbō knew he was playing with fire, but he also believed in his own skills. Should the samurai attack, even without his spear he would beat him to a pulp. So he turned his back on his master to address his brothers.

"We will show the shōgunate we are not to be messed with. They want our spears? I say let them come get them. We are peaceful monks and will not attack, but should they decide to test us, we will show them we are also warriors."

Some heads rose and nodded. Zenbō saw the passion rekindle in their defeated eyes. He had good brothers among them, ready to fight for the right to pursue the way of the Hōzōin spear. In'ei might have been a tough teacher, but they all loved him. They would have been nothing without him, and it was time to pay back his generosity with the fire of youth.

A little more, Zenbō thought, and his comrade would stand with him.

"Zenbō," In'ei called calmly.

The young warrior monk turned to face his master and saw a flash of metal. Then nothing. With a flick of the wrist, the old master had sealed the fate of his novice.

Zenbō screamed and fell to the side, his hands naturally moving toward his ruined eyes. He squirmed and fought the grasps of his comrades who were trying to help him while blood covered his face.

"You're blind to reality," his old master said. "So I took your eyes. When you understand why I did it, maybe you will forgive me."

Then Zenbō fainted.

He woke up a few days later in a bed. Not his bed, nor any of the temple, just a bed. Someone had paid for his stay at a small hospital in Nara. When he asked who, the healer simply said that it was a samurai wearing the Tokugawa symbol on his chest.

Zenbō stayed there for a year, then left Nara. For the next three, he learned to live without his eyes. Then he relearned everything his teacher had taught him.

One day, during his meditation, Zenbō understood that In'ei had saved all their lives by taking his eyes in front of the samurai. A small price to pay for such a result. He had endangered them all with his passion. In'ei had died shortly after expelling Zenbō, and most students left the ancient capital. He forgave In'ei in his heart and only wished he could properly thank him somehow.

Prayers did not suffice, so he put himself harder in his training. Another five years and Zenbō fought better than he ever had. He traveled throughout Japan, searching for any former students of the Hōzōin dōjō. There would come a time, he thought, when his school would be allowed to resurface, but the few comrades he managed to meet would not consider it. He was alone, frustrated, and losing hope.

Then, one morning, while he traveled through Owari province, a man came to him. Usually, when someone approached Zenbō, it was to hand him some coins or some food in exchange *for a prayer. But this man offered for the monk to sit with him and share some tea.*

"I've heard tell of a monk who walks throughout Japan with hopes to revive a sōhei school of sōjutsu," the man said. He spoke well, in an educated manner full of warmth and humor.

"You have good ears," Zenbō replied as he smelled the steam from the green tea with pleasure. "What else have you heard?"

"I've heard about a contest being organized not so far from here. Do you know of a temple named Jokoji?" Hidetada Tokugawa asked the blind monk.

"Zenbō?" Tsuki asked.

The monk could hear her confusion and feel the effect of his betrayal in their hearts. Unless it was his own heart that filled his chest with shame.

"I am sorry," he said.

He had never meant to hurt them. Ame's and Yūki's deaths were on him, he knew it, but just like his eyes, it was a sacrifice that had to be made for a better future. Generations upon generations of men would receive the teachings of Hōzōin In'ei. Hidetada had been honest with him regarding his plans, but Zenbō cared little about it. The world of men was no longer his, or at least that was what he used to think. Now, he didn't know what he believed in, besides the righteousness of his goal. In'ei would not approve, he was aware of it, but what else was he supposed to do if not give his old teacher's dream a second life?

"Sorry, my ass!" Tadatomo spat. "I knew something was wrong with you from the beginning!"

"It is what you were looking for?" Zenbō asked his benefactor, ignoring his samurai friend.

"That it is," Hidetada replied. "You see," he went on, louder, for the six to hear him this time. "My father spread his knowledge of the curse among five of his sons. I learned about this beautiful drum here, though he didn't know exactly how to use it. It took me years to actually find it, and as you noticed along our journey, I needed a few tries to grasp its use. Gifu, that was a mess, sorry about that. But now, as you can see, I'm doing much better."

To prove his point, he beat the edge of the drum once, and the *kyonshī* took one step forward each.

"I didn't like killing two of my brothers, you have to believe me. One knew that the talisman was a *tsuba*, but did not know of which katana. Not much information if you ask me. But the second knew that the altar was in Onijima and that Onijima could be found in Azuchi. Now, that little piece of shit had already ratted it out to Yoshinao, of all people. I should really have killed him first."

"But Yoshinao didn't know you were behind all of this," Mikinosuke said.

"He knew," Hidetada replied scornfully. "He knew, all right. He just didn't tell you because he hoped you would accomplish your mission before finding it out, thus protecting our name. He was always a brave young boy, my brother, though, if you knew how he came to find out about the Samonji, you would reevaluate your opinion of him."

"He wouldn't be the first," Kiba said. Zenbō felt the words targeting him and sighed.

"Now, now, let's all be nice to Zenbō here," Hidetada said, putting his hand on the monk's shoulder. "My brother used spies, I used one too, it's fair. Zenbō deceived you in the name of his master's memory, that is all. Without him, I would never have heard about the Yoshimoto-Samonji, and, who knows, you might very well have accomplished your mission."

"And saved Japan," Rōnin said.

"I'm saving Japan!" Hidetada shouted in rage. His voice boomed several times across the dome, and his breathing remained agitated for a few seconds.

The scent of rotten wood approached the monk and the shōgun, and a broken voice whispered something in Hidetada's ear.

"Apologies," the shōgun went on. "I'm wasting your time, my time, and their time, though time is all they have now. So I will proceed to the altar, and you will all remain where you are, in the company of the dead and some shinobi. Do not try anything, and all will be well."

Hidetada snapped his fingers right after he finished speaking and the pipe players resumed their plaintive music. The shōgun gently tapped on the monk's wrist to invite him to follow. Even if he had not been invited, Zenbō would have gone with Hidetada rather than facing his comrades' ire.

The shōgun walked straight, meaning the six had to move away to let them pass. He heard small wheels creaking on his back but could not comprehend what they had dragged all the way down.

"Is this really what you want?" Rōnin asked when Zenbō passed next to him.

"Do not intervene," the monk replied.

Someone spat. It landed on his foot, but Zenbō did nothing to remove it. He deserved their hatred. For some reason, he thought it had come from the girl, and it hurt even more.

CHAPTER 15
RONIN

Osaka, 1615

From the ramparts of the Sanada ward, the sun falling into the quiet sea was magnificent. The bottom of the clouds was turning to a mix of orange and purple, and the gulls flew in groups of two or three toward their nests. Nagakatsu took in the beauty of the sight with a long sigh of appreciation.

"It's humbling to think it will look exactly the same tomorrow evening," Nobushige Sanada said. *His lord's little finger touched his, and Nagakatsu let his curl over his lord's.*

"Nothing will look the same tomorrow evening," Nagakatsu replied.

"Maybe not in your eyes," Nobushige said. "But to the world, it will be the same."

"My lord, let me fight with you. I beg you," Nagakatsu asked, *shattering his promise not to break this moment.*

"Nagakatsu, you promised—"

"Please, Nobushige," Nagakatsu went on, *grabbing his lord's hand with love.* "I can't do what you asked. Anything but that."

"You have to," Nobushige replied. "You have to leave tonight so that I can fight tomorrow."

"So that you can die tomorrow," Nagakatsu corrected him.

"Probably," Nobushige replied, his beautiful smirk flashing across his recently washed face. Nobushige would face death in all his glory. The plan laid down by Lord Toyotomi would never succeed. It was a desperate last stand, but what kind of honorable samurai would back out now, after months of resistance?

"But it is my choice to fight," Nobushige went on.

"So is mine," Nagakatsu replied as a flock of gulls passed over their heads.

"I can't—" Nobushige said, tightening his other hand in a fist and pinching his lips. "I can't fight if you're there, Nagakatsu. I will lose my will if I see you by my side. Already I struggle. All I want is to saddle our horses and ride far from this lost battle."

"Why don't we then?" Nagakatsu asked, louder than he should have, maybe.

"You know why," Nobushige replied more discreetly, checking around for any sign they were being listened to by anyone.

Nagakatsu knew why. Honor. It was always a question of honor with Nobushige Sanada. This is why he had fallen in love with him, and why he hated him right now.

"You are young, Nagakatsu, so young," the warlord said as he turned to face his lover. "I would not have you die in the last battle of a dying age."

"I should live without honor so that you can keep yours?" Nagakatsu asked, turning his eyes to steel.

"I would have you live tomorrow," Nobushige answered while he worked on the katana hanging at his waist. He slid it off, reversed it, and pushed it into his lover's belt. "So that you can die with honor for a reason of your own choosing another time. And that is an order." As he said the last, he clasped Nagakatsu's shoulders vehemently.

"My lord," Nagakatsu said as he observed the Sanada katana resting next to his. "I can't."

"I always use a spear anyway," Nobushige joked. He had not removed his hands. Their eyes met, and the rest of the conversation happened in them. Nagakatsu assured his lord that he would never love another, and Nobushige thanked him for their time together. He said that the young warrior had been the last and most beautiful note of a well-lived life.

Nagakatsu felt the tears swell in his eyes, and when he understood his lord struggled just as much, his resistance failed him. He started crying, shaming himself on the ramparts, in full view of all those hard warriors he had fought with for the past year. But Nobushige did not let him. He pulled the young man against his chest and embraced him with care. Nobushige kissed his friend and lover on the head, and Nagakatsu felt his lord's tears dropping on his back.

"My lord," he said, his voice muffled by Nobushige's armor. "The others will see us."

"What others?" Nobushige asked. "It's just you and me here."

Rōnin observed Hidetada Tokugawa forgetting about them and advancing toward the pyramid, and he realized something. The current shōgun had fought at Osaka, and if he himself had taken part in this last battle, there was a chance today's situation could have been avoided. It suddenly became his responsibility to end Hidetada's life.

A few days ago, when standing at the bottom of Jokoji Mountain, he had been asked to write his wish on the back of an *ema* plaque. Rōnin had only one wish in his heart, and it was now granted.

"A reason to die with honor," he whispered to himself.

"What?" Tadatomo asked.

"Nothing," Rōnin replied.

Hidetada was walking over the bridge, his priests ahead of him. Zenbō followed right behind the umbrella, then this Kotarō Fūma who seemed to take all of Kiba's attention. Half of the shinobi had vanished within the swarm of dead surrounding them, but the others followed their leaders. The last two were even dragging a huge trunk of hardwood on wheels. Rōnin wondered what it could be, but Hidetada had a twisted mind, and there was no way of knowing what his sick brain had judged good to bring to Onijima.

"In a few seconds," Rōnin said, "I'm going after the shōgun. If any of you wishes to accept his offer, get on your knees, maybe it will be enough."

"I thought you'd never make up your mind," Tadatomo replied as he readjusted his helmet's chin strap.

"Who's with me?" Rōnin asked.

He saw resolve in his friends' eyes, resolve and confidence. Except Musashi. *His* eyes reflected something else entirely.

CHAPTER 16
MIYAMOTO MUSASHI

Musashi could hear the blood pumping on the sides of his head, fast and strong. He could also hear his own breath passing through his nose. Hidetada, the Wind Demon, and the traitor were on the other side of the bridge. The last shinobi dropped the box they had been dragging and raised it up. It would make for a poor blockage. Closer to them, the dead looked bored. Each corpse was facing them, holding rusted swords if they still had arms, though a majority seemed to be armed with nothing better than empty fingers and old teeth. Some shinobi would be among them, keeping to the shadows for now.

They would all fall.

"Musashi?" Rōnin asked, stepping into his field of vision. The lone warrior had been speaking, but Musashi heard none of it. "Musashi? Are you with us?"

Musashi looked at his student. No, not his student. His son. He had long stopped thinking of Mikinosuke as a student. Yet he had one last lesson to teach him.

"Musashi-sensei?" the boy asked. He looked anxious.

Anxious for his teacher. How low had he fallen to have a teenage boy worry for him?

"Rōnin," the swordsman finally replied. His mind was clear. Clearer than it had been for years. "You're mistaken. I'm not with you, you're with me."

"Sensei?"

"A few days ago," Musashi explained as he looked at Kiba, "a friend told me anger was stronger than fear. An angry man cannot be afraid. Well, I am furious."

His son was worried about him, a friend had lost her sister, two companions had died for nothing, and a traitor was walking away. This could not go on. Musashi raged within. A rage like he had never felt in his life. His blood boiled, any drop of fear evaporated from his body, and Musashi remembered his place in the world. It was time to remind the world as well.

"You follow me," he said. "I will get us to the bridge. Nothing will stand in my way. Trust me."

Kiba nodded. Musashi had never seen him smirk as such before.

"Sensei, are you sure?" Mikinosuke asked.

"This is my final lesson to you, Mikinosuke. You think you've mastered my art? Let me show you how far you have yet to climb, boy."

"Yes, sir!" Mikinosuke replied as he bowed respectfully.

Musashi dropped his hands on the hilt of his two swords. It felt like the reunion of lovers who had not shared an embrace in ages. His fingers curled around them and he closed his eyes.

"Tell us when, Miyamoto-dono," Rōnin said.

He focused all his burning anger into a ball, which he pushed down his chest. It vibrated with ire. Musashi felt hot. He clenched his fingers a couple of times and opened his eyes. The path ahead was filled with *kyonshī*, but he pictured it empty.

With passion, Musashi Miyamoto drew his swords, the scrap echoed from Mikinosuke's scabbards, and the master roared.

None of the dead reacted until Musashi beheaded two of them at the same time, but as soon as the heads touched the ground, all hell broke loose.

The master shoved himself between the two falling corpses, ignoring the grunts, the rattle, and the drum calling for the enemies to answer back. He thrust his wakizashi through the next monster's chest, where the heart would have been, and shoved it to the side to block the *kyonshī* on the left. They both fell, and one of his friends would take care of them; only forward mattered to Musashi. One of those monsters tried to stab him. Musashi took a step forward and parried the blade, then broke his opponent's knee with a low kick, and smashed the monster's face with the guard of his katana in the next heartbeat. Pieces of bones accompanied his punch and showered the next body standing between Musashi and the bridge.

He was vaguely aware of the sound of battle at his back. His friends were all capable warriors, and he trusted them. Besides, the enemy would only have eyes for him.

He screamed with rage and with pleasure, splitting a *kyonshī*'s face in half with a flick of the wrist, then grabbed the inert body and used it as a shield to block an expert cut from a once great warrior. Not great enough though. Musashi stabbed through his shield of bones and felt the blade punch through his opponent's spine, then both slid off his blade.

One more step, one more body. Then another, and another. A cut, a thrust, a kick, another cut, another one bit the dust. Musashi twisted on his hips to avoid a set of brown teeth, then elbowed the moving corpses toward Mikinosuke's blade. The master exchanged a proud glance with his student as the boy cleaved the monster's neck. Just a glance, then back to it.

Musashi's roar hurt his throat, and the sound changed. It was no longer rage; it was delight. The master bellowed and cheered as his swords sang. He was back.

Something moved in the corners of his eyes, faster than the dead. Musashi shouldered a *kyonshī* in the direction of the flash, and the shinobi stepped out of his cover. The swordsman stabbed low and caught the shinobi in the thigh. Blood. How long since he had made a man bleed? He tore through the leg with a vicious cut, splashing red all over his victim as the man screamed. Musashi meant to end the shinobi's torment, but one of them got into his blind spot and slashed his straight blade toward the master's wrist. His bestial instinct kicked in. Musashi let go of his wakizashi and the enemy's blade passed through nothing but air. Then he grabbed the falling blade before it touched the ground and jabbed it right through the gasping shinobi's mouth.

An arrow buzzed past his cheek and ended in the neck of a monster about to bite his arm off. It did not stop the undead, but warned Musashi in time. He grabbed the sprouting arrow and prevented the monster from coming any closer. Pulling on the missile, Musashi tripped the dead warrior, who then fell face-first on the island's floor. Kiba appeared out of nowhere and landed on the *kyonshī*'s neck. The head bounced off under the impact and lost itself somewhere in the swarm.

A blade grazed his cheek, but Musashi felt no pain. His trance only deepened when the heat of his blood ran down his face. The master applied himself to his dance of swords, using them both in one movement, then one by one, creating a rhythm that neither the living nor the dead could follow. They fell from his path like wheat to the sickle.

The next he faced wore a once beautiful helmet and stood motionless until Musashi came into his reach. He recognized one of those guardians of the bridge and acknowledged the *kyonshī*'s skills when it lunged in as perfect a lunge as Musashi had experienced. The master crouched under the straight blade and bumped it up with his shoulder right before he rammed his katana into the guardian's chest. The monster moaned, then Musashi shoved him to the side with strength. It fell into the abyss bordering the bridge. He had made it.

A new surge of energy flowed through his veins, and Musashi roared once more as he twisted on his heels. Another guardian came at him with a low cut. Musashi blocked it with his wakizashi, but with a fraction of a second of delay. The rusted sword grazed his waist before the short sword stopped it. It rekindled his rage, and Musashi kicked the guardian away from their path.

"Come on!" he shouted, both for his friends to get on the bridge and for the enemy to try harder.

Tadatomo passed him by first, then followed Tsuki.

"Did you see that?" the master asked as his student walked by him.

"No," Mikinosuke replied with glee. "You were too fast."

"Good lad," Musashi replied. "Now go do what I taught you."

"Yes, sensei!" Mikinosuke shouted as he ran through the bridge.

Kiba nodded at him with respect but said nothing. No words needed between masters.

Rōnin unleashed his sword once behind himself to

create some space, then joined Musashi and put himself next to the master. The bridge was barely wide enough for two men, and would not allow for much movement, so Musashi elbowed the lone warrior back.

"You sure?" Rōnin asked.

"None of them will pass," Musashi said as he focused on his ball of anger. It was intact, vibrating, and feeding him with the will to shatter his opponents. "Take care of my boy for me."

"Only until you join us," Rōnin replied before leaving the master to his task.

Musashi shook the slime and blood from his blades, breathed out once, and roared his challenge at those hundreds of warriors foolish enough to think they could take him down.

CHAPTER 17
HONDA TADATOMO

Jokoji, a few days before

"Dear brother, I apologize for writing these words instead of speaking them. I have tried to find the courage to face you, but I'm a coward. Even sober, my heart is not strong enough to ask for your forgiveness. I don't deserve it. Everything our father and you have fought to build, all the honor attached to the name Honda, I have lost it in a bottle of sake. I want you to know that not one day has passed without me regretting my actions and trying to make amends. I have searched for our father's body north and south, east and west, but there too I failed. Even if I found him, he would be nothing but bones and dirt by now, and my shame is only growing stronger at the thought. But I think I've found a way to find him, or at least his spear, maybe. And I swear that I will not come back home without Tonbokiri. If you never see me again, let these be my final words to you and our family. It was my greatest honor to be born the son of Tadakatsu Honda and to call you my brother. Tadatomo Honda."

Tadatomo ran like the wind, trusting his back to the greatest swordsman of Japan. Their enemy was forward, climbing the stairs to the altar. The identity of the drummer could have shaken him to the core, but Tadatomo's core was already upside down. He had just lost the two most beautiful souls that ever lived, and no matter what the shōgun had said or planned, he would not live under the same sun as their murderer.

As if hearing his thoughts, Hidetada turned to look in his direction. He was too far away to be sure of it, but Tadatomo thought the shōgun stared at him directly and grinned. Hidetada's hand hit the drum, but the sound took a second to reverberate all the way to them. Then the samurai heard a bear-like bellow from right in front of him.

The box left by the shinobi at the end of the bridge shook, then burst open, its planks flying in all directions. In their stead stood a massive *kyonshī*, bigger than any they had faced so far. Its armor was clean, dark, and just as Tadatomo remembered it. The *kyonshī* wore a helmet mounted with great, waving deer antlers, and strapped around the right shoulder hung a series of beads thick as a child's fist. In his hand he held a spear as tall as he was, nearly half of it being a leafy, straight blade. The legend said that a dragonfly landing on its edge would be immediately cut in half, and Tadatomo knew firsthand of its sharpness. His run turned to a walk, then to a stop.

"Tadatomo?" Tsuki asked.

"So that's where you've been," the samurai said, speaking to his father.

Tadakatsu Honda, the greatest samurai of his time, stood like a mountain at the end of the bridge, trapping the six between a swarm of dead and an undefeated warrior. Tadakatsu had been preserved with care. His skin was still intact, though nothing could hide the paleness of his face or the darkness under his eyes. He stood like Tadatomo remembered him, unwavering, strong, and reliable. The general would not attack if they did not go any further, but they had to.

"Move, Tadatomo," Kiba said as he reached them. "I'll take care of him."

"You won't," the samurai replied. "He would shred you to pieces. No offense."

Tsuki held her bow at the ready, but Tadatomo gently pushed her arm down. This was his responsibility, his path to honor.

"I know him better than anyone," he said. "And if anyone has a chance against the mighty Tadakatsu Honda, it's his son."

"Honda-san," Tsuki called, not expecting an answer.

Tadatomo took a couple of steps and bowed with respect and love toward his father. Then he charged.

The *kyonshī* raised his spear in response and thrust it with conviction. His father's strength had not vanished, Tadatomo thought as he crouched under the blade, feeling its wind on his back. He widened his arms and grabbed the dead by the waist. Using all the strength in his legs, and firing himself up with a shout, Tadatomo pushed his father backward the way a sumo would. The *kyonshī* refused to lift his feet, so Tadatomo had to drag him. He was a heavy beast, just as he had been in life, but back they went.

Tadakatsu elbowed his son in the back with such strength that Tadatomo almost fell to his knees. But he hung on. This was nothing compared to Ame's and Yūki's suffering. He saw the bridge end right under his feet and pushed harder. The first thing he needed was to take the *kyonshī* from the others' path.

He felt the hand of his father grabbing him by the back of his belt, and a second later his feet left the ground as he was tossed like a plaything. Tadatomo landed on his belly a few steps from his father, who was already turning his attention back to the bridge. Even dead, Tadakatsu did not consider his son worthy of his attention.

"No!" Tadatomo shouted when he saw Kiba about to engage. "He's mine!"

The massive corpse resumed his stance and did not even bother defending himself when Tadatomo grabbed him from behind. He planted his feet, squeezed his father until his arms bulged, and roared to make the veins along his neck pop. The *kyonshī* finally turned its head toward his son, but already his body was rising. Shouting to the depth of his lungs, Tadatomo lifted his father, twisted on his hips, and slammed the great samurai on its face.

"Go!" he shouted to his friends. He only realized then that he had bitten his tongue when he'd been tossed, and blood poured out of his mouth. His four comrades left without a word. This was his fight.

Tadakatsu stood back up, his armor rattling with each of his movements. He did not urge himself; never had. The man had been undefeatable in life, and nothing, not even the sight of his son drawing his katana on him, would make him react in death.

"For the record," Tadatomo said as he adopted his stance, blade held close to his cheek, "I've been sober for eight years."

The monster lowered his spear, aiming it at his son's

belly, and thrust. Tadatomo slammed it down with his blade, using more strength than he would have with any other spearman. Tonbokiri jammed itself into the rock. While the monster pulled on it, Tadatomo reversed his grip and aimed for his father's face, but Tadakatsu simply weaved his torso and let the blade miss. The son pressed on the attack, knowing he would have no other chance to fight the *kyonshī* weaponless. His cuts were meticulous. He could even hear the voice of his father booming in his mind, agreeing with his attacks, but each missed. Tadatomo feinted and changed the direction of his sword, aiming for the neck rather than the chest. He made it. Or so he thought.

Tadakatsu raised his hand and caught the blade halfway to its neck. A living man would never have tried something so dangerous or so painful, but the dead felt neither fear nor pain.

"Shit," Tadatomo said just before his father pulled on the katana and crushed his helmeted head into his son's.

The pain of his nose snapping almost made him faint, but the sound of Tonbokiri breaking from the ground brought him back to the now. By desperation more than skill, Tadatomo rolled on his shoulder to avoid the next thrust and found his footing after a series of small, unbalanced steps. He turned to face his foe, but his father was already on him.

The *kyonshī* slammed the pole of his spear into his son, who just had enough time to raise his arms in defense. Despite the quality of his armor, the bone of his left arm broke under the impact, making him forget the pain of his nose with another, stronger one.

Tadakatsu shoved his knee into Tadatomo's ribs, and there too he heard a crack. Then the monster aimed for his son's throat with his teeth, but the samurai managed to punch him in the chin with his sword's guard. Tadakatsu stepped backward under the impact but looked as unhurt as ever. As he searched for his breath, Tadatomo saw all the way behind his father, on the bridge, Musashi Miyamoto milling his two swords with skill, killing an enemy for each step back they forced on him.

If the coward can fight, surely the drunkard can prevail, he told himself with a chuckle of desperation.

Tadatomo walked around his father, keeping enough distance to see the spear coming. His left arm was useless and painful. Each breath either hurt his nose or his ribs. For a second he told himself a sip of sake would feel amazingly good at this very moment, but the thought passed. Dying sober, he thought, was a victory.

With the precipice on his back, he took his stance again. Why his father had waited while he got ready, Tadatomo could not know. Maybe a trace of the man still existed behind those dead, white eyes, and if anyone could resist the curse of Izanagi, even a little, it was Tadakatsu Honda. The samurai was proud of his father and hoped that if a spark of his soul still inhabited this rotting body, he too was proud of him.

"Whenever you want, *chichi-ue*," Tadatomo said.

Tadakatsu charged with a loud grunt, spear locked under his armpit to skewer his son. Tadatomo rolled under the spear, twisted on his feet as his father turned around, and cut upward and as widely as he could. The blade passed through both his father's arms as he thrust again and splattered the beautiful armor with slime. Tadakatsu lost his balance with his arms and waved his juicing stumps helplessly. Using the tip of his blade, and the last drop of strength in his weak arm, Tadatomo pushed the husk of his father. The dead samurai grunted as he fell backward, into the abyss, and grunted for a long time before his voice could no longer be heard.

Tadatomo smiled as he fell to his knees. Blood was drooling from his mouth, he could no longer hold his katana, and while he felt his legs, they refused to obey him. The spear deeply embedded into his abdomen prevented him from breathing as he wanted. Tadakatsu had not left this world a defeated man. His last thrust had hit true, and his last victim would be his own son.

The samurai coughed blood. His vision darkened, but he could still see Musashi fighting like a tiger on the bridge.

Tadatomo knew he was dying, and all he could think of was making sure he wouldn't become a threat to his companions. But his legs refused to push him toward the precipice.

His hands moved to the pole of the spear. Maybe, if he pulled it out, he thought, he might be able to drag himself to the precipice and join his father.

"Ah," he scoffed when he grabbed the spear tighter. "I finally got my hands on that fucking spear."

CHAPTER 18
KIBA

Hidetada was already reaching the top of the pyramid with his four priests and the blind monk. By himself, Kiba might have reached them before it happened. But Kiba wasn't alone. He had enemies standing in between, a demon to slay, and companions by his side, and those companions would be needed in the ordeal to come. He counted ten shinobi, plus the Wind Demon. They waited on the second flight of stairs, leaving the first to wind them down before the fight even began.

"Listen," Kiba said as they approached the pyramid, "I have a plan to deal with the Fūma shinobi."

As the old shinobi explained his plan, the *shō* pipes stopped playing. The sudden halt to a sound that had accompanied their progress since before the bridge was akin to ears popping while recovering from a cold. Kiba could hear his thoughts better, but he also knew it meant whatever ritual was necessary to claim the curse had started.

"Are you sure?" Rōnin asked when they reached the

bottom of the structure. He was searching for his breath, Kiba noticed. They all were.

The shinobi nodded to himself, knowing his plan was the only proper way to get through those Fūma warriors. They slowed down midway through the first flight of stairs, climbing the last ten to a walk. There was a world of difference between speed and haste, one of his long-dead teachers used to say. So Kiba and his companions regained their breath as they came into view of the Fūma clan.

Kotarō stood arms crossed on top of the second flight of stairs, looking down at his enemies, while his last ten men had spread unevenly along the steps. Kiba walked slightly in front of the three others and stopped before stepping on the first step.

"You're too late, old man!" Kotarō said as he uncrossed his arms and spread them, his claws making his reach unnaturally long. "The ritual has begun, and soon, *our* patron will rule the dead."

"What do you have to gain from it?" Rōnin asked. His breath was already getting back under his control.

"Gold! Of course!" The Wind Demon scoffed. "Lots of it, and the trust of the most powerful man in the world." His coarse voice irritated Kiba's ears. He so wanted to gut him. A scream came from the top, short and high-pitched.

"Hidetada asked me to give you a last chance to surrender," the Wind Demon went on. "This is not my way, but I will obey his command. Not for you though," he said, pointing his right claw at Kiba. "You must die by my hand, old man. For too long the Iga, the Kōga, and all the other *great* clans have laughed at us Fūma. But look where your precious rules got you. I will put an end to your name for good."

Kiba did not reply to the taunt. Kotarō was right, the Iga

had had nothing but disdain for the Fūma. Ninjutsu was an art built for war, not for profit, and without a proper code, shinobi were no better than mercenaries. The Wind Demon had built himself a fearsome reputation, but he'd been wrong about many other things, and it was time to teach him a lesson.

"What say you, Kiba? Willing to sacrifice yourself for your friends? No? Can't find your words, you coward?" the demon asked, grinning his pointed teeth in a most malevolent smile.

If he could have, Kiba would have replied that he was more than willing to give his life if it meant his friends' safety, but that he believed they would never accept this deal. *They* had honor beyond their years, and still more fight in their hearts.

He would also tell the Fūma shinobi that strength does not mean the absence of flaws, and *they* were full of them. After Sekigahara, during his delirium, as he fought the poison in his body, Kiba found the greatest weakness of his enemies. He could have kicked himself for not realizing sooner. To a trained shinobi with decades of experience, this should have been obvious. Worse still, they seemed unaware of it.

As a farewell to the Fūma, he would teach them.

The old shinobi made a cross with his fingers and closed his eyes. Then he moved his fingers to a different sign and started reciting the nine cuts of the *Kuji-kiri* in his mind, changing hand signs with each syllable.

Rin, pyō, tō, sha.

"Come on, Iga," Kotarō called as a second scream echoed from above. "This is the end of the line for you. No need to pretend anymore."

Kiba held the first two fingers of his right hand inside his left. Pretense, he wanted to tell the demon, was the essence of Ninjutsu, if it served a purpose.

Kai, jin, retsu.

"Have it your way," Kotarō said as he raised his hands, ordering his men to move. They leaped toward the old Iga shinobi without a sound.

Zai, zen!

Kiba opened his eyes right as his fingers uncrossed.

Kotarō had thought him a fool, but had missed the flint stones hidden behind the fingers. He had thought the old man a coward for his lack of words, but silence had its reasons. Silence is the greatest weapon of the shinobi, the Iga used to say. In this case, though, Kiba's muteness did not come from a profound respect for his way, but simply because one cannot speak with a mouth full of flammable oil.

He spat the oil right as the flint stone created a spark, and a tongue of fire bloomed in a loud *whoosh*. The fire enveloped the ten Fūma and peeled a thick burst of shrieks from them. No drugs could negate the pain of the burning flesh, nor remove the innate fear of fire. They fell like flies, their gleaming purple garments melting on their skin. Kiba did not let up on his fire-breathing technique until the last drop dried from his mouth.

"When the fire dies out," Kiba had told the others, *"rush up the pyramid. Do not mind any of them, they're mine."*

Rōnin, Mikinosuke, and Tsuki dashed behind the curtain of fire and ran through the ranks of squirming shinobi. Kiba only gave himself enough time to fill his lungs again and went after them.

The three went straight ahead, even as Kotarō removed his burning cloak and spotted them. He had been too far, but Kiba had not thought the Wind Demon would be taken down so easily, anyway.

Fuming with rage, Kotarō leaped toward the three, claws extended behind him like wings. Tsuki was the closest to him, and the Fūma leader had his sight on her. The girl did not even acknowledge him, her faith in the old shinobi making her blind to the threat.

Pushing any doubt from his mind, Kiba threw the weighted end of his *kusarigama* toward his enemy. It coiled around the left claw and, infusing energy into his old muscles, he pulled on the chain with a shout that would have earned him a thrashing in his training years. Kotarō, like a prized fish at the end of a hook, was taken by the force of the pull, and his massive body flew down the pyramid, back to the first platform. He crashed into the hard ground. Even the Wind Demon would not come out of it unscathed.

Looking over his shoulder, Kiba saw his friends running toward the top, as they had promised they would, just as a third scream echoed from the altar.

Focus! he told himself, returning his attention to his target.

Kotarō was on his back, unmoving. It was time to end his own curse and bathe in the demon's blood. The old man jumped from the second floor, aiming to land by the side of his victim. But Kotarō had other plans. The Wind Demon shook himself up, standing with the sole strength of his abdomen in the blink of an eye, and pulled on the chain coiled around his claws before Kiba could let go of his sickle.

This time it was the old man's turn to be reeled by his opponent, but rather than let him simply fall, Kotarō raised his other hand to impale the old man. Kiba meant to twist from the deadly claw, and maybe in his youth he might have completely avoided it, but age is kind to no one, and the sharp blades tore through his skin and grated against his ribs. A shallow wound, but against the Wind Demon, each scratch was a death sentence.

Kotarō pushed on the attack, shouting in fury as he cut through the air with his claws. Kiba stepped back with each breath, twirling his chain to shield himself, though more often than not, the *kusarigama* did little more than deviate the claws. Kotarō's blades sliced noisily, missing the old man by less than a breath. Any missed step would be Kiba's last. He tried to regain control, but the demon would not let him. Kiba barely touched the ground, jumped back, then twisted, gaining nothing more than a heartbeat of life with each step. And still, Kotarō charged.

The claws found his left wrist, his left eye, and his right shoulder, claiming blood with each successful cut. Kiba was out of breath and out of energy. If only he'd been a few years younger, he might have changed the course of the fight. Kotarō was a beast, but youth was his advantage here. The old man tried his best, using all the tricks a hard life alone taught him. He back-flipped and pirouetted at the same time, letting his chain create a barrier between him and the demon, but as soon as he landed on his feet, Kotarō was there, and his hand found the old shinobi's throat.

"Got you," the demon said as he lifted a breathless Kiba. "I will enjoy watching you die, old man."

He pulled his other hand, aiming his long claws at Kiba's remaining eye. The Iga shinobi challenged Kotarō's stare, fighting his desire to check the upper floor in the second preceding his death.

"*How many arrows do you have left?*" he had asked the girl.

"*Two,*" she sadly replied.

"I'd like you to use one for me," Kiba had asked.

The shot came right as Kotarō's attention was fully on his victim. People claimed he enjoyed killing more than anything, and Kiba counted on it. He had hoped to lure the moth with an unavoidable flame, but Kotarō was nothing if not a well-trained shinobi, and years of hard-gained reflexes moved his hand to catch the arrow before it could do any harm.

Reflexes, the Iga elders used to say, are a double-edged sword, and Kotarō learned his lesson in a most painful way.

Kiba flicked his sickle upward when the Wind Demon caught the arrow and left himself wide open. It sliced through muscles and bones, right before the elbow. Kotarō let go of the old shinobi as he shrieked and went to grab his severed arm. Drugs also did not work on the pain of losing a limb, or two. Kiba cut through the demon's second arm, then kicked him in the chest to send him crashing against the inclined wall of the pyramid.

"Kiba?" Tsuki called from the second floor over the pitiful shriek of the Wind Demon dropping on his ass, the blood loss pumping his energy by the heartbeat.

"I'm all right," the shinobi replied. "Go help the others, I'll be right there. You did good, lass."

"Be quick about it," she said as she left the old shinobi to his ordeal.

Kotarō looked up with dying eyes at his killer, a thousand regrets flashing in them. The paint on his face hid how far gone he already was, but Kiba would rather be sure. He stabbed the tip of his sickle into the Wind Demon's heart as he crouched to his level and left his weapon there. Kotarō already no longer felt pain.

Kiba dropped his hand under one of the severed arms and received the blood as pilgrims received the blessed water of a temple. He passed his hand over his face, leaving four red imprints, and feeling like his life's goal had been achieved at last. It had cost him forty years and an eye, but finally, Nobunaga Oda's curse had been washed in the blood of a demon.

The old man sighed in relief. Kotarō was still alive, and would be a little while longer, or until Kiba removed the sickle from his chest.

"Shinobi," Kiba said as he looked into the demon's eyes, "do not blabber before they kill their targets. We only do it after. Let this be your lesson." He pushed on the sickle as he spoke, pulling a grunt of pain from his victim. "And shinobi do not wear flammable garments."

With that, he pulled on the sickle and let blood escape Kotarō's rotten heart in gushes. His head dropped to the side, and the Wind Demon breathed his last.

Kiba felt his world spin. He backed himself against the wall, next to the departed Fūma leader, and sat down. His vision darkened and his mind buzzed. If not for the pain of his ruined eye, he would have passed out, but it was only a question of time now.

Kotarō smelled even worse in death, and looked uglier still, but Kiba had to admit he had been a formidable opponent. In his last moments of consciousness, he put his hands on the sides of the demon's head as one would a lover, and twisted his neck the other way around.

One can never be too prudent, he told himself.

Then, just as his eyes closed, Kiba heard the drum and chuckled.

CHAPTER 19
RONIN

"Remember," Rōnin said as they climbed the last flight of stairs, "no matter what we find there, we can be sure of one thing. Zenbō will stand in our path."

"Not for long," the boy replied with confidence.

"We fight him together," Rōnin said. He meant to warn the boy against the monk. There was something utterly dangerous about him. His skills were unmatched, maybe even by Musashi, but even more, his unique capabilities made him unpredictable. Rōnin had never fought a man like Zenbō, while the monk had defeated many like them. But time was missing, and they reached the top of the pyramid.

Zenbō was there, standing sideways next to his master, behind a round table of marble lined with silver veins. The altar seemed to shine in the dimmed light of Onijima, except where blood gleamed in a dark red, streaming from four severed heads. Hidetada was dropping the last at an equal distance from the others when the two swordsmen found them. The shōgun looked like a child caught stealing candies in his parents' cabinet, and let go of his priest's hair, then dropped his red hands on his hips. The fresh blood from the fourth head dropped along the carved lines of the table and mixed with that of his colleagues at the center, filling an intricate maze engraved in the stone. Though he could only catch a glimpse of it, Rōnin recognized the talisman at the center of the maze, its holes vanishing with the arrival of the life juice.

Hidetada striking the drum dropped against his hip caught the lone warrior's attention, as intended.

"Two of you left," the shōgun said, nodding. "Impressive."

"Three," Zenbō said just as Tsuki appeared from the stairs.

She nodded at Rōnin, letting him know Kiba had prevailed. In her hands, nocked against her bowstring, the girl got her last arrow ready.

"Did they know what was going to happen to them?" Rōnin asked, snarling at the four heads.

"Did they know?" Hidetada scoffed. "Of course, they knew. They told me about the ritual. Their only regret, they said, was not to be able to come back. Can you believe it?"

"No, I cannot," Rōnin replied.

"Rōnin, Rōnin, Rōnin," Hidetada went on as he casually dropped the drum upside down on the altar and leaned on it. "My offer still stands, you know."

"We piss on your offer," Mikinosuke spat.

"Such a foul mouth at such a young age," Hidetada replied, an exaggerated offended look passing over his face. "Did you speak to your mentor like this? Or, *used to,* I should say."

"Mikinosuke, don't look," Rōnin said, but too late. The boy checked over his shoulder, just as Rōnin had a few seconds before, to see the bridge overrun by the dead.

"You bastard," the boy spat, his voice cracking and tears swelling into his young eyes full of fury.

"I told you not to move," Hidetada replied, his anger resurfacing. "And I'm asking you again. Stay away from my path, or be crushed."

"Tsuki," Rōnin whispered, "when you get a clear shot, take it."

The archer nodded, but the monk had heard it too. Zenbō walked around the table and put himself between the three and the shōgun.

"You sure of this?" Rōnin asked the blind monk.

"Who has eaten the poison might as well swallow the plate," Zenbō replied. His left foot swiped the floor and kicked the butt end of his spear, making it twirl in his hand so that he could take his stance.

"So be it," the lone warrior replied. "Mikinosuke?"

"I'm with you, Rōnin."

Rōnin stepped up first, ran, then leaped into the monk's reach. If he got past the crescent spearhead, Zenbō would be defenseless, so he focused everything he had on the next step and pushed on his ankles to breach the distance before the monk could react.

Zenbō crushed his plan with a flick of the wrists. The pole made a small circle and slammed into Rōnin's face, right when he thought he had avoided it.

Mikinosuke rushed by his side in time to parry the spear coming toward Rōnin's ribs and pressed the attack. Zenbō took a series of steps on the side, avoiding the boy's blades by a hair. Mikinosuke was brutal in his technique, but accurate. He used moves his master had used to get them over the bridge, his blows weaker but sharper than Musashi's. Yet Zenbō guessed them all.

The monk stopped running and held his spear vertically to block both swords at once. They bounced against the pole, and Mikinosuke took an involuntary step back. Zenbō used his spear as a pole and kicked the boy right in the chest, sending him on his back. Mikinosuke coughed hard and the spear already darted toward his face. Rōnin did not let it.

Mae!

He pushed the blade out of its scabbard with the intention of cutting through the spear pole, but again Zenbō saw it coming. He readjusted his thrust and tapped on the katana's pommel before it came out entirely, sending it back into its scabbard. The monk then meant to slam the butt of his spear into Rōnin's face again, but this time the warrior was ready. He bobbed under the pole, letting it pass harmlessly over his head, then stepped forward.

One step to the right, then the sword left its *saya*. One more step, the blade shot up, aiming at the monk's elbow. Rōnin was certain of his timing but felt no resistance. The monk was flipping through the air and landed nimbly at the edge of the altar, dominating the field of battle with his height.

"You can't defeat me," he said, almost apologetically. "Your battōjutsu doesn't work against me, and I've seen your master fight with my own eyes, Mikinosuke. Even if the girl was to use her last arrow, you would not prevail. Stand down."

"We won't know if we don't try," the boy said as he got back on his feet.

Zenbō jumped down and dashed to them this time. He put himself right between the two swordsmen and punched Rōnin in the nose while kicking the boy in the chest again. Mikinosuke rolled backward and up in one fluid movement, then ran. Except that he didn't run toward the monk this time, but at the shōgun.

"Zenbō!" Hidetada called in despair, his hands seemingly incapable of leaving the sides of the drum.

The monk understood what was happening and reversed his grip on the spear. Rōnin grabbed the back of it before the monk could throw it and tightened his grip until his fingers hurt.

Zenbō did not hesitate for a second. His elbow shot backward and damaged the lone warrior's nose even more, and, as Rōnin's eyes blinked, he punched him in the ribs with two curled fingers, forcing his hand to open.

"Mikinosuke!" Tsuki shouted as the spear flew from the monk's grasp.

Rōnin opened his eyes at the exact moment the spear ended its course in the boy's back, right under the left shoulder. Mikinosuke sprang forward with the strength of the blow. His swords fell ahead and bounced against the feet of the altar.

The lone warrior unsheathed his sword and aimed at the back of Zenbō's neck, but the monk simply rolled on his shoulder and leaped toward the spear jutting from the boy's back. Mikinosuke was still alive, but his moaning left no doubt about the gravity of his wound.

"Don't move!" Zenbō shouted, keeping Rōnin in his spot as his hand curled around the pole of his spear. He put his foot on the boy's shoulder and pulled the spear out. There was only a little blood, but the boy screamed. The monk grabbed him by the collar and forced him up. Using him as a shield, Zenbō stepped away from the altar.

"Now, back," he said.

Rōnin obeyed, taking one step back for each of Zenbō's forward. The boy was quickly paling, and the monk had to carry him more than anything else. When Rōnin walked back all the way to the archer, he saw with alarm that the dead were almost at the bottom of the pyramid. Ahead, Hidetada was grinning victoriously. Almost all the blood on the altar had gone, absorbed by the skin of the drum.

"If he doesn't move too much," Zenbō said as he pushed the boy toward the archer, "he won't die."

Tsuki grabbed Mikinosuke before he collapsed and accompanied him gently to the ground. He cried tears of frustration when she let him go. Rōnin could understand the boy. So many had died to get them here, and they were failing.

Rōnin breathed out and straightened up. His blade went back home, and he took a serious step forward.

"Rōnin," Zenbō said, tilting his head, "don't make me do this. I don't want to kill any of you."

"Sorry," the lone warrior replied as he lifted his right hand by his belt.

Zenbō and Rōnin walked together, the monk backward, listening for the swordsman's footing, while the lone warrior judged the distance in terms of heartbeats. Then Rōnin stopped, and so did the monk. They now stood at an equal distance between the archer and the altar.

Zenbō increased the space between his two hands on the pole of his spear. Rōnin crouched and brought his right hand an inch from the hilt of his Sanada sword, ready to draw. On his back, he could hear the grunts of the dead climbing the stairs of the pyramid. It would have to happen in the next bout.

He forced all the air out of his lungs and in the space between two breaths, with no thoughts in his mind, attacked.

Zenbō had been observing each of them during those days together. He knew their strengths and their weaknesses. He knew Rōnin's right step was a little too long. The spear stabbed through the air, aiming at the warrior's knee, just like his old master used to do.

Rōnin unsheathed without thinking and watched the sword flash in a line of silver. He trusted it. The blade moved faster than the spear and cut the pole right behind the crescent blade. The spearhead twirled harmlessly in the air, losing itself outside of Rōnin's sight. His vision focused on a single point, the artery beating along Zenbō's neck. His will flowed to his blade, and he pushed on his left leg just as the katana rose once more.

He heard a gasp as he slid past the monk.

"Beautiful," Zenbō whispered as his hand moved to the gash reddening across his neck. Rōnin shook the blood from his blade and pushed it back into the *saya*, then the blind monk fell.

He turned around to observe the body of a man he had thought a friend, and who perhaps was. Zenbō was a victim of the curse, he thought, and of the war in a sense, just like many others.

"Rōnin!" Tsuki screamed, but too late.

The blade burst out of his belly, right under the ribs.

Rōnin coughed blood, and he looked at the red tip of the sword with curiosity. His hands moved by themselves toward it, and as if the sword wanted to help, it sank deeper into him, revealing more of itself for his observation. Rōnin was about to fall on his knee, but Hidetada did not let him and used his katana to keep the lone warrior on his feet.

CHAPTER 20
MIKINOSUKE

"Rōnin!" Tsuki screamed, pulling the boy from his torpor.

His friend was looking down at the blade coming from his abdomen, hands shaking, while the man behind him used the cover to protect himself from the archer. Tsuki was ready to shoot, her arm tensing the bowstring all the way to her cheek, but not able to find her mark.

"If I pull the sword," Hidetada shouted, "he will die. Don't make me, girl!"

The shōgun kept checking at the altar behind him as one would a kettle of water about to boil.

"Do it," Rōnin said, blood pooling in his mouth.

"I can't," the girl replied through her tears.

Mikinosuke leaned on his elbows and yelped at the pain in his left shoulder. He remembered the monk's spear, and it felt as if a glowing poker of hot iron was being jammed into his upper back. His left arm refused to bend properly, so he rolled on his other elbow.

"Tsuki," Mikinosuke called plaintively.

"Mikinosuke, help me," the girl said, not daring to look anywhere but at her target.

The boy got on his knee, wondering what he could do besides making her realize she had no choice. Then a shape drew itself in the corner of his eye, stumbling up the stairs behind the girl. His right hand moved by itself to the scabbard of his katana, but the blade was nowhere nearby, so he went after the *kyonshī* empty-handed.

Mikinosuke shoved himself in the monster's path and grabbed the spear sprouting from its belly with his one good hand.

Contrary to all the other dead warriors they had fought in Onijima, this man had been a samurai, and a friend.

Tadatomo was snarling red teeth at the boy, snapping them like a hound after fresh meat. The boy curled his arm around the spear pole, clenched his jaw with the effort, and despaired.

"Tadatomo," he said through his teeth, "don't do it, please."

But Tadatomo Honda was blind to his plea. He kept pushing, using the great strength he had developed in life to bring an end to the boy's. His nose had been smashed since they last spoke, and his skin had paled with the loss of blood. He was a far cry from the man who laughed and teased the others so easily. Tadatomo, the boy thought, would hate the idea of harming any of them, and his final act proved how far he had been willing to go to prevent it.

The samurai had used his own belt to tie his hands to the spear, thus making it impossible for him to pull it out and use it against his friends.

Mikinosuke shouted and pushed with all his fading might, but even then his back bent under the pressure of the dead samurai. The mixture of slime and blood made the pole slippery, and added to his sweat, the boy slowly lost his grip.

"Tsuki!" he yelled. "Take the shot!"

"I can't," she replied on his back. "It's Rōnin, I can't."

"Don't let him die in vain," the boy said.

She did not reply this time, but the boy knew she would not release her arrow. Even her elbow started to lower.

From under the samurai's armpit, Mikinosuke saw the other dead warriors climbing the pyramid. The stairs slowed them but they would reach the top, eventually. He prayed with all his heart that his master wouldn't be among them.

An idea popped into his brain, and Mikinosuke put all his weight on top of the spear end, bending it lower until it tapped against the last step of the stairs. The spear locked against it and the boy gave himself a second to breathe as the dead shell of his friend squirmed against the sudden resistance.

"I'm sorry this happened to you," he told Tadatomo. The monster moaned and growled against the spear, his hands unable to twist from the binding he had forced on himself while alive.

Mikinosuke was about to rush toward Hidetada and push the situation somehow. Maybe if they killed the drum master, the dead would cease their attack, he thought. But then he felt Tadatomo's presence even closer and realized with alarm that as the monster agitated himself, the spear was sinking deeper into him. And just as he understood it, the slippery part of the pole entered Tadatomo's belly, and the monster fell on the boy.

He screamed as the samurai landed on him and both crashed against the stairs. Mikinosuke put his arm under Tadatomo's chin, but the samurai was heavy and the closeness of his prey only seemed to energize him. He snapped its teeth so close to the boy's face that Mikinosuke could smell death on the monster's breath.

"Tsuki!" the boy screamed.

CHAPTER 21
IKEDA TSUKI

Jokoji, a few days ago

"Ready?" Yūki asked, looking first left to her lover, then right to her sister. "Now!"

The three women flipped their *ema* tablets together, revealing to the others the wish they would impose on Yoshinao Tokugawa, should they make it to the top of the mountain.

"War?" Ame signed with an air of confusion when she saw the one character Yūki had brushed in black.

"Not war per se," Yūki replied. "I just want to experience it. What's the point of training so hard if we never use our skills? Why? What did you write?"

Ame tilted the tablet to give them a better view of her wish.

A life with Yūki Ikeda *was written on her plaque.*

"Damn, now I feel silly," Yūki said.

"How about you, Tsuki?" Ame signed.

The girl felt even sillier than her sister and blushed when the two other women leaned to check her ema.

"A purpose?" Yūki asked. "You're asking a daimyō for a purpose?"

"I couldn't think of anything else," the girl replied, hiding behind her palms. "When I see you two, I'm envious. You know what you want so vividly. Me, I just want everyone to be happy."

When she peered through her fingers, she found none of the judgmental look she had expected from her sister, only a loving smile.

"Tsuki," Yūki said as she put her calloused hand on her little sister's face. "What characters make the word purpose*?"*

The archer looked back at the plaque and read the characters she had written, wondering where her sister was going with this.

"Eye, and Target," she read.

"Eye and Target," her sister repeated. "No one can give you your purpose. It is there, somewhere, and when your eyes fall on their target, you will know. So don't ask something so silly," she went on, slapping her sister's back.

"Ask for a ton of cash instead if you don't know what you want," Ame signed, prompting a bout of laughter from her lover, and a discreet giggle from the archer.

Her arm was tiring. She had to shoot soon, or her aim would fail. Yet Tsuki could not let go of the arrow. Rōnin was still alive and would be for as long as she kept her missile from flying. Even if she released it, she might miss, and the shōgun would kill the man she had come to love. Then nothing would stop him from completing the ritual.

"Tsuki!" Mikinosuke screamed at her back.

She could hear the boy struggling against a grunting

kyonshī. Maybe she could help him first, then the boy could decide what to do with Rōnin and the shōgun.

"Tsuki," Rōnin rasped when she was about to turn around. He nodded reassuringly, telling her in his simple gesture that she could do it.

She drew her arm once more, aiming right between the deranged eyes of Hidetada Tokugawa. He was looking at her daringly, his tongue stretched out and licking his lips. Only this part of his person stood out from Rōnin's frame.

Tsuki calmed her thoughts, focused, but failed.

"I can't," she said as tears streamed from her eyes.

CHAPTER 22
THE FOUR

Kiba sucked his breath in when he regained consciousness and felt the panic of the moment shake his whole body. He blinked hard while trying to remember what was happening, then saw the inert, carved-up body of Kotarō Fūma sitting next to him, and all came back at once. The sound of hundreds of grunting dead registered in his brain, and when his vision allowed him, he saw them climbing the stairs, passing so close to him that he could hear their feet dragging against the steps of the pyramid.

"Tsuki!" Mikinosuke screamed in panic.

Kiba was on his feet before he thought about it. Some of the dead spotted him and left their procession, rushing on the flat ground of the first platform to do their worst. The shinobi did not let them.

Using Kotarō's shoulder for support, he pushed himself up the inclined wall of the pyramid and ran along it with all the speed his tired legs could muster. Flashing past the legion of the dead, he saw the familiar shape of Tadatomo's back, and for a second felt joy in his heart at seeing his comrade alive. Then he noticed the spear jutting from his lower back and saw the feet of the boy thrashing from under the samurai.

Kiba was on Tadatomo in the blink of an eye.

He grasped the samurai's helmet between his hands and raised the head trapped in it from the boy's throat.

"Farewell, Honda-san," Kiba said just before snapping the samurai's neck.

Tadatomo stilled right away, and the shinobi gently pushed him to the side, revealing the tear-covered face of the boy instead. Tsuki was standing right above him, her bow at the ready, but he could see her lack of conviction from her posture. He meant to ask her what was happening, but the grunts from the dead called his attention backward. They were a few seconds from them.

"Grab the spear," he told the boy as he turned around and picked his half-empty bottle of oil from his belt.

"Almost done," Hidetada whispered in Rōnin's ear after his eyes flicked to check the altar behind them.

Rōnin's thoughts were quickly fading away, but one thing was certain, the girl would not shoot. He was dying though, and only she refused to see it. It might take a long time before the blood loss took him from this life, but eventually, he would die. Only the blade sticking from his abdomen kept him alive for now. He chuckled at the irony, but the pain almost made him pass out.

Tsuki, he tried to call, but the words did not pass his lips this time.

A flame erupted from the girl's back, darkening her silhouette for as long as Kiba breathed fire at the coming *kyonshī*. But they would keep coming, and eventually, they would all die. Only Hidetada would survive, and the world would crumble under his crazed ambition.

His life, Rōnin realized, meant their death. Then he knew what had to be done.

"A reason to die honorably," he whispered to himself, though he heard the voice of his beloved lord.

He looked down at the blade jutting from his skin once more and grabbed it with all the strength contained in his fingers.

"No!" Tsuki screamed when Rōnin grabbed the katana by its blade, for she immediately knew what he meant to do.

The lone warrior twisted the blade with the sole strength of his will and pulled it to the side, cutting through his skin and guts. Rōnin screamed but did not stop, not even when the shōgun realized what was happening and tried to retrieve his katana. Rōnin did not let him. Even if his fingers were bleeding, even if his palms were being severed, he would not let it go. He pulled the blade upward, dissecting more of his insides, and yet did not relinquish his grip.

Rōnin, no matter what, would die.

The shōgun understood it, and the girl did too.

Hidetada let go of the katana when his shield offered him no more protection and turned to grab the drum from the altar. He pulled it away from the talisman, revealing the butterfly mark from the Samonji's guard against the blood-soaked skin of the *kotsuzumi*, and dropped it on his shoulder. His right hand moved to hit the drum, and Hidetada heard the twang of the bowstring.

When she saw her friend take his own life, and the fear on the shōgun's face, and the butterfly on the drum's skin, Tsuki found a target for her swelling rage. She found her purpose.

The arrow darted from her bow. She saw its course in her mind even before that, and her aim was true. Truer than ever before.

It punched through Hidetada's right hand, then through the skin and the wood of the drum. The butterfly shredded as the missile flew through the hourglass shape of the instrument, but the arrow did not stop. It pierced through and emerged from the other side as if nothing had stood in its way and finally ended its path in the dome wall of the island.

Hidetada's shriek drowned in the rattle of hundreds of corpses falling inert, many of them tumbling from the pyramid.

"What have you done?" the shōgun screamed as he grabbed the wrist of his ruined hand. His fury seemed even stronger than his pain at this instant, but when Kiba and Mikinosuke came to stand by the girl's side, he shivered and remained quiet.

Moving like a snake, he grabbed the broken drum and rushed the opposite way. Kiba was about to go after him, but they heard a sound like the call of a wounded stag, and the earth shook.

"What is that?" Mikinosuke asked.

Then it started raining inside the dome.

"Onijima is dying," Kiba said.

"Rōnin," the girl called with dread.

They rushed to his side, but Rōnin did not have long left. He covered his wound with his hands to prevent the girl from seeing it. He did not want her to remember him covered in guts.

"Come on," she said as she put her arm under his.

"No," he replied, not having the strength to say more.

"Rōnin, come on," she called. "Kiba, help me."

But neither the shinobi nor the young boy now carrying the spear moved to help her. They knew just as she did that Rōnin was leaving.

"Tsuki," Mikinosuke gently called. The rain from the lake above their head was getting stronger. Dust and bones from the wall had started to crumble as well.

"We need to go," Kiba said. He dropped to one knee and put his hand on the rōnin's shoulder. He said nothing that the lone warrior did not already know.

"Wait," Rōnin whispered. "The tsuba."

Mikinosuke moved to the altar on cue and picked the talisman from the center of the table. It looked almost new. With care, he put it inside Rōnin's wounded hand and closed it into a fist for him.

Rōnin took a last look at his friends. What a beautiful bunch, he thought. He wanted to tell the girl her shot had been amazing, and that he was lucky to have seen it. He wanted to wish the old man a happier new life and warn the boy to treat his master's memory with respect. But already Rōnin felt himself rise from his body.

Tsuki moved first. She had to go now before her heart broke even more and kept her feet from running.

The pyramid was littered with unmoving dead bodies.

Even now that they were gone, the corpses obstructed their path. The girl treaded carefully but with speed through them. To the shinobi, it was no trouble at all, but the boy was quickly vanishing now that the tension of the fight did not keep him alert. When they reached the bottom, he collapsed, and Tsuki helped him on Kiba's back, but even then the boy refused to let go of the spear in his hand. She only realized then that the shinobi had lost an eye during his fight.

The earth shook more violently, and the rain turned to a downpour. Great blocks of bones and mortar fell from the sky, and wide cracks streaked like scars across the dome.

Kiba ran as fast as possible, considering his condition and the semi-conscious boy on his back. When they reached the bridge, Tsuki worried from his uneven gait that maybe this was too much for him. Now that he had killed his demon, Kiba was fallible at last.

The shinobi took a step to the left shortly after they got on the bridge, but it seemed on purpose, and when Tsuki saw the next body, she understood why.

Musashi had died on his knees, and even in death had refused to fall. Though she could only glimpse at him, she saw dozens upon dozens of cuts along his arms, clothes, and face. She could not see which had taken his life, but the master was snarling like one of those stone lions protecting the temple on their backs.

Mikinosuke saw it too, and while he said nothing, he did not even try to stop the tears from falling.

A block fell right ahead of them at the end of the bridge, and Tsuki heard an extremely loud *boom* from somewhere near the pyramid. Water gushed into the dome, and the sky crumbled much faster now that its integrity was gone.

They rushed back into the corridor. Her lungs were fire, and she could hear her own heartbeat.

"Tsuki!" Kiba called ahead, taking her from the darkness she was falling into.

The hallway was still lined with fire and they had to climb over the bodies left here and there by nine warriors on their way to save Japan.

Her feet got wet when they crossed the room where the *kyonshī* had waited for centuries, and even there the walls were falling to pieces. Mikinosuke rasped, and she saw fat pearls of sweat on his face. Then the boy vanished from her sight when they dashed through the darkness again.

"Follow the sound of my feet," Kiba said as he purposefully stepped louder, like a regular person.

How the shinobi kept running in the dark, Tsuki could not comprehend, but she listened to him and even caught the moment he stepped on the first step of the stairs.

Looking up, she saw the sunlight at the end of an impossibly long tunnel. Was it even the same day? she asked herself.

She heard Kiba breathing loudly, like a horse at the end of a race, and realized after a short time it was actually her. Kiba was gaining ground, his body getting smaller at the center of her vision. She could hear the water filling the corridor at an alarming speed, then crashing against the stairs.

Her feet moved by themselves, but soon she bumped one and hurt her shin against a step. Tsuki tried to pull herself up, but her arms gave up. For some reason she could not explain, she discarded her bow, as if its weight dragged her down. She looked up when the water reached her feet again, failed to call Kiba, and saw the light dimming to complete darkness.

Almost there, she told herself. *I was almost there.*

"Tsuki," Kiba called gently, "Tsuki, wake up." There was

no urgency in his voice. She hadn't moved and felt the lower part of her body drenched in the cold water of the lake. It was no longer rising.

"I think we're fine," the shinobi said as he helped her sit up.

When she looked up again, she saw the end of the stairs, like a door made of light. She gave herself a minute, and they left Onijima for good, knowing that the souls of five brave warriors protected the place and that the curse of Izanagi was gone.

CHAPTER 23
TSUKI IKEDA

Lake Biwa, one year later.

Lake Biwa was as peaceful as ever. It was hard to imagine that a year ago the battle for the fate of Japan had taken place under it. Some folks living off the fish from Biwa claimed the level of the water had dropped suddenly a year ago, but their neighbors called them crazy. Nothing, they said, could disturb the sacred lake. And after Yoshinao Tokugawa had the gate of Onijima sealed, Tsuki believed the cursed island would never be sought after.

She sighed with pleasure upon the sight of the sun slowly setting over the tip of the lake, stretching lanky shadows toward the east.

As she had done when the stones had been erected by the lake's shore, she planted a stick of incense in front of each. The smell caressed her nostrils when she sat back from her offering to Ame and her sister.

"I miss you, you know," she told the stone. "Knowing that the two of you left together helps, but it still hurts. And

Mom misses you too. She speaks of you with pride, though it hurts me not to tell her why you died. Yoshinao made us promise. He said that if the faith in the Tokugawa name dwindled so soon after the war ended, it might spark a new wave of conflict. I think he's right, but I don't like it."

She used a burning match to light another stick, which she reverently put in front of Musashi's stone.

"Mikinosuke really did not like it either," she said with a chuckle. "You should have seen your boy when Yoshinao asked for our silence. I thought he might kill him with his eyes alone. But I guess he has grown, and he managed his temper long enough for us to leave. Then and only then he cursed the daimyō with the foulest swear words I ever heard."

She smiled at the memory, then soured when she remembered it was the last time she saw the boy.

"You should know," she went on when the next stick found the ground in front of Tadatomo's resting place, "that he took your father's spear to your brother. He wanted to do it alone, and I think it was a pilgrimage of some sort for him. A way to truly end this journey. I heard he then became a retainer of the Honda clan."

She turned her attention back to Musashi and waved some life back into the stick.

"Apparently he has discarded his name and taken yours as his. And now all of Japan is buzzing with surprising words of a young Miyamoto Musashi resuming his path of duels and training. You would be so proud of him, Musashi-san."

A grey heron passed far over her head, its wings covering the six shadows for a moment as the bird flew toward the sun.

"I also miss you, Rōnin," she said when she sat back

from her next offering. "I know you belonged to someone else, but sometimes I think of you. You helped me find my purpose, and I will never forget you, though I'm sorry I still don't know your name," she said, chuckling and wiping a tear from her eye.

"As I traveled back here, I wondered if I should tell you or not, but I guess you ought to know. I'm tracking the curse. Kiba and I are. Someone helped Hidetada, and Nobunaga before that. Someone has been working to revive the curse for a long, long time, and I will track him down, and end it all for good. This is my purpose."

She opened her fist when she realized how sullen the mood had turned, and let her natural smile back on her lips.

"Kiba apologizes for not being here, by the way, though he says it's silly to speak to a bunch of stones. He had a quick errand to run before I meet him. Then we'll be gone for some time, I'm afraid."

Not knowing what to say next, Tsuki bowed until her forehead touched the ground.

She hesitated when she sat up but looked at the last stone. She would not give him incense, but fished a small pouch from the bag on the floor and dropped it in front of Zenbō's gravestone. The girl opened the pouch, revealing a stack of candies from Kyōto.

"Mikinosuke would be mad if he saw it," she said. "And I haven't forgotten you. I don't think I will. But I'm not angry anymore. Not all the time, at least. And you should know that some of your old comrades petitioned the new shōgun, who allowed them to reopen your dōjō. Apparently, Hidetada had left some vague instructions about it. So, I guess he did one good thing after all."

The light was quickly fading away and the shadows from the stones soon merged with the evening's sky.

Watch out for my sister, Tsuki silently signed to Ame. *And watch out for me too, please.*

Tsuki stood up at last. She picked up her bag, her quiver, her bow, then bowed one last time to those heroes she had journeyed with, then left.

Following the sun, she moved toward the sea, to Osaka, where a boat awaited her.

EPILOGUE

Hidetada Tokugawa curled up into a ball, pushing himself as much as he could in the corner of the dark room he had called home since Onijima. Nights were filled with nightmares of dead warriors coming for him, tearing his flesh apart with their rotten teeth. Even in his dream, if he opened his eyes, it was to see the demon of revenge lurking over him. The demon tortured him with his presence as much as with his threats. Sometimes he asked questions, sometimes he simply observed his victim from the ceiling. Hidetada had told him everything about the drum and the curse of Izanagi; as much as he had learned from the man who had given him the cursed drum in the first place, the one who called himself Shinigami. But even when his curiosity was quenched, the demon never left without promises of future pain. Hidetada woke every morning in a bed soaked in piss reminding him of his miraculous survival from Onijima. The dome had crumbled on him, and great waves of water gushed around him. His head hit the pyramid when the dome filled with raging waters, and the next thing he remembered was waking on the shore of Biwa, confused, and terrified.

He had come so close. So close to the ultimate power.

His frustration tortured his day like his nightmares did his nights. Insanity was clear to all but him. They would not believe him when he said monsters were coming for him. There were eyes lurking in the dark, even in his very room.

It didn't matter what others said; he knew it in his heart, death was coming, and not a pleasant one. Not even his son, the new shōgun of Japan, deigned to visit him anymore. The decision of his retirement had promptly been forced on him upon his return. Apparently, ordering the destruction of the Ikeda and Honda clans was not a wise idea, and the members of the court feared another civil war if power remained in Hidetada's hands.

He suddenly covered his ears when a wave of voices and grunts flooded his mind, then closed his eyelids to hide the glowing eyes looking down on him from the ceiling.

"Leave me alone!" he screamed, waving his hand against nothing.

When he looked again, the eyes glowing red were still there. They blinked, then twisted. And the demon dropped from the ceiling without a sound. He stepped up from the darkness, putting himself in the dim light of the candle by Hidetada's bedside. An angry, yet quiet beast, with fangs protruding from scowling lips.

The former shōgun wanted to scream, but no sound passed his lips, so strong was his panic.

The demon crouched and caressed Hidetada's face with a gloved finger.

"Cockroaches have an amazing lifespan, haven't they?" Kiba said, his voice barely more than a whisper. "But don't you worry, drum master, this is my final visit."

"Why?" Hidetada asked in a trembling voice. "Why now?"

"Because one is never too prudent," Kiba replied as his second hand came to Hidetada's face.

"What?"

"Maybe one demon's blood isn't enough," the shinobi replied. "I'm still alive after all."

"I... I can give you anything," Hidetada stuttered.

Kiba shushed the former shōgun by putting a finger over his lips.

"A friend of mine is waiting for me," Kiba said. "And I hate to be late. But for you, Hidetada, I'll make an exception. I will take all my time."

His thumbs gently forced his victim's eyes shut.

"And don't worry about screaming. No one will hear you."

AUTHOR'S NOTES

Dear Reader,

Thank you a thousand times for giving *Undead Samurai* a chance, and congratulations on reading it to the end. What started as an impromptu thought somewhere along the lines of: "Hey, a novel with samurai fighting zombies would be cool," quickly became the novel I enjoyed writing the most (so far), and then ended up in your hands. If you've enjoyed reading half as much as I adored putting it on the page, I will consider it mission accomplished on my side. Also, if you did, I'd like to ask for a few seconds of your time for a short review on Amazon and/or Goodreads. Cheers!

While *Undead Samurai* isn't nearly as realistic as the other novels I have published, I have tried to keep it within a tight historical frame. Bar the swarms of undead warriors, most of the events related in this novel before Jokoji are true to history. This being said, I allowed myself more freedom than I usually would, and I owe it to you and to the charac-

Author's Notes

ters who appeared in this novel to reestablish the truth on some matters.

Musashi Miyamoto is probably the one character whose life story changed the most in *Undead Samurai*. In reality, he lived until 1645 (twenty years after the events of this novel), and nothing indicates that he was a coward. While there is a certain level of doubt regarding his life's tale, even from his time, he remains by far one of the most famous swordsmen of Japan's rich history, and he left his mark in various arts, philosophy, and, of course, with the creation of his Niten Ichi-ryu school of martial arts.

The master adopted several sons, the two most famous being Mikinosuke and Iori. The Mikinosuke in this novel is based on both those men, though neither met Musashi as described in *Undead Samurai*. The actual Mikinosuke died in 1626, aged 22 or 23, when his lord Honda Tadaoki (the son of Tadamasa and thus nephew of Tadatomo) passed away, which forced Mikinosuke to commit seppuku according to the tradition known as junshi. I didn't feel like ending things this way for him.

Tadatomo is one of the two characters I love the most in this novel and is the one who surprised me the most during the writing process. The real Tadatomo did lose a battle at Osaka due to being drunk; however, he died in a subsequent battle, regaining his honor with a valiant victory. Before this last battle, he is said to have voiced his regret over his drinking habits, and is now considered in Japan as the "God of alcohol quitting." People pray to him to gain the strength to quit drinking, and I wrote his character in *Undead Samurai* as an homage to him.

Author's Notes

The other characters among the nine are all fictional.

Rônin, also called Nagakatsu, is very lightly based on Tamiya Tsushima-no-kami Nagakatsu, an important figure of the Tamiya-ryu school of Iaido, though, besides his name, school, and some anecdotes, they don't have much in common.

Tsuki and Yūki Ikeda did not exist, but their mother did and she was by all accounts an amazing woman. Ame is purely fictional as well, but I didn't give her the name Suzuki by luck, and I must admit I have some plans for her, though that will be for some novel in the distant future. By the way, in case you were wondering, she is the second of the two characters mentioned earlier.

Kiba is a member of the shinobi clan from Iga, which was attacked by Nobunaga Oda in 1581, though he left a few to escape. One of the most famous shinobi in history, Hanzō Hattori, is actually from that clan and maybe his image helped shape the character of Kiba.

Zenbō did not exist, but his school did. The Hōzōin-ryū was founded by Hōzōin Kakuzenbō In'ei (that's where I got the name Zenbō from). The school was never forced to shut down, though In'ei meant for it to close upon his death. Thankfully, his nephew and successor disobeyed and the school is still active to this day.

I might need to make a short trip to Hitetada Tokugawa's resting place because he did not come out of this story nearly as grand as in reality. He lived until 1632, and at the

Author's Notes

time of this story was already Ogosho (a retired shōgun) and no longer the shōgun himself.

Yoshinao Tokugawa is also a fairly remarkable character who is not discussed often, maybe because he lived mostly when peace was restored. His mausoleum can be visited at Jokoji Temple, a place I've been to on several occasions and truly adore above all other temples in Japan.

This novel is really a love letter to Japan, its culture, and its history. I have lived in Japan for more than seven years at the time of this writing and would consider myself lucky to be here for twice longer. I have many more novels planned in this country, and cannot wait to create more stories set in ancient Japan.

I also left the door open to some future stories related to this one, taking place before, after, and in various places. So if you want more of this, please share the word about *Undead Samurai*, and let's make it something truly great together!

ACKNOWLEDGMENTS

Much gratitude to the beta-readers who shared their time, opinions, and kind words with me at various stages of the editing process. I was lucky to find some kindred spirits in them, and hope to receive their help again in the future. Thank you, Kate, Thomas, Dean, and James.

Cheers to all the reviewers, booktubers, and podcasters who will mention this novel, hopefully in a positive light. It's always a pleasure working with you.

Thank you to my brilliant editor, Christine, for spit-shining my writing into something decent enough for people to read. I love being an author and one day I will be a great writer too. In the meantime, I will continue to need help from master editors such as you.

As usual, and forever, thank you to my stunning wife for being in my world and giving me the space to write. I guess she secretly hopes that I get rich thanks to my novels someday. Poor thing...

And finally, thanks to all of you, dear readers, for making my dream come true.

Now go review this book somewhere (please)!

ALSO BY BAPTISTE PINSON WU

The Three Kingdoms Chronicles:

Yellow Sky Revolt

Heroes of Chaos

Dynasty Killers

THANK YOU

If you've enjoyed this story, please take a second to share your thoughts on Amazon or Goodreads, and feel free to get in touch with Baptiste Pinson Wu on his social media platforms or directly through his website.

Printed in Great Britain
by Amazon